THE REASON FOR HIS WIFE'S RETURN

TARA PAMMI

ONE NIGHT IN MY RIVAL'S BED

MELANIE MILBURNE

MILLS & BOON

First published in Great Britain 2023
by Mills & Boon, an imprint of HarperCollins*Publishers* Ltd,
1 London Bridge Street, London, SE1 9GF

www.harpercollins.co.uk

HarperCollins*Publishers*, Macken House, 39/40 Mayor Street Upper, Dublin 1, D01 C9W8, Ireland

The Reason for His Wife's Return © 2023 Tara Pammi

One Night in My Rival's Bed © 2023 Melanie Milburne

ISBN: 978-0-263-30681-1

06/23

MIX
Paper | Supporting
responsible forestry
FSC™ C007454

This book is produced from independently certified FSC™ paper to ensure responsible forest management.
For more information visit: www.harpercollins.co.uk/green.

Printed and Bound in the UK using 100% Renewable Electricity at CPI Group (UK) Ltd, Croydon, CR0 4YY

Tara Pammi can't remember a moment when she wasn't lost in a book—especially a romance, which was much more exciting than a mathematics textbook at school. Years later, Tara's wild imagination and love for the written word revealed what she really wanted to do. Now she pairs alpha males who think they know everything with strong women who knock that theory *and* them off their feet!

Melanie Milburne read her first Mills & Boon novel at the age of seventeen, in between studying for her final exams. After completing a master's degree in education she decided to write a novel, and thus her career as a romance author was born. Melanie is an ambassador for the Australian Childhood Foundation and a keen dog-lover and trainer. She enjoys long walks in the Tasmanian bush. In 2015 Melanie won the HOLT Medallion, a prestigious award honouring outstanding literary talent.

THE REASON FOR HIS WIFE'S RETURN

TARA PAMMI

MILLS & BOON

PROLOGUE

Eleven months ago

> *Greek Billionaire Breaks Hearts by Marrying a Nobody American!*
>
> *Brilliant international corporate lawyer and daredevil playboy Aristos Carides, thirty-three, broke fans' hearts all over the world by marrying a nobody American, Mira Reddy, also thirty-three, over the weekend in party city Las Vegas.*
>
> *While the playboy's numerous fans have taken to posting their disappointment all over the internet, Carides's new bride is conspicuously absent from social media. However, one of our reporters has unearthed a picture of the plump, plain Mrs. Carides, which clearly boggles our minds as to how she landed the favorite bachelor on the planet.*
>
> *Sources close to Mr. Carides have leaked that Mrs. Carides has tied up the playboy in a watertight contract marriage of five years through nefarious means known only to the couple. We're trying to learn more.*
>
> *Here's a montage of the clips posted by adoring fans of Mr. Carides...*

AristosLover23: OMG howz the world fair? Why did Aristos marry such a boring old woman?

Carides'sFavCoochie: Wonder what she did to land him…

ArisBootyCall: A gold-digging skank if you ask me.

HackerNush: My sister's not a nobody, you assholes. She's pretty and smart and a wonderful doctor. Get your facts straight.

BeautyYana: And they're in love. Jeez. Stop corrupting everything.

IamAristos: My wife is a gorgeous piece of ass. Why wouldn't I marry her?

HackerNush: Aristos, that you? Can you sue this trashy website? Or should I try my hand at it?

IamAristos: Bringing the whole thing down might be the easier way, Nushie-kins ;)

HackerNush: On it then. :)

CHAPTER ONE

Ten weeks ago

MIRA REDDY CARIDES hid her trembling hands by her sides and greeted friends and colleagues who'd come to pay their respects at her grandfather's wake while stealing glances at her estranged husband like a covetous other woman.

Aristos is here, her mind kept repeating in an awed voice. In California. Tall and broad and devastatingly gorgeous. After zero communication in the eight months since she'd left to take care of her grandmother and stayed behind after her death when her grandfather, her Thaata, became ill.

Of course, the fact that his grandfather and hers had been friends for five decades wasn't a small thing. Very possibly he was here on Leo Carides's behalf to pay final respects to an old friend and wanted nothing to do with his estranged wife.

Mira scoffed, knowing it was wishful thinking. From the moment he'd arrived, she'd felt his gaze on her back like a knife, flaying her hard-won armor apart, ripping through her shields, delving for her secrets, demanding she let him see into her head and her heart.

Really, Mira, Aristos has no interest in your stupid heart. Isn't that why you ran away? a rational voice whispered and Mira clung to it.

But it was impossible to ignore the speculation among the guests even as she played host alongside her grandfather's protégé and heir, Caio Oliveira. She could hear the awed whispers about their marriage, their subsequent separation. His name floated around her, making her pulse race...

Aristos Carides, the international corporate law genius and the man who donated millions to orphanages around the world.

Aristos Carides, the daredevil playboy and the man with the Midas touch.

Aristos Carides, the magnificent male specimen who'd broken hearts all over the world by marrying the most boring woman on either side of the Atlantic.

But to Mira, he'd always been someone no one else knew, no one else saw.

To her, he was the adolescent companion she'd once adored with all her heart. The orphan who'd suddenly found himself heir to billions that she'd found common ground with. The naughty, brilliant, live-wire teenager that had made her heart sing and laugh with his daredevil stunts. The stunningly handsome young man she'd fallen in love with. The gorgeous, coveted young lawyer-in-the-making she'd let herself be persuaded into getting engaged to by their grandfathers.

What could be more thrilling than spending the rest of her life with such a dynamic, gorgeous guy who accepted her for the calm, boring, staid teenager who barely took any risks or sought fun.

They'd had the same goals in life—to make something of themselves, to not let their pasts become hurdles in their lives, to make a difference in the world.

At least that's what she had thought.

It hadn't mattered that the match had been arranged by two sly old men or that Aristos himself had never asked her. He'd looked happy enough when he'd put the ring on her finger. Those dark gray eyes had shone with that wild fire when she'd kissed his cheek. He'd been his usual charming, aggressive social self at their engagement party.

She'd been incredibly naive at eighteen and the fact that love was nothing but a sweet, poisonous lie hadn't completely taken yet. Luckily, Aristos had fractured her delusions of fantasy love the very night after their engagement party and the truth had come to light thanks to his cousin Kairos.

It had been a timely reminder that Aristos, like her father, was a man to whom everything in life—wealth, women, extreme sports—were challenges to be conquered and then moved on from. At least, her pride had remained intact as she'd never betrayed her foolish feelings for him.

The very next day, she'd called off the engagement, telling her grandfather that she'd realized getting married at eighteen would only hamper her ambition to become a doctor. To quote Thaata when Leo had complained, "No one can shake my stubborn, fierce granddaughter once she makes up her mind." Her decision had been validated when Aristos hadn't even asked her the reason for canceling the engagement.

But she'd never been able to erase Aristos from her heart. Never stopped wondering if everything they'd shared during their teen years when she'd visited Greece for long, glorious summers had been anything but a sham.

She'd kept obsessive track of his meteoric rise in the corporate world, his worldwide fame for his charities, his penchant for extreme sports and his escapades with women, eavesdropped on Leo Carides's calls to her own grandfather over the uncontrollable devil that was his grandson.

The devil she had been determined to stay away from, despite Thaata's constant urging that she give him another chance.

Only Aristos had walked back into her life one crisp September evening last year when she'd been in Vegas to watch over her sister Yana at her latest photo shoot.

He'd walked into her suite, all dark stormy eyes and sensuality, with the shocking proposition for a convenient contract marriage that served both their purposes. Because, of course, Thaata had shared her plan to have a child through an anonymous donor with Leo Carides, who had passed it on to his grandson.

Their contract marriage would give her the child she wanted, Aristos had argued, born of a father who didn't mind being a part-time parent and the contingency of a support system should anything befall her. Being a doctor by profession, Mira saw enough devastating life changes to want to cling to that. Unnervingly, but unsurprisingly, shrewd of Aristos to capitalize on her needing such reassurance even when he hadn't seen her in years.

For Aristos, it would give the illusion of settling down and stability that the board of Carides Inc. demanded he show, extremely put upon as they were by his constant exposure to near-fatal thrills. It would give him the heir for the Carides legacy that Leo Carides was desperate for. Since his "bloody grandson kept throwing himself off mountain cliffs and helicopters."

Despite turning it around in her head, Mira hadn't found a single reason to say no to him.

That it had appeased their mutual grandfathers, that they had seen it as some grand reunion of a romantic match, had been the icing on the cake. Not one soul knew about the quiet divorce they intended to acquire after five years. Or at least that's what Mira had thought until she'd seen the scathing article online.

Aristos, with that annoying amusement that grated on her skin, had sprawled on a heavy recliner and watched her from under those thick lashes, as she'd planned their arrangement to a T.

It had taken Mira two months to realize that she hadn't foreseen two small but important nuggets. That she might actually fall in lust with her own husband and that Aristos, per his behavioral patterns, would find it impossible to be faithful to her beyond a mere two months.

So when her grandmother had fallen sick, she'd come home running. Used it as an excuse to rid herself of the naive hopes and possessive fire his proximity raised in her. The silence on his end had only confirmed her suspicions that he regretted their arrangement. She'd been waiting with bated breath for annulment papers for months.

But he was here now, his mere presence like throwing fuel onto slumbering embers. Her grief at losing her grandparents back-to-back—the only real parents she'd ever known—the sense of restlessness that had haunted her the last few years, the debilitating fear that she'd always be lonely and all her worries came back with a vengeance.

Why? What was it about the blasted man that her own needs and desires took on new, hungry shapes around him?

What was it about him that made all her vulnerabilities come crashing to the surface?

She looked across the vast, high-ceilinged room, her gaze immediately locking with Aristos's. He hadn't moved from his lounging position against the wall since he'd arrived. Only following and cataloging her every move like a quiet predator sizing up prey.

Dark gray eyes held hers, a mocking glint to them. As if he knew why she'd run away. As if he knew that beneath her wariness lay a thirst for something darker and more real than anything she'd known in…forever. As if he remembered the moment when the thin veneer of polite apathy between them had been knocked down with a single touch.

Awareness arced between them—as potent as it had been the one time they'd kissed as husband and wife.

The folded note in her fist called her attention, giving her the strength to look away.

A handwritten note from Thaata, who'd left notes for her, Yana and Nush, as if he'd known that his time had been near, that the three granddaughters he'd raised with such love and affection would be desperate for more from him.

Tears she'd somehow held at bay for weeks returned. Mira excused herself, ignoring Yana's and Nush's curious looks, and walked toward the large kitchen where she'd spent most of her childhood, hanging on to her grandmother's words. Her fingers trembled as she unrolled the note and caressed the crisp stationery.

Nothing real can be built on a foundation of transactions, Mira. Or by burying your real desires. If you truly want the King, be the Queen I raised you to be.

Mira's breath hitched. Laughter bubbled as she sank

against the large island block where she and her half sisters had laughed and cried and fought and helped her grandmother cook a million meals.

Had Thaata known that marrying Aristos had been nothing but a glorified transaction? Had he known that Mira's heart had never really left the cocoon of safety and comfort, petrified of being shattered if she used it? That her strength was only a mirage, hiding her deepest fears?

In this moment, it had left her with nothing but a desperate clawing for more.

Thaata was right. Nothing had been real in her life. Not the endless dates she'd gone on in the last decade based on some app's algorithm, not the men who were supposed to be her perfect matches on paper. And definitely not the way she'd locked up her heart so tight that she could feel no pain.

Only Aristos's touch made her feel the pulse of something real. Something so effortlessly carnal that a kiss had shattered the icy frost she'd encased her desires in, fractured the fortress she'd built around herself for so long.

And he was here, now.

Sending her possessive, smoldering glances that said he hadn't forgotten the kiss. That said they were still bound by contract and something else. Even with grief and loss tossing her about, it was the first spark of life she'd felt in months.

What if for one evening, one hour, one moment, she allowed herself to feel something real? If she let herself drown in sensation and pleasure and forgot her plan and her rules and everything rational?

Aristos Carides willed himself to last just a few more minutes under the blisteringly cold spray. Despite his grandfather Leo's twenty years' worth of speeches and sometimes downright threats, he'd never quite learned how to control his baser instincts. Had never learned how to temper the yawning emptiness within him that wanted more and more. More thrills to prove he was alive. More high-stakes cases. More status and wealth.

As if he could never rid himself of the hunger and thirst he'd known on the streets.

But even as a child, on the streets of Athens where he'd grown up until twelve years of age when Leo had found him and dragged him home to be civilized, fighting for scraps to live on, he'd always been a master at deception. He'd simply used those skills and pretended that he had everything under control. That there weren't any moments when he saw himself in the mirror and only a sense of dissatisfaction and restlessness looked back at him.

The entire world thought he had something to prove, that it was an unquenchable need to defy nature, physics and his demanding grandfather that drove him. Instead it was something else he relentlessly pursued under extreme conditions. Something else that he wanted to purge.

Not that anything had ever helped keep his needy desires in check when it came to *her*.

Mira Reddy, the golden princess with large brown eyes that sized up everything with a look, with lush curves that had sent his adolescent body into fits of lust, with a kind smile so broad and so big that one felt drenched in it. The fiercely magnificent lioness who'd been dangled in front of him as the ultimate prize he hadn't imagined he could have in his wildest dreams fifteen years ago. Only to be told that he came secondary to her ambition to become a doctor.

Except he'd known in his heart, as had Leo, that the golden princess had found him inadequate at the end. He'd been good enough to be her pity project as a wild, almost feral teen, but not enough to share her life.

He'd never forgotten the feeling—like offering a feast to a starving man and snatching it away just when the scent of it drove him wild with hunger.

She's yours now, though, that same feral voice whispered. *She's Mira Reddy Carides and you've got her where you've wanted her for years.*

Even with the cold water freezing his skin and other important parts, a hot rush went through him at the mere thought. He pressed his forehead to the cold tile, scoffing at himself.

Wanting his wife with a desperation that bordered on unrequited longing was not a good feeling. It was the same "not good" feeling he'd indulged in on and off for over two decades now. Ever since he'd seen Mira when he'd been twelve, awkward with his sudden birthright and inheritance and she'd smiled at him, he'd lost a part of himself to her and gained an impossibly ridiculous dream.

A dream that had come close to being real, only to be snatched away, again and again.

For all the media claimed him to be a playboy who changed partners as fast as he won litigation cases, every woman he'd taken to bed, every thrill he'd chased, had been to seek escape from that blasted feeling. A chase to rid himself of that "longing."

Ergo, even now, he was failing to drown out the intemperate reaction he had to seeing her after months. To seeing her hanging on to the Brazilian Caio Oliveira's arm, looking like they were made for each other.

Even though she belonged to *him*.

Seeing her large brown eyes shine with wetness, knowing that she was brokenhearted over her grandfather but wouldn't welcome any kind of comfort he offered, made him feel helpless. Inadequate. Like the runt Leo had picked off the streets two decades ago. Like he'd never measure up, where it mattered. Like he'd always be the poor little boy who'd been neglected by his mother in favor of her drink.

And Aristos hated feeling helpless. Hated remembering how small and powerless he'd once been. Hated that even after she'd abandoned their arrangement yet again, he still felt this pull toward her, this gnawing need to...

With a filthy curse, he turned off the shower.

Enough was enough. He'd given her enough time to look after her grandparents, given himself enough time to cool down after she'd run again.

It was time to bring her home where she belonged. Time to make her his in a way that would kill this ridiculous longing he felt, once and for all. He'd locked her tight in an arrangement for five years, hopefully enough to extinguish the hold she seemed to have over him. Enough to make sure she was tied to him for the rest of their lives through their child even when it was over between them.

The white lie he'd told her to entice her didn't bother him one bit. He'd never take their child from her but neither would he simply fade into the background as he'd let her believe.

Christos, the elaborate scheming it took to get her into his life... He hadn't seen such handiwork in the wildest cases he came across in his corporate career.

Walking into the room he'd been shown into for the night, he was shaking his wet hair like a mongrel when he felt that telltale tension that always took root in his body when Mira was close. Like a rubber band being stretched tighter and tauter in his abdomen, threatening to snap at one more breath, and yet continuing the burn endlessly.

The room was in relative darkness, but the moonlight spilling through the open French doors was more than enough to make out Mira standing there. Inside his room. Like his wildest wet dream coming true.

With her back pressed up to the closed door. With one side of a loose robe hanging off her shoulder, baring the smooth arch of her long neck. Open wide at the front, the robe taunted him with a hint of those lush curves he'd dreamed of far too often for his liking, white lace kissing the flesh he wanted to mar with his mouth. The silky material stopped mid-thigh, fluttering at the breeze that seemed to have poured in just for his benefit. Thick thighs he wanted to bury his face between and shapely calves that he wanted around his back, with white-tipped toes peeping out of slippers.

He'd never seen Mira's legs; the errant thought struck him out of nowhere. And the unfairness of it burned.

Even as a teenager, she'd always dressed with an old-fashioned sort of modesty, covering up her plump curves in voluminous skirts and blouses, as if she could contain the sheer sensuality she held in her body. Even when he'd found her at Yana's photo shoot in Vegas, surrounded by stunning models with every inch of skin on display, she'd stood out, regal and gorgeous in her pale pink pantsuit, wrapped up in poise and confidence and an indefinable mystery that made his skin thrum. That brought out the greedy conqueror in him.

Her innate sophistication had always been compounded by how tightly she guarded her emotions...the perfect counterpoint to his roiling extreme. The temptation that made him want to unravel all that poise and polish and perfection until she was panting with need for him. Until she was reduced to the basest desires with him. Only with him. Only for him.

He let his gaze rove back up her body, lingering on every inch of her and yet too greedy, too needy for more of her. As always.

"What a pleasant surprise to see you *here*, Mira," he said with a bow that mocked everything from the transactional nature of their relationship to her standing inside his room in what was clearly a revealing negligee to his near nakedness.

But she one-upped him as she always did.

Instead of her signature brow raise or tightly wound smile, he saw the shiver that wracked her. He noted her gaze landing and skittering away from his naked body. It was mild and breezy in the room and that shiver was not out of cold and that she let him see it…

The rubber band snapped and lust poured through him, warming up every frozen tip of his limbs, every inch of his flesh within seconds. Flesh he'd brutally punished mere minutes ago under an ice-cold shower.

She pushed off from the door with an elegant sensuality, walked to the giant bed with its invitingly cozy quilt and leaned against it, facing him. The traitorous breeze brought the scent of her to his nostrils. He took a deep breath, filling his lungs with that subtly sweet rose scent, diving deep into the very abyss that beckoned him.

His body reacted as it usually did in her presence, saluting her at full mast. It had nothing to do with the uncharacteristic stretch of celibacy he'd taken since he'd seen her again in Vegas almost eighteen months ago. Once he'd cast his eyes on her again, even before she'd accepted his proposition, he wanted no other woman. He couldn't even conjure another woman's face or body when he jerked off. It was an obsession, a madness, and it was time he purged it from his system.

If he'd hoped his erect cock would chip away a bit of his wife's poise, Aristos was denied the satisfaction. But she... her distinct beauty...from the arrogant blade of her nose to the thick brows that spoke so eloquently for her... It stole his breath afresh.

Her long, silky black hair had been braided and it hung over her right shoulder, the thick rope of it hanging past her breasts. Aristos had always wanted to wind that braid in his hand, to pull her closer, to hold her to him as he moved inside her from behind, to simply arrest her long enough to see what lay beneath the calm surface. Her face, freshly washed and free of makeup, gleamed with soft silkiness he wanted to test with the tips of his fingers.

Her lips, thick and plump and a light brownish pink... He wanted to sink his teeth into them. She'd liked it when he'd done it the one time they'd kissed. The only time. He'd come in his hands like a horny teenager that night just thinking of how sweet she'd tasted, of how she'd melted against him and moaned her demands.

A week later, she'd left, leaving him a note on that damned to-do pad of hers, as if he were just an item to check off.

Nanamma had a heart attack. Have to look after her and my sisters. Don't know when I'll be back.

That had been eight months ago. Weeks had piled into months, he'd been busy with a high-profile case, but Aristos had known as soon as he'd seen that note that she'd run again. But knowing how close she was to her sisters, how much she loved her grandfather Rao and his wife, he'd decided to give her the peace and the space before he reminded her of their agreement.

Having heard from Leo that Rao was worse—of course she'd kept in touch with his grandfather—he'd been preparing to visit when he'd learned that Rao had passed away.

Questions buzzed in his head like a swarm of bees, demanding to be asked. Demanding that she behave like a wife. Demanding that she cry and rant and vent and cajole him into acting like a husband.

That she hadn't completely ignored him tonight, that she was here in his bedroom, dressed as she was, told Aristos something was up. Other than him, that was.

As she leaned against the bed, her brown gaze sought his, determination written into every inch of her pretty features. Except he looked deeper this time.

The pulse flickering at her neck and the ragged rush of her breath that made her chest rise and fall betrayed her tension. The dark smudged circles under those huge brown eyes, the pinched set of her lips betrayed her grief. The rawness of her emotions hit him like a stinging slap of air, shocking him.

He resisted the urge to grab her by the shoulders and soothe her with nonsensical words he didn't even know he could utter. "I know how much you loved him," he heard himself say, softly, in a gruff tone he couldn't shift. "And how much he adored you."

She nodded, tightlipped, her eyes filling with tears he was sure she hadn't let anyone see in weeks. Because she was brave Mira. She was the strong, confident older sister that her younger sisters looked up to. Because she was a fierce nurturer at heart.

If it was madness to be jealous of one's own as-yet-not-conceived child, Aristos was definitely a contender for it.

Suddenly, he felt like a fool who'd fallen for his own deception. Another average, powerful man who judged a strong woman and called her lacking in feelings.

Just because she didn't seem brokenhearted about their past didn't mean she didn't feel them at all, did it? So why had Mira stayed away? Why had she broken their engagement fifteen years ago?

"Is there anything I can help with?" he asked next, feeling as if he was trying to find a foothold on the steep, rocky incline of her and his own emotions. Every time he thought he had a grip on what made Mira tick, she pushed him off the cliff to dangle from a lifeline, and begin the upward trek all over again.

A shake of her head this time. "Caio has it all under control." Her lower lip trembled and she bit down on it. "I don't know what I'd have done without him this past week."

His jaw tightened at the hint of admiration and genuine affection in her tone. If he didn't like the bastard Brazilian who was full of honor and integrity and all that shit Aristos had rarely seen in powerful men, he'd have invited him into the ring and beaten him to a pulp for cozying up to his wife. "Of course."

Mira Reddy Carides...was his.

It was a chant in his head.

"You were glaring at him the entire time."

That she had noticed his reaction made satisfaction sizzle through him. "That's what you came to discuss with me, in the middle of the night? After leaving your poor husband to his own devices for eight months?"

One bare shoulder rose and the robe slipped farther down to her elbow. "Why, Aristos?"

"Will you answer my questions too, *glykia mou*? I have two decades' worth of them."

She licked her lower lip, a flash of trepidation in her eyes that she quickly masked. "Yeah, sure."

He took a step closer, hoping to shake the equanimity she wore like a second skin.

Craning her head up to look at him—he'd forgotten how small and curvy she was—she said, "Why?"

"Why what, Mira?"

"Why were you so angry with Caio?"

He shrugged. "I was jealous, not angry."

A quick, all-consuming perusal of him. "What do you have to be jealous of?"

He shrugged, wondering how such a clever, beautiful woman could have no clue when it came to him. "I don't like him touching you so much. Don't like how bloody perfect you look together. Even Rao thought so at one point."

Her mouth fell open, and her eyes grew into large pools. "Caio's like a brother to me. And he belongs to Nush, even if she never acts on it. I'd never even dream of going there."

"Nush and Caio, huh?" he said, feeling a sudden expansiveness in his chest. Suddenly, it made complete sense. He'd liked the sneaky little hacker from the moment Mira had introduced her little sister Anuskha to him. Just as much as he liked the troublemaker sister, Yana. There was something about seeing the three Reddy sisters together and the bond they shared that called to the wounds that had never healed inside him.

She nodded, her chin tucking down into her chest. Her

head popped back up, as if it worked on a spring, and Aristos smirked.

Her palm landed on his chest and gave a gentle push. Pink scoured her round cheeks even as his heart thundered under her touch. "Could you please use the damned towel while we talk? It's… You're distracting me and I have something important to talk about."

"You're the one who interrupted my nighttime routine," he said in a sulky voice, masking the tension that dug into his muscles. "You do it." There was a fire he'd never seen in her eyes tonight and Aristos followed the thread of it. "I dare you, Mira," he whispered, like he used to do all those years ago when she still liked him.

When she'd laughed with him. When she'd treated him with kindness and affection that had been like rainfall over parched earth.

Her brown eyes blazed with anger. "Is everything a game to you? A challenge? A dare?"

"Is that why I gave you so much space and time to be with your family? To let you care and mourn for your grandparents without intruding on what you consider sacred, without demanding you stick to our arrangement?"

Her eyes kept searching his, as if she could see into the truth of him if only she tried. With a sudden huff, she grabbed the towel from his shoulders. Aristos swallowed as her fingers danced over his bare flesh, branding his skin, burning through him.

They lingered over his abdomen before she cinched the towel around his hips. His erection was now nothing but a source of pure torment.

Leaning back against the bed, she took a deep breath. Preparing her spiel, he'd no doubt.

"How much longer do you need?"

"For what?"

"To come back home."

Hesitation danced in her face. "I…"

"I let you go once without question, *pethi mou*. I won't be repeating that mistake. This time, we have an ironclad contract, Mira."

"What do you mean 'once'? And what will you do if I break the contract? Sue me for deserting you?"

The unusual break in her usually infuriatingly even temper goaded his own. Gritting his jaw, he carefully measured his words. "Fifteen years ago, you broke your promise. But we were young and foolish and it's…long over. As to your second question—"

"Wait, so you actually noticed that I broke our engagement back then?"

CHAPTER TWO

DARK GRAY EYES watched Mira carefully, searching, seeking, delving. A predator who wouldn't stop until he had the prey, squirming in place, giving him everything he demanded.

God, why was she digging into things better left alone?

And how was it that Aristos became calmer and quieter the angrier he grew—for all his usual high spirits—while she lost her temper and started yelling like a fishwife at the market?

Mira pressed her face into her hands, calling herself all kinds of names. Even the gesture was betraying of her state of mind and she immediately corrected it.

He was still watching her, those thick brows tied into a frown. Examining her from all the angles. Turning her inside out.

Say something to distract him, Mira. Do something.

She could hear it in Yana's voice. Yana, who thought herself an expert on men and was forever giving her and Nush advice on how to deal with them.

But nothing came to Mira. Not when her rational mind was lost in devouring the stunningly gorgeous man in front of her who was by all rights her husband. Not when she didn't understand anything but the desire thrumming through her.

Thick jet-black hair and a wide, almost cruel mouth and a jawline that she could write sonnets about... If it had been just that, Mira could have resisted his appeal. She'd dated ballplayers, actors, all kinds of handsome men. Nothing special there either.

But Aristos's eyes—dark gray and stormy, full of mirth as he seemed to be forever laughing at the world—had always drawn her in. Drawn her in and held her captive. Invited her to drown deep and give in.

For all that he lived a reckless lifestyle, for all that he courted media attention for his high-profile cases, for all that he was a man full of contrasts with donating millions to charity...there had always been something fathomless about him that had called to her. She'd never been able to pin down Aristos and yet felt the most overwhelming urge to conquer him, tie him down to her, make him...hers in a way he belonged to no one.

Sensible, strong, self-sufficient Mira, even as a teenager...had found a tempting abyss in Aristos's eyes. A spine-tingling challenge. And had never quite recovered.

"Would you like me to answer the question, Mira?" Aristos prompted in a soft, yet implacable voice that had her gaze jerking to his. "I would answer, *agapi mou*, but then there's a price to pay, as you so cleverly put it. You're racking up quite the debt with me."

"No," Mira said, straightening her shoulders. "I... I misspoke." Coward.

She could see it in his eyes too. He nodded, as if convincing himself to move along. "Shall we try the present again?"

She frowned.

"At the risk of sounding like a needy, petulant husband," he said smoothly, sounding anything but, "when are you coming home, *honey*?"

"I need time."

"No."

At least she could always trust Aristos to bring her back up, despite grief and loss and whatever brought her down. "I didn't come here to fight."

"Why do you need time? I didn't force you to marry me."

No, he'd somehow discovered her deepest wish and dangled it in front of her. *Donkey, meet carrot.*

"You didn't contact me for eight months. I thought our marriage was null and void," she said, sounding prim and tightly wound even to her own ears.

"And why didn't *you* contact me, Mira? An even better question—why did you stay away for so long?"

So many excuses—real and fake—rose to her lips but Mira discarded them. There was something about seeing him here in her childhood home, sounding so gruff and concerned about her, something about the look in his eyes that made her question the truth of her own assumptions.

"Space and time to be with your family. To let you care and mourn for your grandparents without intruding on you."

His words came back to her in sharp relief.

"My grandparents, my sisters... They're everything to me, Aristos. Family's sacred to me."

She'd said that to him almost fifteen years ago and he'd remembered. No, he had not only remembered but acted on them. He had given her space when he could have acted like he usually did—all business-minded and transactional.

"I did want to look after Thaata and Nanamma," she finally said, meeting his eyes. "But it was also just a very convenient excuse."

His chest rose and fell as if he'd surpassed an insurmountable obstacle. "For what?"

"I was having second thoughts about our…arrangement."

He pushed a hand roughly though his hair, his mouth twisted into a sneer. "Because you enjoyed our kiss? *Theos*, I never thought you a coward of all things, Mira."

"No. It wasn't just that." It wasn't the passion of their kiss that had scared her. It was how much more she wanted along with it that had. But she wasn't going to talk about it. Now or ever. "It… Truth or dare, Aristos," she said, chickening out when she should simply demand the truth.

Aristos was notorious for his dares. He would never pick truth, especially with her, right?

Wrong.

"Truth."

She stared at him—the glint of challenge in his eyes, the satisfaction thrumming from every gorgeous naked inch of him. He'd beaten her at her own game. She could simply cheat and ask him something else but every inch of her revolted at the very thought.

Because this was sacred between them. Suddenly, with a sharp clarity brought on by grief and loss like nothing else could, Mira knew Aristos would always give her the truth. Only she'd never actively sought it before.

But she wanted it now—a little morsel of truth and a little piece of something real between them. Even if their contract marriage had entered a gray area thanks to her abandoning it.

Even if all he would give her was one night of pleasure and escape. Even if he'd fractured her heart fifteen years ago and it had never recovered since.

"In the two months that we were married, did you…" Her heart thundered in her ears. "…were you faithful… I mean, did you do stuff with other women?"

Everything about him stiffened. The mirth and playfulness immediately erased by something dark and the laugh that escaped was entirely too empty. "Would you believe me if I answered you?"

"Yes, I would. I will. Please, Aristos…just this once. Tell me."

"Then I would use that word you discarded so easily, Mira. I was faithful to you. I haven't…*done stuff*—" his mouth twisted in a sneer "—with anyone since I…hunted you down to Vegas."

"But that was eighteen months ago," she said frowning. "Before we even…decided on this."

He simply inclined his head again in that mocking bow of his.

Mira's stomach flopped, falling…falling, her entire world turning upside down. Because she believed him. She believed everything he said and everything he didn't.

Even though she'd seen him with his PA—the ever-present shadow of his—that dark evening at Carides Towers. Elena was possessive of him, protective of him, and Mira was pretty sure it was Elena who'd leaked the details of their contract to the media.

Aristos was oblivious to it all. Because Elena was loyal and hardworking and had been one of the tutors Leo had engaged for him.

On a rare impulsive visit to his office, buoyed up by their passionate kiss and her own pent-up longing, Mira had seen Elena sliding her arms around his waist, seen her push herself up against him. Seen her sink her fingers into his hair and pull his face down.

It had lasted only a handful of breaths. It had felt like a hundred eternities.

Like someone had hollowed her out and Mira had run from the premises as if her life had depended on getting away. It felt like she'd fallen down a time hole into the past again.

Aristos with another woman...

She wanted to mention Elena now, demand he explain what happened that evening, but discarded the idea. That woman was not allowed in this space between her and Aristos. Not tonight. Not when Mira was finally claiming a small slice of it for herself.

"So that's why you ran," Aristos said, breaking her out of the replay of the ghastly scene.

The sudden absence of his body heat enveloping her, the empty space he seemed to leave around her, told her he'd stepped back.

When she met his eyes, blazing anger had turned them dark. His mouth was a picture of distaste. "You thought I cheated on you. You thought I had the morals of an alley cat. You *think* I'm still that feral dog who's loyal to no one. And instead of asking me about it, instead of..." He sucked in a deep breath, his self-control masterful.

She saw a flicker of the teenage Aristos in his eyes, though he hadn't learned to control his temper as well then.

The Aristos that had found himself off the streets but in an equally ruthless and confounding world all of a sudden. The Aristos that had been found lacking in every way by the tutors Leo had hired to whip him into shape to be his heir. The Aristos that had been alternately horrified and bemused by the fact that the very family he'd craved all his life could include conniving cousins, and vulture-like aunts. The Aristos that had been full of raw vulnerability and reckless stunts, the Aristos that had delighted in making her laugh.

The Aristos she'd tried for years to erase from her mind, her heart, her memories even. But he'd been her first love. Maybe the only man she'd ever loved.

"So that's what you think of me." He was standing half-naked in front of her and yet he'd never been more wrapped in armor, more inaccessible to Mira. "A man who goes back on his word, a man who has no loyalty. A man who would make a mockery of you and our marriage the first chance he gets. A man who doesn't even deserve a chance to defend himself."

"Our marriage was...*is* a convenient transaction, Aristos." Mira had never hated her hard heart more than at the moment. Never hated her inability to let herself be vulnerable and open.

How many precious things had she lost in her life because she'd never gotten over her mother's abandonment of her? Because her father had disappointed her again and again and again by never being even remotely interested in her existence? When did strength morph into brittleness that blinded one to all the good things in the world?

"We never..."

"If it was only a transaction, why did you run?"

And there was the crux of it. The small kernel of truth she'd been refusing to face for months. Even now, a part of her wanted to hide from his relentlessly prying gaze and from her own self. But she also wanted to touch him and kiss him and soothe his ruffled feathers and claim just a little of him for herself.

Something real.

He had given her that even in the midst of the ridiculous contract. But she'd been too stupid to see it, to take it. To know it.

Lifting her chin, she faced him. "Because I realized I did want it. Even if it was all a sham, I wanted it to be real for as long as it lasted."

"You had it, *thee mou*, and you threw it away."

An echo of something unsaid lingered in his words but Mira couldn't see it.

Before she could recover, he moved away from her, as if he couldn't bear to be near her. Something urgent and panicky filled her veins. She'd never been so wrong in her life. Never been so dependent on someone for her own peace of mind. A part of her wanted to slink away with her tail tucked between her legs, say it was over before it began.

The other part that had read and reread Thaata's note won.

His suitcase was flung open on the island in the closet and he'd pulled on black boxers by the time Mira gathered enough nerve to reach him.

One night... she kept chanting to herself. She'd live for this one night first and then sort out the rest.

She froze on the threshold though. For long minutes. She'd gotten an eyeful of his lethally honed body before but in sparse moonlight. But now... Heat flushed her from within, a sudden outpouring of desire. Her skin felt two sizes too tight.

His boxers hung low on bony hips—really, the man should be eating constantly for all the energy he burned through in his extreme lifestyle—and her eyes traced the dark trail of hair that ran down from his abdomen and disappeared into his underwear. Happy trail, wasn't that what Yana called it? Aptly named since Mira could happily explore where that led for hours.

Every bit of him was pure muscle. Including the sculpted V at his groin.

Her gaze moved up from that spot—a favorite of hers now—to his hard abdomen and then higher to his lean chest, smattered with springy chest hair. The man even had a sexy

Adam's apple, if that was possible. Mira licked her lips, myriad images of all the things she wanted to do with him flashing vividly in her mind.

Aristos had stilled too. And had caught her thoroughly shameless appraisal of him. But there was no knowing smirk dancing on his lips, no challenging glint in his eyes. No mocking taunts, no using their situation to touch her and taunt her and inflame her senses. And suddenly, she wanted that Aristos back.

She wanted him back, *period*.

"No, it's not shameless," she muttered to herself, shaking her head.

"What's not shameless?" he asked, instead of throwing her out, and Mira thought maybe there was a chance she could save the night at least.

"Me ogling you is not wrong or shameless," she replied, some of her confidence coming back. "You're mine to look at. Naked or otherwise."

Now where had that bold possessive declaration sprung from? And yet, she was damned if she'd take it back.

One arrogant brow rose in his face, but no warmth dawned in his eyes.

She'd never seen such cold frost in Aristos's eyes and something else struck her. She had hurt him—hurt the mighty, powerful, brilliant Aristos Carides. The man that nothing touched. And even more alarming was that he hadn't hidden his anger either.

It felt like she'd arranged her life into a rigid, unbending jigsaw puzzle, only to realize she not only had it wrong but there were important pieces missing.

"I'm sorry for not confronting you with my...doubts."

He barked out a laugh—loud and jarring and full of a

bitterness she'd never seen in him. "But not for doubting me in the first place?"

"I had my reasons to form the assumption in the first place. But I admit that I jumped to a conclusion that might not have been arrived at."

He cursed—a filthy word that his cousin Stella had taught her in the two months she'd lived at the Carides mansion. "*Christos*, Mira. You're the most infuriatingly stubborn, arrogant, tight-lipped woman I've ever met in my life."

"That's quite the distinction as I know how *many, many* women you've *met*, Aristos," she retorted.

God, where was her common sense? Why was she riling him up like this?

He advanced on her and she stood rooted in place, despite every rational instinct urging her to flee. Oh, Aristos would never hurt her in any way, she knew that. She'd always known that. It was her own heart that built unfounded expectations and ridiculous notions around him.

Reaching her, he grasped her by the nape of her neck and pulled her closer. How he managed to do it without actually being rough, Mira had not enough sense to figure out. Only that it felt possessive and hot and she liked it. Like really liked it. Liked it enough to feel dampness gush between her thighs, enough for her breasts to feel achy and heavy, enough to want to chase more.

"I want to know why you came to such a ridiculous conclusion."

Mira arched her back, which pushed her chest onto his and felt an answering shudder run through him. Satisfaction zinged through her. She swallowed at the stark need that filled her every pore. "Pity we all don't get what we want, then, isn't it? Even the powerful, brilliant Aristos." She licked her lips and his gaze zeroed in on that spot.

"Actually, you're not really that brilliant, are you? Because you're missing the obvious point here."

"You're playing with a street dog, *thee mou*. They don't play by rules. They might look and act domesticated but they never lose that ruthless edge."

She scrunched her nose. "I really object to that analogy, Aristos. But if we must use it, I've never, ever shamed you for your origins."

"No?"

It was her turn to frown. "Of course not," she said, a sinking feeling in her gut. "I'd be the worst kind of person to hold that against—"

"What did I miss?"

"Don't change the subject," she said, stiffening up in his hold. "You're not the only one who could get angry by unfounded accusations."

"What did I miss, Mira?"

She huffed out a breath, knowing that she'd just be butting her head against an immovable wall. When Aristos shut down, she remembered like it was yesterday, he shut down hard. "You're angry with me, I know. Probably enough to dissolve our arrangement," she said, testing the waters.

"Wouldn't you like to know, Dr. Carides?"

Really, the man was far too perceptive for his own good. "Fine. You have every right to be angry. But you missed the fact that I came into your room tonight, Aristos. Dressed like I am," she said, ignoring the heat climbing up her chest.

His gaze shifted down, and gleamed. Her big breasts were just about falling out of the lace negligee's neckline, pressed up tight against his chest. Between the lace chafing her sensitive nipples and the heat from his body, it was a miracle she hadn't melted into a puddle at his feet.

Something like a growl escaped his throat and one large

hand cupped her hip with a possessiveness that made her want to whimper with need. "*Why did* you come into my room tonight?"

"Losing my grandparents so close together made me realize how…lonely I've been. Not just these last few months, but before we met again in Vegas too. How I've pretended like it's enough and the pretense became reality. I wanted to feel something real tonight. To feel alive. To grasp something for myself. And you… Kissing you was the most real thing I had felt in so long, Aristos. Selfishly, I wanted to ask you for more. I wanted to forget contracts and clauses and transactions and just ask you to give me something real again. Something no one else can give me."

His chest rose and fell, as if he felt gripped by the same emotion that held her. "And what are you dressed for, *yineka mou*?"

Pushing to her toes, she let more of her weight fall into him. His grunt cinched the knot in her lower belly tight. Nuzzling into his stubbled jaw, she reveled in the rough graze of it against her soft skin. "To be seduced to within an inch of my life. To seduce you too though I really don't have much experience with that."

As if granting her unspoken wish, he rubbed that stubble against the soft underside of her jaw, her neck, his fingers drawing mindless circles against her lower back and buttocks. God, they hadn't even kissed yet and she was this close to climax. The scent and heat of him surrounded her, bringing back memories she'd shoved so deep that her heart thundered in her ears. Pulling back to look at him, she tried to hold on to the last thread of sanity but it was a losing battle. "I could've asked Yana for pointers but then I'd have to illuminate her and Nush about the state of affairs between us. And I couldn't have that because they adore you and idolize you and think we're this great love match going through a rough period and I didn't want to break their hearts."

He bopped the tip of her nose, his smile wide. "You're cute when you're nervous."

"I'm not nervous. I'm…horny and needy and if you don't—"

His other arm wrapped around her waist and he was lifting her until her pelvis rocked against his and Mira went giddy with pleasure. His hard length pressed against her core and she ground her hips, begging for more. His mouth opened against her neck, warm and damp, and then he bit that sensitive spot and he timed it to his rocking hips and his filthy words about what he was going to do to her and how many times he was going to push her over the edge.

And beneath the heat spreading through her like molten lava, Mira's chest tightened with emotion. She'd needed him tonight, only him. But a part of her hadn't been hopeful that he'd give her this. That he wouldn't—justly as she'd found out—laugh in her face at her request. And yet he was here, his kisses hungry, his caresses designed to drive her to the edge but his smile and his eyes, present, here with her. Holding her through one of the hardest nights of her life.

Gratitude sat like a lump in her throat but he'd hate it if she thanked him. Instead, she dug her fingers into his thick hair, tugged his head up and kissed the hollow of his throat. Her heart felt like it might explode out of her rib cage as his large, lean body suddenly stilled and Mira knew he was remembering just as she was.

The first time he'd asked her to kiss him, she'd buried her face in his throat, shy and tentative, and then she'd kissed him there and told him it was her favorite spot to kiss in the entire world and he'd held her like that for long minutes, his arms wrapped tight around her.

"That was enough then, *ne*?" he said, his dark eyes all inscrutable, the pupils blown wide with lust. "Not anymore, *yineka mou*."

There was a warning in his words, even anger, and yet Mira didn't care right then. "No, it's not enough," she said, sinking her fingers into his hair. She'd wanted this man like she wanted no other for fifteen years. And tonight, she was going to have him.

Tonight, he was all hers.

Tugging his head down, holding his challenging gaze, Mira pressed her lips to his. The first contact singed all the way to her toes. His lips were soft and firm and warm and she rubbed hers up and down, side to side, intent on learning and kissing every inch of him. She poured all the things she couldn't say into the kiss, teasing him with her tongue, taunting him with nips of her teeth and doing it all over again. Slow and soft, she had her way with him, all the pent-up longing and frustration and desire of years flowing out of her. And then she bit his lower lip and tugged it into her mouth and when he growled, she swallowed the sound, then lapped at his lip with her tongue.

Her eyes flew open as her back met the wall. Locking her against it, Aristos rocked into her again and Mira thought she might just come from that. "Shall I show you how I like to kiss, Mira?" he asked, his fingers deep in her hair, her scalp stinging.

"Yes. Do whatever you want to me, Aristos. Just please, I don't want to think. Only feel."

"Your wish is my command, *thee mou*."

And he did take over and how spectacularly he did. The kiss had none of the finesse and tenderness of the other kiss.

None of the soft entreaty or the slow exploration of hers. It was all teeth and tongues and greediness and pulse-pounding pleasure and stolen breaths. Mira gave herself over to all of it—to the sensations, to the freeing she felt in her soul, and to him, her husband, Aristos Carides. At least for now.

By the time Aristos pulled back, she was half sobbing, half panting, thrusting her hips into his, chasing that mindless rhythm where nothing but sheer pleasure existed. The only place, it seemed, where Aristos and she could meet each other in perfect communion.

It was more than she'd expected when she'd signed her name on the marriage contract. More than she'd ever wanted for herself. Maybe it was even enough to sustain their relationship over a lifetime instead of five years, came the errant thought with such fervent hope and blinding clarity that she came to herself.

Only to realize that her feet were on the ground again and Aristos was not kissing her anymore and why was Aristos not kissing her anymore?

With a shaking hand, she pushed a stray lock of hair from her face and met his gaze. He wasn't touching her but he hadn't moved away either. "What's wrong?" she asked, a thread of fear snaking around her. If he walked away now, God, she'd go mad.

One hand on the wall behind her head, he was breathing hard and watching her face. Always watching her, studying her, delving into her as if she was some big mystery he wanted to unravel.

A long time ago, the way he looked at her had made her feel on top of the world, it had made her feel like a...*queen*. There was that word again.

"What?" she said, feeling unnerved by the intensity of

his scrutiny. She licked her lips and found his taste there. Lapped at it again, greedy for more. "Why did you stop?"

"I thought we should sort things out before this went further."

Her mouth fell open in a gasp and she punched his stomach with her fist. Not that the man even grunted. "It's clearly not that good between us if you can stop to scheme, Aristos."

His palms clasped her cheeks when she'd have made her escape. "No, *agapi*. Stopping this is the hardest thing I've ever done and I've scaled mountains that killed other men." He took in a deep breath. "But you should know, if you don't already, that I'm a scheming, strategizing man to my core, Mira. I don't take a step in a sport or in a case without planning ten steps ahead. It's what kept me alive for the most part."

Mira swallowed, uncaring what he saw in her eyes. "I'm listening."

"Are you coming back to me? After you use me tonight?"

The laughing glint was back in his eyes but she had this knowing in the pit of her stomach that it was forced. That he had brought it in on purpose to lessen the gravity from the first question.

But his cover only proved her exhaustion at having to provide one of her own. It seemed she didn't care anymore what he saw.

"I think so."

"Not good enough, *thee mou*. There's a reason I made the proposition to you. Carides's board still needs to see me settle down. Leo still wants his heir in case I end up dead. If your answer is you think so, then this ends now."

"No, wait," Mira said, grabbing onto his arm. Words rushed out of her, fueled by something she didn't understand. "Yes, yes, okay. I'll come back and see our...arrangement through." How that word stuck in her throat. "I still want a…baby. But I want some amendments to the conditions."

"Agreed to any and all amendments," Aristos said so fast that Mira's head spun.

Only when she looked into his devilish eyes did she realize he'd been bluffing when he'd said he'd walk away.

"Yes, to anything? Without demanding explanations?"

"Yes," he said, studying her.

"You're so confident that you can seduce any kind of common sense out of me, aren't you?" she said, half smiling, half in awe.

"Maybe." And then he was dragging her into his arms, and his mouth was at her neck and Mira thought she could die right now and it would be a happy death. Another breath-stealing kiss. Another climb to the edge. Another thorough ravishment of her in which this time, his clever fingers joined in.

"Truth or dare, Aristos," she whispered against his chest, her legs jelly under her. The man was using her like his personal wind-up toy, bringing her to the edge and then talking her down.

"Truth," he said, laughing against her mouth.

"Would you have let me walk away if I hadn't agreed?"

"No, Mira." His large hands went down her back, down, down, down until he had her buttocks in them and he was squeezing them, and pulling her hard against him, until his erection was once again notched at her sex and she was melting away into a million molecules of pleasure. "Your stubborn, infuriating, sexy ass is mine for the next five years and I don't mean to waste a single day of it."

Mira pretended like her heart didn't swap five years for

something else and protested that it was four years and four months.

By the end of the night, the wily, cunning, ruthless man that was her husband had persuaded her that the clock had reset on the five years and Mira couldn't find it in her to disagree. Not when he brought her to the edge, again and again, and made her body soar with pleasure. Not when after three orgasms, the man had spooned her from behind and thrust into her again, as insatiable as she was for him.

Five years with Aristos—more real and more intense than anything she'd ever asked for. Would they be enough to sustain her for a lifetime? Or would it be impossible and heartbreaking yet again to walk away from him?

When she shivered at the very thought, he gathered her to him until his very breath was hers. His fingers were at her forehead, smoothing away the frown as he whispered, "No overthinking this, wife."

Mira smiled and nodded.

Queen for a day, she told herself, before falling asleep against the warm cocoon of her husband's body with a wide smile.

CHAPTER THREE

Present day

THE DOUBLE DOORS to his office suite swung open so suddenly that Aristos gritted his teeth. An expletive hovered on his tongue about being disturbed when he was in the middle of reviewing case notes with his team, when silence fell around the noisy room like a muffling blanket.

Massaging the nape of his stiff neck with his fingers, he looked up and stilled.

Mira stood framed by the double doors, a large blush-pink shoulder bag dangling from her fingers, an overnight bag in the same color by her feet.

That bag wasn't big enough.

He shoved the errant thought aside, reminding himself that she was here.

After years of being denied the thing he wanted most, after all the years of waiting, Mira was finally here. *As his wife.* Right, then, he would enjoy the success of the first step of his plan *and* the sight of her.

Dressed simply in dark blue skinny jeans that hugged shapely legs and wide hips, and a white V-necked T-shirt that showed off the hell out of her breasts, she looked sensational. Stunning. Delicious enough that he wanted to throw his staff out, seat her on his desk and lick her up all over.

Every inch of his body was hurting today. He was main-lining painkillers as if they were coffee after a brutal physio session, and still, Aristos felt the hungry clench of his abused muscles as he took in the glorious sight of her limned by light against the entrance.

Evening sunlight bathed her round face, showing him everything he was greedy for. Thick silky strands escaped her usual no-nonsense French braid, giving her a slightly disheveled look. A thin sheen of perspiration made her light brown skin glow. But there was also a pinched look to her features, fatigue drawing tight lines around her mouth.

Aristos frowned.

Mira had always had a plump face with big eyes, an ar-rogant nose, a wide mouth and a curvy figure—*Christos*, everything about her had become his type, and yet there was none of her usual radiance to her today. The hollow-ness of her cheeks said she'd clearly lost weight in the weeks since he'd seen her.

Was it just grief or something else? Should he have stayed and helped, despite Caio's reassurances that he had every-thing under control? Did the stubborn woman even real-ize it was okay to lean on someone else from time to time?

Across the vast room, their gazes met. And held. Time itself seemed to come to a standstill as neither of them blinked. As if they were starring in one of those old West-ern movies Leo laughed at, engaging in some shady stand-off, betting on who would win.

He grinned, wanting her to see his pleasure at her arrival, gave her another lengthy, shameless perusal, wanting her to know where his mind immediately went. Wanting to rile her up. Even though grinning at his wife like a lecherous creep in the middle of a staff meeting meant the muscles in his jaw pulled up and his cheekbone hurt like hell.

Even across the distance that separated them, he could see the flare of awareness in her eyes, the subtle defensive stance she took as if she could hide her response to him. Like clockwork, anger followed. Along with a glimmer of wetness in her eyes that made his hackles rise. She blinked and then glared at him again, making him wonder if the painkillers were making him loopy.

Like insects beginning to buzz, whispers started around them. His staff was clearly reaching the obvious conclusion about her. No one—man or woman—would dare to interrupt one of his strategy meetings. And of course, having never laid eyes on his mysterious, "boring" wife ever, they were lapping it up as if they were at the first showing of a successful drama.

"Welcome to my office, Dr. Carides."

"I'm disappointed, Aristos," she said in that crystal-clear voice of hers that rang like a bell, her chin lifted with that belligerence that equally disconcerted and excited him.

Everyone and everything fell silent again.

"And why is that, *thee mou*?" he said, just as loudly, pouring all the charm he had into the words, making them thrum with the pleasant tension in his muscles that wasn't from the painkillers.

If she wanted a public argument, who was he to deny her? Who was he to stop the media from reporting tomorrow that Aristos Carides's darling American wife had stormed back into his life in the most magnificent way possible?

"All through the flight, I had these elaborate dreams of being carried over the threshold in your strong arms in a grand gesture of loving welcome." Her voice barely dipped in tone but her hard swallow belied her composure. "Only to find you can barely move."

The simpering, pouting tone of her voice sent a fresh wave of shock through him.

Aristos reached for one of his crutches leaning against the desk, hiding his confusion about her state of mind under a smile. "Your wish is my command, Dr. Carides. All you had to do, ever, was ask." The tendons in his forearms bulged as he tried to push himself up and sweat pooled at his neck and under his arms.

Of course, his dear wife had to pick this precise time to show up in his life.

Mira was at his side in the next blink, looming over his chair, her face wreathed in blazing anger. "Stop it," she said, slapping him lightly on his wrist, as if he were a recalcitrant child. "Stella told me about your accident, that your injuries are bad."

Out of the periphery of his sweat-clogged vision, Aristos noticed that his PA, Elena, had also rushed to his side, almost mirroring Mira's stance.

"I didn't know you were into rougher stuff," he whispered, shielding Mira from curious eyes with his shoulders, defaulting to mocking her.

Streaks of pink appeared on her already flushed cheeks. When he didn't relent, she muttered, "I should've known better than to challenge you."

Aristos grinned up at her. He hated losing in life, in any way or form. Especially to her. Keeping the smile on his face took all the energy he had.

She sighed. "Please, Aristos. I was only kidding. Don't… hurt yourself further."

He sat back and took her in—the folded arms and the unusual concern glinting in those eyes. "I had all kinds of dreams too, you know, about how I would welcome you," he said, following the sudden impulse to shake her dark mood off. He'd not foreseen the frustration his injuries would cause when he was around her. "That is, when I could convince myself that you would come back without further... persuasion from me."

"By *persuasion*, you mean *coercion*."

"All's fair in marriage and war," he retorted, his voice taking on an edge.

"As you can see, I'm here. So neither is required," she said softly.

"You took your sweet time getting here, *yineka mou*," he said, twisting his mouth into a mock pout.

"Why didn't you let me know you were..." She bit her lip and he could almost see her grapple for control, "If I had known how seriously you were injured..."

Again, she stopped herself, casting an eye around their intent audience.

Aristos watched her, willing himself to be still, as her gaze rounded the vast conference table. Her blandly polite smile went into icy territory when it lingered on Elena for just a nanosecond longer before moving on and rounding back to him.

Realization pressed on him, the sensation akin to when he'd been wedged under a flaming piece of metal during the accident.

His suspicion had been right.

It was Elena she thought he'd cheated on her with.

Instantly, he remembered the rainy evening when Elena had, out of nowhere, made her feelings known to him in an aggressive manner he'd never seen from her. It was one of the few times shock had frozen Aristos into inaction. His fast reaction times and his ability to foresee everything coming at him were the reasons he hadn't ended up dead so many times. And yet, he had been thrown for a loop at

Elena's actions. So much so that it had taken him several seconds, maybe even minutes, to untangle himself from her untenable, cloying embrace.

He'd immediately made two things clear in no uncertain terms—their one-night fling fifteen years ago, when he'd acted like a fatally wounded animal looking to make the worst kind of decisions to bury his pain, had been a huge mistake he'd erased from his mind, never to be repeated again. Secondly, and more importantly, he was married now and that meant his wife had all his loyalty. Even though she deposited a body pillow between them like some fortress wall he needed to scale every night. That thought he'd kept to himself.

To which, Elena had guffawed loudly—until it had dawned on her that he was utterly serious.

Aristos had forgiven her two blunders that evening—one that she'd apparently been so sure of his response that she'd unwisely acted on it and the other that she'd intended to be cruel to both him and Mira and their arrangement. But Elena was… Elena. One of the very few people who had known him when he'd been nothing and still remained by his side.

Not out of duty or familial pride, like his grandfather reminded him at every chance.

Not out of false loyalty and induced by greed and ambition like most of his cousins.

But out of choice.

Yes, there was the fact that he paid Elena extraordinarily well but still… He liked to believe they had a bond of some sort. Just not the kind she'd imagined.

It had been easy to move on from the awkward incident with Elena returning to her usual sensible, no-nonsense efficiency.

Only it had had a consequence Aristos hadn't imagined—

Mira had run away from him yet again. Just the reminder of how low she thought he could sink set his teeth on edge.

"Ask everyone to leave," Mira said now, in a quietly demanding voice that brought his head up with a jerk.

"We're in the middle of an important strategy meeting that we're already behind on. We can't just stop for...personal reasons," came Elena's soft reply from his other side.

A murmur of assent followed from his most diligent staff members.

He turned his gaze to Mira, let the pregnant pause prolong, despite his need to placate her. As his PA and right-hand woman and the one who was shouldering the brunt load of work because of his damned accident and required rest, Elena's polite dismissal of Mira's demand was not... wrong or confrontational. But he wanted to see his reluctant wife's reaction to it, see if she'd betray the smallest chink in the iron armor she swathed herself in.

With this fresh start, he wanted Mira to come to him with the truth, assert her role in his life.

Christos, how was it that he wanted the one woman in the entire world who had no desire to be his wife? Or had that always been Mira's appeal—that she was icily untouchable, perfectly unattainable for someone who had crawled out of the gutter?

"I understand," Mira said softly, holding Elena's gaze.

Disappointment curdled in his stomach, more sourly than the medication he had to consume every few hours.

"But this is a rare occasion," she began again, with a polite smile, "and I can assure you all I won't make a habit out of interrupting your important meetings on a regular basis. So, please, see yourself out." Steel wrapped in silken, soft tones.

His tired body flooded with arousal.

"Will ten minutes suffice?" Elena asked, even though most of his staff had already shot to their feet.

Aristos hid his dislike. With that question, Elena was hovering on the very firm boundary he drew around his personal life.

Mira, though, looked in everyone else's direction, effectively communicating that responding to Elena's quip was beneath her. "My husband's clearly not at his best and needs his rest. I know he pays you all astronomical salaries for your expertise. Do as much as you can in his absence. I'll forward any directives he might have tomorrow morning."

If he hadn't been coached relentlessly by tutors and his grandfather that it made him appear common and cheap and vulgar and even weak to his enemies, to express his astonishment at life's little blips, Aristos would have had his chin hitting his chest in soundless wonder.

When Elena sent him a beseeching glance, unwisely requesting him to trump Mira's dictates, his wife made the decision for him in a soft tone that would brook no opposition. "Oh, and I'll also be communicating how he'll be conducting business in the near future. Because he's not going to be coming into work again. For several weeks at the least."

Mira sank into the leather chair next to Aristos, fighting the urge to bury her face in her hands and moan loudly, with both relief and mortification.

She shouldn't have bossed around his staff. For one thing, it was highly unprofessional. Secondly, it was beneath her to engage in the sort of possessive behavior that only seemed to broadcast the worst kind of insecurities.

But the sight of his PA rushing to his aid, the reality of that woman, who had been such an insidious, important part of Aristos's life for so many years, questioning Mira's sensible decision, had pushed her into a danger zone where she reacted emotionally.

It was bad enough how alarmingly pale Aristos's skin looked in utter contrast to the colorful map of bruises on his face. Neither had she missed how fast and shallow his breathing had become when he'd tried to push up to his feet. It was bad enough that he was here at work, looking and feeling like he did.

Did the blasted man have no sense of when and where his strength might desert him? That he could permanently injure himself if he didn't give his body enough time and space to heal?

His PA was very possibly just doing her job. But it was not her call to decide whether Aristos should be at work or not. If he wasn't going to take care of himself, then she was going to do it for him.

"'My husband is not at his best and needs his rest...'" Aristos parroted in a mocking voice. "That sounds like some awful poem that rhymes."

Mira turned to look at him and her breath fled her body afresh for more than one reason. His thin and yet wide lower lip was split right down the middle. There was a yellowing bruise covering his entire right cheekbone and there were stitches that hadn't yet healed beginning at the middle of his left eyebrow and inching up into his forehead.

And these, she knew, were only the cosmetic ones.

Still, none of them even remotely minimized the appeal of the man. Which confirmed something Mira had always known. His stunning good looks were only the smallest part of what made Aristos so dynamic, such a deeply dominant presence in any room or crowd.

Even now, his eyes danced with unholy delight as she studied him with a desperate greed she couldn't deny. She shied her gaze away from the shadow of bruises at the V of his loose, long-sleeved gray T-shirt, which was clearly camouflage.

"I'm wondering if I should apologize," she asked, uncaring that the ridiculous question undid her assertive declaration. As long as it gave her emotions time to find steady ground.

"Why?"

"It's your office, a professional environment. Not the local fish market. I had no right to barge in here and definitely had no right to act like I...like some jealous, overeager wife keeping an eye on her schmuck husband."

"Ah... But you are my wife, Mira and I would say you have some right to assert yourself over me, whichever way you want, schmuck or not."

Assert herself over him... How did he make the most innocuous of statements sound like the most delicious lure, Mira would never know.

"Only some?" she said, humor at his made-up words washing away some of the fear that had gripped her all through the flight. He looked battered and bruised and she still had to look at his reports to know the exact detail of his injuries. Outwardly, he definitely looked damaged. But... seeing him in the flesh, teasing and taunting her like three months hadn't passed, the roller coaster of emotions with her hormones in the driving seat came to a temporary pause.

How she wished she could talk to Nanamma right now, about her fears about the pregnancy, about how irrationally upset she kept getting over things that had never bothered her before. About how much she yearned to share the abundance of her joy with Aristos and have him reciprocate it fully. But she wasn't here now and when she had been, Mira had held her cards too close to her heart. Even convinced herself her heart didn't feel much to begin with.

Her sisters would definitely share her joy, shout it out from the rooftops, she knew. But it wasn't right to tell them before she told Aristos.

Which should be any moment now. Only that seeing him hurt…was doing a number on her. Her chest felt like a dangerously inflating balloon that might pop as she thought of what his reaction might be.

What if he'd changed his mind about being a father? What if he wasn't happy about the news? What if…

"Only some—the basic minimum—are granted by the contract," he said, hooded gaze watching her. Assessing her. "The rest have to be earned."

She raised a brow. "By being your biddable, caring wife?"

"By cohabiting with me under the same roof. In the same bed, more importantly."

She laughed then, tears pooling in her eyes, and only some of it was due to humor. Relief coursed through her in waves, making her suddenly cold. Turning her face away from Aristos, she made a show of searching for a cardigan in her large handbag.

A sweatshirt fell into a perfect drape over her shoulders. Mira took a deep breath, the scent of ocean surrounding her in comfort. "You are not okay, Dr. Carides," came his even-toned statement.

It drove tears into her throat, that casual way he smothered the concern. "I really don't like being addressed as such."

"But you're a real doctor about to specialize in palliative care, are you not?"

"Of course I'm a real doctor." How did he know what she'd wanted to specialize in? Was Aristos privy to everything in her personal life? "I meant that you can't call me Dr. Carides. I worked damned hard to get my degree and it is Dr. Reddy."

"I'm too much of a feminist to deny your right to decide that," he said with such genuine sincerity that Mira felt the overwhelming urge to grab his battered face and kiss the hell out of it. He raised a finger in that dramatic way of his, energy radiating from him even in his exhausted state. "But I would also like to point out that I too have made a big sacrifice—unwilling at best and screaming denial at worst—in you attaining that damned degree, *thee mou*. I demand and deserve at least a little credit."

Her mouth falling open, Mira stared at him. Did he mean what she thought he meant? Had her bald-faced lie that her career and her calling were more important than getting married—the reason she'd given for breaking their engagement—still carry weight with him? "You're mad."

"Some call it genius."

Challenge glinted in his eyes.

Take the bait, they said. *Take me on.*

Pressing her palm against her belly, she shied away from it.

His low, humorless laugh mocked her.

"I probably should say sorry for my bossiness but I won't."

"Lucky for you, I like your bossiness, Dr. Carides."

Her gaze jerked to his and warmth speared her at the slumbering heat in his. It was impossible to not react, to not feel something in the presence of the very real desire in his eyes.

"Now, please tell me why you felt the need to throw my staff out. If it is so that you could have your way with me, know that I'm most willing in spirit. My body, however, might not quite cooperate just yet."

"Like I said, you're mad," Mira whispered, heat flushing her from within. "Wait a second, so you can't get it up?"

Dark color streaked his sharp cheekbones. "Of course I can get it up, you wicked woman." His gaze swept over her, from her hair to her feet, lingering in places, possessively invasive and yet warmly intimate at the same time. "But you will have to do most of the work. At least for today."

"A few weeks is more like it," Mira said with a sigh. "You're clearly not fit for sex or to be here." She squared her shoulders. "Are you going to fight me on this?"

"I love fighting with you. It's the only time you play for real."

Every word, every sentence, every look from him was a tease, a taunt. A double-edged sword dipped in honey that he dared her to dance on. "Why didn't you let me know how bad the injuries were? I'd have come immediately."

"Because I do not want your pity. If that's the reason you're here, please turn around and go back to your clinic. I'll have my PA text you as soon as I'm in working order."

"That's not how a marriage works," Mira said. Even the thought of that woman playing intermediary between them made her want to growl. "Even one with a five-year shelf life."

When she grabbed one of his crutches so that she could hand it to him, his long fingers stilled her.

Storms swirled in those gray eyes, turning them dark as his starkly handsome face drew close to hers. Close enough for her to see the deep lines of strain around his mouth. One long finger traced the plump jut of the veins at her wrist. "I'll have one of the chauffeurs drive you. Go home and rest, Mira."

Mira flinched at the dismissal in his tone. "And where's home? Carides mansion or California?"

"The mansion—your home." The tips of his fingers danced lightly over the skin under her eyes. "You look like you're ready to drop out of exhaustion."

"I'll rest once I see you settled into your bed."

"I have attendants and round-the-clock nurses to look after me. You're not here to play nurse at my bedside."

"No, I'm here to play wife at your bedside, Aristos."

"I'm of no use to you until I recover."

Hurt lanced through her.

Yes, their marriage was a contract because they both wanted children. Because they both wanted a convenient arrangement with none of the emotional hassle. That's how this had started.

But was it still just that to him, even after that night? Did he think she wanted nothing more of him than his services as a...stud?

She threw the sweatshirt he'd draped over her shoulders back at him, hurt and anger making her movements erratic. "You're so...arrogant and reckless. You think you're invincible. But you're wrong." She grabbed her handbag then and hitched it over her shoulder.

"Where the hell are you going?" Aristos demanded in a quiet tone, pushing himself to his feet and getting the crutches under him.

"You can't dictate that I can be your wife only when you're hearty and healthy. And if it sticks in your craw that much to let me see you like this—" she was shouting the words at him now and God, she never shouted "—then you should've thought of that before you decided to drive some beastly car around a curve that kills most men just to show off your macho power."

"Mira, you're crying."

The quiet desolation in his voice perversely made the tumult of her own emotions still. She ran the back of her hand over her cheeks, feeling as shocked as he was.

Around them, evening had given way to twilight. The floor-to-ceiling glass wall behind him showed the city's brilliant lights and cast dark shadows over his bruised face.

Aristos, in her mind and her heart, was dynamic, impossible to pin down, larger than life. The thought of him stuck under thousands of pounds of hot, scorching metal made bile rise in her throat.

"Come, Mira. Let's go home."

She stared at his hand, extended between them. The long, elegant fingers with square nails. The rough, abrasive texture of his palm. The sprinkling of hair over his arms. The corded strength in his arms.

"I don't know," she said, clutching her neck where a giant boulder seemed to have lodged, cutting off her air. "I should've known making a deal with you is tempting the devil itself. I shouldn't have—"

His hands clasped her cheeks and she jerked at the warmth of him. "Look at me, Mira. The injuries look worse than they are right now."

"I should've never gotten involved with you—"

"It's too late to back out now."

Mira buried her face in his chest, drawing long, deep breaths to quiet the building hysteria.

"You're scaring me to death right now—"

It was the fear in his words that did it. And the thundering beat of his heart at her cheek. And the solid hardness of him around her. She laughed, wiping her hands over her cheeks again. "Serves you right. Because that's what you did to me when it should've been the opposite. When you should be making things easier for me. When you should be…" Wrapping her arms around his waist, she burrowed into him. If she could lodge herself under his skin, she'd have done it. "You could have died, Aristos. Where would that have left me?"

"A wealthy widow."

Her hands on his chest, she pushed him, anger sending her to the other end of the seesaw. "I'm pregnant. Do you still want to talk about leaving me a wealthy widow, you bastard?"

Whatever color remaining in his face fled, leaving the colorful bruises to stand out even more. "You're pregnant," he repeated, his gaze going to her belly and then combing back up to collide with her gaze.

Mira nodded. "Not just…" She licked her lips, the intensity of his scrutiny making the words harder to come. "It's twins. We're having twins."

His features were frozen into a mask, and tension thrummed through him. "Two babies?"

She smiled then, and the joy of sharing her news washed away everything else. "Yes, twins means two babies."

"And everything is okay with you? With…them?" he said, waving a hand around her midsection.

"Yes. Everything's fine and as it should be."

His throat moved on a hard swallow and a part of her wanted him to wrap her up in his arms. Wanted to burrow herself into him until she didn't have to be strong. Wanted to give herself over, completely.

She'd been prepared for the news and still, it had been a shock. What was he thinking? What was he feeling? Why did he look…*trapped*? Or was that her own fretful mind adding fuel to the fire?

But even the sudden tension that seemed to bathe him

couldn't help Mira shed the wretched feeling when she imagined him gone from the world. She couldn't even grasp the deeper meaning of that feeling just then.

"I just lost my grandparents in the last year. And even though there are times when…" Deflection escaped her. "I'd be devastated if you died, Aristos. Especially now." She gathered her tattered composure and raised her chin. "So if you plan to continue on this…reckless path and end up dead sooner or later, then tell me now. Because I can't go through that again. I won't go through another death, another loss. I won't put my children through it. It's better they don't know you than lose you because you have to constantly prove yourself. That contract means nothing to me then."

"What does that mean?"

"It means I'll walk away now and never return if you don't put a stop to your ridiculous, death-defying stunts."

CHAPTER FOUR

A COUPLE OF hours later, Aristos walked slow laps around the manicured gardens, his thoughts refusing to settle.

Before Mira could make real on her threats, they'd been interrupted by an excited Stella and his grandfather, who'd heard that Mira had returned. Returned to their marriage, returned to him. At least, his grandfather and his cousin seemed to view Mira's return as an inevitability and were happy for them.

He'd half expected Mira to start their argument back up again when he'd suggested that she was tired, and refuse to come home with him. As much as he'd wanted to think that she'd pounced on a new excuse to break their arrangement, her tears and the fracture of her even temper had been far too real.

God, he'd never seen her like that. And he never, ever, wanted to see her like that again. The realization that he'd been responsible for it sat like a boulder on his chest, hours later.

Mira's wide smile and warmth when she'd hugged his cousin had been real too. Aristos had never been more thankful for Stella's spectacular entry than that evening. He'd forgotten how much Mira hated confrontations, how her self-possession had always driven him up the wall. And yet today, she'd let him see how fragile she was feeling.

"I'd be devastated if you died, Aristos. Especially now."

Which brought him to the huge, glaring truth he still couldn't seem to settle with.

They were having twins! Twins—Christos! Two babies... two real, tiny individuals...

Sweat beaded on his brow and his chest contracted again in a weird spasm.

Wanting a child with Mira was one thing and hearing her say she was pregnant with twins was a whole different thing.

He would be father to two children...two little lives he could ruin and traumatize and corrupt in a thousand different ways. Ignoring the twinge of discomfort in his hip, he went inside the gym and ran through the strength routine his physiotherapist had been insisting Aristos do since the accident.

The aches and pains fell away as his mind churned the same thing over and over.

What the hell did he know about being a father?

He'd never even seen the face of the man who'd fathered him. The man who had abandoned his mother long before Aristos had been even the size of a kidney bean. He'd dumped her the moment he'd learned that her billionaire father, Leo Carides, had washed his hands of her, said that she was nothing but a spoiled princess playing at rough love, Mama had told him in one of her drunken ramblings.

Sperm provider, that's what the man had been. Nothing more.

Wasn't that his role too? a mocking voice asked and Aristos found he had no way to refute it. And he didn't want to let it stand true.

It had seemed simple enough in theory when he'd concocted the plan. By marrying her, he'd give her what she so desperately wanted. And he would settle down and build the legacy that Leo and the Carides board wouldn't stop carping about instead of using his stunts to undermine his charity efforts. *And* he would have finally Mira in his life as his wife.

The concept of fatherhood had been a vague, far-fetched thing he'd barely thought of. At best, he'd assumed he'd be a generous, busy father and would keep his involvement to a minimum. He had no doubt—then or now—what a phenomenal mother Mira would be. He'd seen her with Yana and Nush—how completely she loved them, how unconditional her support of them was. He'd remembered her dream even as a teenager to build a family of her own.

Christos, what an arrogant, thoughtless ass he'd been. The very same reassurances did nothing to dispel his escalating confusion now.

And the thought of Mira leaving him in five years with their children in tow—because for all that he was the arrogant, ruthless bastard that she called him, he'd never separate their children from her—left him with a visceral fear he couldn't get a hold on.

Growing up on the streets of Athens with an alcoholic mother who barely remembered to feed him, all Aristos had ever wanted was a family. When Leo had brought him home years after his mother's death, he'd thought he'd found one—for all of two minutes. In the end, he'd realized he'd have a family only if he made one and he'd wanted to build it with only one woman.

Now the blasted contract stood between them like a wall. And the fact that his wife thought the worst of him.

She thought he'd cheated on her.

She thought he would be an irresponsible, uncaring, even reckless parent.

She thought very little of him. With the tiring routine siphoning away some of his anger, a bit of sense returned.

Had he given her cause to think any better? Yes, she should know better, know him better, but that was a faulty assumption. He was dealing with a woman who, after summers of falling in love with him, had broken their engagement overnight. With a woman who didn't fall for sweet words or cute promises but demanded action.

So he'd simply have to prove to her what he could be as a husband and as a father-to-be and as a provider.

He wasn't going to let go of Mira or his children or the family he was finally building. Not now. Not in five years. Not ever. That much was clear to him. Which meant he'd have to teach his dear wife that threats and intimidations didn't work on him. Especially not the ones about her leaving him.

He'd just finished his routine, dumped water over his overheated head and returned to his bedroom when Mira stepped out of the attached bathroom. They hadn't spoken again since he'd left her in Stella's capable hands as soon they'd returned and he'd fled to the state-of-the-art gym he'd had built in one wing of the mansion.

Seeing Mira in his bedroom settled something in his chest.

Except for the quiet swishing sound of the waves from the ocean past the veranda attached to their bedroom, heavy silence blanketed them. Overhead lights flickered on with each step he took toward the center of the room, illuminating her face more and more. He let his gaze sweep over her body with a lazy leisure he was far from feeling.

Her hair, damp and braided, hung over one shoulder. She'd changed into a baby-pink silk negligee that fluttered far above her knees and a matching robe tied at the waist that invited a closer look at the cleavage it proudly served up. *Christos*, he'd forgotten about his wife's fascination with silk-and-lace lingerie. During the day and to the general population, she was Dr. Mira Carides—self-sufficient, smart and almost always conservatively dressed in pantsuits. A woman who was ruthlessly sensible and let none of life's fancies or silliness touch her.

By night, she was his sensuous wife who loved tormenting him in one sexy outfit after the other. That he was the only one who got to see this Mira, touch this Mira, know this Mira…went a long way to calming him down.

In the minimal light, he realized now that she'd lost weight. Her round cheeks had a sunken, taut look. Even with exhaustion etching itself into the lines of her face, her skin gleamed with that dewy silkiness that invited his touch.

He wanted to pick her up and wrap her in his arms and tend to her. He wanted to place his hand on her belly and let the sheer wonder of the children they'd created together fill him. He wanted to revel in the feeling of something bigger than him for once in his life.

He resisted the urge to do it all with a patience born of a fight for survival. He was a master strategist, forever planning in business or his charities or his dares, ten steps ahead.

He'd stay away tonight, deny all the clamoring needs in his mind and body. And as many nights as it took for him to get control over his emotions. For as angry as he was with her, he didn't want to make his pregnant wife cry.

Once was more than enough.

Just as he took an inventory of her, she did one of him.

Aristos cursed the fact that he'd walked back with nothing but his workout shorts on. Those light brown eyes of her went rounder and bigger as they took in the map of colorful bruises and scars on his torso. Over the burn on his lower hip, which was healing but left a large scar. Over the scratches on his chest. Over the dark bruise inked across his abdomen.

Suddenly, he found himself offering thanks that she hadn't returned weeks ago, when his injuries had been much, much worse.

When he passed her by en route to the bathroom, she stalled him, her fingers wrapping around his wrist. Something combative entered that soft gaze, teasing out the desire he wanted to keep a grip on. "Those look…awful."

Even the catch in her tone couldn't temper his mood just then. "They *look* awful."

The tip of one pink-tipped finger traced the edge of the biggest bruise on his ribs that had turned purple. On and on, her finger went, even as her hand trembled, past his ribs, past his abdomen to the seam of his shorts, like some intrepid explorer mapping uncharted territory.

His stomach tightened, desire a deafening whoosh in his ears. With a hard swallow, he arrested her exploration. "Go to bed, Mira. We're both exhausted."

Her trembling fingers fluttered over his lower abdomen, possessive and hot, even as her mouth set into a stubborn line. "We need to finish our discussion."

"Let it go, Mira."

"Your entire upper body is a map of colorful bruises and you never gave me your promise. So no, I won't let it go."

"I told you earlier. But I will again since you seem to be operating on zero energy. They look worse than they feel."

"Zero energy? I'm not the one who flinches when they have to get up."

"That was just the result of a brutal physiotherapy session this morning. I'd pushed myself too far."

"Just because I didn't force the issue in front of Leo and Stella, just because I followed you home like a dutiful wife, doesn't mean the issue's resolved to my satisfaction."

Aristos leaned an arm on the wall right above her head. Lemon and vanilla filled his nostrils, sweet and tart just like her, inviting him to drown in the scent.

All he'd need to do was bend down another inch and he could shut that stubborn mouth up in the best way possible. He'd have what he'd been dreaming of feverishly since the accident and facing his own mortality. He could drown in her hot, sweet response, he could give them both what they desperately wanted but were too stubborn to ask for.

And she'd let him do whatever he wanted to her, he knew that too. Even now, desire and something else warred in her beautiful face. They could seal the good news in the best way. But while wanting Mira had always been a weakness he didn't mind indulging in, reveling in, the stakes were much higher now.

He had so much more to lose now if he didn't control his emotions, if he gave in to the easiest path.

"I don't respond well to threats, *thee mou*. You would have realized that if you paid attention to our history together. But you've conveniently erased every single part of our past."

"I was not threatening you." When he raised a brow, she flushed and licked her lips. Her fingers toyed with the edge of her top, flashing him glances of her belly that he desperately wanted to touch, and cradle and kiss. He wanted to experience the wonder of their children growing inside her with a longing he barely contained.

"Okay, yes, I was threatening you. But I… I didn't mean

to." She rubbed a hand over her face, her shoulders slumping forward. Her obvious exhaustion gnawed at him, pushing his own temper toward the edge. "I didn't mean to sound so dramatic and…mean."

"Mean? You think I'm angry because you were mean to me back there?"

"Wait, Aristos. Let me explain properly. The last few weeks have been a lot and when I walk in, I find that—"

"The last few weeks, Mira? Doesn't that tell you something?"

"What?" she said, raising her clueless gaze to his.

His words came in a torrent of anger, the only available and acceptable outlet to the ache he felt deep in a place he'd sealed off a long time ago. "You've had *weeks* to get used to this. Weeks to make your plans and perfect your ultimatums. Weeks to decide how this was going to play out between me and you, *ne*?" He pushed off from the wall, his throat an achy mess it hadn't been in a long time. Not since he'd been a child and discovered that his mother preferred to drink what little money she had instead of feeding her son. "I had *two* hours to sit with this news that you threw in my face. So, if I were you, I'd be very careful about throwing ridiculous threats and illogical demands in my face just now, *thee mou*. I never react well when I'm pushed into a corner. No wounded animal does."

CHAPTER FIVE

HE WAS ANGRY. Of course he was angry. He had every right to be angry.

She hadn't told him about the pregnancy in weeks and then she'd threatened to take herself away, his unborn children away, two minutes after telling him. Never to let him see them or her again.

Jesus, what the hell was she thinking? How could she talk like that to him? And if he'd threatened her with something like that, even as a joke, she'd have been devastated.

But then, Aristos would never do that, a voice whispered with a conviction that came from deep inside her. Beneath Aristos's anger always lurked a far deeper, stronger emotion.

Mira rubbed her pounding temples, cursing herself for going about it all the wrong way. What she'd wanted was to rip up the contract and ask him to give their marriage a real chance. That they begin all over—a fresh start for their new beginning.

It was the reason it had taken her weeks to get here. Because she hadn't wanted to return to that big house. She hadn't wanted to look back and let fear rule her again. What she'd ended up doing was make him wary of ever trusting her again.

This was why she hated romantic relationships. And this was why she hated dealing with him, especially.

Aristos was her kryptonite, always had been. Turning her from a sensible, self-sufficient Mira to this irrational creature at the mercy of deep emotions, at the mercy of things she knew she shouldn't want.

Seeing those bruises on his body, seeing him exhausted and pale, had stolen her common sense away. Imagining him in pain and torment had pushed her to irrationality. She couldn't help thinking she'd come so close to losing him.

But did she truly, really ever have him?

Could anything ever contain the maelstrom that was Aristos Carides? Was it anything but foolishness to think he would ever be a responsible father? Was it anything but pure stupidity on her part to think she could somehow convince him that she didn't want their arrangement to be temporary? Especially when they couldn't trust each other?

Mira paced the vast bedroom, straightening things here and there, rubbing her lower back and mulling things over.

She had to fix what she'd unknowingly ruined.

Trust between them was a tenuous, fragile rope that they were still braiding. She didn't want to go through this pregnancy or childbirth, facing Aristos across the table as if they were enemies. Or worse, dispassionate people who were held together by just the pregnancy and that flimsy piece of paper. She wanted trust between them, she wanted the closeness and connection they'd shared that night and she wanted...*him*.

And yet, it seemed she couldn't just wish it into existence, could she?

"Planning your escape route?"

She turned to find him rubbing his hair with a thick towel. A white T-shirt and black sweatpants covered up the gorgeous body. Dismay filled her at the realization that he might be leaving again.

"Are you going out again?" she countered.

Before he answered, a knock sounded on the bedroom door. Frowning, Mira glanced at her watch. It was half past ten. An array of staff walked in, carrying dark wooden trays bursting with food and drinks. She'd barely thanked them when the whiff of pizza hit her nose.

With big, juicy chunks of pineapple—just as she'd been craving earlier.

Her mouth watered as the doors closed. "How did you know I—"

Without glancing at her, Aristos picked up a bottle of beer from one of the trays and popped the cap open. "Stella texted me that you asked about where to find pineapple pizza."

"So you had them make it?"

He shrugged. "It took longer because they had to have fresh pineapple brought in by a chopper."

"You had someone bring in fresh pineapple by chopper at night to make the pizza I asked for on a whim?"

"That's the one disadvantage of living here. Something we have to address soon."

Mira simply stared at him, her mouth hanging open. Even the delicious smell of pizza and her hungry belly weren't enough to pull her attention away from the man in front of her. Who was clearly pissed off at her and yet had the room in his head to have that small wish of hers seen to immediately.

"So you don't want it, then?" he said, laying a hand on the large circular tray. The pizza slices were hot and the scent of cheese and pineapple summoned her like a call from the mother ship.

"No, of course I want the pizza," Mira said, dragging the tray toward her. But she couldn't eat. Not yet. Not when something was sitting in her throat like a huge boulder blocking her airways.

Leaning his forearms on his knees, Aristos bent forward. It was almost like an attack—if attack meant drowning her in the scent and sight of him. "Will you eat or do I have to force-feed you?"

Without responding, Mira served herself two slices of pizza and leaned back in her seat. The pineapple was juicy and sweet on her tongue, the cheese hot and melting, hitting the exact right spot. He watched her like a hawk as she finished two slices in record time and chased them down with a glass of ice-cold water.

"Still not eating any meat?"

She shook her head, not even surprised anymore that he'd remember. "I tried to, just for the duration of pregnancy. It made me gag."

He nodded. "You need protein."

"I like yogurt cups."

He picked up his phone and sent off directions for a metric ton of yogurt to be delivered, she was sure.

Ignoring the temptation to reach for a third slice of pizza, she reached for a bowl of fresh fruit. Like a rubber band being stretched, the awkward silence and tension filled the space between them. Once she finished the fruit bowl, she resumed her walk around the sit-out area, wondering what she could do to keep him near.

"Why do you keep doing that?"

She turned around to find him standing not a foot from her. Now that one appetite had been seen to, her other one came roaring back. He smelled like the ocean and all Mira wanted to do was take a dip. To just rub herself all over him until she smelled of him. "Do what?"

"You keep rubbing your lower back. You did that at work too. You're doing it again now."

"Oh." She should've known he wouldn't miss that. "I've always had a weak back. Thanks to the—"

"You fell as a nine-year-old from a horse and landed on your back. You told me that once."

Warmth drizzled through Mira at the small fact that he'd remembered. God, she was a goner if Aristos's brilliant brain remembering small tidbits about her was enough to melt her from inside out. "Yeah, that. It's come back since... It makes itself known more. Especially when I've had long days."

"Then why not get into bed, give your aching back a break and rest, *yineka mou*? Are you refusing it just to spite me?"

Mira pressed a hand to his chest and he stepped back as if she'd burned him. "Of course I want to lie down. But I... I had quite a sedentary day and it would be good to get steps in," she said, pointing to her smartwatch.

"Why?"

She sighed, knowing he wasn't going to let it go. And was going to get angry all over again. But suddenly, her own actions seemed peevish. "Because the damned flight was long and I was stuck between these two old men who grumbled and whined every time I asked to get up. I spent too long sitting down."

He pressed a hand to his eyes, tension pouring from him as if he were a radiator. Damn it, why did she keep doing and saying things she knew would piss him off? "You flew commercial."

"Yes."

"Not even first class."

"No."

His curse was long, and loud and downright filthy, which she knew thanks to Stella trying to teach her Greek the last time she'd been here. "Your grandfather owned a billion-dollar IT company. Don't tell me Caio gave you nothing out of it."

"You know better than to insinuate that Caio would cheat any of us out of anything. The inheritance from my grandparents…" She hesitated, knowing this would also make him angry, but she didn't want any more lies and half-truths between them and maybe the only way to build trust was by baring her innermost self. "I've locked it up to be used in the future." She licked her lips, second-guessing all her decisions now. What she'd thought strength only felt like a brittle veneer of self-sufficiency. Because when it really mattered, she needed Aristos. And it was getting easier to accept it, every moment, every day. "A first-class ticket felt like unnecessary expenditure when I still have outstanding student loans."

"So let me get this straight. When I asked you over and over if you needed money, before and after our wedding, and you kept saying you didn't need anything, you were lying?"

"Yes. No," she said, pressing a hand to her forehead.

"You didn't use the inheritance from your grandparents on anything for yourself?"

"No."

"Why the hell not?"

"It's…complicated to explain."

"Try me, Mira."

"I wanted to save it. For the future. Especially now that there will be two babies. That's a lot of…expenses that will snowball me soon." The throbbing vein in his temple made it explicitly clear that she was once again in the danger zone with him. "Us soon."

"Ah… So you decided that your husband might be unwilling or unable to pay for these expenses? For his own children? You have zero trust in me in every matter, *ne*?"

"Aristos, you're reading this all wrong."

"Am I, really?" He rubbed a finger over his temple, as if willing that vein to not pop. "Tell me, Mira. Have you made plans to raise the children all by yourself even before our contract ends?"

"No, that's not what it means at all. I didn't even think of you—"

A long shuddering exhale left him.

"Look, it's not a reflection on you, okay? You know me, Aristos. I'm a penny-pincher. If Yana operates on one extreme, I operate on the other. I always, always prep for the worst-case scenario, for disasters, for…" When he'd have moved away, she caught his hands, willing him to understand as she splayed her deepest vulnerabilities open. Self-indulgent tears threatened. "It's a defense mechanism against…being hurt, against the risk of being abandoned. Materially and emotionally and… It will take me time to trust someone other than myself. It doesn't mean I don't trust you." His jaw was so tight that the man was going to need dental work if he didn't relax. "In retrospect, I should've booked myself a first-class flight." She rubbed her lower back again, willing the twinge to go away. "I just needed to walk more."

"Why? Is something wrong?"

"No, nothing's wrong."

"Unless you want me to wake up the entire household and have a team of doctors here within the next half hour,

Mira, you will tell me why it's so imperative that you have to walk right now."

"My BP is a little out of… It's been a little erratic. Nothing to worry over at this stage." She cast a look at her feet and he cast a look at her feet and Mira dropped the robe to cover them up but it was too late.

Before she knew it, Aristos nudged her to the bed, dragged her ass to the edge with a firm grip that she wanted to sink into, pushed the flimsy robe up her thighs, took her foot in his broad palm and gently pressed at her inflatable balloon-esque flesh with the tips of his fingers.

Mortified at his scrutiny and more than aroused at his other hand cupping her knee, the tips of his fingers spread out toward her thigh, she tried to pull away. His dark head bent, the thick hair begged to be caressed by her fingers.

"Should I call a doctor?"

"It's just swelling, Aristos. I was sitting for too long without moving. It happens even to people who are not pregnant. It's just water retention. And please," she said, trying to jerk her foot free of his hold again, "will you let go of my foot?"

His head jerked up, his mouth twisted into a snarl. "Why? Is there a condition I have to meet before you'll allow me to touch you again, *thee mou*?"

The words were soft, silky, and yet full of so much bitterness underneath. She hated herself for making him doubt her so much.

Mira sunk her fingers into his hair, and tugged, fear that she'd already lost him pricking like needles. A vein flickered in his temple, his nostrils flaring at the rough grip of her fingers. His gray gaze threatened to devour her. But she didn't care. "Right now, my feet are fat and swollen and… I'd just rather you didn't look at them too closely. It hurts my vanity, okay? My body's changing every day. My clothes fit weirdly already. I feel ungainly most of the time, *and* I don't want you to look at my swollen feet." She closed her eyes, hating how insecure she sounded. Dratted hormones!

His fingers under chin made her eyes pop open. Tenderness filled his eyes, and Mira wanted to drown in them. "You're growing two babies inside you. I couldn't even begin to imagine all the changes your body's going through. And yet, you're more beautiful today than I've ever seen you. Even with exhaustion leaving its mark on you."

His fingers drew trails of heat over her thighs, his throat moving on a hard swallow. "You don't believe me?"

"I want to believe you," Mira whispered, her heart inflating to a size bigger than her damned feet.

He didn't break eye contact with her as he gently lifted her foot and brought it to rest on his crotch. They hadn't even touched except for his fingers on her feet—her swollen feet—and yet, he was hard and thick and so...ready. A surge of excitement and arousal jolted through Mira, her breath releasing in a soft whimper.

"You want me."

A smile curved his lips, no humor reaching his eyes. "I always want you."

He said it like the sky was blue or the earth was round or that the world was a green wonder. It stole into her like a blessing, a benediction. Her sex contracted and released, making its achy emptiness known. She wanted to blame her horniness on the hormones too but God, she'd always panted over Aristos.

Mira wriggled her feet gently, tracing the heavy weight of him with her heel, and his breath shuddered out of him in a sibilant hiss. His shoulders rose and fell, the muscle in his jaw jumping.

With a shake of his head that made her belly swoop in

disappointment, he lifted her foot from him and scooted back. Something about the tightness in his face told Mira she'd done him a disservice—months ago and now.

"I'm so sorry I didn't tell you sooner."

The temperature between them dropped immediately. Apparently, her husband could still blow hot and cold as if all it required was a button to be pressed. Before he could push her away, Mira slipped off the bed and into his arms, landing awkwardly on her knees between him and the bed. Her knees straddled his and if he'd only give her a little welcome, she'd have crawled into his lap shamelessly.

"*Christos*, Mira! Be careful."

"If you leave before letting me say what I want to, you're forcing me to chase you, and believe me, I'm exhausted already."

He regarded her with a pensiveness she didn't like seeing in his eyes. His words came back to her. *A wounded animal...*

"Say what you have to say."

"There's no big conspiracy behind why I didn't tell you sooner. First, I didn't want to do it over the phone because you'd have just asked me to jump on a plane immediately and I still had things to sort through. Second, I... I didn't even realize that I had missed my period for almost four weeks. Something happened to me at the house after Yana and Nush left. I..."

"What? What happened?"

"No, nothing dangerous. Between making sure my father was settling into rehab again, Nush and Caio's sudden wedding and taking care of my grandparents' home—which they left to me... I lost track of time. They could sense two heartbeats on the first checkup. That's how late I went to see the doctor."

"You shouldn't have been alone when you found out."

"It wasn't by design. And I wanted to tell no one more than you." She covered his hand with hers, willing him to believe the sincerity in her tone. "After that, I couldn't wait to get away. I… I couldn't wait to tell you, see your expression."

I don't want to go back. Not in five years. Not ever. I want to stay here with you and build our family and our future together.

The words lingered on her lips, begging to be given voice. "And what I said earlier about leaving… I was reacting out of fear. Out of anger. Seeing you hurt…" She pressed a hand to her chest. "…it's not an easy thing. It's not…something I can process fully yet."

"Okay."

"Okay, you're not mad at me anymore? Okay, enough already of my pathetic attempts at begging for forgiveness?"

"Okay, I heard what you said. Okay, I'm still angry," he said with that brutal honesty that she'd never appreciated before. "I understand saying the wrong thing when acting out of fear. But I don't appreciate threats, Mira. Especially about your leaving me. Especially now that you're carrying my…*them.*"

Mira nodded. She'd never felt as small as she felt right then. Because, once again, it was becoming clear that she'd hurt him where it would pain the most.

"As for my ridiculous, death-defying stunts, I'll think about it."

It was more than she'd hoped for, after messing it up so badly.

Gratitude and relief made her throw herself at him. "Thank you," she said, pressing her mouth to his cheek, and he turned right at that time. And then her mouth was on his and Mira gave in with a long groan.

She'd needed this since the moment she'd left that morning. The heat of his hunger, the warmth of his body wrapped around her, the sheer intensity of being alive as his mouth plundered her... It was all she needed to go on. Her breasts ached to be touched, her sex damp and ready. She moaned against his mouth, begging him to take it deeper, and he complied. With filthy words whispered against her jaw and a hard nip of her lower lip that stung.

Mira rubbed her cheek against his, like a cat sunning itself, her entire body a mass of ache and want. "Will you come to bed?"

Pushing to his feet, he reached out for her and pulled her up. Mira would have stumbled if he didn't keep an arm about her until she was steady again. Her head felt dizzy in the best way possible.

With the maturity of a woman that her teen self lacked, she realized now that the kind of heat between them was not normal. That sex between them would always be a flame that would start up at the slightest flash. And yet, she had a feeling it wasn't fueled just by chemistry. It almost felt like their bodies understood something that their minds refused to or simply couldn't.

Licking her lips, loving the taste of him there, she raised a heated face to him.

Whatever passion she'd spied earlier in his face was gone, leaving an inscrutable look in his eyes.

"As tempting as your invitation is, I have work to attend to and you need rest."

Mira flushed and wondered if the large bed could open up and swallow her whole. "Work now?"

"There are things I have to see to, people I have to talk to, schedules I have to rearrange now that you're expecting," he said, with an infinite patience that bordered on condescension.

Shock at his swift but curt rejection had her responses dulled. She called out when he reached the door. "Aristos?"

"Yes?"

"You didn't... You didn't say anything about the pregnancy. About twins. About...us being parents."

"Is there anything to say other than wow to our reproductive organs, *thee mou*?"

There was a flatness to his tone that Mira couldn't cut through. The lack of humor in his words made it all sound clinical, like another project he'd finished, another deal he'd cut.

"It's what we wanted, *ne*?"

She nodded, wondering where he was going with this.

"And like you pointed out so brutally earlier, this is bigger than both of us now. Bigger than our contract and little arrangement and our past even."

It was everything she wanted Aristos to say, everything she'd wanted to hear ever since she'd been told there were two heartbeats. That this pregnancy had changed both their lives in ways they couldn't even comprehend yet. But his words... They felt wrong, they sounded wrong. The way he looked at her was all wrong.

"Good night, Mira."

He didn't even wait for her response. Mira went to bed, feeling that same loneliness she thought she'd never have to bear again fall over her like a shroud. He needed time and space to process their news.

Only their kiss had been right. Nothing else. She fell into restless slumber holding on to that.

CHAPTER SIX

IT WAS PAST five in the evening when they arrived at the penthouse at Carides Towers in the business district of Athens about three weeks after Mira returned to Athens. Returned to Aristos, as she'd been calling it in her mind.

"Keep your day open."

It was all the notice Aristos had given her the night before. As if she was the one working fourteen-hour days, pushing their body to its limits after a major accident, and acting the model spouse.

And yet, she'd barely slept, she'd been so excited.

Dressed in a loose white summer dress that flirted with her thighs, her hair braided away from her neck and face, she'd been elated to find Aristos waiting for her at the helipad that morning, dressed in a white linen shirt and dark denim. Even dressed casually, he'd stolen her breath away. It had been enough to simply watch him as he strapped her seat belt in the chopper he was piloting himself.

Being the naive fool this pregnancy and her hormones had turned her into, she'd assumed that meant she'd get to spend the entire day with her husband, who could give a master class on how to ignore one's spouse without crossing the line into negligence.

Because he'd been doing exactly that for three weeks now. He was there for breakfast, lunch and dinner. He was present for all of her doctor's appointments, including with a masseuse and a physical therapist. He lavished her with back massages and foot rubs every night. He brought her vitamins and reminded her to go to bed when she'd been studying hard for her specialization exams. He was there to hold her hair back when nausea began showing up mid-morning as her second trimester began and he was there with a glass of sparkling water with a slice of lemon just as she liked it, exactly when she needed it. He was there to kiss her and hold her and rub her back when her sleep turned restless and to whisper words of comfort and endearment as if he'd learned the exact words she'd need to hear by rote. He was a warm, hard, solid presence on the bed next to her when she didn't want to be alone.

And yet, it wasn't enough. It wasn't what she wanted. Mira wondered if she was being selfish, entitled, more than a little lovesick in her expectations.

But in her heart, in the deepest, most vulnerable part of her, from where she was trying to operate in this new stage of her life, she knew that there was a long list of things Aristos didn't do anymore with her.

He didn't tease and taunt her anymore. He didn't seek out her company, he didn't demand she give in to him with that feral seductive quality that she'd never been able to resist. He asked her nothing that didn't seem to come out of a caregiver questionnaire. He didn't laugh with her, didn't provoke her, didn't cajole her into long, warm kisses.

It was as if he had a manual—*Being a Good Provider for Dummies*—and followed it step by step without ever going off script. But she'd had enough.

Enough of seeing her husband while away hours upon hours on work in his study with that PA of his.

Enough of him treating her like some…fragile possession given into his safekeeping, of him keeping her at a distance.

Ironic that it was exactly what she'd envisaged when she'd signed the contract with him. And yet, the brittle, perfectly sterile quality of their marriage was a limbo Mira didn't want to live in for another moment.

The long summer day had been unbearably hot and muggy. Even the cool, pristine white marble floors of the vast penthouse as she went in search of Aristos weren't enough to bring Mira out of her rotten mood.

They had toured three different estates, beginning with one in Mykonos at ten this morning. Mansions with whitewashed walls, magnificent views of the sea and lush, manicured gardens abounded at all three estates. And while the real estate team awaiting them at each place had sung praises of the properties, Mira hadn't been able to discuss the necessity of a new home with Aristos. His PA had been an ever-present shadow, winding Mira up with her mere presence.

Other than to ask her if she was tired or hungry—which he asked at the top of the hour, every hour as if he'd set a damn alarm—her husband hadn't given her a single private minute. He had an agenda apparently not only for their day but also for their life—one she was only beginning to see now.

She couldn't, however, blame Aristos for tiring her out because not only had they dined at a restaurant overlooking the beach right when she was getting hungry, but he'd even brought her to a suite at a nearby luxury hotel for her standard one-hour nap right after. And when she'd woken up refreshed and ready to tackle the day, there had been ginger chai and little buttery croissants waiting for her.

She'd no idea how Aristos managed to have the ginger chai made exactly the way she liked it when they were in a luxury hotel away from home, but he had. But sadly, drinking the chai, overlooking the snowcapped mountain range in the distance, while he'd pounded away at his laptop with his team hovering over them, had been the only high point in a day where her mood had been steadily spiraling.

Now, she walked through one expansive room after the other in the penthouse, furnished in light grays and navy blues and soft golds with sleek, modern pieces that were very much to her taste, as she followed the murmur of soft voices. Unlike the first two estates, which had reminded her of museums with their pristine white furnishings and priceless sculptures and paintings, the penthouse, for all it was in the middle of a concrete jungle, was refreshingly welcoming and warm.

Finally, she pushed at double doors and arrived at the study that was the size of a mini library. To find Elena mopping at Aristos's chest with a dainty napkin in hand.

Her stomach curdled instantly as Mira noted the large brown stain on his pristine white shirt.

The image of the same woman draped all over Aristos in that darkened corridor right here in this very building flashed in front of Mira's eyes, triggering that very same flight response. She wanted to flee. She wanted to hide her hurt, cut off the tentative hope and affection that were growing into deep roots for their budding family.

If you don't open yourself up to hope and connection, people can't hurt you. Like her mother and father had done all her life.

It had been her guiding principle most of her life, something she had internalized without her knowledge. Only Yana and Nush had earned a piece of her heart, chipping away at her resolve one day at a time. But Aristos *had* shattered her tender heart once.

What was the guarantee that he wouldn't do it again? That he wasn't already doing it with his remoteness and distance?

But she couldn't run. Not this time. She couldn't act out of fear and the compulsive need to avoid hurt at any cost. That's how she'd ended up with such loneliness, such a deep void in her life.

"Mira?" Aristos said, moving toward her immediately. The scent of the spilled coffee from his shirt made the ginger chai come back up her throat. Though it had more to do with the woman wiping the stain than the coffee itself. "You look pale."

"Hmm?" Mira said, her mind insistently replaying the intimacy between her husband and his PA of years.

She didn't doubt Aristos at all. She'd never do that again. But that didn't mean she liked the status quo either. It wasn't irrational to not want…that woman near him. Not when Mira recognized the adoration in her eyes.

Aristos's touch on her shoulder jolted her. She met his gaze and swallowed the excuse that rose so easily to her lips. To deflect away from her own fears, to pretend that things didn't hurt, to suppress her own needs had been her default for so many years. But not anymore. "I need to speak with you. Now. In private."

His hand cupping her shoulder with a tenderness she was beginning to hate, Aristos frowned. "You have that cranky look in your eyes. I'm sorry we tired you out."

Mira jerked away from his touch and regretted the gesture when his mouth tightened. "I'm not a child whose energy you have to manage."

"The pilot is on hold if Mrs. Carides wants to return, Aristos," his PA piped up from behind him.

Mira closed her eyes, fighting the urge to scream like a banshee. Suddenly, she wished her sisters were there with her. Nush would have hugged her while Yana would have dragged that woman out of here by her hair. That image made it easy to reach for the frayed threads of her composure. "I said I want to speak with you."

"You have a meeting in fifteen minutes." Elena piped up again, not crossing the line but hovering over it, testing and pushing.

Mira simply stared back at Aristos, uncaring of what he saw in her face.

"I think we're done for the day." While his words were humorous, the steel in his voice was enough for his PA to walk away on the very next breath.

The tap-tap of her heels and the closing of the doors should've sounded triumphant to her ears, and yet all Mira felt was flayed open.

She closed her eyes, wary of meeting his gaze, her heart thundering in her chest, locking away stupid tears. Before she could arrest it, one lone tear swept down her cheek and she didn't even have it in her anymore to care that Aristos was catching her in another vulnerable moment. It seemed all her false armor had fallen away.

A finger caught the tear, while another lingered at her jawline, a tantalizing caress that every cell in her wanted to lean into. "I never realized it would be near impossible to make you happy," Aristos whispered, a remote, distant thread of something like longing in his words.

But that couldn't be true when they both knew he already *had* her.

She hurriedly scrubbed at her cheeks with her knuckles.

"The coffee spill was an accident, Mira." His soft tone belied the gray storm in his eyes. The tendons in his neck stood out. "I know how little you think of me, but there's nothing but professional—"

"I don't."

Conviction rang in her voice, crystal clear. She was done hiding—from him and herself. Slowly, the bleak fury in his eyes abated.

"I was wrong that day. But I didn't think...*that* today." When he just frowned, she took a deep breath and plunged ahead. "I returned because I promised I would. I returned because I'm pregnant. But Aristos, more than anything, I returned because I want this to work between us. For at least as long as that contract stipulates," she added at the last minute, taking the easy way out.

One step at a time...she reminded herself.

His nostrils flared as if he wanted to say more but he closed his eyes. Deep brackets straddled that mobile mouth and she couldn't help notice how exhausted he looked. He worked such long hours and constantly watched over her, his energy so dynamic that she'd forgotten that he'd been in a major accident not two months ago. Come to think of it, he'd been pushing himself brutally the last three weeks as if a demon was chasing him.

"Then why are you upset?" he asked before she could bring that topic up. Really, she should've made a list—it was the only way to feel a little in control while everything about her life, everything about her, was in constant flux.

"I'm not upset so much as bracing myself to..."

"To what?"

"To tell you what's going on in my...heart."

His head reared back in an infinitesimal manner—like a predator cocking his head for one moment, as if surprised by the prey's attack. She tensed, wondering if he would mock her use of the word *heart*, remind her that they were only bound by the contract. But the silence only stretched, gaining weight with each passing second.

In the end, he nodded, encouraging her to go on.

Mira breathed in deep and brought down another wall she'd built around her own heart. "If it's hard for me to rely on you financially, it's near impossible for me to bare my... insecurities. Emotionally. That night in your office when I saw you two... It was easier for me to run away, easier to assume you were cheating on me—" she forced herself to say the ghastly words, half choking on them "—instead of showing you how hurt I was, showing you how much I... had begun to care about our stupid arrangement."

His hands clasped her face, his forehead bent to hers in a nuzzle that made her heart expand. God, she'd been starved for his touch. "And you're telling me this now because..."

"Because I want something from you."

He laughed then, his eyes full of that wicked humor she'd missed so much. "I should've known."

"Also because I promised myself that I'd stop acting out of fear."

He stared at her, his hand reaching for hers. "And once you decide something, nothing and no one can stand in your way, can they?" Something almost like admiration glinted in his eyes, the first hint of true emotion in weeks.

He brought her knuckles to his mouth and kissed them one by one. Rewarding her for what she'd shared, she knew. Could it be that simple? Could she have the old Aristos back if she simply kept her thoughts and feelings open, her heart open?

His gray gaze held hers, leaving her no quarter to hide. "What is bothering you, Mira?"

"Your PA... I don't want her near you."

He uncoiled from his lazy stance, some dark emotion

flashing across those starkly beautiful features. "And why is that?"

"Why do you always send the sullen, morose Nikos to guard me when I go to that little café to study? Why not that stud Boris?"

"Boris flirts with you."

"You and her… It's probably the longest you've kept a woman in your life, *ne*?" she said, saying it like he did when he challenged her. "I'm supposed to simply tolerate her devouring you with her eyes, hoping your shrew of a wife would disappear so that she could have a chance?"

"*Christos*, Mira! You don't pack your punches when you are ready to fight, do you?"

"You won't let Boris near me because he's talkative, Aristos."

"Stop mentioning him."

"You're taking a huge risk by allowing her to…undermine my confidence in us. In *us*, not you. Do you hear the distinction?"

"Yes." Color crested his too-sharp cheekbones. "It was once, a long time ago, after you left. I was in a bad place and I stopped it before it could…"

Mira pressed her hand to his mouth, loath to hear more. The very idea of him with that woman…even years ago, made her want to bleach her eyes. Now she wished she'd thrown the woman out herself.

He grabbed her wrist, gently moving her hand but holding on to it. "What you saw a few months ago, I stopped it immediately and told her she'd crossed a line. I thought she got the message."

Beneath everything else, hurt pierced Mira.

They had wanted their first time together—both their firsts—to be special. But she'd run away after what she'd seen and heard that night after their engagement. She'd thrown herself into her studies, into preparing for medical school, banished him and that night from her thoughts until she felt absolutely nothing. Until she wasn't hurting anymore.

And yet… He had so easily admitted that he'd been in a bad place after she left. That he'd made a mistake by letting it get even that far with Elena. But what his cousin Kairos had shown her that night at the party he'd thrown for Aristos… Was that not the truth? How could it not be when she'd seen Aristos and heard his words?

Would they ever be able to leave the past behind? Or would it haunt them forever?

One thing was for sure. This time, she wasn't going to let her own fears throw away what was hers. "It's not because I don't trust you, but I just can't…have her near you. I don't care if that makes me an insecure, jealous wife. *You're mine, Aristos. Only mine.*"

CHAPTER SEVEN

THE NAKED EMOTION dancing across Mira's gaze... Aristos felt the tightness of weeks in his chest relent just a little. There was conviction and something else in her words that soothed him, that he'd wanted to hear for a long time. And while a part of him wanted to reject those words, reject the deeper emotion ringing through them, he resisted the urge.

If she was trying to act away from a place of fear, he, it seemed, was cursed to forever act out of some deep wound. He wanted to be selfish and demand why she'd suddenly decided that the tenor of their relationship had to change.

But he knew the answer and he loathed it with every fiber of his being. He'd been caught in his own trap and if that wasn't irony, he didn't know what was.

Self-sufficiency and composure was armor for the woman she'd become. But the girl he'd fallen in love with, the girl who'd laughed at his feral antics and told him he could conquer the world if he wanted to with such conviction... That girl had been without this armor.

And he kept waiting to see flashes of that Mira.

Here was that Mira...but there for all the wrong reasons.

Christos, between poisonous doubts about what had made Mira flee the first time and the damned contract between them and his own doubts about being a father, his head felt like it was full of vague, intangible fears that he couldn't take action on. Add his own vow to himself that he wouldn't let the attraction between them, her need and his, to further entangle his head... Now it seemed like the most ridiculous punishment.

He couldn't forget, for one moment, that even her words were coming from a place provoked by hormones, the changes in her body and mind, the changes she'd embraced with that devotion he knew she was capable of.

All of it wouldn't have been possible if they hadn't conceived so fast. If the rug hadn't been pulled from under them with the news of twins.

He had everything he'd ever wanted. Mira in his bed. Mira looking at him with hope and something else fluttering in her words, in her eyes, in her actions. She was fully committed to this, as only she could be. And yet, it was nothing but a false victory. A hollow one.

"I've never been claimed with such possessive fierceness before," he said, letting the ever-present thrum of desire wash away his bitterness for the moment.

"If you still didn't get it, that's the way things are going to be now," she said, lifting her chin with that stubbornness he'd once adored.

He laughed, the sound bursting through him. "Thank you for the warning."

Her own shock was written across her face. "You haven't laughed like that in a while." Her words were tremulous, her desire written across every inch of her. "In fact, you haven't looked at me like that in a while. Not since the night we...conceived."

"That's not true."

Her shoulders slumped. "I'm not going to argue about something I know to be true. But..." She licked her lips and his blood fled south. "I miss it, Aristos. I miss you teasing me and needling me and pricking at my composure, and I miss you looking at me as if you want to devour me whole."

Evening light diffused through the high windows in the study, limning her with a golden glow. He took her in—the way the sundress hugged her voluptuous curves, the ever-growing bump of her belly and the damp tendrils of her hair framing her achingly beautiful face.

Everywhere the rays of the sun touched her—the silky flesh bared by the square neckline, the globes of her breasts, which were already bigger, the lush pink of her lips, even the toned length of her arms—he wanted to touch and kiss and caress. Despite her intermittent nausea, she was glowing and yet Aristos knew it wasn't all just the pregnancy.

He'd seen a determination, even a new kind of courage, in her eyes and it was changing her from the inside out. Suddenly, he wanted his hands all over her, lust and something else underscoring itself through him. *Christos*, he was a fool to think he could resist her. And even if he did, why should he deny her what she needed? Every night in bed, she draped herself all over him—sometimes in sleep, sometimes seeking relief for the ache in her lower back and sometimes awake and alert and begging him with her eyes to kiss her. He'd indulged her, taken it as far as he could before he'd slipped out of bed, claiming work called.

"Come here, *yineka mou*."

She shook her head. He wanted to believe that she was refusing him just to be contrary. But he wasn't sure anymore. Had he ruined their truce already?

"It would be to your advantage, *thee mou*."

"There, that's another thing," she said, her voice rising, agitation written all over her. "You haven't called me that in weeks. In fact, I have a feeling you took those words away from me on purpose."

"You're imagining things, Mira," he said, keeping his voice light, hiding his surprise at how unerringly she'd pinpointed his intentions.

Her throat moved in a swallow, her big eyes wide as pools. "Are you still punishing me, Aristos?"

"Of course not," he said, feeling a surge of protective tenderness that had been his companion for as long as he'd known her. That had always been the crux of his conflict. He wanted to protect Mira from himself, from the dark, hungry thing inside him that demanded so much but not enough that he'd ever consider giving her up. And yet, if she were unhappy because of him... No, he refused to accept that scenario.

"You have no idea how desperately I want to believe you."

"Come, Mira," he repeated, letting her hear the thrum of desire pulsing through him like an ever-present beat. "I know what would make you feel good, *agapi*, and I promise to give it to you. Now."

The pulse at her neck fluttered, her incredibly soft mouth falling open in a whispered gasp. Eyes wide, she looked around the vast study, half covered in darkness and half in fading light. The city was coming alive around them, beneath them, for the night. He saw her glance out the French doors into the balcony that overlooked the business district, saw her swallow at other skyscrapers that tried and failed to win against the Carides Towers.

"No one will dare disturb us here, Mira," he said, pushing away from the desk he'd been leaning against. "This penthouse is mine. *Ours*," he amended.

"Someone could see us." And yet there was a whisper of excitement in her tone that made his cock stiffen impossibly hard.

"Just as shadows writhing against the wall. Would that bother you?"

"Against the wall?" she said, licking her lips. "I've gained weight and you're not in prime condition. That would be—"

"Ah… There's my ever-sensible wife," he said with another laugh. And she looked at him again with that same hungry glint in her eyes. As if she wanted to wrap herself up in his laughter. For an indulgent second, he let himself believe that she was driven by the same thing as him. "Leave the logistics to me, *yineka mou*. I've not disappointed you so far, have I?"

"No. Sex with you is…something else. Granted, I have almost zero experience and you have loads, so maybe that's the reason. Not some unknown magic as I foolishly assumed."

"You've seen my schedule, Mira. No man can have as much sex with as many partners as the tabloids make out while he runs an international conglomerate, runs million-dollar charities and participates in outrageous, death-defying stunts," he said, using her own words. "As for between us, yes, sex becomes something I can't define either."

"I want it too, because you want it," she said, with a harsh exhale. She rubbed a hand over her neck and chest in a sensual gesture that tightened his own body. *Christos*, seeing her aroused by just his words… It was a high unlike any he'd ever known. And he'd chased them all through the years, looking for this…this sensation of falling and yet somehow feeling grounded. "You like the danger of it. The thrill of it," she said, studying him, but not hiding the fact that it thrilled her too.

Theos, if she continued in this vein, he was going to be putty in her hands soon.

"Watching you want me is the biggest thrill I've ever

known, *yineka mou*. Watching you fight that innate composure and decorum and that starchy sensibility of yours just for me... That's the thrill I've always chased."

She walked toward the French doors, her eyes watching him the entire time. "And yet I've been throwing myself at you since I've come back." Her tone carried more than a hint of pain and self-doubt and suddenly, he loathed himself for putting it there.

"You can't doubt my desire for you. You shy away your gaze right now but you can see the proof, *ne*?" Her gaze slid to his crotch and then back up, setting him on fire. "Stop arguing and come to me, Mira."

She shook her head, the stubbornly infuriating woman, continuing the ridiculous game he'd started. "You've been keeping me at a distance, in more ways than one. I want to know why."

"We've both been exhausted by the end of the day, Mira. You know that."

"Too exhausted for sex at night? Even if I swallow that, what about during the day when you're no more than a few doors away from me? Don't tell me the reckless playboy Aristos Carides, known for his risky escapades, doesn't have sex during the day?"

"Mira—"

"Too exhausted for sex...look at you lying through your teeth to spare my fragile feelings. This day is full of surprises, huh?" Another snort as she rubbed her temple with her fingers. "You know I laughed when Yana showed me this article about how married couples have less sex or some such nonsense. I guess at least we can claim that we're truly a married couple now."

He didn't smile this time, watching her thoughts play out across her face. He wished there was a way to turn on the subtitles to those emotions with the flick of a button. He wished he could take back the distance he had imposed between them, even though the decision itself had been a rational one.

He rubbed a hand over his head, pulling at his hair in frustration. That's what he got when he tried to be rational and honorable—an upset wife.

Theos, Mira had opened herself up to him today. No, she'd been doing it ever since she'd returned. It was that stubborn tenacity of hers—once she set her mind to something, she didn't back down. She'd been waving a white flag that he'd not only refused to acknowledge but actively discouraged. And instead of rewarding her as he should've done, he'd let his own doubts and fears ruin their truce before it began.

He'd hurt her yet again while he'd tried to figure out his own head.

The silence in the darkening room stretched, and he felt as if they were standing on the cusp of something. Would they move one step forward or two steps back again? Had he crushed the tentative hope she'd been trying to bring to their relationship?

"As tempting as the idea of providing you with a thrill is—" she pressed a hand to her abdomen "—I don't feel so good anymore."

"What's wrong?"

"This whole day I thought…"

"Mira, what did you—"

"I'm hungry *and* I feel a headache coming on." As if to confirm her claim, her stomach let out a loud growl right on time.

He straightened from the desk, reaching out a hand to her. "Then let's satisfy at least someone's appetite tonight."

If his barb landed, his wife didn't betray it even by the flicker of an eyelid. And that's how Aristos knew that damned armor of hers was back. As clearly as if she'd slammed a door in his face.

Mira wiped her mouth and settled back into her seat with a groan that seemed to have sprung from the very depths of her.

Seated across from her, Aristos sighed as the satisfied sound sent a jolt of lust through his body.

"That pasta and that chef are a gift to the universe. Do you think I could bribe him with my...charms?" she said, adjusting the neckline of her dress until her cleavage was more prominent. "I mean all of this is going to waste anyway."

Anger and something else glinted in her eyes as she held his gaze. Aristos let his own dip to her chest, let her see the full force of his desire for her. "Not funny, *yineka mou.*"

Even knowing that relief for his current state was far away, he still enjoyed the near-painful clench of his aroused body at the sight and sound of her. At least, he seemed to have gotten one thing right.

His wife seemed to love the upscale Italian restaurant he'd commandeered for the rest of the evening. She'd had two servings of the pasta primavera, and a slice of dark chocolate cake. His appetite, on the other hand, had deserted him the moment he'd realized he'd hurt her.

"I feel horrible about the poor people who'd been waiting in line for hours to eat here."

"You were hungry and we couldn't risk your sugar falling too low," he said, with a shrug that told her the topic was over. "You shouldn't have waited that long to tell me you were hungry anyway."

"But so were they," she said, looking around the empty restaurant with a kind of horror. Leave it to Mira to find the gesture horrible rather than romantic. "Couldn't we have eaten without throwing them out?"

He shook his head. "My security can't isolate threats among so many. It's the downside of being a—"

"A playboy that has women all over the world panting over him and sending him skeevy gifts like their underwear?" she quipped, some of her natural assertiveness and composure returning.

He sent a silent thanks to the steely strength at the core of her. *Christos*, he preferred this strong, resilient, no-pulling-punches Mira to the quiet, withdrawn Mira she'd been in the short drive to the restaurant. Her reflection in the dark-tinted window glass had shown him how stricken she'd been.

She hadn't done it as payback for his own behavior of the last few weeks. He knew that as well as the vanilla scent that was lodged in his very cells. She'd truly been disturbed by "his ploy," as she called it.

He tried to ignore the heat rushing to his cheeks. Another irony of his life: he had the interest and obsession of women world over and yet not from the one he'd wanted most of his adult life. "How did you know about that?"

"How did the media learn about the contract we signed without a third soul's knowledge? Or were there three souls involved already?"

Elena, of course. He bit back a curse. How had he been so sloppy with his trust? More importantly, how had he not realized how fragile Mira was? For the first time in years, Aristos thought of everything Mira had shared as a teenager with him—being abandoned by her mother as a baby, dealing with her alcoholic father, the requirement of perfection and strength they had imprinted on her—and still, she'd managed to love her grandparents and her sisters wholeheartedly.

But sharing the pain only offered a momentary solace, as he very well knew. So why had he imagined that all those past hurts wouldn't dictate her actions in the now?

A thoughtful expression took over her face as his own weighty thoughts consumed him. "Aristos?"

"Yes?"

"It will be like this when the babies are here too? With the security team trailing us everywhere? Will they follow us for checkups and playdates and first day of school and...whatnot?"

"Yes. It's an unfortunate downside. I'll do everything to make sure you and the babies are not exposed to the media. But in terms of safety, the team has to be there. There's an unhealthy interest in my life and I can't take the risk of it touching you."

"Some of it could be minimized if you didn't court it with your stunts," she added, a sneaky twist to her mouth.

He was so glad that she was sparring with him again that he let it slide. "Since we're on this topic, let's talk about what you've planned for the future."

"The future?"

"Yes, the future. We both know you probably drew out a five-year, ten-year and twenty-year plan for your life and the babies, Mira. I don't want you to leave the country when the five years are up. I don't want to have my...children across the ocean thousands of miles away."

Her head jerked up and her mouth trembled. But in this, he refused to budge. Refused to let her stubbornness win in any way.

"I wasn't planning to." When she finally looked up at him, there was something in her gaze that arrested his spiraling temper. "Can we not discuss this right now please? I… You'll only get a defensive response the way I'm feeling right now."

"And your career?"

The shadows instantly left her. "You know, Stella and I were talking about that. The other day, even Nush asked me if—"

"I'm the one you should be discussing our future with. Not my cousin or your sister."

"I would have if you had been available, Aristos. If you'd given me the slightest encouragement to talk about the thousand things I want to say to you and share with you and…" When she spoke again, her voice was soft, small. "Whatever's going on in that head of yours, you shut me out. You were working out of some damn checklist as if me and this pregnancy are some special project. That's not how this works. That's not what I need."

He felt as if she'd struck him and yet she was doing nothing but being honest. Behaving exactly as he'd wanted her to behave and act for years. "I don't know how else to be, how to be…what you need right now. I just can't."

She reached for him, her pink-tipped fingers running over the veins on the back of his hand. Her touch, the open guilelessness of her expression, stunned him. "That's more honesty than you've given me in three weeks. And as for my career, my hands and my brain and my…my life feels incredibly full. I'm going to look into getting certified to practice here, in Greece. But even that is a…vague plan for the future. I'm not giving up my career per se, but I'm going to put it on hold. I… I want to be a hands-on mom, for at least a few years. Give or take ten." She scrunched her nose, her smile turning a little stretched as he stared at her in silence. "Does that make sense, do you think? I mean, you did say I shouldn't worry about finances right now."

"It makes perfect sense."

As he stared at her full face with those intelligent eyes and stubborn nose and painfully lovely mouth under the brilliant strips of light the cut glass chandelier threw on her, Aristos felt one of his own assumptions crumble to dust.

Just because she could bury her hurt and other emotions deep inside didn't mean she didn't feel them as strongly as he did. He hated when people made assumptions about him and yet he'd done the same to her.

"I'm glad you ate before your appetite was ruined by... this. By me."

She grimaced and reached for the glass of water. "I'd have eaten even if I wasn't ravenous. I can't let your mind games mess with the care I need to take."

He deserved that, he knew. And still, that comment made him...resentful. Like a schoolboy who'd been denied his treat. "This pregnancy, those unborn babies mean the world to you already, don't they?" The words left his mouth before he could control them.

A frown marred her face. "Why do you say it like it's a bad thing?"

"I didn't," he lied.

"I don't want to fight anymore tonight," she said, not quite meeting his gaze. "Please, Aristos."

He took her hand in his then, across the table. She was warm and soft and he couldn't help but trace the plump veins at her wrist. He brought her hand to his mouth and kissed the center of her palm. Emotion held him in one of its hard grips and he forced himself to breathe through it.

It was relief, he supposed, that even though he'd hurt

her, she was here. She was staying. She was…where she belonged.

Whatever she saw in his face, her question seemed to be designed to pull him back to the now. "You never gave me an answer about… Elena."

He let her distract him, knowing that she needed his reassurance, glad that in this, he wouldn't fail her. "Her days with me have been numbered ever since I saw your face the evening you arrived and the way she challenged your authority in front of everyone. She crossed too many lines. I knew then it was time to send her away." He couldn't stop bitterness from drenching his words when he said, "I did wonder if you'd ever speak up, let me defend myself."

"So you were just throwing her in my face by having her at the mansion every day and enjoying the show?"

"Only partly," he said. "You have to remember that Elena has been with me for more than a decade. It takes time to decouple her from that position."

"I hope you're not firing her though. That seems unfair."

"She's moving to another team." He studied her with that intense scrutiny, shadows masking his thoughts from her. "I guess I should say thank you for believing me," he said with arch sarcasm. "Even though I've never given you reason to distrust me."

"That's not…" She caught her words just in time and looked away.

That's not what? What had he done that she forever doubted him? That she cast him in such black light?

Aristos waited to see if she'd pick up the gauntlet he'd thrown down yet again. And yet when she didn't, when she once again refused to discuss the past, it bothered him less than it ever had before. Maybe because he finally believed that Mira was committed to this life with him.

But he wasn't sure if he would ever stop wondering why she'd abandoned the idea of them so easily. If it would always prick like a thorn lodged deep inside, festering there.

They were heading home to Carides mansion in a chauffeured car, instead of taking the chopper, as Aristos really did have to call into a meeting. The drive was two hours long and Mira dozed off to the sound of his deep voice lulling her into comfort.

She woke with her head neatly supported by a corded arm in dark silence. And the shoulder strap of her dress at her elbow. And her breasts smushed against a corded bicep and she herself lying half across Aristos's lap.

"Sorry," she said, wiping her mouth with her hand. Thank God, she hadn't drooled on him.

"You kept shifting on the seat trying to find a comfortable position."

"Thank you."

"Are we back to that kind of politeness, then?"

"You started it," she said, and then sighed. "My throat's parched."

Having finished a bottle of water, she straightened her sundress and pulled the jacket he'd draped over her shoulders tighter around her. The moment she settled onto the opposite seat, Aristos pulled her feet into his lap.

She jerked as the warmth from his calloused palms instantly lit a fuse somewhere else in her body as if there were wires attached. When she looked out the window, she noticed that they'd left the city behind long ago. And with each mile they put between his work and them, she felt a little better.

"You never told me why we were touring those estates," she said, suppressing a groan by the skin of her teeth.

God, the man could weave magic with those fingertips. On her feet, on her neck and shoulders and elsewhere. Suddenly, she felt stupid for churlishly refusing what he'd offered back in the penthouse. And sitting in relative dark with his fingers pressing into her feet, with his eyes devouring her, tension thrummed through her, seeking release.

"Because we're looking for a new home. We won't move for a little while but before your due date. Which one did you like the best?"

"I like the Carides mansion best. And Leo would be heartbroken if we moved out just when the babies are about to come. And Stella too."

"He can live with the disappointment. Although he will have an invitation to come live with us if it pleases him."

"Why are we moving at all?"

"The mansion is only accessible by the chopper or it's a two-hour drive to the nearest city. What if you need something in the middle of the night? What if something goes wrong and we have to visit your specialist?"

"But you already employed an army of people to see to my every need, want and demand, Aristos. I don't know if I should be ashamed or proud that this pregnancy and I have created an entire new economy."

"It's not enough to put my mind at ease, Mira."

"And what about my peace of mind?" she said, unable to stop the words.

"Would it really bother you if I continued with my racing?"

"Of course it would. Why else would I make a big deal out of it?" She studied his gleaming gaze in the dark, wondering what he was thinking. "Please, Aristos. Tell me what's going on in your mind."

"I was angry that you didn't tell me immediately. Angry

enough that I wondered why I should make so many changes in my life for someone who doesn't trust me. Who thinks the worst of me. Who doesn't wish to—"

"None of that is true. Not anymore. And to show you good faith, I'm also willing to compromise, to put your mind at ease."

He raised a brow.

"We—including Leo—will move to the penthouse a month before my due date. And stay there for a few months after the babies come. I checked the floor plan and there's enough rooms to accommodate my sisters and Caio. Oh, and Stella. She'll kill me if I exclude her. But eventually, I wish to move back to the mansion. Maybe after the first few months and we all get into a routine."

"I didn't know you were that attached to the Carides mansion."

"I... I have good memories associated with that house. The summers we spent together... They mean something to me. They...were some of the most wonderful times of my life."

"You want me to believe that you're sentimental about the place because that's where we—"

"We fell in love once, yes. Is that so hard to believe?" Mira didn't wait for him to answer her. Because she knew where that road would lead. And she was so tired of looking back, of letting the past dictate her present and future. "And the fact that it's only accessible by chopper works in my favor."

"I can't wait to hear the why of this."

"Leo told me that you'd never return home every day if you returned to work full-time. Especially after the long break you've been forced to take due to the accident."

He smiled and the warmth of it teased out her newly fragile hope. "My grandfather is a traitor."

"I'm grateful for his advice on how to deal with you."

"How to manipulate me, you mean?"

"We have hurdles enough as we navigate this... I don't want to take the chance that I might become an afterthought once you go back to your corporate world and your thrill-seeking ways. It's not selfish to want you close through this pregnancy and when the babies come, is it?"

"But you're inviting the whole world into our lives, into our very home for the birth, *ne*? Do you still need me?"

And Mira heard it then. The doubts he hid beneath the silky taunt. Saw the tight jut of his jaw, the tension wreathing his frame. She didn't understand the source of it—not unless he shared them with her. Not unless he trusted her enough to share them with her, and she had no idea how to bring that about. But for now, she did have the courage and hope to give him the truthful answer.

"Not the whole world, Aristos. Just my sisters and Caio. And Stella, of course. I want them all here. I want our babies to be surrounded by people who love them and adore them from the first moment. Did you know that they absorb everything around them—the sights and sounds and feelings—from the moment they come into this world?" Her throat ached but in the best way. "I want them to feel so much love that they never doubt how much they're wanted. I want my sisters and Stella and Caio and Leo to spoil them rotten while you and I teach them right and wrong. And as for your second question... I want you close for myself. I need you there because I want to do this with you by my side. I want to share every high, every joy, every pain and every flinch with you during this whole thing and after because I—"

She never finished her thought, for Aristos was lifting her and depositing her in his lap. And then he was kissing her with a breathtaking intensity, lapping at her mouth, invading it with his tongue, stroking every inch of her, and Mira thought she might die of the sheer pleasure of his need.

His hands and mouth were everywhere on her, stroking and cupping, caressing and nipping, his words drawing a trail of heat wherever they touched.

"I want to give you what you want, *thee mou*. Let me, Mira. Let me make it up to you."

Mira buried her face in his neck, licking at the salty taste of him, breathing in the wild scent of him. At the back of her mind, thoughts floated like a low-level hum. They hadn't really sorted anything out. He'd purposely put distance between them. And the past was a specter that seemed to cut through the present.

"I need to touch you, Mira."

Every concern melted away at the feral hunger in his words. Here in the now, she was surrounded by his hard warmth and she just wanted to stay there. Forever if possible. "Yes, God. Now, Aristos."

"Tell me, *agapi*. What do you need from me?"

Bringing her mouth back up to his ear, Mira told him, with no hesitation in her voice, no inhibition in her flesh. Nothing but pure pleasure.

And how he delivered. With his fingers strumming at her core, his wicked mouth coaxing and cajoling and tormenting her aching nipples, his words—his hot, filthy words—vibrating against her skin, and his other hand coasting all over her trembling body, he kept her at the edge for so long that she was nothing but sensation.

And when she fell, she fell apart in a spectacular way,

pleasure splintering her. His teeth nipping at the pulse in her neck made it keener, sharper, just…everything more.

And when she floated down to earth, he held her close and kissed her temple and held her as he'd held her once, a long time ago.

Mira clung to Aristos, the afterquakes of her orgasm leaving her panting and limp in his arms. Beneath her buttocks, he was hard and heavy and she wished she had enough energy to straddle him, to take him inside her, to give him what he clearly needed but was determined not to take.

"If you can lift me and flip me around so that I straddle you, you can have me," she said, licking the shell of his ear.

He chuckled, and sudden, inexplicable tears filled her eyes. "As inviting as that sounds, you can hardly keep your eyes open, *thee mou*."

"I give you my blanket consent, Aristos. You can finish even if I fall asleep on you."

He was still laughing, his face buried in her neck, and it sent vibrations through her body. "What a thoughtful wife you are, Mira. But when I'm inside you, I'd rather you participate than snore in my face, *agapi*."

She was laughing too then, and his arms tightened around her, and however the day had started, the ending was perfect. She'd changed him a little, she thought, chipped away at the remoteness just a little today. And it left her with a giddy joy.

This moment was so perfect that her heart lurched into her throat, a painful yearning filling her chest. She wanted to bottle that laughter and hide it away. She wanted to always make him laugh like that. She wanted a chance to… learn and love the man he'd become. If only…

No, the past and its hurts didn't belong with her anymore.

Not when the present was a thing to be savored, not when they were finally building a foundation for their future. And somewhere in the last few months, she'd even begun to understand what might have driven him all those years ago.

For so long, she'd viewed the past through hurt and betrayal and a shattered heart. But now... Now she could see them both for who they had been—teenagers masquerading as adults with their hearts bearing the weight of their love for each other and past hurts and new fears.

God, the initial pull between them was because they both intrinsically knew what it felt to be abandoned by parents who should love them. Their baggage had been astronomical. Still, she'd at least had the security of having grandparents who'd loved her, the security of knowing her place in the world and what she wanted to do with it.

But Aristos... He'd had a whole heap of expectations crushing his shoulders, even as cousins and aunts had been waiting on the sidelines for him to fail. He'd barely turned eighteen with enormous pressure from Leo to mold himself into something, although he'd grown up on the streets with no education.

Was it any wonder he'd seen her as a prize, especially when she'd been dangled as such in front of him by both their grandfathers?

Could she truly let the past lie and build a new foundation?

Yes, came the resounding answer.

Dipping her hands into his hair, she pulled his head down for a rough tangling of their mouths.

"I want to ask you something," she whispered, the lingering echoes of pleasure making her bold and brave.

"What else would you have of me, Mira?" he asked. Even

his sudden stillness couldn't puncture the haze of happiness that pervaded her very limbs.

"I want us to leave the past where it is. I…want this to be a fresh start, Aristos, a real start. I want us to truly forgive and forget."

A jaw-cracking yawn took hold of her and his answer was lost to her in the fuzziness of exhaustion-driven sleep. Sliding her off his lap, he gathered her to him and sleep began to claim her deep.

CHAPTER EIGHT

MIRA ARRIVED AT dinner two weeks later to find Aristos's family gathered around the giant dining table. She could feel Aristos's gaze running over her face with that intense scrutiny that made her skin tingle but she didn't answer the overwhelming urge to look.

A lot had changed between them and yet, it felt like nothing had changed. He wasn't operating out of a checklist anymore, but he wasn't all there with her either. And if she was being truly honest with herself, his heart wasn't with her. And like some mirage teasing her in the distance, the more he held it back from her, the more she wanted it.

She'd slept well into the morning that day blissfully unaware that whatever she'd said in the limo after her climax had set them back to square one. God, she'd been exhausted, and buzzed from the orgasm, and she couldn't even remember what she'd asked of him.

And his displeasure at whatever she'd said had diluted their physical intimacy too.

Had she admitted that she wanted more than he was giving her? Or that she was falling for him, all over again? Was he finally realizing what this pregnancy and the changes meant and was feeling trapped?

She was about to make an excuse that she was too tired when Aristos reached her, his gaze searching. "If you're too tired for this, just say so, Mira." His chin notched onto her shoulder, and his body beckoned her with its warmth. "We will reschedule."

Over her shoulder, she studied his face. "No. I'm fine."

He pulled her chair out, and then walked around to the opposite side.

While it wasn't all of Leo's daughters and his grandchildren and various cousins around the table—Aristos's mom had been the youngest of six and the only one who'd given birth to a boy—her least favorite aunt and her least favorite cousin of his were seated across from Leo at the other end of the table.

Tia Camilla and her stepson Kairos.

Thank God, her favorite of his aunts was also present—Stella's mom, Sophia.

Mira forced a smile as Stella hugged her with one arm. Her skin crawled at the idea of Kairos next to her but she swallowed her dislike of him somehow.

Conversation flew around her in Greek and for once, Mira didn't mind at all. She was ravenous as always. And though she didn't enjoy the food as much as she usually did, she forced herself to eat, her thoughts in a jumbled whirl.

She'd known Kairos from the first time her grandfather had brought her to Greece to meet Leo when she'd been six. It had been common knowledge even then that Leo had been grooming Kairos to be his heir.

Even as a girl, Mira had never liked Kairos that much. The man was full of himself—all shiny surface with no substance beneath.

Aristos, even wild and near-feral, and extremely prickly as he was when they'd first met, had been the exact opposite of the smarmy Kairos—full of ambition and energy, bursting with a strength of character that had fascinated her from day one.

And of course, everything had changed for Kairos the moment Leo had discovered that his youngest daughter had borne a son—the very daughter he'd adored but thrown out when she'd defied his will and ran away with a man he had refused to give a blessing to.

To give Leo credit, he hadn't immediately shunted Kairos to the side. But his secret gambling debts coupled with Aristos's incisive intelligence had made the latter a clear winner in a race no one had entered except Kairos and his insecurities.

Even now, as she watched him beam a fake smile at her, Mira struggled to keep her own straight.

Seeing him brought the episode of their engagement and the entire debacle that had happened the following night into sharp focus. Not that it was ever far from Mira's mind. Especially now when she and Aristos had gotten together again. Especially when she was coming to truly know him more and more.

She'd seen the gleam of lust in Kairos's eyes even as a teenager who'd barely understood her own body. She'd seen his jealousy of Aristos as he toppled every one of Leo's expectations. And yet that night when everything had fallen apart, Kairos had been her friend.

And she knew now that something was innately wrong with that very picture in her head. There was no way she could ask Kairos about that night, not without betraying her own doubts and the state of her marriage to him.

And Aristos… Asking Aristos about it would destroy every bit of their relationship all over again. God, she couldn't take that risk. Not today. Not ever.

* * *

"Mira and I are expecting. Twins."

The quiet announcement by Aristos at the dining table, full of pride and something else she couldn't make out, landed with the impact of a meteor. At his command, the staff brought out a couple of bottles of iced champagne. Leo's congratulations and Stella's whoops surrounded them as champagne was poured into flutes and passed along. But of course, they'd both known that something was up—thanks to the team of people Aristos had going in and out of the estate.

But this was their first official announcement and she didn't begrudge him the moment. She'd shared the news with her own sisters almost a week ago over a video call. They'd screamed so loud that Mira had to slap her hands over her ears.

Mira dipped her head in a nod when Stella's mom expressed her congratulations in that quiet way of hers. She didn't speak English but the genuine affection in her voice was enough for Mira. Especially since her nephew didn't even meet her eyes. Aristos had avoided his aunts for as long as Mira could remember.

Tia Camilla and Kairos though… Mira wished she could keep her gaze straight ahead and yet, the cold silence from their end of the table made it impossible not to look.

His mouth set into a stiff line, his beady eyes flinty with anger, Kairos let out a low peal of laughter. A sudden hush fell over the table.

"Kairos! This is good news for our family," Leo said, an inherent warning in his tone. But Aristos's cousin had already imbibed too much alcohol and he didn't have control over his tongue at the best of times. He rose from the seat, and Mira drew in a relieved breath.

Until he walked around and slapped Aristos on the shoulder hard enough to make her flinch.

"Ah… So you've finally given Leo what he wants, *ne*? Forced yourself into a marriage, put yourself to stud just to cement your control over Carides Inc.?" Kairos began, not even trying to cover up his bitterness. "Your ambition knows no morals or boundaries."

Her glass sloshed water over her fingers as the words registered. Fear kicked in her chest about what Kairos might say about the past, ruining the present. Mira reached for Aristos's hand across the table, her throat aching. "Aristos, he's drunk."

But her husband had a savage edge to his temper that belied his steady heart. "You should be raising your glass to me, Kairos, thanking me for taking care of another duty that you have failed." Unable to cope with his drinking and his gambling, his wife had left Kairos years ago. And yet, his arrogance hadn't dimmed one bit.

Mira would've found satisfaction in his words if fear didn't beat a tattoo in her heart.

"What the hell is that supposed to mean?" Kairos demanded.

"Carides heirs means the cushy allowance and maintenance fund that Leo grants you will be guaranteed for another few decades. It means the board will stop complaining about my actions. And even if I perish—as you've been praying for for years—it will still be my children who rule the Carides empire." Utter silence blanketed the room. "As always, I've shot past Leo's expectations for me, giving him two heirs. And you won't mock them as you used to mock me, *ne*? Born in wedlock, made of good stock—because really, Mira beats all the socialites you've been panting after in both brains and beauty, and I bet you anything they're going to be as smart and—"

"Aristos, that's enough," Mira whispered, each of his words landing like lashes against her skin. Was this what he thought of their children? Mere pawns and accomplishments in his ambitions? Like check marks on his list of attributes? But then, that's how he'd been acting. She turned to Leo. "Please stop them."

"Spread your sperm around enough and it was bound to happen," Kairos continued before Leo could even speak.

"That's you and your ill-fated progeny you speak of," Aristos retorted, pushing to his own feet. "Mine are legitimate."

It was the quiet before a storm, a wide, ugly smile contorting Kairos's face, and suddenly, Mira knew whatever he'd told her that night, whatever he'd shown her, was somehow lies. All lies. And she'd thrown away a lifetime's happiness based on his words.

"The whole world knows she made you sign a contract, cousin. That she intends to leave you after five years." Kairos made a leering face at Leo, taunting the patriarch. "Did you know that bit of delicious truth about your precious heir?" Then he turned to Aristos, a knowing grin twisting his mouth. "I know that she only chose you because you offered her what she wants the most, *ne*? Your little secretary was happy to share those facts with me. Apparently, your pretty little wife was desperate enough for a baby that she overlooked the fact that you're still nothing but a feral animal under all that polish you've acquired. It's the only reason she came back into your life after dumping you the first time. You bought her just the way you've bought your-self into the entire family's good graces."

"Stella, take Mira to the bedroom," Aristos said in a calm, quiet tone that fooled no one.

Pressing a hand to her throbbing temple, Mira sighed. "I'm not a child you need to dismiss from the table because it's about to get ugly. As for him, he's nothing but a jeal-ous drunk."

But Aristos... Something bleak and cold lit his gray eyes. His anger, his loathing, his ire... They were all directed at himself. Why? Her chest felt so tight that she wanted to rub a hand there.

"This is an old war finally coming to its conclusion, *yineka mou*. I don't want you caught up in the crossfire."

"I'm in the crossfire whether you like it or not," Mira said, shaking her head.

"Just leave, Mira."

"No. His filthy words don't even touch me. It's you who can..." She turned to Stella, a steely resolve taking over. "Will you please get him out of here?"

Stella nodded and with her mother and aunt's help, she herded a swaying Kairos out the door.

Aristos's grandfather got to his feet in a slow movement that spoke of his tiredness. He cast one warning look at Aristos, patted Mira's shoulder and left them to the storm brewing in the room.

It had been brewing for a while. Kairos was simply the catalyst. And Mira was ready for it. For weeks, she'd won-dered at Aristos's lack of reaction to her news. On paper, he'd done everything and yet, his heart hadn't been in it. And now to hear him boast of their babies as if they were... That she couldn't tolerate.

Even now, he was turned away from her, tension wreathing his tight shoulders. "I wish you'd do as you're told just once, Mira."

"And I wish you didn't treat me as if I was some special project, Aristos." She went to him then, the scent of him immediately calming her, even as the man himself twisted her inside out. "I don't understand why you're letting him get to you. Kairos has always been jealous of you."

His shoulders shook, his hand pressed to his temple. "And yet, he seems to have drilled down to the truth."

She turned him around with a hand on his shoulder. "What truth would that be, Aristos? How can anything he said be worse than the fact that this is the first time I've heard you mention our unborn babies and that too as if they were some kind of pawns in a big game? As if they were your accomplishments?"

"That's not what they are, Mira."

"And yet that's all I heard." She sucked in a long breath, putting that concern aside for now. Yes, Kairos was an ass, but his words could prick her husband, who'd always been mocked for his background. Who'd fought his way to the top through sheer willpower and hard work. Who'd always been treated as an outsider even when he'd had a family. And she... Even unknowingly, she'd judged him and found him guilty too. It was eating away at her already. "I don't care what they say about us, Aristos. You and I know the truth."

"Who's distorting the truth now, *thee mou*?" he asked, his tone dangerously silky, stepping away from her as if he couldn't bear to be touched. "What we have is a contract that works in both our favor. You know why I signed it. They're the heirs that Leo wanted, the heirs I need to shut the board up. They will be the face of the new Carides generation. My legacy—the only thing in the whole goddamned world that are truly mine. My children will rule the Carides board unchallenged, the very same board that made me run through so many hoops."

"Yes, they're the new generation. But they're not the only—"

"Why should I not crow my success to him and my cousins and to the world that has always stood against me? You got what you wanted. Why are you denying me what I wanted out of this?"

Mira grabbed the glass of water and threw it in Aristos's face before she even realized she was doing it. Fury and hurt were like twin jets of flame, rocketing through her. The sound of the glass hitting the table and then the floor at her feet was like a deafening explosion in the silence.

"Is this all a joke to you, Aristos?" Her voice wobbled but she refused to let a single tear through.

"Far from it, *pethi mou*."

"Then when are you going to act like it?" The question shot out of her like an entreaty. But that was personal. To fix her mistake, to bring things between them to an even keel, she'd beg Aristos, if needed. But that weakness began and ended with her. Not with her children. Her voice was rock steady when she said, "My...babies will not be your achievements to be shown off to the world, or some cardboard puppets that you will manipulate beyond belief for the grand, great Carides name."

Only when the words were out and her breath shook out of her in a raw, jagged exhale could she bear to meet Aristos's gaze again.

He hadn't even wiped the water she'd thrown on him. It

plastered his wild hair to his skull. One lone drop dripped from his temple, flew down the slanted slope of a sharp cheekbone and then slipped past a tight jawline. "As for me and you, you're not just some…sperm donor and I'm not just a convenient womb…"

And then it struck her—the painful truth he'd been dangling in her face since the moment she'd arrived but she refused to accept. Had hope made an utter fool out of her? "You still consider us bound only by the contract?"

"Yes," said Aristos, before he could swallow the urge. Before he could become weak.

Whatever little color was there fled Mira's face but she didn't break or bend. If anything, her chin lifted in direct challenge to his rejection of the hope in her voice.

"I'm just reminding you how particular you were about the clauses and subclauses, *yineka mou*. Reminding you that as my children, there will be certain expectations of them too."

"They're ours, Aristos, the best parts of the both of us. And whether you accept it or not, I know that you'd never manipulate them or neglect them or do anything that would harm them in the smallest way," she said with a simple conviction that threatened to take him out at his knees.

"Once you had no faith in me. Now, you have too much, Mira."

"I know what I know," she said simply. Her chest rose and fell, that quiet dignity of hers wrapped around her. Her voice didn't waver one bit when she said, "So that night, at my grandfather's house, you were performing per our contract's demands?"

There was that stupid spasm in his chest again, with nowhere to go. But he wasn't going to let the avalanche of emotions trying to bury him win.

Kairos's filthy words hadn't hurt him, but they'd released his worst fear. Released a reminder of the rejections and struggles he'd faced even before Leo had found him. Of the pain he'd felt when Mira had left without a word all those years ago.

If he didn't clip the tenuous wings of hope spreading through his chest right now that he couldn't seem to contain when he was near her, if he didn't cauterize himself against that very hope, it would leave him wingless.

Untethered. Powerless.

Because a part of him still couldn't trust that she wouldn't leave again. A part of him was still terrified that he would fail as a father. A part of him wondered if she and those precious babies would find him as worthless as his mother had found him. And he simply couldn't take that chance.

"I've never hidden the fact that I've been lusting over you forever, Mira. Maybe your recent grief and loss made it appear more to you. It *was* explosive but please let's not rewrite history and make it more than it was."

She nodded, even though they were both aware that he'd hurt her. "Then we have to agree to disagree over that night. For me, it wasn't fulfilling a contract. It wasn't the set course we'd decided on for our marriage. It wasn't just sex."

A sudden breeze from the open French doors threw tendrils of her hair away from her face. It also plastered her cotton dress to her body, taunting him with the outline of her belly. Her skin, always silky and smooth, seemed to shimmer in the afternoon light. And her eyes—they shone with a conviction and a fire that would scorch him if he let it.

Reaching him, she kissed his cheek—a soft buss of tenderness that threatened to undo him. Nuzzled that silky-smooth jaw against his harsh stubble, as if he were a wild horse she hoped to tame. Made his gut tighten with thick, slumberous want. But it wasn't just that. Her arms came around him, and her belly grazed his side, and his distasteful words seemed to burn through him.

"That night was something I reached for after years of loneliness, something I wanted desperately. It was real and beautiful and as necessary as breath. And the thing is… No one else would have been enough, Aristos. It had to be you." Pulling back, she caught his gaze again, trapping him, pinning him, forcing him into a stillness that had never been possible for him, except with her. "Our babies…" She grabbed his hand and placed it over her belly. His heart gave a thunderous thud against his chest, rattling in his rib cage like a bird trapped, thrashing to be let free. "…were conceived under the magic of something raw and real. And that's the way I'll remember it for the rest of our lives."

"Are you running away again, Mira?"

Leo Carides's softly spoken question halted Mira's frenzied packing.

Throwing another pair of pants into the traveling bag, she turned to find her grandfather's oldest friend hovering over the threshold. "Come in, please." Scrubbing a hand over the trail of tears that seemed to have no end, she faced him. "To answer your question, no. I was going to camp outside his office though."

"I have been informed he hasn't been to work in three days."

Three days since he'd been gone… Where was he, then?

Leo walked past the bed to the veranda, poured water into a glass and beckoned her close.

Mira drank the water and turned to look at the blinding blue of the ocean. But for once the view lost against her emotional turmoil.

"Rao and I were so sure that you were the girl to ground my grandson, the one to civilize him—"

"He's not an animal to need civilization," Mira interrupted, inflamed by the choice of his words. "He was a mere boy when you decided to put the weight of the world on his shoulders. When you decided to set him impossible challenges. You made him fight when you should've shown him love and acceptance and…"

If he found her words offensive, Leo didn't show it. "That was the only way to ready him for what lay ahead. You have seen his cousins and his aunts. They're all useless vultures who would've torn him apart if I didn't make him strong. But you're right. I did starve him for something more important in the process."

Mira lifted her head, shocked at his candor.

Leo laughed and her breath caught at the flash of resemblance between him and his grandson. "I made many mistakes with him, Mira. And it is right that Aristos merely tolerates me."

"That's not true. He adores you. But of course, being the stubborn dickhead he is, he can't show it. He probably thinks it's a weakness to care about you. That is your fault, *ne*?"

This time, Leo's laughter was loud and booming. "Now I see why he's never forgotten you, why he…" He shook his head. His gaze was fond and searching as it returned to her face. "Even then, I remember how he bloomed under your friendship, how he laughed around you, how happy he was, and I made a deal with Rao. For his happiness and yours. So much for two old men matchmaking, eh?"

Mira looked away, frowning at the disappointment threaded through his words. "The past is full of mistakes, Leo, including mine. Please tell me why you're here."

"His words were rash and crude the other night…and yet, you think Aristos would have let anyone tell him how to run his life? Do you think anything but his own wishes motivated him to enter this ridiculous contract marriage between you two?"

"He did it for you and the board and…"

"He did it for himself. My grandson is nothing if not a man full of complex emotions that he barely understands. And the fault of that lies with me."

Mouth falling open, Mira stared at the older man. "You're saying Aristos wouldn't have given in to anyone's pressures? Not even yours?"

"Carides's board whines from time to time, but they know where their fat stocks come from. And as for me, I have pressured him, badgered him because his stunts were getting riskier and riskier. I wanted him to settle down." He sighed. "You're right that I have demanded the impossible of Aristos and despite all the odds stacked against him, he rose to the occasion. And yet, this is the first time I've seen him do something for himself."

"You're saying he wanted this marriage for real? That he wanted me for real?"

His silver gaze searched Mira's face. "Of all the things Rao says about you…" He swallowed and corrected himself, a yawning chasm of loneliness in his eyes. "…said about you, I thought one thing true. That you're clever, Mira. But maybe he was nothing but a foolish old man like me, hmm? After all these years, if you still don't know the depths to which you have driven Aristos, if you still don't understand the impact you've had on him…then you're not only naive but unworthy of him."

"Please, Leo. Enough riddles," Mira said, fairly pleading the old man to explain. "Tell me what you mean."

He shook his head. "I can't betray my grandson's secrets. Not even for his own good."

"Do you know here he is?"

"He was scheduled to appear at a race in Monaco two days ago. His new assistant confirmed his presence. But only as a guest for some kids' charity the race is sponsoring," he said in a rush, his gaze shrewd.

"I don't know what to do, Leo. I… I have tried…"

His arm around her shoulders, Leo squeezed her into a gentle hug that sent tears crawling into her throat. God, she missed her Thaata. She missed his hugs, and his kind words and his gentle nudges…and she missed Aristos. And she wondered for the first time, if she could do this if she didn't have Aristos's heart involved. If she could put aside her own need for…

"What do you think he's expecting of you?"

Leaning her head into his embrace, Mira frowned. "He's expecting me to…leave. Especially after that disastrous fight."

With a final wink, Leo walked out.

Mira pushed the bag away and flopped onto the bed, her thoughts in a whirl, her lower back aching. Leo had given her a lot to think about.

She'd slipped away from Aristos's life all those years ago after she'd been paraded in front of him as the ultimate partner, rejected him in front of the whole family and she knew better than anyone that Aristos Carides didn't take easily to losing.

His proposition in Vegas had unsettled her on a deep level that she'd refused to examine then. Because in one thing, Leo was right.

Aristos could have chosen any woman on the planet—at least a thousand willing and better suited and less combative and maybe more loving and open—to be his wife. To be the mother of his heirs. To be his convenient wife.

And yet he'd chosen her despite their bad history, despite the fact that it rankled him that she'd broken their engagement. He'd "hunted her down to Vegas" in his own words.

Why had Mira been his choice? Was it simply a sop to his bruised ego, to his masculine pride, to "conquer" the woman who'd once had the gall to walk away from him?

Or was it possible, her foolish heart thudded at the mere thought, there was more?

CHAPTER NINE

ARISTOS RETURNED THE next night. After four long days and nights where she'd worried herself in endless loops. Holding on to Leo's words like a talisman.

"He married you for himself."

His soft footfalls into the room as he passed the bed, the sounds of the shower, the faint light peeking out of the closet—everything twisted Mira into a mass of nervous anticipation. Nothing she'd done had helped her fall asleep. A part of her had wanted to escape to another bedroom, or banish him from here. Even his proximity right now felt unbearable. And yet a part of her didn't want to be alone in some far-off bedroom, wondering if her hope was truly foolish.

Minutes later, the bed dipped under his weight, her super-aware senses immediately thrumming at his nearness. His scent soothed her and wrapped around her like the embrace she desperately wanted from him.

Fluffing her own pillow, she turned on her side and away to face the rich, impenetrable darkness of the ocean beyond the veranda.

She felt him shift on the bed, until she could feel the heat of his body like a warm blanket at her back. He'd moved closer to her. Every inch of her tightened into a ball, bracing for his touch, wishing she didn't want it, but needing it anyway.

"I'm sorry." The words were a hard rasp but easily given.

She considered ignoring him—for about three and a half seconds.

"For what exactly?"

"Mira, look at me."

He didn't touch her, even as everything about him pulled at her like the moon did the tides. She rubbed her palm softly over her belly, seeking and giving reassurance and love. "I'm too tired to discuss your sins, Aristos."

"Sins, Mira?" Gravity weighed down his voice. "Not mistakes?"

"Mistakes are made without intending to cause hurt. You had to have known that talking like that about the babies..." she said, taking the easy way out even now, "would hurt me."

For a long time, he didn't answer.

A shuddering sigh followed. She felt him thrust his fingers through his hair, felt his reluctance and hesitation and his internal struggle as if they were her own. But that didn't mean she could simply forget the pain and doubt he'd caused her in the last few days.

"You know how...savage I get around Kairos. He pushed all my buttons and I let him. I said things I never even thought about the...babies. I'm not a man who cares about legacies and... *Christos*, you know that about me, Mira. But there's no excuse for the fact that those words impacted you. For that, I am sorry. More than I can say."

He meant it. Every word.

Mira couldn't shake the conviction nor did she want to. Neither did she miss the stark hesitation before he said "the babies." The careful, dispassionate way he said it broke her heart a little for him. So she offered an olive branch. Turning around, she said, "I believe you."

His fingers gripped her wrist loosely as if he meant to bring her hand to his face.

"Truth or dare, Aristos," she whispered, invoking the one game that wasn't a game between them but their sacred ritual. A vow that had bound them before they'd even understood their own hearts.

"Truth."

Her gaze met his. "Are you feeling trapped?"

He frowned. "Trapped?"

"By the pregnancy? Are you having second thoughts? Because if you are, the least you can do is be up-front with me. Then I can amend my plan. Or make other plans." Her voice shook on the last words but Mira couldn't live in some limbo world. She'd rather know now before she was even more enmeshed in his life. Even more entangled with his heart. "Ever since I told you that it's twins, you've been detached. You can't even say *babies* without flinching. When you did talk of them, it was as if they were stepping-stones in some game. If you want out, Aristos, this is the time to say it."

"Mira, look at me," he said, his fingers gripping her chin.

She did it because he left her no choice, but what she saw in the swirls of his gray eyes held her arrested. He looked angry and shocked and tormented—at himself.

"No." The word rang around them—loud and harsh and resonant. "No, I'm not feeling trapped. No, I don't want you to make new plans. No second thoughts. None."

She searched his gaze, as if she could plumb it and find more. Because that question had been for herself. For her selfish hope.

"Tell me you get it, Mira." Looming over her, he shook her shoulder none too gently, his eyes carrying that haunted look she hadn't seen in a long while. "Tell me you understand that my actions have nothing to do with you and… the children."

Relief stole her breath and panic she hadn't let herself feel until now made tears pool in her eyes. They slid down into her hair, leaving her trembling.

"Shh… Mira. Shh…" Leaning over, Aristos managed to gather her up until she was sitting by his side, his arms enfolding her shoulders in a tight grip. "I'm sorry, *agapi mou*."

"Don't… Don't you dare call me that," Mira retorted.

And still hope lingered in her breast. Audaciously so. It was an endearment that he had never used before—he was only offering it as an apology and yet it soothed the tender edges of her heart that had taken a battering the other day.

He crooned at her temple, words Mira couldn't understand, the warmth of his body an inviting cradle around her. "Mira, tell me what I can do to make you believe that I regret my words."

The answer came easily. It was the one place where they'd always met as perfect counterparts. And Mira needed the magic of his touch now. The magic of his worship, his want, his wondrously skilled hands upon her.

Because she wanted to believe that Aristos would continue on this journey with her. Because if that's all he could give her, she would live with it. She would make do and build a family and pour all her love into it.

"Touch me. Kiss me. Give me so much pleasure that I forget the fear, Aristos."

The warm press of his mouth was a brand against her temple and Mira pushed into it. "First, you will tell me why you tremble like a leaf, *yineka mou*."

When she'd have protested, he pressed his finger to her mouth.

A shuddering exhale left her and she struggled to not kiss the rough pads of his fingers. To not draw that digit into her mouth and suckle on it until it rendered him as mindless and lost as she felt already.

"Give me this, give me your fears, Mira, and I promise I will never let them touch you again."

Mira pressed her head into his chest, and let out a groan when his fingers found her lower back. When he held her like that, when he touched her like that, she felt no fear, only hope spreading through her like sunlight.

"When I told you I had to sort through a lot of things, I wasn't lying. OneTech and Nush and the company's interests, Caio had in hand. But the house and Nanamma's jewelry and other pieces of his estate, Thaata left all of that to me. Nush had already left with Caio to Brazil and Yana was at a shoot in Bali. I was completely alone in the house that had loved me more than either of my parents ever had. I went through every room in the house, sorting through decades of accumulated stuff. It began happily enough."

"What do you mean?"

"My grandmother never threw away a single thing of mine. Every card I ever made them, every silly bracelet I spun, every essay and poem I wrote, every Halloween costume I ever wore, every Diwali craft she and I made together—she kept everything. Every single thing. But in all of it, in the mountains of stuff, there wasn't a single photograph of me with my parents. Not a single one.

Something possessed me and I searched like a mad woman. I went back to the storage unit and opened every box again. I found nothing. I spent weeks lingering there, walking the empty house like some kind of wraith, trying to remember her face. My mother's face."

Mira closed her eyes, the same resolve filling her again. "Until I woke up one morning and threw up the meager breakfast I had. I got a blood test done the same day, went to see my doctor the next week and because I'd left it so late, the doctor could detect two heartbeats already. The moment I came home, I threw up again.

"I… I have never been so scared, Aristos. Never. Not when I held Thaata's hand in mine and knew he was slipping away. Not when my father left me outside a bar for hours when I was seven because he'd gotten drunk inside and forgot all about me."

His hand cradling her cheek, the warm press of Aristos's mouth against her temple was an anchor calling her back to the present. "It was strange, the confluence of those two things. I realized for the first time that I was so…lonely. And that I didn't have to be. That I'd done that to myself."

But the hollowness of the memory was fleeting when Mira grabbed his hand and brought it to her belly. She found his gaze in the darkness, refusing to shy away from the moment, from her own heart. "From the moment I boarded the plane to return to you, I knew what I wanted in my heart."

"What, *yineka mou*? Whatever you ask for, it's yours."

Your heart. Your love. You.

Instead Mira said, "I want to burn down that stupid contract. I want us to make vows to each other again, just for ourselves. I want us to be a real family…"

His sudden stillness stole away her words.

Fear slithered through her veins, but she wasn't going to turn back now. "And if that's not what you want, if you still want to stick to our five-year rule, then I want out now. I'm sorry for changing the rules on you midgame, sorry that I'm not the sensible, practical woman you bet on, but I—"

"Yes. Yes. Yes," he whispered against her mouth. "Yes, for burning down the contract." And then Aristos was kissing her.

Kissing her as if his life depended on it and yet, it wasn't hard or urgent or just full of lust. It was a promise given in reverent touch. His mouth left hers and trailed all over her face, even as he whispered words she couldn't understand. And then returned to her mouth again and again, as if it were a shining beacon in an ocean of darkness. And every time he returned to her mouth and kissed her again, Mira discovered something new in it.

And it would be enough to sustain them over a lifetime.

CHAPTER TEN

ARISTOS PUSHED HIS guilt and his regrets aside and decided to verbalize his own fears. This woman was worth pushing aside the harmful patterns and beliefs that had helped him survive once.

With her sweet taste thrumming through his blood like some miracle drug, her hands reaching for him hungrily, her words burrowing into his heart, it was the easiest thing in the world to do.

Christos, it would haunt him for the rest of his days—the specter of fear and pain in her eyes. The vulnerability she hid beneath the stoic, strong mask she wore.

Her brave words swept over him again and again, washing him free of his own fear. "Vulnerability does not come easily to me, *yineka mou*."

"No, not for me either. And why would it, Aristos? You've been taught to equate it to weakness. First for survival, alone out there in the world, and then for a different kind of survival after Leo found you. You've never been given a safe space to do so."

Wonder flickered through him at the depth of her understanding. "Maybe you should specialize in psychology, Mira," he said dryly, feeling as if she'd cut him open to peer at his insides. Even now, his instincts screamed at him to not bare himself so fully to her. To protect himself.

"It's a lesson I learned the hard way too. Shutting out vulnerability meant shutting out so many other things too. Like joy and wonder and abundance. Before I came here, I made the decision to stop acting out of fear. To stop getting in the way of my own happiness. Loneliness is perfectly safe and sterile but settles deep into one's bones."

"You were right." He looked away, ashamed of what she might see in his gaze. It was useless because even in the darkness, she could hear the thread of disquiet in his words. "When you told me it was twins, I was...terrified. For the first time since I made that proposal to you, what that meant hit me like a ton of bricks." He pressed a hand to his head. "It's taken me weeks to even verbalize the fear. I've never known...what a healthy, thriving family looks like. Only conditions and agreements and clauses and rewards and punishments... You've seen how Leo and I still fight like dogs, *ne*? How I can't tolerate anyone but Stella in the family? You must have lost your usual good judgment that day in Vegas, Mira, that you chose me for the one role I can't just learn for."

"No parent is ever perfectly ready, Aristos. I'm just as at sea as you are."

"What if I mess up this whole thing about being a father, Mira? What if I can't love my own children? Worse, what if they see that?"

The wide shimmer of her smile was like a beacon in the thick darkness of his own fears. "That you worry about doing right by them is more than enough of a start."

Her long fingers clasped his cheek and she took his mouth in a soft, tender kiss, swallowing away his words, swallowing his fears. Filling him with hope and desire and faith in himself, in them. Nothing in the world felt insurmountable when Mira kissed him, when she gazed at him with such wonder as if he was the answer to her every wish. "We will learn, Aristos. We will do it together. And when we make mistakes, we will try to do better."

A fierce longing swept through him, drenching him, drowning him. "I want this just as much as you do." Some lingering reservation in her gaze reminded him of his actions not four days ago. "I will prove it to you, *yineka mou*."

"Is that a dare, Mr. Carides?"

"It is the only way I understand the world, Dr. Carides."

Closing her eyes, she trembled again and it became his mission to rid her of that last remnant of fear. To fill her with the very faith she'd given him.

Slowly, softly, he stroked his hand over her face, plunging it into her thick hair, murmuring soothing words, gentling her, willing the fear to leave her body. He dipped a trail of kisses over her forehead, her temple, the smooth skin of her jaw, over and over again. Going back to her mouth for a taste in between.

Lust roared through him, driving him to deepen the kiss, goading him to drown her in pleasure, urging him to bind her to him here, where there was never any doubt between them.

He resisted the overwhelming urge—he wanted honesty between them. He wanted to return her faith back to her— faith he didn't deserve—a thousand times over. He wanted to wipe the lingering emptiness in his gut despite the fact that his biggest risk had paid off.

She wanted the contract torn and burned. She wanted to build a real family with him. She wanted to do this for real… But all of it, all her newfound desire, all her deep resolve, it was for those innocent lives in her belly. It was because she was already a fierce mother.

It was for the children, their children.

Victory had never seemed so hollow to him. And yet, Aristos continued to kiss her, continued to cling to his good fortune, continued to remind himself that he had her. Forever. Nothing and no selfish desire would come before the babies for Mira. Not when she had resolved to make a go of this permanently.

The hollowness of it fled fast enough when Mira sank her fingers into his hair and brought his mouth to meet hers.

This time, he let her feel the roaring desire he'd nipped until then. The dark craving for her every night when he found her nuzzling into him. Tugging on her hair to hold her like he wanted, he plunged his tongue into her mouth. And *Christos*, she paid him back in explosive response. Teeth and tongues danced, no hold, no grip, no nip close enough, hard enough, warm enough. He groaned when she dug her teeth into his lower lip, vying for dominance, telling him to go deeper, rougher, faster.

When he cursed, she skittered out of his hold, her thick braid lashing him in the chest. "Your hip... Your physio said you pulled a muscle the other day. That you were in pain."

Flopping onto his back, Aristos laughed. "Spying on me, *yineka mou*?"

"He called to say he'd upped your pain meds and you weren't here and I demanded he tell me what was what."

When she continued to stare at him as if she was scared to even breathe near him, he grabbed the end of that braid and tugged her closer. "It's more sore and tight than real pain."

"Okay. How do you want to do this?"

"This?" he said, grinning at the frown tying her brows. His wife was ever a problem-solver and he liked when she looked at him like that. A lot.

"I want to have sex with my husband. In fact, I've been

panting for it for over…a month now. Pawing at him when he's asleep like a creep."

"How creepy did you get?"

She flushed and he laughed again. "Nothing south of the border. I like—" there was that vulnerability turning those eyes into molten pools again "—hearing your heart thud in my ear."

He easily understood her unspoken fear and sobered up. "Mira—"

"That's a discussion for another day. Especially since it will break our fragile peace if we go there now."

"Turn on the light. I want to look at you. Properly."

She reached for the remote, but hesitated. "My body's already changing."

"And I want to map every change, learn every rise and dip anew. Just looking at you, lying next to you in the most innocent ways, makes me rock hard, Mira. It has always been like that."

The lights came on and Aristos looked at his wife. Whatever blood remained in his brain flooded south instantly. *Christos*, she'd always been his wet dream. But now, whether it was the pregnancy hormones or some inner resolve, she was glowing from inside out.

The baby-pink sleeveless silk top and matching shorts made her skin glow golden. The lacy neckline barely contained her breasts and even as he watched, the plump nipples he loved wrapping his tongue around pushed up boldly against the silk. A thin, long gold chain with a tiny pendant played peekaboo in her cleavage. Her shorts hung low on her hips and bunched against her thighs, leaving the bump of her belly bare.

"You're so beautiful you take away my breath, *yineka mou*," he whispered, giving her everything he felt in this.

Wrapping his fingers around her nape, he pulled her forward and tugged down the flimsy top and rubbed his stubble against one fat nipple.

Mira's groan, long and guttural, made his cock impossibly, painfully hard.

He repeated the same motion against the other breast, knowing how sensitive she was there. Realizing she'd grown even more so with the pregnancy. Again and again, until she was the one undulating against him, the one driving his mouth over and over again to each peak, the one urging him to taste the turgid tip begging for his attention.

When he swirled his tongue over the taut bud and gently suckled her with his lips, Mira dug her nails into his shoulders. This was pain he welcomed, pain he relished because it told him that she wanted him. That Mira needed this from him. From the man he was. Only from him.

With his mouth devoted to her breasts, and his hands learning her all over, the smooth planes of her back, the tight indentation of her waist, the luscious swells of her buttocks, every inch he caressed with increasing fervor.

Laced by the knowledge that she was his. That she had asked to be his for the rest of their lives.

It was not exactly what he wanted, for he was a greedy bastard, an avaricious little mongrel who wanted everything when it was Mira. But still, that their arrangement was turning into a union they were both committed to, added a layer of renewed force to his desire.

He'd always felt possessive of Mira, even when she wasn't in his life. But now, something visceral held him in its grip as he licked a trail down her cleavage.

With the same mindless urgency as his, Mira stroked her hands down his chest, his abdomen, his thighs and then back up again over and over and over, as if she was committing him to memory.

Her touch stalled, as her long fingers trailed over his damaged hip. Pulling away from him, she scooted herself into a kneeling position down the bed. She tugged his shorts down with an impatience he couldn't hold against her. And then she touched her mouth to his hip.

Aristos groaned at her lush, swollen mouth lingering so near where he needed it desperately but hadn't asked for.

She kissed the jagged lines and raised flesh of his hip with a reverence he didn't deserve, that made his chest expand and tighten at the same time. Mumbling something he couldn't even hear, she pressed kisses all over the damaged area, kneading it just right with her long strong fingers. His groan when he let it escape was filled with both relief and pleasure.

"Does it hurt?"

He shook his head, unable to master his voice.

"You know I regretted something about that night all those months ago."

"I don't want to hear this. Because I have no regrets."

She smiled then. And it was full of delight and wickedness and desire. And he wondered if he could drown in it. He wondered if she had bewitched him from that first day almost twenty years ago. He wondered if one day he would stop wanting to see something else in her eyes when she looked at him.

"I didn't touch you to my heart's content. I regretted that I let you take the lead. I regretted not doing this," she said and then she licked up his cock like it was her favorite Popsicle.

Aristos threw his head back and groaned, every nerve ending vibrating with pleasure, with need that wanted complete scorching. Her fingers fisted around his length, dragged up and down, urging his body on and on.

Fingers and lips, she worked him into a ravenous spiral. He followed them along with a thrust of his hips, chasing his climax.

Stars exploded beneath his eyes when she released him with a loud plop. "Mira," he said, his voice guttural, "straddle me. Take me inside you before I spill all over you. Ride me, *yineka mou*."

Brown eyes turning molten from lust, Mira nodded. She gave him one long lick before she released him. His erection plopped against his abdomen. Hands thrust beneath his neck, Aristos watched as she slowly shed her pink shorts.

His luscious wife, he'd noticed last time, wasn't shy exactly but neither was she blatantly comfortable with her nakedness. The complexity of this woman, every hard and soft edge he discovered, fascinated him even more. Like he could spend his lifetime trying to learn her, chase her, conquer her and yet, the thrill would never abate. "Don't cover yourself, Mira. You're glorious."

She nodded, lifted her hips and peeled down the panties. Pushing onto his elbows, he rubbed his stubble against the smooth skin of her thick, muscled thigh. Grinned when his stubble left a mark.

The moment the panties came off, he sent his hands on a quest, her lush beauty sending him into a tailspin all over. From her breasts—wet from his ministrations—to her swollen belly, and then down through the patch of trimmed curls.

She scooted her butt closer to him and Aristos let out a loud thanks.

Her delightful giggle was cut off when he delved between her legs. With a soft, inviting rasp, her thighs fell away as he caressed every slick curve and then dipped one finger into her sex. Her tight flesh closed about him greedily and he had to swallow the raw lust that had always driven him when he was with her. His fingers came away damp and shiny and pink crested her cheeks.

Holding her gaze, Aristos licked his finger and groaned at the musky, salty taste of her. "One of these days, *agapi*, I will convince you to sit on my face."

Her gasp was mortified but her wide, blazing eyes couldn't hide her interest. So many layers to unravel still. But she found her wits fast enough. "Maybe when I'm not pregnant with your twins and they aren't playing soccer in my belly and there's no risk of me accidentally choking you because my center of gravity is off."

He laughed, pleasure and joy twin birds in his chest, fluttering away, crowing delight. His body reacted just as much to the easy humor between them as it did to the slick evidence of how much she wanted him. "For now, I'll make do like this," he said and went back for more.

He learned her with every stroke and caress, letting her moans and groans guide him. He wielded his fingers as if they were his weapons, his only weapons, in bringing her down. He delved and caressed and thrust and searched. When she was panting and begging him to touch her clit, only then did he grant her wish.

With two fingers inside her and hooked to find her sweet spot, he let the pad of his thumb ravage her clit. His sensible, practical wife needed fast, rough up-and-down strokes—he knew that already, and he gave it to her now. One hand on his wrist—as if she was scared he'd stop—and one caressing his chest in wide, long strokes, she chased the rhythm of his fingers, hips moving back and forth, eyes closed.

He didn't let up until she came with a shiver, his name on her lips. Not until she fell onto his chest, her forehead damp, her eyes hazy with completion. Not until she begged him to let go because she was too sensitive.

When she closed her eyes, and said, "Wake me tomorrow, please," he laughed.

Not a second later, her eyes popped open. She studied him with an intensity he was beginning to notice and understand only now. "I love it when you laugh, Aristos," she said, her fingers lingering over his mouth. As if she meant to touch his smile. "You used to do it a lot more in those early days."

Warmth drizzled through him like a summer shower that drenched the parched earth, that made everything look bright and fresh. "I used to," he said, in a gruff voice that forbade further discussion of their shared past.

She pressed her cheek to his chest, her fingers constantly moving over his flesh, touching, lingering, seeking.

"What, Mira?" he asked, sensing her hesitation. Hating that she still didn't trust him completely. Not enough to bare her innermost desires.

Her fingers reached his hip and lingered. Like clockwork, her magical fingers worked on him. She automatically kneaded and massaged the forever-sore flesh with efficient strokes she'd learned from the physical therapist. "I don't want to tell you how to live your life. I don't want to be that wife who curbs her husband. But I have to say this." She scoffed and the exhale sent a warm breeze over his damp skin. "I don't even care that you'll remind me that isn't..."

"Spit it out, *agapi mou.*"

Large, soulful eyes regarded him with a clarity that seemed to burrow under his skin. "Are you going to continue your...pursuit of whatever the hell it is you chase with your extreme sports?"

"Is that wifely concern?"

She shrugged. "I hate seeing you hurt. I can't stand the

thought of this happening again. I'm not threatening you with anything, Aristos, but if anything happened to you the next time…"

"As you reminded me so wisely," he said, running his fingers through her hair, "the doctors told me my hip would have that lingering pain for the rest of my life. So you can be content that the most extreme sport I'm looking forward to is lifting both the twins at the same time."

Joy flashed through her eyes, there and gone too soon. "And if you'd fully recovered?" she threw back, her frown forbidding. "I never understood why you…" She sighed. "I'm glad, Aristos."

"How about you show me your gratitude by mounting me and riding me, *yineka mou*? As I remember, you are a talented horseback rider."

She giggled and it held the same beauty as a sunrise he'd once seen after scaling the side of a mountain. It stunned him and humbled him and yet, it felt just as much of a thrill. "You're a greedy man, Aristos Carides," she said, kissing him, awakening him all over again, scorching his senses.

"Avaricious when it comes to you, Dr. Carides," he said, watching her as she rose to her knees. Her movements were slow, ginger as she adjusted herself. Cheeks turning dark red, she seated herself over him. Even then, she took care not to jostle his hip. Kept inquiring if he was okay.

With her luscious thighs straddling his hips, her breasts bare, the end of her thick braid hanging between their bodies and tickling him, she looked like a queen.

His queen, he amended.

And then her fingers fisted his cock and she notched him at the opening of her body and Aristos let himself be taken to heaven all over again.

He drank in every nuance of her expression as pleasure painted itself over her face, immensely glad that they had this.

That they would always have this and their family. And that had to be enough.

Mira threw her head back and groaned as she slowly lowered herself onto his shaft. Every inch of her tightened with relief and pleasure and something more as she thrust down the last bit and he was fully seated inside her.

A filthy curse escaped Aristos's mouth, his features set into stark hunger she loved seeing in his face. His hands were gentle over her hips, adjusting her, and another arrow zoomed through her, pooling where he filled her.

"This is okay? You're good?"

She nodded, her throat tight with a bunch of crowding emotions.

"You're always the perfect fit, *yineka mou*."

"I missed this. I missed this with you," she said, every last inhibition, every last fear thrown away to the wind, blasted into pieces by the pleasure rocking through her.

"So that's why you want this to be permanent," Aristos said, a devilish delight to the set of his mouth.

Leaning forward onto her knees, Mira bent lower, until her bare breasts rubbed against the hair on his chest. Their raw groans melted into a symphony that only seemed to feed back into their pleasure. A sudden prickling in her scalp made her realize Aristos had wound her braid around his fingers and was tugging her closer. Mira stared at this beautiful man who had given her more than anyone ever had by admitting to his mistakes, to his fears, and his desires.

Bending down, she took his mouth in a rough kiss that said so much more than her words could. "I will admit that

I have never found such a connection with anyone else," she said.

He bit her lip, the beast, and then licked the nip with a soft lave of his tongue. "I do not like when you think of other men even usually," he said, in a growl that reverberated through her. "I hate it if you do it when you're in bed with me."

And then his hands, those clever wicked fingers, stroked her everywhere.

Palming the heavy weight of her breasts, pinching the needy knots of her nipples, stroking every inch of her skin until Mira was chasing another climax.

She pulled herself up and then thrust down again. Soon, she built a rhythm that had her undulating over his body, as natural as breathing. It wasn't as fast and devouring as the night months ago when they'd conceived.

Speed was not their ally today. And that scarcity only made it even richer, slower, more exploratory. They took their time, course correcting a couple of times to accommodate his hip and her growing belly, and by the time they found their new rhythm, their damp bodies reaching and separating with her movements and his thrusts, they crossed over into a new level of intimacy. Something steadier, and richer and deeper than mere lust and want.

When he pinched her sensitized clit and pitched her headlong into her climax, Mira whispered his name over and over. With one hard upward thrust of his hips, Aristos followed her into oblivion and Mira knew that her dreams and happiness and joy had always been tied to this one man.

Giving in to the tide of emotions that had always swamped her when it came to him felt like coming home.

CHAPTER ELEVEN

MIRA STARED AT her reflection, turned sideways and cradled her baby bump. Even to her critical eye, she was glowing from within. Of course, the fact that she'd spent most of the afternoon being pampered from head to toe or that for the first time in years, she was truly happy, probably made a big difference.

Not that pretty feathers didn't help.

The elegant emerald green dress crisscrossed over her chest in rectangular panels hugging her breasts with as much reverence as Aristos showed them almost every night. He seemed to think it was his job—the competitive devil—to learn every change in her and worship it until she was moaning and panting.

The dress fell in a flowing drape over her belly and fell to her ankles, the thigh-high slit making it easy for her to walk around.

It had been one of the fifteen outfits that her newly appointed, very own personal designer had brought in on a helicopter for Mira to pick from, for tonight.

Just as there had been a masseuse, a nurse, a doula and a nutritionist who regularly flew in over the past few weeks. They'd need a fleet of helicopters at the rate Aristos had people flying into the mansion, Mira had joked when Aristos had informed her of the schedule. To which, the arrogant billionaire had smirked and retorted that he had a fleet ready.

She hadn't dared look at the price tag or the designer label of any of the dresses and outfits in her entirely new wardrobe. Thanks to her sister Yana, she'd gotten a thrill out of ordering clothes and pregnancy essentials and everything for the nursery from women-owned businesses and artisans from all over the world.

Granted, Mira had grown up in affluence all her life but her grandparents had never been given to excess and had always encouraged their three granddaughters to save for a rainy day and give back whatever they could to the community. She'd never forgotten how many of her fellow medical students had overwhelming debts, or that her alcoholic father had blown through his trust fund and every bit of allowance he got from his daughters—after his grandfather had washed his hands of him—in a matter of days.

Mira herself had always bought classic, long-lasting pieces for her wardrobe but she'd never been one for blowing her savings on clothes and jewelry like Yana did.

Aristos, on the other hand, seemed to believe that no designer label or jewelry was good enough for her.

Beneath the beauty and poise the professional makeup and the designer dress gave her this evening, Mira could see the radiance in her eyes. The last few weeks had done her a wealth of good, physically and emotionally. Whoever had said that happiness made time pass far too fast had been absolutely right. There were barely two months left before the babies were due.

The thought sent a flurry of butterflies through her chest.

Days, almost five weeks, had flown by since she and Aristos had had the showdown, as she liked to refer it in her head. Or rather the moment where she'd been at her most vulnerable.

But her raw honesty had paid off a thousand, no, a million times more than she had ever imagined. Her every need was catered to, her every wish—even the unspoken ones—fulfilled.

Sometimes, in one of those magical moments where they connected, she felt as if Aristos had been waiting for her to ask him to make a commitment to her. Waiting, all these years, for her to come back to him.

Mira didn't know what to do in those moments—to hold on to them with everything in her and immerse herself in the magic or to let them go as foolish thinking and simply be glad for what she did have.

Her happiness mattered to him and that should be enough. Especially when he showed it in myriad ways.

He'd even arranged the greatest surprise of all for her by flying in her sisters for an entire weekend. It had been the most amazing two days and exactly what she'd needed from the moment she'd locked up their grandparents' house in California. They'd binge-watched old classics, given the chef that Aristos had appointed just for her a list of dishes to pig out on and generally reminisced about their grandparents. The icing on the cake had been to see Nush so deliriously happy in her marriage to Caio that she practically glowed with it. Yana and she had left with promises to come back for a longer stay as soon as the babies arrived.

Mira had sobbed for an hour after they left, her hormones going haywire with fear, their departure triggering the loneliness and sorrow she never wanted to feel again.

So much so that Leo, Stella and a harried-looking Aristos had spent the entire evening by her side, sitting through old Hindi movies they didn't even understand—movies that had reminded her of her grandparents and given her a sense of comfort, sending terrified and yet somehow hopeful looks in her direction.

It had made her burst into laughter, her emotions coming the full circle.

And Mira had known then, had understood that despite the fact that she and Aristos had not married for love, her babies would be okay. That she would be okay.

And it was all down to him.

She'd known Aristos at different times in her life, at different milestones in his own. She'd known the feral teenager who did not trust his new family, she had known the daredevil who'd tried his best to make her laugh, she'd known him when he decided that he would study law against Leo's dictates. She'd known him the night of their engagement when he'd looked at her as if she was the answer to his every prayer. She'd known the smooth businessman who had made her the deal she could not refuse.

But the version of Aristos she had gotten last month… It was impossible to not drown in him. To not weave silly, foolish dreams around his every word, every act, every touch.

Not that Mira ever forgot that it was all for the babies. Aristos might have been afraid that he wouldn't know how to be a father, but the few he considered important, the few he considered family had all of his loyalty.

Every bit of concern he showed when she complained about her lower back aching, every frown he got when he couldn't magically make pregnancy easier for her, every smile he bestowed on her when he felt one of the babies kick—they were all for the pregnancy. For the babies.

He was more than she'd ever expected, especially for a man who had always struck her as impossible to pin down. A man who sought one extreme challenge after the other to spice up his life. He was, and had always been, larger than life. And yet, he had taken to the part of being a husband and an expectant father so well. As if it was all he'd needed to ground him.

And he made it impossible not to wish that it was for her too. That she wasn't just the Carides wife or the mother of his unborn children.

That he would see her as just Mira and still want her.

That he would see her and maybe…even love her. Just a little.

Because she was falling in love with him, all over again.

Mira was jostled out of her wishful reverie when a palm landed on her lower back, exactly where it had begun to ache almost every day. It seemed to have become instinctual to Aristos to knead that muscle as soon as he touched her, to try to give her relief immediately.

"You look beautiful." He whispered the words at the juncture where her neck met her shoulders. Where she was the most sensitive. Arousal flooded her body and Mira gasped in a much-needed breath.

As always, he stood behind her, one arm gently draped around her waist. Long fingers spread out over her belly. His body was a solid, hard presence at her back. Mira didn't even know when it had become a thing between them. He would come stand behind her and she would immediately lean herself against him, let go of some of her weight.

It was trust. It was comfort. But it was also much more—one of those thousand little rituals couples engaged in. That Aristos and she were building their own repertoire of those little things made joy beat at her. That they were just theirs.

Arms wrapped around her gently, he did a little thing with his hips that made Mira's eyes roll back in her head when he was inside her. The thick length of him against her buttocks made her wish he was inside her now, driving them to the edge. "*Christos*, how do you turn me on so easily, *yineka mou*?"

"That's a gift you return in a million ways, Aristos," she murmured lazily, arching her neck a little more so that he could get to all her sensitive spots. He licked up a trail obligingly, leaving whispered pockets of heated endearments. Filthy jokes that made her laugh and crude promises that made her shiver.

She loved how vocal he got during sex, how he twisted her inside out with anticipation with just one look, how he could be across the room from her and still communicate how much he wanted her.

Passion like theirs, the explosive physical connection they shared, she knew, was rare. Because she'd tried to find it with someone else, tried to replicate it with men that dating apps matched her with. Sensible, practical men who were her perfect matches on paper, men who didn't make her lose all common sense. To no success.

It was something to do with their chemistry, maybe even the genuine friendship they'd forged in those earlier years before it had fractured. They had this...a true communion of their bodies. It had to mean something. *It had to.*

It helped Mira forget the hollowness in her heart when she remembered it wasn't love that he felt for her.

She grabbed his fingers and pulled them up until they rested beneath her breasts. A gruff grunt expunged into her skin was her reward, as was the way he cupped her breasts, and let those clever fingers weave mindless circles over her aching, taut nipples.

Mira pressed back against him wantonly, groaning at the feel of his erection nudging her back.

"Don't tempt me, *agapi mou*," he said, nipping at her skin, easily driving her to the edge.

This too had become a game between them—he called her his love, she argued vigorously, he nipped some part of her flesh, causing little pain and lot of pleasure as if he meant to bind him to her, and she let it stand.

She knew not to take it to heart, that it was his way of taunting her to provoke a reaction and still, every time he said it, her heart missed a beat. Clenched tight with hope fisted within.

"Why not?" she said, meeting his gaze in the mirror and pouting. "Your recovery has turned a new leaf and I'd like to reward you for all your hard work," she said, stressing on the last two words.

He laughed against her skin, and it vibrated along her nerve endings, burrowing deep within her. "A reward? Am I allowed to pick?"

She giggled and he nipped her skin again. "As if it's a big guess." She wriggled her butt against the hard length.

He grunted, rocked his hips up into her and gruffly muttered, "Asking my very pregnant-with-twins wife to go down on her knees would make me a beast of a husband, *ne*? Not that you let that small temporary obstacle stop you from giving your everything. I knew all that steely strength of will would pay off in some way."

Mira laughed, remembering the very illuminating and highly entertaining night she'd spent learning what and how to drive Aristos to the edge of his limit. "I'm sorry I didn't see it through…all the way," she said, laughing and groaning at the same time. "For leaving you with no recourse at the last second."

His laughter joined hers and that was her true prize. "I

did like painting your chest, Mira. Dirtying you up just a little bit."

"Next time, I'll be prepared."

"Will you pen it into your planner, *agapi*?" he teased. Her eyes rolled back now as he snuck his fingers under the paneled bodice and pinched one taut bud just the way she liked. "I promised myself I'd be the very best husband to you, *yineka mou*."

But even under the avalanche of pleasure he rained down upon her, Mira felt the uncertainty pinch her. "Competitive in this too, Aristos?"

"As long as I'm the only winner that rides this particular—"

She gasped in outrage—at least tried to. But it was impossible to hold a coherent thought together.

Breath panting, bodies moving in a feverish symphony, they humped like teenagers who couldn't get enough of each other. Like they had the night of their engagement.

Until Aristos had backed off suddenly and said he wanted to do it differently. That he wanted it to be special.

Even the memory of a promise that had fallen apart spectacularly wasn't enough to cool the heat racing through her veins. Solid and warm and so hard against her flesh, he was here now. And he'd chosen this future with her.

Tremors shot down to her lower belly, pooling into dampness between her thighs. He snuck his hand under the slit and cupped her core, all the while watching her with a languid heat. The other hand pushed the panel of her bodice aside until her breast was bared. Long fingers flicked at her nipple as his other hand busied itself tugging her flimsy panties away.

And then he was thrusting two fingers inside her, pressing his thumb pad to her clit in perfect harmony. Her climax hovered close but Mira wanted more tonight. She needed everything.

"No. Not fingers, Aristos. Not tonight." She looked up into the mirror, grabbed his nape and kissed him. "Please, I need more…"

"*Thee mou*, you set me on fire, Mira."

"That's the idea," she said, digging her teeth into his lower lip.

"Our guests will be here any minute, *yineka mou*."

"Then you better hurry. Oh, and please don't muss my dress."

With a rough growl and a curse that made her giggle, he picked her up and shuffled her an inch to the left. A firm palm on her back pressed her until her hands were resting on the dark wood chest that Mira was suddenly grateful for. Legs kicked apart, her breasts achingly heavy, she waited with panting breath. Closed her eyes as she felt the silk slide up her bare skin, heard the rasp of his zipper and then he was probing inside her already wet heat with a gentleness that brought tears to her eyes.

She bit the rough pad of his palm that was caressing her nape, needing his usual wickedness. Tenderness would do her in right now. Because it was for so many reasons except the one she wanted it to be. "I'm not glass, Aristos. I won't break if you speed it up."

"And yet you feel incredibly fragile in my hands, *thee mou*."

Mira pushed her hips back into his next thrust and heard his rasping groan. He went deep that time, hitting the exact right spot where she needed him.

And slowly, they found the rhythm that worked best at that angle, Aristos upping his pace just a little bit more and

Mira letting him know that she was more than fine with her vocal grunts.

The soft thud of his pelvis against hers, the rasp of his hair-roughened legs against hers, the incredibly gentle hold he kept over her hip through every stroke and thrust…and the counterpoint to his tenderness, the very filthy words he gave Mira, telling her how hot and hard she made him, how he adored every inch of her silken smoothness, as if to make up for his slow torment, she was thrown headlong into her climax.

Tears filling her eyes, Mira gasped at the pleasure fragmenting through her in a million fragments, biting off the words that wanted to pour out, hating that a small, tiny part of her was still afraid of saying them. Still afraid that he'd never say it back.

Her dress was not only wrinkled from where he'd bunched it in his hands, but Aristos noticed, way too late for his own comfort, that his wife was crying.

Big fat tears pooled in her eyes and flew down her cheeks and down her forearms that he'd clutched to arrest his own momentum as he'd reached climax. His thighs were still trembling from the aftershocks of how explosive it had been. How disjointed and out of this world his own body felt.

With a rough curse at his own lack of control, he cleaned her up, and then straightened both their clothes. Through it all, she stared at him, with a glazed look in her eyes, tears still clinging to her lashes, being far too biddable for a woman who refused to be caged.

"Is it the babies? Was I rough?" His voice rose with every second she didn't respond. "Mira…"

"I'm fine. Just crying at my climax, like I do at everything these days. NBD."

Holding her close, Aristos peered at her, as if he could look down into her soul.

She wasn't telling him the complete truth.

She never told him the complete truth, always holding a little bit of herself back.

A part of him hated it. Hated that she gave of herself so completely to this marriage and the future but not to him. Hated that she was evasive even to this day when he brought up their engagement and why she'd broken it.

But a big part of him focused on the raw need she let him see in her eyes, the want she let him hear in her words, the laughter she evoked in him when she suddenly turned naughty to pay him back.

That she was fire and heat and sensuality itself underneath practical self-sufficiency—he'd always known that. But that she could be playful and wicked and enjoy every little thing he threw at her in their sex life…that she could make him laugh when he was deep inside her…it was something he hoped he'd never get used to.

He hoped she'd never stop surprising him with how much she invested into their relationship, into their future. Into their present.

In the last few months, his life had truly changed. A change he'd planned for—in colorful, scheming detail, as a man who always planned things before he walked into the blizzard. He'd known that bringing Mira back into his life would be something similar. And yet, it was nothing like he had thought it would be. He had only ever pursued excellence—a necessary evil for his own survival. He never let himself be still or stop on the way up the climb.

And he'd never once considered his own happiness.

He had known it only once, and even then it had been fleeting, gone before he had sense enough to recognize it.

And for all the changes Mira had brought into his life, it was the bursts of sheer happiness that threw him now. Because he had been happy in the last few weeks, he had been content. And yet the fear remained, like a niggle at the back of his head, a constant voice that kept saying he shouldn't get attached to those moments, because it wouldn't last. And he was beginning to hate that voice.

He was beginning to hate how it pulled him away from this current moment, from enjoying the woman who stared at him as if he was everything to her. He had waited eons for Mira to look at him like that. To see him and recognize someone equal, but also someone worth spending her life with.

"If I didn't feel awful about all the effort Stella and Leo have gone to, for my benefit, I'd manipulate your overprotective instincts to get out of this party."

And just like that, the voice of disappointment curdled his joy. He clasped her cheek and turned her until she could meet his gaze. "You refused to have a big wedding. You refused to let me show you off to the world. You refused to let me squash all those nasty rumors and gossip. And then you left." Like embers barely put to bed, his discontent flared every time he thought of the damned contract and all the rumors his vile cousin had spread about them. "I'm done hiding you and this. I want the world to see that you're mine. If, however, it makes you ashamed to be tied to me or the Carides name, then that's your problem."

"That's unfair. It's only the wild exploits, the utter gossip they write about you, that bothers me. That they painted me like some pathetic woman you rescued bothered me. That your so-called loyal PA leaked our contract to the entire damn world bothered me. You…and us and this… I like this life we're building, Aristos. What do I do to make you believe that?"

"Look happy about it tonight, *thee mou*. I want the world to see you next to me. I want the world and the damn board and my entire extended family to see that you're mine and you're happy and that—"

"You never care about others' opinions, like ever." She stared at him, her eyes wide. "I didn't… I didn't realize it was so important to you."

He tried to swallow his acidic response but it slipped out anyway. "I don't think you've given thought to what drives me, Mira." He thrust a hand through his hair, suddenly feeling too tight in his own skin. "If you had, you'd not run away from every mention of our past, as if it haunts you."

Every inch of satiety and satisfaction left her face, leaving confusion and pain behind. "That's not…" Ever the brutally honest woman, she swallowed her lie. "I just… I like our present so much better than the past. I like that we discuss things when we fight. I like that we're both compromising and communicating what we need."

She came to him then and kissed his mouth with a breath-taking reverence that threatened to bring him to his knees. "I love our life, Aristos. I love what we're building together." She sighed against his lips and looked into his eyes. "But you're right that I haven't been the dutiful wife. Not learn-ing what is important to you, not realizing how much pres-sure you're under after your injury, not realizing your head is scattered in so many spaces. That's on me. I'm sorry, Aristos. Truly."

He waved her apology off—it wasn't the thing he wanted anyway. *Christos*, he had hoped he'd learned some sem-blance of control around her. But he found himself floun-dering at the most trivial of things.

He wanted to push her still, demand she tell him why she'd broken their engagement all those years ago. Demand that she give him closure. Maybe she hadn't loved him. Maybe she'd been scared of being tied down. Maybe, maybe, maybe… He could think of a thousand *maybes*. And yet the little boy in his head whispered it had been something to do with him.

That it was him she had run away from.

Why else would she hide from it?

It seemed however hard Mira tried the past wouldn't leave them alone.

"I just… I feel like we're in a bubble, safe from the world and everything else." She tried to explain to him because he deserved to know the reason behind her reluctance. "I don't want it to burst. I don't want—"

He frowned. "Nothing that you and I don't want will happen, *pethi mou*. This life is ours."

"But we don't live in a complete vacuum. Others influence our thoughts and actions, however much we'd like to believe our will is our own."

Turning her around so that she could face him, he searched her gaze. "You're not just being your usual self-sufficient, antisocial self, are you?"

"You make me sound like a crotchety old woman who hates everyone."

"That makes me feel special, knowing that you don't hate me." He grinned and pressed a quick, hard kiss to her lips that left her panting. Thank God his good humor had returned. "I do know you have no interest in playing the billionaire's socialite wife or even in simply sitting back and enjoying your privileged life when you can give something valuable back to society."

Her large eyes widening, Mira opened her mouth in a soft gasp. "Do you remember every word I ever said to you?"

"The important ones at least. The ones that made me think, made me see the world a little differently. The ones that made me a better man."

"I don't know…"

"Did you delete the memories of every moment we spent together all those summers? Was it so ghastly?"

"No, of course not," she said, pressing a finger to his lips, forestalling his questions as she always did.

She searched for some other topic to divert his attention and shamelessly used the one that came to her. "The other night, how did you know I should drink juice to make the babies active again?" Even now, Mira felt the thread of re-membered fear shake her. Two days ago when she hadn't felt the babies kick for a whole two hours. She had no one to ask about it. She'd panicked and left a message for her gynecologist but she had been unable to sleep.

Aristos had stumbled out of bed and had come back ten minutes later with a glass of orange juice. Mira drank it un-thinkingly and then not half an hour later, the babies had started kicking. She'd fallen asleep smiling, cuddling into Aristos without question.

"I called Tia Sophia."

"Stella's mother?"

"Ne."

"In the middle of the night? She must have been shocked."

"Not really. I had already spoken to her a couple of times. Met her for coffee outside of Leo's knowledge."

Mira met his gaze in the mirror, her own shock evident in her wide eyes. Tia Sophia was Stella's mother, the only one among his five aunts that had ever shown genuine interest in Aristos. At least, that's the impression Mira had always gotten. And yet, Aristos had never let the older woman close. Had chosen to keep all of his extended family at a distance. It was credit to Stella and her stubborn tenacity that she had made any headway with him at all.

"Why?"

His broad shoulders shrugged, even as he ran his fingers over her arms. Touching her, anchoring her. And if she were being fanciful, even loving her. But she wasn't going to be fanciful and ruin the happiness she had found in this new, fragile hope between them.

"I heard you mention it to Yana, how much you missed your grandmother, how you wished she were alive today. How mothers and grandmothers and aunts pass down generations of wisdom and advice about pregnancy... So I called Tia Sophia. She said she is more than happy to share whatever wisdom she has with you."

Mira stared at him. "You did it for me," she said, butterflies running around in her belly.

"I was thinking about what you said, about raising our children surrounded by family, love and not just us. I want them to have that but I also want you to have it. Everything you've ever wanted."

"I don't know what to say. But tell me, please. How did it go?"

"It wasn't as hard as I imagined it would be."

"No?"

"Looking back, I see now that Tia Sophia has always tried to build a relationship with me. I learned only last year that she'd tried her best to find Mama even though she'd been so stubborn after her fight with Leo. Even after he found me, Tia Sophia fought him on how he was only treating me as the heir he'd always wanted but not his grandson. But back then, I lumped all my aunts together, refused any overtures she made toward me."

He rubbed his fingers over his face, a tell she had come to recognize when he was disquieted.

"What's changed now, Aristos?"

"Does it matter what? Isn't it good?"

"Of course it's good. I just... I want you to do these things for yourself. Not for the babies or me."

He frowned before he said, "My inability to trust her, to let her into my life, should not affect my kids. It should not rob you of the things you want. Tia and Stella have agreed to stay with us for a few weeks after the babies are born. Maybe after your sisters leave. That way, the babies and you will have a rotation of people who care about you, around you."

I only need you, Mira wanted to say, her thoughts in a whirlpool.

How could she ask for more when this gorgeous man had somehow turned making her happy into a competitive game with himself? Why else would he go to such thoughtful lengths after years of shunning his family?

"If you don't like having her here," he said, watching her carefully for her reaction, "we can ask them to leave."

Mira shook her head, giving herself a moment to find her voice. "No, not at all. Stella often talks about how much her mother wants a better relationship with you. And the few times I met Sophia, she struck me as a genuinely kind woman."

"Good," he said, tapping her cheek. "I have to warn you, though. It will be third world war between Tia Sophia and Leo but it could also be entertaining."

Mira threw her arms around his neck.

Gratitude, relief and something else she didn't want to

closely examine engulfed her. She kissed his neck, continued to pepper kisses up his jaw, over the very faint scar on his cheekbone and then his forehead.

Tears filled her eyes as they always did these days—far too easily. She sniffed inelegantly, and then buried her face in his neck. "Thank you, Aristos."

As he held her tightly, his heart thudding against her cheek, Mira knew it was time to face her guilt and her biggest fear. Before the babies came. Before everything got ruined again.

CHAPTER TWELVE

MIRA HAD NOT imagined in her wildest dreams how much she'd like being referred to as Kyria Carides. Or the genuine camaraderie shared among Aristos's executive staff. Like her, almost all of them seemed to consider him larger than life.

Meeting the Carides family went better than she'd expected. Especially with Stella and Tia Sophia, and even Leo sometimes, running interference anytime Aristos had to leave her side.

With maturity of age and having decided on a fresh, bold approach to life, it meant she recognized people among the extended family and friends who wished Aristos and her the best.

Especially among the younger generation of Aristos's cousins, most of whom were happily married and didn't really care one way or the other that Aristos was the heir Leo had picked by spurning the rest of them. Especially when having Aristos head Carides Inc. meant their stock prices soared and their children's trust funds got fatter and cushier.

The outpouring of love and affection and best wishes from friends and staff and even his cousins who'd once considered him competition only cemented that conviction.

Aristos was a man who inspired loyalty—with his brilliant skills in the corporate law world, his charity works and with his enduring prowess in pitting himself against extremes.

Feeling eyes on her, Mira turned to find Kairos walking through the party with that exaggerated swagger that only made him look like a fool. Every inch of her wanted to get away from him, even hide from him, pretend like he and his foul lies hadn't messed her up back then.

But for Aristos, she'd face him.

Mira followed Leo the moment he stepped away from family members and friends, and stormed into his study after him. She'd known talking to Kairos, clarifying the past, would be a fool's errand. Instead, the bitterness and poison he harbored toward Aristos, toward her and their budding family had truly scared her.

"Mira, what is it? Why do you look so pale?" Leo asked, walking around the desk to her.

"You have to get rid of Kairos. Throw him out of Carides Inc. Get him away from Aristos. Immediately."

"Sit down, Mira. That much agitation is not good for you."

"You aren't listening, Leo. I know you're fond of Kairos but you cannot have him near Aristos. You've seen how he talks to Aristos and that's only the surface. He… He's so full of resentment and hatred and poison for Aristos that I'm scared he might do him harm."

Shock dawned in the old gray eyes so much like his grandson's. Before he could respond, someone else entered the room.

Mira didn't have to turn to know it was her husband. On a hunt for her.

"What's wrong? Leo?" Aristos's voice was full of steel, threatening to cut at the smallest provocation.

Leo simply pointed a gnarly hand in Mira's direction and said, "She wants me to remove Kairos from the company. From anywhere near you. He has scared her."

Within the next breath, Aristos was kneeling in front of her, rage radiating from him in dark waves. One large hand descended on her thigh, and then moved up from her belly to her arm until he was caressing her cheek. "You're trembling."

He cursed, barked what sounded like instructions to Leo too fast for Mira to catch. His grandfather left the room and closed the door behind him.

"Did he hurt you? What did he do? Mira, are you in pain?"

Mira grabbed his hand in both of hers and shook her head. "I'm not hurt, Aristos. Come on, look at me. I'm fine. I'm just…angry and shaken."

Some of his rage seemed to abate but his glare remained. "Maybe he did not hurt you, but he has you scared. And that's not acceptable."

"I am worried for you," she said, "worried about what kind of harm he might do you. The way he talks of you… Aristos."

"You should have more faith in me, Mira. He cannot touch a hair on my head. But clearly, he can get to you, so today we will get to the bottom of that. Did he follow you? Threaten you in some way?"

There was a reason she hadn't gone to Aristos directly and instead approached Leo. And her brilliant husband hadn't missed that. She'd meant to talk to Aristos tonight about everything but after her discussion with Kairos, her fear had gotten the better of her. Mira shook her head, gathering her strength. "No, I went to him."

God, why had she been such a naive fool back then? Why

such little trust in herself? Why hadn't she asked Aristos for clarification once in fifteen years? Useless questions battered at her, twisting her nerves even tighter.

Aristos bit his lip and studied her. "Why, Mira? You've seen how delusional and volatile he can get. Why would you go near him?"

Still, she fought for time. She bent her forehead to his and let out a shuddering exhale. "I just… Please, Aristos, first promise me you'll talk to Leo about this. That you'll take some kind of action. You're not invincible, you know."

"Close to, anyway," he quipped, though without real humor.

"No," she said, leaning down toward him and biting on his lower lip, hard. Just the way he liked it. And then she swirled her tongue against the tip of his, playing, running away, teasing. Just the way that got him hard, fast.

Soon, his fingers were wrapped around the nape of her neck and he was stealing away her breath, her heart, her very soul in a tender kiss that only amplified her fear that she'd lose him. A sob burst through her and Aristos swallowed that too, his palm a warm, steadying weight on her back.

In the end, he pulled away. Gray pupils danced with lust, his breath came fast and he rubbed his face. "You're not distracting me from this, Mira. You want Kairos thrown out of Carides Inc. But I know you. I know that you would not demand such a punishment unless he deserved it. I would like to know what his crime is."

"He hates you so much, Aristos. Isn't that enough? I wouldn't sleep a wink knowing he's near you."

"Feelings are not enough to ruin a man's livelihood, Mira. Because that's what it will be. Kairos has a position in the company because he's family. He'll not find another job anywhere else. Not with his addictions."

Mira closed her eyes and willed herself to let it go. The past was over. She knew the truth. She had known it even before Kairos had spilled it. She could just say she'd approached him with some misguided intention of calming him down. Or some other innocent lie. But God, she couldn't hide anymore.

Feeling Aristos's palm cradle her cheek, she nuzzled into it. Tears pooled and one rogue drop trailed a path down her cheek.

Opening her eyes, she gave voice to the pain that had haunted her for fifteen years. Only to discover that it was no one else's fault but her own, that it had been her own cowardice. "That night—the night after our engagement party—I know where you went."

His brow cleared in one flicker of a breath. In the next, his frown returned tenfold. "The night after our engagement? The night I was supposed to meet you in the greenhouse? Our special night?"

Mira nodded and wiped away the lone tear.

She had to be strong now. Strong enough to withstand his justifiable anger, his raw hurt and whatever he threw at her. Strong enough to show him that she wasn't running this time. Not ever again.

"You never gave me a chance to apologize for it. I'm sorry I never showed up. I... I went to a party I shouldn't have gone to. I got...drunk and other things happened. By the time I came to the next afternoon, Leo told me you'd broken our engagement. You'd left that very morning without even saying goodbye."

"I was there at the pool house where Kairos threw you the party."

"No... You couldn't have been. How?"

"Kairos drove me there. After I waited for an hour, he

came by the greenhouse. He told me he had something to show me, something related to you. You'd been acting so strange that whole summer, I'd have followed the devil if he said he'd bring me to you."

Aristos's nostrils flared. "And?"

Mira grabbed his hands with hers. "I know that what I thought I saw was not true. What I thought you said is not the truth. I knew it even before tonight. Please, Aristos. You have to believe me. I didn't need proof. I knew the truth."

"What did you see, Mira?"

"You were sitting between two girls, shirtless, your... trousers undone. One of them was kissing your neck and the other had her hand on your...stomach. Your head was thrown back and..."

"Kairos spiked my drink. I was more than half out of it."

"It wasn't just that. He and that friend of his, they kept pushing you and finally you said, *'Yes. Fine. Leo bought her for me—a prize of good breeding. Yes, she's boring and intellectual and not at all the sort of fun, party girl a Carides heir requires, but she brings his seal of approval. Marrying her means getting closer to the real power.'* When they joked about you giving up your freedom just for power, you said, *'She's the type you marry and have sons with.'* And that it didn't mean you'd stop partying with other women."

Every exact word fell from her lips from memory, the words that had tormented her so much. "I ran from the room then and the most awful part was that he drove me back to the villa. He acted like he was my friend."

Aristos rubbed his hand over his face, slow anger building in his eyes. It was a stillness that never took hold of him unless he was in the grip of a raging emotion. Dark stormy eyes met hers, that sinful mouth twisted into a bitter edge. "I wanted them to leave you alone. I wanted Kairos to leave you alone. All evening, all week, he and his gang of thugs had been asking questions about you. Wanting to meet you. Mocking you. Asking if I'd already... I just wanted them to shut up. I wanted them to leave us alone. I wanted them to think I didn't give a damn about you. Or else they'd have tormented you like they did me for years. Especially since I was traveling so much and I couldn't be there every minute with you. However much I wanted to."

"I don't need an explanation. I know now..."

"Do you, *agapi*? Are there any more sins that I should know about? You never trusted me, did you? You never thought I could be more than my alley cat morals."

"That's not true, Aristos. It was me, all me. I was so... insecure. You'd been gone all summer... You hadn't even proposed to me. You'd been avoiding me for days before the engagement..."

"Because I was afraid that I'd push you to sleep with me when you might not be ready. Because I was afraid that I'd persuade you to elope with me and not wait the whole year like our grandfathers decided before we married. Because I was afraid that you'd sense my desperation to be near you, to keep you by my side, to own your heart like you owned mine."

His angry declaration gouged a hole through Mira. Regrets upon regrets piled on her, making it hard to breathe. But she tried. "I... I was so in love with you, Aristos. But I didn't trust it. I didn't trust that I deserved it. I didn't trust that such happiness, such love, such devotion...could be mine. It was like..." She closed her eyes, and drew a deep breath in. "I was waiting for the slightest sign for it to fall apart. And when Kairos showed you to me that night... All my fears came true."

His hands on her knees, Aristos dipped his head until

his forehead lay in her lap. And when he spoke, the words seemed to come from some far-off place. And Mira knew that even as he touched her with that reverence, even as he gave her the words she'd wanted to hear for years, she was losing him.

"He knew how much I loved you. He knew what it would do to me to lose you—the one person who didn't care where I came from and where I was going. The one person who accepted me for whoever I was right then."

"I did, Aristos. I loved you then and I love you now. I do. You're my heart. You're my everything. You're my present and future and I…"

Shooting to his feet in an economic movement, he pulled himself away from her.

"A future based on a lie? Without trust?"

"No, a future based on us."

"You married me thinking I cheated on you. Thinking that I had no morals. *Christos*, Mira, did you want a child that desperately? Were you going to forgive me with your generous heart?"

She stood up and wiped her hands over her face. "No, listen—"

"What if Kairos hadn't made such an ass of himself that afternoon?" Aristos said, already making himself remote and inaccessible. "Would you have ever doubted what you saw? Would you have ever told me, asked me for clarification? Or would you have held that against me forever?"

Aristos ran another hand through his hair, making it stand up every which way, his lean frame trembling with anger and something else. And even in the grip of it, he gave her his hand when she tried to get up.

He released her fast enough though, as if even that minimal contact was unbearable for him. As if she'd broken his heart all over again.

And she had, she knew that now. She had broken his heart back then and she was doing it again. This wasn't a short misunderstanding from fifteen years ago that they could get over with a proper talk. Because he'd loved her with that depth and intensity that only he was capable of and she'd thrown it back in his face. Once fifteen years ago, and now again.

"Aristos, please listen to me—"

"I fell apart after you left. You wouldn't take my calls... You wouldn't reply to my emails. I almost boarded a flight without telling Leo, I was that desperate to see you. And then he told me what your grandfather said. That you realized pursuing your medical career was more important. That the engagement had been a mistake you felt pressured into. That you and I had nothing in common and you never wanted to see me again."

"I was talking out of my own pain. I thought you..."

"Then why the hell didn't you stand and fight?" His mouth became a study in bitterness, his eyes so dark that gray was nearly swallowed up by the black. "Everything you gave me, the trust and affection and love, you took it away in a minute. I felt like I had been orphaned all over again. I...thought I'd never be worthy of you. And to forget you, I threw myself into everything. Into law, into sports. I was determined to make you come crawling back to me."

Tears poured down Mira's cheeks, even as fear fisted her stomach tight. "I'm sorry. I can't say it enough. But I love you, Aristos. I have fallen in love with you all over again and I'm not worthy of you. But I'll prove to you that I—"

With one last look at her, Aristos walked out of the room.

And Mira wondered, as a sob rumbled out of her chest, if she'd lost his trust forever this time.

It was pitch-dark in the bedroom when Mira felt a hand on her temple and immediately jolted into alertness. She grabbed Aristos's wrist, her nightmare suddenly turning into reality when he said, "I will be back in three weeks."

He was pressing a kiss to her forehead. She tried to get up but her body was already off-balance and awkward. She ended up reaching for his hand, turned sideways and then pulled herself to sit up on the bed. Even then, he adjusted the pillows at her lower back and Mira fought fresh tears.

"Please, Aristos. Don't go. Not like this."

He let her pull his hand to her face, let her nuzzle his palm, let her kiss the rough abrasions at the center of his big hand. Let her cling to him. "This trip has been scheduled for a while, Mira. You know that. This way, I can clear the calendar for when the babies come."

"And what about me? I need you now."

"You have everything I can give you, Mira."

Her head jerked up, her every little fear turning into stark reality. His face was set in taut lines and there was a blank note, a resignation to his words, that terrified her.

"I have apologized a hundred times and I will, another thousand times. It wasn't you I didn't trust. It was myself. I'm allowed one mistake, Aristos."

He said nothing, held her for what felt like a long while, until she fell into an exhausted sleep. And when she awoke the next morning, Mira had known immediately that he had left.

And while she wasn't sure she could bear it if he tormented her for too long, she knew she'd wait him out. She'd wait out his anger, and his fury and his hurt and everything he was feeling.

This time, she wasn't running. Whatever mood he came back in, whenever he decided to be back, she'd be here, ready to tell him what he needed to hear, to understand that she loved him.

With all of her. And that he was worth waiting for. Worth loving even if it took her an entire lifetime to prove it.

CHAPTER THIRTEEN

THE CALL CAME when Aristos had just poured himself a glass of Scotch. He'd given up the pretense of working by noon. For the first time in his adult life, his head refused to cooperate. So he'd ordered his new PA to cancel everything on his plate, given half his staff a heart attack when he lost his temper at some innocent question and walked out of his office. Had spent the rest of the day running through his physical therapy routines, looking at his calendar over the next few months without really seeing it.

A harried Stella rushed on, speaking ten sentences where one might do, sending his heart into a tailspin, not unlike how his car had spun out of control. His glass fell from his shaking fingers as three words registered on his slow mind.

Mira was hurt.

His throat in his heart, Aristos yelled into the phone until Stella calmed down. Even then, his cousin couldn't speak in rational, clear sentences. Mira had fallen, somehow and hurt her head, and had lost consciousness.

He gathered that much and that was more than enough.

True fear gripped him then. He hadn't known anything like that, even as a kid fighting for survival. Only Stella's continued reassurances at silence on his end, that while she had lost consciousness for a while and had a hard bump on her head, Mira and the babies were fine roused him out of it.

Even then, she had to repeat it a few times for it to sink through.

"Don't go, Aristos. Don't leave me now. I need you."

Those words haunted him all through the short flight back to Athens and then the helicopter ride to Carides mansion. She had begged him not to go, she'd asked him to stay because she needed him but he hadn't listened. Because what?

His ego had been hurt? His fragile feelings had been dented by her lack of trust in him a decade and a half ago?

What was she supposed to think when she found him drunk out of his mind, surrounded by scantily clad girls, talking shit about her to his cousin? After he'd promised to spend the night with her—their first night together, a special night they had been planning on for months and then disappeared without word?

"I love you now. I didn't need proof, Aristos."

It was what he'd wanted to hear for more than fifteen years and she'd offered it to him that night. Eyes full of tears, trembling from head to toe, she'd offered the benediction he'd craved, from the moment he'd seen her shy smile, the moment he'd met her generous heart.

Why hadn't those words been enough?

Why had he thrown them in her face and walked away?

What the hell had been wrong with him?

Fear, the answer came up every time. And it galled him to admit that for he'd pretended and believed his entire life that he was fearless.

"You're not invincible," Mira had said in his office and she was right. He'd been afraid that he'd never be good enough for her. That she'd abandon him as his mother had done, as she'd done all those years ago.

He'd had what he'd wanted all his life and yet he'd been scared to believe he was worthy of it. And now she was hurt, alone and terrified for the babies, probably, and he hadn't been there.

By the time he jumped out of the helicopter, Aristos was sweating profusely, his legs barely holding him up.

He walked past his family, and hers, and made his way to their bedroom. She was sleeping. Reaching her side, he swallowed the tears that crowded against his throat.

Tenderness and fear and an avalanche of love welled up within him, consuming him, drowning him, choking him.

Her face looked pale and wan and small against the stark white pillow. He went into the bathroom, took a shower, dressed in pajamas and crept into bed by her side. It wasn't enough that the doctor had reassured him that Mira was fine and the babies were fine. That it had just been a simple bruise.

He needed to touch her, to hold her, to feel her warmth against him. He wanted to feel the babies kick against his palm. He wanted to see the delight and sheer joy in her eyes when they did.

So many people who loved her, so many whom Mira loved and yet she had found it in herself to love him too. And yet he ran away from her and her love. And more importantly he'd run away from himself.

Because he had messed up once but Mira had given them a new chance. How did he know that he wouldn't do it again? He hadn't committed the mistake that Mira thought he had. But he had deserted her when she'd begged him not to.

Aristos didn't know how long he was awake. Around dawn, he felt Mira move on the bed, go into complete stillness and then with a soft cry, she cuddled into him. Her hands moved over him with a frenzy he couldn't calm but thoroughly understood. In the end, he simply surrendered. Like he should've done a long time ago. He kissed her, and held her wordlessly.

He'd barely gotten his arm around her and his mouth pressed against her temple when he realized she was fast asleep already.

His throat contracting at her trust and love, something he'd callously walked away from not a week ago, he gathered her to him. Only when the warmth of her body thawed the frost around his heart, only when the lush heat of her breaths caressed his cheek, did the fear that had gripped him leave.

He fell asleep within minutes, for the first time in his life, feeling satisfied about his place in the world.

He belonged with the woman he loved, he'd always, loved.

When Aristos woke up, it was to find midmorning sunlight showing him an empty space next to him on the bed. Somehow, he managed to brush and shower in record time, without peeking at the gaggle of voices that he could hear floating up through the backyard.

Dressed in dark denim and a white linen shirt that Mira loved seeing on him, he walked past the large kitchen and dining area. His heart was beating a rapid boom by the time he arrived at the cozy setup at the large patio in their backyard.

Breakfast had been served buffet style, and there were any number of people surrounding the one woman he wanted to get to.

If it were just his family members—Stella, Leo and Tia

Sophia—he'd have thrown them all out with one gesture. But no. As if they meant to protect her from him, his wife's sisters enfolded her between them on top of a cozy sofa, with Nush's husband, Caio, standing sentinel behind them.

That they'd noticed him coming down the steps wasn't in doubt given the combative look Yana cast him and the deep frown Anushka subjected him to.

But he only registered it in passing, like you noticed little tidbits around the world even when your heart was crawling into your throat.

As if aware of her sisters' antagonistic glares, Mira looked up. Her smile froze, and a wariness entered her large eyes that would fell him to his knees if he let it.

He caught the thread of words Yana whispered to her and his heart iced over as they sunk in.

"Jesus, give him a break," Caio mumbled from behind them. "He looks bad enough."

It was support from a quarter Aristos hadn't expected to get. Though it felt good, Caio wasn't the one he needed to convince.

When Mira sighed, Yana and Nush walked past him, the younger one squeezing his hand in an encouraging gesture.

"She adores you. And once Nush gives her heart, she'll stick with you no matter what."

He nodded, glad that she was talking to him. It took him a while to break the awkwardness building up. "Caio is very lucky."

"And he knows it," she added softly. There was no rancor or complaint in her words.

"Yana has asked me if I want to have the babies in California. They both promised they'd be there the entire time, if I'd like."

Aristos covered the distance to her between one breath and the next, terror stealing words from him. Lowering to his knees, he bent his forehead against her thighs.

"I said no," she said, running her fingers through his hair. "That I was done running. That I didn't need to be chased by you anymore."

"So sure, *thee mou*?"

"But if you—"

"I love you, Mira. I have loved you from the moment I saw you when we were thirteen. You wore a denim skirt and loose T-shirt and you told me you had recently found a new sister and now, a new friend in me and did I want to join you for a picnic near the pool?" He fought the sob rising through his chest, attempting to steal his words. "I fell in love right then, *yineka mou*, and I knew my happiness lay with you. I swore to myself that I'd have you in my life forever. That I'd prove myself to you over and over again. No one had ever looked at me with such…open welcome and artless affection."

Mira laughed and then cried, and scooting forward with an awkward grunt, threw her arms around Aristos's neck. "I'm sorry it took me so long to see it. That I didn't trust you back then. I was an immature, foolish, terrified girl, Aristos. I…couldn't believe that you'd want me that much, that you could truly love me like you did." She wiped her hands over her cheeks. "It wasn't you so much as I was so scared of love, of—"

"Shh… Mira. No more tears. No more, *thee mou*. It is my turn to apologize, my turn to admit to my own fears. I spent most of my adult life needing to be worthy of you, Mira."

"But there's no deserving when it's love, Aristos. I loved you from the moment you offered me that pink frosted cake even though you were ravenous. You put me before you and it was…everything to me." She clasped his cheeks and kissed his temple. "Thank you for coming after me, for binding me in that contract, for not giving up on me. For choosing me."

"I'll always choose you, Mira. I'll always love you. You gave me happiness when I didn't know what it was."

Under his palm, one of the babies kicked and they stared at each other and then burst into laughter.

He took her mouth in a warm, hard kiss then and Mira knew she'd reached home. That there was never going to be a doubt again. That she and Aristos had found their way back to each other, despite everything. That they and their love could not be stronger.

That no matter what, they would always find their way back to each other.

Rubbing herself against his chest, Mira gave herself over to the magic of their kiss, knowing that this time, it would still be there when the kiss was over.

Eira and Eros Carides were born two months later, exactly on time, without causing their mother any further complications. Though their father, their exhausted but exhilarated mother whispered to them, had collapsed in exhaustion in the armchair next to her massive bed two nights after they were born after being awake straight for two nights, and turned into a complete basket case by the time they had arrived.

The mighty, nearly invincible and thoroughly reckless Aristos Carides had been reduced to a walking, talking, sleepless bundle of excitement and fear alternately, in the weeks leading up to the birth.

They had fought a lot in those last couple of months, given Aristos's overprotective instincts after Mira's fall.

Mira had borne them with as much forbearance as she could muster, at least for a little while. Not that she'd needed a reason to be irritable in those last few weeks. Her back had ached constantly, her pelvis had felt like there was ten times more gravity constantly pulling on it. And she'd pretty much waddled everywhere, giving up any pretense to a normal gait.

Aristos's incessant hovering hadn't helped. So much so that her sisters had commandeered Caio for one weekend to steal Aristos away to Athens to release her for some much-needed girl time.

Of course, the moment he had left, Mira had missed him like a hole in her heart, had been miserable about how tetchy she'd been with him not an hour ago.

Her sisters and Stella had been gob smacked when she spent two hours of their planned movie binge marathon time chatting with Aristos on a video call.

The one thing they had agreed on, though, was that they wanted the sex of the babies to be a surprise. They had also fought about names for the babies. So of course, that meant they both had to come up with two names each—for a girl and a boy. Her husband's competitive, almost ruthless instincts had taken over almost immediately. He had been adamant that he wanted to name both his children because he'd claimed he already loved them more than she did.

Mira had not given an inch, though she'd thought the entire thing so adorable that she kept kissing him every time the issue came up. In the end, they had compromised and were each allowed to name one child, whatever the sex.

Mira had known the minute she stared at the little girl who had jostled her brother for position and come out first.

Large brown eyes and a thick mane of jet-black curls had instantly reminded her of her grandmother. "Eira… She is Eira," she had said, tears running down her cheeks. His own gaze large and wide and full of undisguised terror and wonder, her husband had reached for their daughter, buried his nose in her chubby belly and simply whispered, "I love you, Eira. Papa loves you so much, *koritsi mou*." To which, their daughter had given him an adorable half smile as if she understood him perfectly.

And just like that, Aristos swore, he'd fallen in love all over again.

Their son, like their stubborn mother, had been a different issue. He had refused to leave his mother's protective womb, had cried endlessly even after he'd been coaxed out, and when his father named him Eros, he'd screamed his lungs out as if he found the whole thing extremely offensive.

Mira had had to bite the teasing laughter that wanted to pull out of her at the fright in Aristos's eyes. It had taken them both a day to realize how high-maintenance their son was going to be. Competitive to the bone, Aristos had spent the last few days, after they'd returned to their home, learning to quiet and comfort their son, determined to get it right. It had involved walking endlessly through the house, at all hours of the night with Eros strapped to his chest. Driving their son, strapped in his car seat, around the estate until he fell asleep.

And Aristos had won too, for Eros had napped this afternoon for a whole two hours, which meant Mira had been able to cuddle Eira as much as she wanted.

Mira cast one look at the double bassinets in a corner of their bedroom. When she'd put forth her proposal about not using a nanny during the nights and that she'd try co-sleeping with each of her babies on alternate days, she'd expected a fight on her hands. Instead, within minutes, Aristos had ordered another set of bassinets to be arranged in the adjoining bedroom, in case one of the babies woke up and disturbed the other.

So far, it hadn't been easy but with her sisters and Stella and Tia Sophia giving them breaks during the day, she and Aristos had managed okay.

When her silent phone flashed another text from her impatient husband, Mira ran her knuckle down both the babies' cheeks and went in search of him.

She found him sitting at the cozy dining table in the nook. Light from the tall candles on the table cast flickering shadows onto his face. His stark beauty stole her breath all over again. But it was the wicked light in those gray eyes and the wide smile digging grooves around his mouth that made her heart beat faster.

"What's this?" she said, reaching him, glad that she'd taken the time to shower and blow-dry her hair.

"We haven't spent an hour together in the last month. I adore our babies but I miss you more, *yineka mou.*"

And just like that he stole her heart all over again.

"I know you won't be comfortable leaving for someplace else, but Stella and Yana have promised to look after Eira and Eros for three hours." He raised a hand, grinning. "Under Tia Sophia's watchful eye."

When she smiled, God, he knew her so well and he loved her even better, he whispered in a gruff voice, "Come, take pity on your husband, *agapi mou.* He's been parched for you."

Shaking her head at his antics, Mira passed the chair he'd pulled out for her and settled herself on his lap instead.

"I missed you too. And I love you, Aristos, so much that I…" Her throat closed up.

Clasping her cheeks with gentle hands, he simply said, "I know, *agapi*," and then proceeded to kiss the hell out of her.

Mira sank into the kiss, remembering Thaata's note. She didn't know or care if she was the queen or not, but she had a kingdom all right.

Full of love and happiness.

* * * * *

ONE NIGHT IN
MY RIVAL'S BED

MELANIE MILBURNE

MILLS & BOON

To Cliona Kennedy,
who looks after our pets when we need her to.
You are such a wonderful caretaker of our fur family
and we appreciate you so much.
We can truly relax with you in charge!

CHAPTER ONE

I WAS MEETING my younger sister Niamh for a drink after work at one of London's swanky hotels. Now, you might think there is nothing unusual about two sisters catching up over a cocktail but it's nothing short of a miracle I still have a sister. It's also a miracle Niamh could not only book the venue but get there without her support worker. And it's an even bigger miracle I arrived at the hotel more or less on time.

I'm normally a super punctual person but my last client of the day wanted some changes to the plans I was drawing up for his luxury villa in Italy. Before you get too excited, the client is nudging eighty and he's building it for his grandchildren. Lucky grandchildren. The only thing I got from my paternal grandparents was a chip on my shoulder. Long story. I won't bore you with it.

I spotted Niamh sitting in the brass and glass mezzanine level area, surrounded by gorgeous fresh flower arrangements that made it look like summer had come inside. Which was kind of nice because even though it was June, summer certainly hadn't made much of an appearance outside. It had rained for twenty-two days in a row. But I live in hope.

I moved through the chairs and tables, and I noticed with a pulse-tripping jolt that Niamh was not alone. A stop-your-heart-handsome dark-haired man was beside her seated in a wheelchair. He looked vaguely familiar and I narrowed my gaze as I tried to place him. Neither he or Niamh were looking my way, they seemed completely absorbed in each other. Yikes! They were even holding hands.

Okay, so now you're probably wondering why I was so surprised to see my sister holding hands with a gorgeous-looking man. Why shouldn't my sister be happy in love or lust or whatever?

Because while my sister is twenty-seven years old, she is still in many ways a child and it is entirely my fault.

Niamh looked up and saw me standing there and waved me over with an excited gleam in her eyes. 'Ash, come and meet Ethan Barlowe. Ethan's older brother Grayson will be here soon.'

Grayson Barlowe? I had to force myself to walk without stumbling. I had to force myself to smile as if everything was okay. But everything was not okay. It was seriously not okay. Barlowe was not an uncommon name but…surely Ethan's brother couldn't be…? I swallowed a furry thickness in my throat and looked at Ethan's darkly handsome features again. That glossy black hair, those grey-blue eyes were so incredibly familiar, and yet Ethan had laughter lines I had never seen on Grayson Barlowe's face.

I offered my right hand to Ethan. 'Nice to meet you, Ethan.'

There was an awkward moment when he offered his left hand instead of his right but then I realised he couldn't use his right hand at all. It lay limply on his thigh. I noticed then that his wheelchair was a motorised one, no doubt because it would be impossible for him to wheel himself about without the use of both hands.

'Lovely to…m-m-meet you, Ash. Niamh's t-t-told me so much about…you.' Ethan's voice had a slight stutter and he paused and frowned fiercely in concentration before he said some words, as if his brain had trouble deciding which word to use. I'm an architect, not a neurologist, but I can recognise an acquired brain injury when I see it. Besides, for twenty years I've been managing my sister's.

There was the sound of someone approaching and I didn't need to turn around to see who it was. I could recognise that slightly uneven gait anywhere. A shiver ran down my spine like an ice-footed spider and my heart began to pound like I was having some sort of medical event. I caught a whiff of expensive aftershave, one I had smelled three months ago at the Architectural Awards event where I was pipped at the post by Grayson Barlowe, who took home the major award that I had coveted for months and stupidly thought would be mine. Not because of an overblown sense of my own creative ability but because so many of my colleagues had said my entry was sure to win. It didn't.

And it particularly rankled that Grayson Barlowe had won it instead.

We've been business rivals for years. The rivalry didn't start with us, it started with his grandfather and my father. They were at war the entire length of their careers and even though they are both now deceased, the battle hadn't gone to the grave with them. Out of respect for my father, I continued to resent Grayson Barlowe and all he represented. Not that he isn't a creative genius. I've lost count of the number of awards he's won for his stunning and innovative designs. I'm just insanely jealous of his success that seems to come so easily to him. Oh, and the fact that he's a playboy who only has to look at a woman to get her to fall at his feet in a swoon. Not me, though. I'm fully vaccinated and completely immune against his polished brand of male charm.

'Grayson,' Ethan said, smiling broadly at his older brother. 'Come and meet my...my fiancée.'

'*Fiancée?*' Grayson Barlowe and I spoke in shocked unison—although his voice was low and deep and kind of raspy and sexy. Mine was more like the sound of someone inadvertently stepping on a squeaky toy.

Niamh's smile was even wider than Ethan's. She held up her left hand and an expensive-looking engagement ring flashed with brilliance that rivalled the sparkles in her eyes. 'Ethan proposed to me earlier this week. That's why we wanted you both here to celebrate with us this evening.'

I was having trouble finding my voice. I was having

trouble believing my sister had met and fallen in love with someone without me knowing anything about it. I was having trouble standing next to Grayson Barlowe without dropping at his Italian leather clad feet in a swoon. He was wearing a charcoal-grey business suit that highlighted the width of his broad shoulders and the long lean length of his legs. His ink-black hair was swept back off his face similar to his brother's but, unlike Ethan, Grayson had flecks of grey at his temples, giving him a distinguished, older and wiser look that somehow made him even more attractive.

His ice-blue eyes met mine and a current of energy hit me like a lightning zap.

'Did you know anything about this?' There was an accusatory quality to his voice that reminded me of a high school teacher I had a showdown with when I was fifteen. I wasn't so sure I could win a face-off with Grayson as my opponent, but I was going to have a red-hot go at it. But don't get me started about my combative nature.

'No, nothing. Did you?' I shot back.

Grayson's lips thinned into a grim flat line. 'Of course not.' He turned back to face his younger brother, a frown carved deeply between his eyes. 'How long have you known each other?'

'Six weeks,' Ethan said with a defiant light in his eyes.

'Six weeks!' Grayson and I did the speaking in unison thing again. Well, he spoke, I screeched like a startled cat.

I looked at Niamh. 'How can you be sure he's the one in such a short time?'

Niamh's chin came up and her eyes took on the same defiant gleam as Ethan's. 'We knew the minute we met each other at the gym. I thought you'd be happy for me. I haven't had a boyfriend before and Ethan is so kind and good and—'

'Rich.' The cynical note in Grayson's voice made me want to slap him. Not that I'm an advocate for violence of any sort but it riled me that he was suggesting my sister was a gold-digger. He had only just met her. How could he make such a snap assessment of her?

I swung around to face Grayson with a glare so hot I could have moonlighted as a welding machine. 'How dare you?'

Grayson's eyes glittered with the same cynicism I'd heard in his voice. A worldly cynicism that made me feel wrong-footed somehow, which was weird because if there was an award for being a hard-nosed cynic it would surely go to me.

'Come with me,' he said, jerking his head in the direction of the exit. 'I want to speak to you in private.'

There was no possibility of me saying no. I suspect there were very few women on the planet who could say no to Grayson Barlowe. Besides, I wanted to speak to him where Niamh and Ethan couldn't listen in. We had to stop this nonsense between our siblings before it went any further. In love with someone after only six weeks? It was ridiculous. Niamh was naïve and innocent and way too trusting. It had taken me three years to get engaged to Ryan, but of course it had ended in tears. His, not mine.

Grayson led me to a private room on the other side of the hotel. It was furnished as a sitting room—twin soft sofas in plush velvet, long elegant silk curtains at the windows with a pelmet above. There was an antique writing desk and chair set on one side of the room, bookshelves on the other. The carpet was ankle-deep and hand-woven and it was a gorgeous shade of shell pink to match the silk curtains. It would have been a feminine room except for the cold marble statue of the hotel's founder placed near the window, as well as a stern-looking portrait hanging on one of the walls. Those beady eyes seemed to glare at us as we made our way in, as if to ask us why his peace was being disturbed. *Rest in peace, old man*, I said to myself. *This fight is none of your business.*

Grayson closed the door once we were inside with an ominous-sounding *clunk*. His eyes drilled into mine and I resisted the urge to look away. I balled my hands into tight fists, my spine ramrod-straight, my chin high—it had to be held high in order to maintain eye contact with him. He was well over six feet and I couldn't help recalling how my ex-fiancé hated it when I wore heels. I reckon I could wear stilts around Grayson Barlowe and still have to crane my neck.

'This has to stop and it has to stop now.' His voice had a determined edge to it, hinting at a personality not unlike my own. Once I make up my mind, that's it. I don't back down.

Although I agreed with him, I was unwilling to be on his side due to his insulting assumption my sister was a shallow gold-digger. I found myself looking for reasons for Niamh and Ethan to continue their relationship in spite of my own reservations.

'What's your main objection?' I injected my tone with cool crispness. 'They're both consenting adults.'

His dark eyebrows snapped together in a tight frown. 'My brother has obviously been blindsided by your sister's looks. And she clearly wants someone wealthy enough to take care of her.'

I know my sister is stop-the-traffic stunning, but it was insulting that Grayson couldn't see past Niamh's looks to her sweet, gentle and caring nature. 'Ahem, it's the twenty-first century. Women don't need a man to take care of them.' Call me a hypocrite but, feminist though I am, I sometimes fantasise about a man taking care of me. A man who would have my back and stand by me and encourage and support me. Who would love me for being me. Not a single man in my life past or present has ever done that for me, so you can see why it's just a fantasy on my part. *Sigh*.

Grayson's mouth tightened even further. 'I will not allow my brother to be exploited by someone who's only after a meal ticket.'

'She's not looking for any such thing.' I knew it wouldn't take him long to see how limited my sister was in some areas. Unlike his brother, Niamh has no visible disability but if you spend enough time with her it soon becomes apparent she has some limitations.

Not physical but intellectual. She has a reading age of an eight-year-old. She can only do simple maths. She has a small working memory, so complicated tasks can easily overwhelm her. Her support worker has helped her enormously, and of course I do everything I can, especially since Mum died three and a half years ago. It's been Niamh and me against the world ever since and, let me tell you, it's not always a nice world for people with acquired brain injuries. Or their carers.

Grayson scraped his broad-spanned hand through the thickness of his hair. I stared in fascination at the deep grooves his fingers left behind. I started to think about those long, tanned fingers gliding down the bare skin of my arm, or my legs… I shivered, and then swallowed thickly and quickly realigned my shoulders and spine back into a stiff don't-mess-with-me pose. It's kind of become my default posture in life, to be honest. Always bracing myself for a fight. I had no idea why I was suddenly fantasising about Grayson Barlowe's fingers on my body. It'd been a long time since I'd been intimate with anyone but surely I could find someone a little more suitable than my number one business rival?

Grayson's eyes came back to mine and a frisson coursed through my body. He had arresting eyes, a glacial ice blue with tiny flecks of grey. They were fringed with thick and long eyelashes that gave me an instant pang of envy. I had to use three coats of mascara and an expensive lash serum to make my lashes even vaguely noticeable.

'What sort of work does your sister do?'

'She doesn't have full-time employment…as yet. She volunteers at a pet shelter.' I moistened my dry lips with the tip of my tongue and added, 'Is your brother employed?'

Grayson's eyes followed the movement of my tongue with an intense focus that made something soft and feathery flutter across the floor of my belly. He rapid blinked and screened his expression like a shutter being drawn on a window.

'He works for me in a part-time position.' His curt answer contained a weight of information about him. Information I suspect I was able to decode only because of my own situation with my sister. There was a world of regret, guilt, pain and quiet despair in Grayson's reply. A world I was all too familiar with and knew I could never leave, even though I wished I could turn back time and do everything differently at that playground twenty years ago.

Grayson suddenly frowned again. 'Are you okay?'

It was my turn to rapid blink as the sting of tears at the backs of my eyes took me by surprise. I was caught off-guard by his assessing look. I was caught off-guard by my spiralling emotions. Emotions I had stuffed so deeply inside myself I had almost forgotten they were there. Almost.

My baby sister wanted to get married and I couldn't allow her to do it. Or at least, not in such a hurry. Not until I could guarantee she knew what she was doing. She had no experience when it came to men. She had

never had a boyfriend before. I had spent my life trying to protect her from further hurt after the one time
I failed to protect her. I could not bear to see her in any
sort of pain, and emotional pain is one of the worst to
experience. I should know, I've experienced it for years.

I brushed one of my hands over my eyes in an impatient manner. 'I have hay fever. All those fresh flowers
in the restaurant.'

He reached into his jacket pocket and took out a
neatly folded snowy white handkerchief and held it out
to me. I stared at it like it was something I had never
seen before. But then, it had been years since I had seen
one. Most people use tissues these days. Grayson's possession of a freshly laundered and neatly ironed handkerchief seemed to suggest he was a traditionalist at
heart. Or maybe he was doing his thing for the environment, saving our forests from being made into paper.

'Take it.' His voice had that note of drill sergeant
command in it again, which made me want to refuse
on principle but I mentally did a stocktake of my tote
bag hanging on my shoulder and I wasn't sure I had
any tissues in there. Tampons, breath mints, lip-gloss,
paracetamol, hand sanitiser, swanky new business
cards that had cost me a fortune... No tissues. Then I
recalled I gave my last purse-sized pack to Niamh two
days ago when she had a nose bleed and I had forgotten to replace them.

I took the handkerchief from him and my fingers
accidentally brushed against his. A ripple of energy
flowed from his body to mine like a live electric cur-

rent. I held his handkerchief up to my eyes, dabbing at them and trying to decide if I should blow my nose to give more authenticity to my claim of experiencing hay fever. I decided against the nose blow. Unfortunately, I have never been a dainty nose-blower. Seriously, I could stand in for a fog horn.

Along with the cleanly laundered smell, his handkerchief held a trace of his aftershave fragrance—an alluring blend of bergamot and citrus, and male body heat. I lowered the handkerchief from my face and folded it into an even smaller square. I needed something to do with my hands because, right then, I was tempted to reach up and touch Grayson Barlowe's stubbly jaw. The dark regrowth generously peppered his chiselled jawline and my gaze was magnetically drawn to the sculpted perfection of his mouth. His lower lip had a sensual fullness, his top lip sharply defined as if his Maker had spent an inordinate amount of time getting it right, like a sculptor works on their career-defining masterpiece. It was a mouth that hinted at a passionate nature that was carefully, vigorously held in check but once unleashed could be dangerous.

I suppressed another shiver, trying not to think of how dangerous it would be to be in bed with Grayson Barlowe. Dangerous and exciting and mind-blowing.

I stuffed the handkerchief in my tote bag. 'I'll wash it and get it back to you.'

'Keep it.'

I shrugged as if I didn't care either way, but I have a thing about returning borrowed things to their own-

ers. Good manners and all that. Speaking of manners...
Grayson and I had been invited to share in the celebration of Niamh and Ethan's engagement, but here we were behind a closed door instead of raising our glasses to their happy union in the flower-filled restaurant.

'So, what do you plan to do about your brother's engagement?'

'Stop it, that's what.'

I raised one of my eyebrows in an imperious arc. 'And how do you plan to do that?'

He let out a harsh-sounding breath that made his nostrils flare. He reminded me of a thoroughbred stallion ready to fight for his territory. 'I'll talk some sense into him.'

I gave a cynical twist of a smile. 'Good luck with that. He looks quite smitten with my sister.'

Grayson's expression hardened like quick-setting concrete. 'You can't seriously believe they're in love with each other?'

'Maybe they're in lust.' I immediately wished I hadn't mentioned *that* particular L word. I could feel my cheeks blooming with heat, as if by the very mention of the erotic word I had allowed something forbidden into the room. Something forbidden and dangerously tempting. Something that threatened to get out of control like a lit match to dry tinder. I could almost hear it crackling in the silence like tiny flames gathering energy to start an inferno.

His eyes held mine in a lock that sent a hot shiver rolling down my spine like a burning ember. I don't think I've ever had a man look at me quite so intensely. The air seemed charged with tension, a throbbing tension that increased as each heart-stopping second passed. He broke the eye contact and his gaze dipped to my mouth. And stayed there for endless seconds...

I held my breath.

My pulse quickened and my blood pumped and my heart jumped.

Grayson licked his lips and swallowed, returning his now inscrutable gaze to mine. 'Whatever they're feeling, I know it won't last.'

'You don't believe in true love?'

'Do you?'

I know I do it myself at times, but I hate it when people answer a question with a question. I suspected Grayson was very good at deflection. He wasn't the sort of man to give too much away about his feelings or his personal life. I gave a stiff smile that didn't show the brilliant job my cosmetic dentist had done on my once crooked teeth. It's taken me years to learn to smile properly but I still only keep them for special occasions.

'Some people get lucky.'

He glanced at my bare ring finger. 'You didn't?'

That's another thing I hate—how so many people in the architectural community knew about my broken engagement. But I guess, since I broke it off only days before the wedding it did kind of cause a bit of a scandal.

'Let's say I had a lucky escape.'

Grayson made a soft snorting noise but I couldn't tell if it was one of amusement or cynicism or something else. He was standing at least a metre away but I could still feel the male energy coming off him. A potent energy that made me aware of my femininity in ways I had never been to that degree before. My skin prickled, my heart raced, and liquid heat pooled in my dark secret places. Places I didn't want to think about right now. Places I hadn't thought about in years. I hadn't had a lover since my ex. I hadn't even felt a flicker of desire…until now. But what was I thinking? Sleeping with the enemy was a no-no. Besides, I couldn't afford to get distracted away from the issue of my sister and her…*gulp*…fiancé.

Grayson placed his hands on the back of the sofa he was standing behind and set his glittering gaze back on mine. 'Are we on the same page about getting Ethan and your sister to rethink their relationship?'

'How do you suggest we do that?' I knew my response hadn't actually answered his question but I was unwilling to commit to anything that would hurt my sister. Niamh believed herself to be madly in love. She was thrilled with the giant bauble on her ring finger. She had been dreaming about getting swept off her feet since she was a kid. The fact she was still a kid in some ways didn't mean she wouldn't be shattered if Grayson and I forced her to give up her dream of living happily ever after with Ethan.

Who was I to burst her big fragile shiny bubble and break up what could be her first and only chance to have a relationship? It was my fault she was the way she was and, while I was committed to protecting her and providing for her, I didn't want to sabotage her happiness. She deserved to be loved. Didn't everyone? And while I wasn't entirely sure of Ethan's motives, on the surface he looked like he was absolutely besotted by her. But that might be a temporary infatuation. It might fade and then my sister's heart would be broken and I would have to pick up the pieces.

Not that I'm without considerable experience in that department—my mother fell apart when my father took his life after a business deal went wrong a couple of years before Niamh's accident. A business deal with Grayson Barlowe's grandfather, no less. Hence the ongoing feud between the Clancy and Barlowe camps. My father's death was as unexpected as the failed business deal that left us basically penniless. Mum fell apart, even though she and my father had had a rocky relationship at the best of times. I finally managed to get her back on her feet but then she fell to pieces again when Niamh was injured, which was totally understandable. It was a double blow to lose her husband and then have her favourite child permanently damaged in the space of two years. To say I'd had to grow up fast is an understatement. There wasn't time to process my own grief. I was too busy carrying my guilt.

'We sit down with them and talk them through the issues.' Grayson's voice cut through my painful thoughts.

We? He wanted me to join forces with him? The thought of teaming up with him gave me a weird feeling in my stomach. A kind of shivery feeling that was part thrill, part dread. I sat on the sofa, not because

I wanted to but because my legs were feeling a little unsteady. Grayson's presence was so intimidating and yet I couldn't take my eyes off him. He was so damn attractive, even when he was frowning.

'Issues such as?'

His eyes hardened to flint. 'My brother has a trust fund left to him by our late grandfather.'

I upped my chin a fraction. 'So?'

'I don't want him to be taken advantage of by a supposedly love-struck beautiful young woman. It wouldn't be the first time it's happened.'

Anger was a fire in my blood that threatened to boil its way out of my veins. 'My sister is not the type of person to be influenced or impressed by how much money a man has. She's not the least bit mercenary or worldly.' I wanted to say *And nor am I*, but it didn't seem relevant at that moment. I wasn't interested in impressing him with my self-sufficiency. I just wanted to protect my sister from being hurt by his ruthless approach to the situation.

'It's obvious Ethan's been taken in by her act of doe-eyed innocence,' Grayson said, moving away from the sofa. He opened and closed his hands, as if trying to release some tension. 'He's not mentioned a word to me about dating anyone and now suddenly he's freaking engaged? She must have made him promise to keep it a secret.'

I widened my eyes in outrage, even though, like him, I was a little peeved Niamh hadn't told me a thing about dating Ethan either. I was used to knowing *everything* about her, far more than most older sisters would know. But then I've had to know everything in order to make sure she has all she needs and to keep her from being exploited by others.

'Look, I don't know the full extent of your brother's disability but I think you're doing both he and Niamh a disservice without a proper conversation with them first.'

'Marriage is out of the question. I'll do everything in my power to stop it.' His adamant tone riled me more than it should have. It was like I was programmed to adopt the opposite stance even though I actually agreed with him. But then he was a Barlowe, and I was a Clancy. We had a long history of going head to head.

I rose from the sofa and nailed him with my gaze, still playing devil's advocate. 'You know, some people do actually fall in love quite quickly. Or don't you believe in love at first sight?'

His mouth slanted in a smile right out of the cynical playboy's playbook. 'No. But lust at first sight? Yes.'

There was a pulsing silence. A silence so intense that I could just about hear my own heart beating. I could certainly feel it hammering away in my chest like an industrial piston.

Grayson's eyes roved over my face in slow motion. He studied my grey-green eyes for a heart-stopping moment. Then he shifted his focus to my mouth and paused there even longer. I was having trouble breathing. I had forgotten how to do it. My breath was locked somewhere in my throat as the seconds ticked on and on and on. Niamh is always saying what a nice mouth I have. I am less complimentary about my features. But right then, with Grayson Barlowe's gaze staring at my mouth as if it were the most beautiful and fascinating mouth in the world, I was starting to wonder if I needed to reassess my opinion on my physical assets.

But suddenly, as if someone had snapped their fingers to break a spell, Grayson shifted his gaze and glanced at the door. 'We'd better get back to the restaurant and talk some sense into them.'

He strode purposefully over to the door and opened it for me, standing to one side as I walked through. I was aware of the difference in our height as I walked past him. I was aware of the citrus and bergamot fragrance of his aftershave that was as intoxicating as a mind-altering drug. I was aware of him following my every movement, making my body feel different somehow, more feminine, more graceful…*desirable.*

And I was acutely aware that *I* was the one who needed some solid sense talked into them.

CHAPTER TWO

WE MADE OUR way back to the restaurant but when I looked at the table where Niamh and Ethan had been sitting it was now occupied by another group of people. I swivelled my gaze around the restaurant but there was no sign of my sister and her... Ethan. I still couldn't bring myself to refer to him as her fiancé. Niamh was mentally too young to be married. Too naïve to know what she was doing. I had to stop her from screwing up her life and I had to do it now.

I swung around to look up at Grayson. 'Where are they?' My voice was kind of scratchy as panic climbed up my spine.

His frown carved a deep trench between his eyes and he muttered a filthy curse not quite under his breath. 'They can't have gone far. Wait here. I'll ask the staff.'

I'm not used to being ordered around but this time I did as I was told. The thunderous expression on Grayson's face was enough to freeze me on the spot. For a decade.

But while he was off interrogating the staff, I did my own investigation. I pulled out my phone from my tote bag and opened the app that could locate my sister's whereabouts within seconds. But for some reason Niamh was not showing up any more. She had either turned off her phone or blocked me from keeping track of her. I didn't even realise she knew how to do that. Or had Ethan done it for her? My sister could be impulsive at times, it was one of the things that had changed about her personality since the accident. One of many things that had changed. But, until now, I had always managed to stop her from doing anything rash.

How could I stop her if I didn't even know where she was?

Grayson came back to me with an even more furious expression. 'They left the restaurant soon after we left them to talk privately. Damn it. I should've known something like this would happen.'

My heart was thumping like I'd been administered with a shot of adrenalin. It threatened to beat its way out of my ribcage. 'We didn't leave them for long. Is Ethan able to drive? Or did they come in a cab or ride-share?'

A flicker of something passed over Grayson's face, something I recognised because I had seen it on my own face for the last twenty years just about every time I looked in a mirror. A flash of pain, a ripple of regret, a gnawing ache of guilt. The trifecta of ghastly feelings one has when one feels totally responsible for a loved one's injuries. I had heard about the serious car crash Grayson and Ethan were involved in when Ethan was a teenager. Someone had mentioned it to me at an architectural conference but they hadn't given me many details and I was too polite to dig for more information. Besides, I didn't want anyone to think I was showing too much interest in my business rival's background. But, as far as I knew, Ethan had been the one driving. Or did Grayson blame himself for not insisting on driving himself?

'No, he no longer drives. What about your sister?'

'No. She mostly uses public transport or I take her where she needs to go. Oh, and sometimes her support worker.'

Grayson looked at me oddly for a moment. 'She has a support worker?'

'Yes, not a full-time one, though. She only needs help with some tasks, I fill in the rest.'

A perplexed frown wrinkled his brow. 'I didn't realise she was disabled.'

'Most people don't until they spend some time with her. She has an acquired brain injury from an accident when she was seven.' I didn't tell him the rest of the story. The horror story that had changed my family for ever. I had turned my back for only thirty seconds while she was on the swing, possibly even less time than that, and yet it had been enough for her to fall off and fracture her skull. Those few seconds had changed everything for all of us, most of all for Niamh. Her potential stolen. Her brain no longer functioning the way it was meant to.

Grayson sent his hand through the thickness of his hair again and I wondered if it was a stress thing. A habit he had adopted without realising it.

'I'm sorry.' His voice was deep and rusty. 'I thought she was yet another gold-digger after Ethan's trust fund.'

'But she told you she met Ethan at the gym. It's a specialised one that has tailor-made classes for each client.'

His jaw worked for a moment as if he was mentally chewing over something. 'I thought she might be a care worker or fitness trainer or something. Ethan was taken in by a carer a couple of years ago. He was convinced she was the real deal but, of course, she wasn't. She knew about his trust fund and wanted to set herself up in life. I knew what would happen. A costly divorce in a year or two's time. I paid her off in the end. It was cheaper and easier and saved a fortune on legal fees.'

'How did Ethan take it?'

'He was shattered.'

'I'm sorry to hear that, but I can assure you Niamh will not break your brother's heart.'

Grayson's eyes glinted with his trademark cynicism. 'Not if I can help it, she won't.'

I tightened my mouth and glared back at him. 'Firstly, you won't be able to pay her off.'

One dark brow rose in a perfect arc. 'How about you?'

I stared at him for a thumping heartbeat or two. What was he implying? That I could be paid to go away and take my sister with me?

'You think you can write a cheque to get rid of me? Think again.'

He moved closer and looked down from his considerable height into my upturned face. I stood, totally mesmerised. I wanted to look away but I couldn't. My body was disconnected from my brain. My brain was saying, *Step back, put some distance between him and you*, but none of it was getting through. The Wi-Fi was down or something, or too weak to pick up the message. And I was too weak to do anything but look into his darkly handsome features. I was transfixed by the intractable light in his eyes, by the sudden flare of his nostrils, by the alluring smell and heat of him that dazzled my senses as no one had ever done before.

'How do I know you're not behind them getting together?' he said, through thinned lips. 'For all I know, you've probably facilitated their getaway, all the while pretending to be as surprised by their announcement as me.'

I was shocked by his cynical assessment of me, shocked and angry, but I was keen to keep a lid on my emotions. He was a powerful opponent and I didn't want to give him any advantage by behaving like I had zero emotional regulation. But right then I wanted to swing a savage kick at his shins. I wanted to scrape my nails down his too-handsome face. I wanted to grab a fistful of his hair and tug and tug and tug. Another secret part of me wanted to grab the front of his crisp business shirt and lift my mouth to meet his hard one.

But, instead, I drew in a quiet and calming breath and held his gaze with cool composure. 'I'm as completely in the dark as you. And we're losing valuable time arguing the point here.'

He held my gaze for a long pulse-stopping moment.

Then he let out a harsh-sounding breath and raised one of his hands to the knot of his tie, tugging at it as if it was choking him. 'I need to find my brother before he does something he later regrets.'

'At least we live in London, not Las Vegas. If so, they could have been married by an Elvis impersonator by now.'

Grayson didn't appear to appreciate my attempt at humour. He glared at me so darkly I thought I might turn on the spot to smouldering ashes. Or maybe it was because I was already feeling so hot in his disturbing presence. I'm no naïve innocent like my sister but I have never met someone who stirs my senses into such a frenzy. I'm normally so logical and sensible but I had trouble keeping my thoughts in order. My brain kept coming up with X-rated images of Grayson Barlowe and me in bed together, naked limbs entangled, his muscled arms and legs pinning me to the mattress. Or the floor, or the ground, or up against a wall…

I gave a tiny shudder and gave myself a concussion-inducing mental slap. I had to stop thinking about him in such an erotic way. He wasn't my type and I was certainly not his. I'd seen him in the gossip pages, and at awards events, with blonde bombshells who looked so perfectly put together they could have been supermodels. Some of them *were* supermodels. Interestingly, Niamh is a blonde bombshell with her white-blonde hair and stunning figure. I haven't cracked any mirrors lately but I can safely say I do not look anything like a supermodel. Not even close. I fall into the category of mousy girl next door. Or maybe girl down the road, so far down the road you wouldn't notice her at all.

Grayson shoved his shirt cuff back to check his designer watch. My gaze was drawn to the dark hairs that covered his wrists and tapered over the backs of his hands and long strong fingers. He glanced back at me and my heart skipped and tripped.

'We'd better check Ethan's apartment first, then we can widen the search.'

'We?'

'Yes, we. It will be quicker if we stick together. Besides, I don't want you out of my sight until I'm sure of your motives.'

I gave him a gelid look. 'I can assure you my motives are the same as yours. Exactly the same.'

Grayson's brows rose ever so slightly and a devilish glinting light appeared in his gaze that made my pulse pick up its pace like a runner dashing for the finish line.

'So you want the same as me.' It was a statement not a question, but I wasn't so sure he was still talking about his brother and my sister. The electric energy was back in the air again, fizzing around us like a wayward current. Tingles ran up and down my spine, hot little pinprick tingles that made me aware of my escalating pulse and increased breathing rate. Seriously, I had to either get fit or get laid. Eek, why was I always thinking about sex around this man?

'I want to find my sister before your brother breaks her heart,' I said. 'I'm sure he's a nice guy and all that but she has no experience around men.'

Grayson moved towards the exit, signalling for me to follow him. 'Come on then. We'll try Ethan's place first and go from there.'

A few minutes later, I drew up behind Grayson's car outside a block of apartments in a lovely tree-lined street in Islington. Before I could unclip my seatbelt he was by my driver's door, opening it for me. I didn't know whether to be flattered or furious. The feminist in me insisted I was perfectly capable of opening my own door, thank you very much. But another part of me lapped up the old-world chivalry with relish.

Grayson led the way to the entrance of the building. He typed some numbers into a keypad and the doors opened. We walked across the shiny marble foyer to the lift and he pressed the call button and the doors whispered open at his command.

He waved me to go ahead of him. 'After you.'

I stepped into the lift and he followed and the doors locked us in together. I was doing my best to avoid his gaze but my eyes kept tracking back to his face as if drawn by a magnetic force. He was still frowning, the twin pleat between his brows deep and tight enough to grip a pencil.

'Does your brother live alone?'

'Yes, he insisted on it a couple of years ago. He has a support worker to help him in the morning to get ready for work but he spends the rest of his time alone.' His jaw tightened like a clamp and he added, 'Or so I thought.'

The lift stopped on the top floor and the doors opened on another gentle whisper. Grayson held the lift door open with one muscular arm while I stepped past him, conscious of his inscrutable gaze on me, and doing my level best not to trip or fall flat on my face.

He led the way to an apartment down the wide carpeted corridor and then pressed some more numbers into another keypad outside the door.

'Wait. Aren't you going to knock or ring the doorbell first?' I asked. 'Ethan and Niamh might be...you know...busy.' As euphemisms go, busy didn't quite cut it but I was determined not to mention the word 'sex' in front of him. I could already feel the heat in my cheeks and in my lower body.

Grayson glanced down at me, still frowning. 'Right...' He pressed the doorbell with his eyes still holding mine. Then, when there was no answer, he arched one dark eyebrow. 'Do I have your permission to enter now?'

I wasn't one hundred percent sure if he intended it as a double entendre but, all the same, I could feel myself flushing to the roots of my hair.

'Yes,' I said and blushed all the more because I was starting to think if he asked me to have sex with him I might indeed say yes. Not because I was interested in a relationship with him—I was over long-term relationships with men. But I figured it would be kind of interesting to experience a one-night stand with Grayson Barlowe. For research purposes. To see if the chemistry I was sensing between us was a real thing or a figment of my imagination.

The apartment door opened. The penthouse apartment door, actually. I tried not to look too impressed at the stunning décor, or gape at the view of Finsbury Park out of the large bank of windows in the spacious sitting room. I see gorgeous houses and apartments all the time. Many of them I've designed myself. I earn a very comfortable living and I've paid heaps off my pretty little townhouse's mortgage but it could be years and years before Niamh and I could ever live in a penthouse. Or have a view over a park.

Well, it seems Niamh could do if she married Ethan Barlowe. *Just saying...*

I pushed the thought away as quickly as it formed. My sister could *not* rush into marriage after only six weeks. She didn't know Ethan well enough. Marrying someone was a big commitment, and there were issues to consider regarding their levels of disability. Issues they might not have thought through in the heady rush of falling madly in love. If indeed they had fallen in love. I've had my fair share of infatuations over the years, so I understood how convincing those feelings can be at the time.

Grayson wandered through the apartment but I stayed put in front of the windows overlooking the park. I chewed my lower lip, mentally working through some of the issues the young couple might have to face. They both had disabilities that might impact on how they lived together. Surely they needed to spend a little more time considering how well-suited they were *before* they got married? It's too late once the ink is dry on a marriage certificate. I wish my parents had thought a little more about it before they said, 'I do.' Of course, in blindingly bright hindsight, I now realise I too should have considered whether or not Ryan and I were as well-suited as I wanted us to be. But I was in stubborn denial and had my head buried so deep in the sand I'd hit water and I couldn't see through the bubbles for how bad things actually were.

'They're not here.' Grayson spoke from behind me.

I turned to face him, struck again by how flipping gorgeous he looked even when he was frowning and glaring.

'Where else could they have gone?'

'Your sister's place?'

'Niamh lives with me.'

His hands were resting on his slim hips and his frown deepened. 'And you *still* didn't know anything about Ethan and her being involved?' The heavy scepticism in his tone annoyed me.

My back straightened, my gaze blazed, my blood boiled. 'Why do you keep suggesting I've colluded with them over their relationship? I had absolutely no idea she was seeing him. How do you know it wasn't him manipulating her, hmm?' I folded my arms in a defensive pose and added, 'That's the more likely scenario, in my opinion.'

'So when and where have they been alone together?' He seemed to be saying it to himself rather than me, his right hand going to his head to do that finger-combing thing again.

'Maybe they haven't been alone together a lot. Maybe you don't need to be when you meet The One.'

Grayson's steely gaze came back to mine and my stomach shivered like a shaken jelly. 'Since you have more experience than I do in such matters, I'll have to take your word for it.'

'Actually, my ex wasn't The One,' I found myself confessing. I unfolded my arms and dropped them by my sides and sighed. 'I just pretended to myself for way too long that he was.' Even three years on, I still cringe at how stupid I was to think Ryan and I were going to be together for ever.

'Who broke it off?'

'I did.'

There was a beat or two of silence.

'Why?' Grayson asked.

'He didn't want Niamh to be my bridesmaid.'

His eyebrows rose ever so slightly. 'Good call. You were together for what, a year or two or more?'

I was secretly impressed he didn't question the curtain coming down on my relationship but I wondered how he knew how long I had been going out with my ex. Ryan worked in the financial sector. He had no interest in architecture—another madly flapping red flag I should have noted earlier. I hadn't taken Ryan to any architectural awards ceremonies after the first time I was nominated for an award early in our relationship. He'd drunk too much because he was nervous for me— or so he said. Looking back now, I think he'd drunk because he was jealous of the attention I received.

'Three, actually. But it wasn't just about that.'

'What was it about?' Grayson's voice had softened to a gentle burr of sound that did strange things to my heart rate. As far as I know, I haven't got a heart condition but when I'm around Grayson Barlowe I swear I could have a hole in my heart or a murmur or a leaky valve, or all three.

'Ryan didn't understand my commitment to my sister. That she was always going to be a part of my life, especially after our mother died. Niamh needs me to watch out for her, to protect her from being exploited. We're a package deal. Buy one, get one for free.'

He lifted a dark eyebrow. 'Buy?'

'Bad choice of word but you know what I mean.'

Grayson let out a long sigh. 'Yes, I do indeed.'

There was another immeasurable silence. A silence in which I was conscious of only one thing—Grayson's blue eyes holding mine.

I licked my suddenly dry lips and he tracked the movement of my tongue with his hooded gaze. Something fizzed and tingled at the backs of my knees like a cocktail of sherbet and champagne had been injected into my bloodstream. I could feel it working its way through my body, sending tingling sensations to my core. Not the core I concentrate on during Pilates but that *other* core. The feminine core that most of the time I ignore.

But then the spell was broken when Grayson's phone began to ring. He grimaced and slid his hand into his jacket pocket, glancing at the screen before saying to me, 'Excuse me.' He turned slightly away to answer it. 'Mum?'

Okay, I admit it, I'm a terrible eavesdropper. Good manners aside, I just can't help myself. I do it all the time. Coffee shops, restaurants, the supermarket, museums, the gym, even walking along the street, I listen in on other people's conversations. I find them fascinating and revealing, sometimes even inspiring. Of course, I've perfected the art of eavesdropping, like now, for instance. I moved a short distance away—my hearing is good but not superhuman—and picked up a book that was on the coffee table, pretending an avid interest in robots.

'You *knew* about this?' Grayson's voice was loud enough to hear from outer space. Only joking. He didn't seem the type to shout at anyone, much less his mother. But his tone was certainly stern and disapproving. 'How can you encourage them? They've only known each other six weeks.'

It seems I underestimated the superhuman powers of my hearing because I could clearly hear Grayson's mother's response. 'How could you deny Ethan this chance to have a life with someone? He's in love and he wants to get married.'

'Have you met her? Niamh?' Grayson barked back, frowning like he was auditioning for a role as Chief Frowner.

'Yes, I have, as a matter of fact. I met them for lunch a few days ago. Niamh was charming and sweet and is obviously very much in love, and so is Ethan,' his mother said. 'Don't ruin it for him, Grayson. He deserves to be happy. He's been miserable for so long but now he's got his old spark back, and it warms my heart to see it.'

I saw a flicker of emotions pass over Grayson's face. His jaw worked, his eyes flinched as if the light was suddenly too bright and his broad shoulders tensed, as if the invisible weight he was carrying was finally wearing him down. He lifted a hand to his face and pinched the bridge of his nose, his shoulders now hunched forward.

'Look, I understand you want him to be happy. So do I. But he's rushing into this without doing due diligence. I think he should slow down a bit. Spend a bit of time getting to know Niamh and her circumstances a little better.'

'Niamh is nothing like Donna,' his mother said.

'And you've made that assessment after only one lunch meeting?' Grayson shot back.

'I'm a good judge of character.'

He gave a cynical sound that wasn't quite a laugh. 'Your track record on choosing husbands isn't great.'

There was a tight silence.

'I loved your father and he loved me. The accident changed everything. Your father couldn't cope with seeing both of you so badly injured.'

'I only broke my leg.'

'Everything that was you before that night was broken in that accident, Grayson.' His mother's voice had softened but I could still hear it. 'And of course, Ethan changed irreparably too. Your father couldn't handle it. He still can't. It's why he limits his contact with both of you.'

'How can you excuse his behaviour after all this time?' Grayson's voice was so bitter I could almost taste it in the air. 'He cheated on you, repeatedly, while Ethan's life was hanging in the balance.'

'Because somewhere underneath all that pain and anguish is the man I fell in love with.'

'Yes, well, that man is now shacked up with a new wife and family,' Grayson said through lips pulled so tight I could see the white tips at the corners of his mouth. 'His *perfect* family.'

See what I mean about eavesdropping? You find out so much information about people. I was intrigued by Grayson's backstory, not just about the accident and how it impacted his family but the comment about his father's new family. The way Grayson leaned on the word 'perfect' in such a scathing way. I know from experience that a lot of people find a disability in someone else confronting. Even small children stop and stare and ask questions that are hard at times to answer. Of course, adults should love their children no matter what. Had Grayson's father found the changes to his son Ethan all too difficult and sought comfort elsewhere?

It is a challenging time when the full extent of a patient's disability is made clear by the medical professionals. It can be devastating to find out your child can no longer do the things you dreamed and hoped they would do. Even as a sibling I found it nothing short of heartbreaking to see how Niamh's injuries permanently changed her, especially when it was my negligence that had caused them.

It sounded like Grayson's mother had a far more forgiving and accommodating nature than Grayson. How could she still have feelings for the man who had deserted her and her sons at their most vulnerable? To be perfectly honest, I lean a bit more towards Grayson's camp of unforgiving hard-nosed cynicism.

Forgiveness is definitely not my second name. It's Florence.

CHAPTER THREE

GRAYSON WAS STILL frowning as he asked his mother, 'Do you have any idea where Ethan and Niamh are now? We left them for a few minutes at the restaurant, where they'd asked us to meet them, but when we got back they'd disappeared.'

'*We?*' his mother asked, like she was a detective homing in on a suspect's conflicting evidence.

Grayson glanced at me and then rolled his eyes. 'Niamh's older sister Ashleigh.'

'Ash,' I interjected quickly. No one ever calls me by my full name. Only my father called me Ashleigh and since he's been gone I can't bear hearing it on anyone else's lips.

'Is she against their relationship too?' his mother asked in an affronted tone.

'We both have some serious concerns, yes,' Grayson said.

'Well, I'm not sure I should tell you in case you try and ruin things for them,' his mother said.

'We don't want to ruin anything,' Grayson said with a note of frustration in his voice. 'We just want them to slow down a bit.'

'So says the man who changes lovers by the week, or even less,' his mother said with a generous dollop of disapproval.

'We're not talking about me, we're talking about Ethan,' Grayson said, pinching the bridge of his nose again until his tanned skin turned white under the pressure.

'Ethan is an adult. He might have a disability but he can decide how to live his life and if he wants to spend it with Niamh, who are you and her sister to oppose it? I don't want to see him end up alone and lonely...or give up...' The quality of his mother's voice changed over those three little revealing words, 'or give up.' Had Ethan tried to end his life after his last relationship ended? Grayson had said his brother was shattered by the previous breakup. That was understandable, given he had been set up and exploited by his carer. But shattered to what extent? To the point of wanting to end it all?

Niamh had dipped in and out of depression a couple of times over the years, wondering if anyone would ever love her the way she was. I had always supported her through those dips in mood and was always watching out for another one. Believe me, after losing our father to suicide, I have become extremely hypervigilant about subtle shifts in mood. But over the last six weeks I'd become a little more relaxed about her. She had been happier and more positive in her outlook than I had seen her in years. I'd put it down to the very expensive psychologist I had organised for her. But clearly it had more to do with Ethan Barlowe. Maybe

I needed to be a little more positive about their relationship. It wasn't just money and security Ethan could give my sister—he could provide emotional support. Love. Commitment.

Grayson ended the call with his mother a short time later. He slipped the phone back in his jacket pocket and looked at me in a world-weary fashion. 'I'm sorry you had to listen to that.'

'I wasn't listening,' I said. I'm actually quite a good liar. I can control all the so-called tells people watch out for—the micro expressions that give most people away. But I got the feeling I wasn't fooling Grayson Barlowe. He held my gaze for a long moment, the silence stretching, stretching, stretching...

Then he looked at my mouth and I had the sudden urge to moisten my lips. I rolled my lips together instead and he continued to stare at my mouth as if it was something of unique and profound interest to him.

His gaze came back to mine and my heart skipped a beat at the bright gleam in his eyes. 'What if they didn't go far when we left them?'

I was having trouble keeping up. I was so focused on that gleam in his eyes and wondering if he was going to kiss me.

'Erm...' I chewed at my lower lip, not sure of what to say, which, let me tell you, is way out of character for me. I am never lost for words.

'What if they stayed where they were?'

I frowned in confusion. 'But they weren't in the restaurant. I looked at every table. Besides, the wait staff told us they'd left the restaurant.'

'Not in the restaurant but in the hotel?'

Now I understood the gleam in his eyes—he thought he had solved a mystery. I was a little annoyed I hadn't thought of the possibility of Ethan and Niamh booking a room myself. It made sense they couldn't have gone far with Ethan's mobility issues.

'But how will we find out for sure? The hotel reception staff won't release private information about their guests,' I pointed out.

'I'm Ethan's legal guardian. They will have to tell me.'

'How come you're his guardian and not your mother or father?'

'My father wasn't interested, and my mother didn't want to do it on her own, so she signed it over to me.'

'Why?'

'Because I insisted.'

I raised my eyebrows. 'And no one ever says no to you?'

His eyes locked on mine with a searing heat that sent liquid fire through my blood. 'Occasionally.'

The atmosphere tightened. My heart rate escalated. My skin prickled and my palms moistened. Grayson's gaze dipped to my mouth and this time I didn't resist the urge to sweep the tip of my tongue across my lips. I couldn't resist. It was beyond my self-control. He triggered in me a desire so ferocious and feral it frightened me as much as it excited me.

But I had to stay in control. I couldn't allow myself to be distracted by a man like Grayson Barlowe.

'You know, I really thought you were going to do

something really stupid back then,' I said in a voice far huskier than I'd intended.

Grayson quirked an eyebrow. 'Like what?'

I turned to pick up my tote bag from where I had left it on the floor near the sofa. I hung the strap of my bag over my left shoulder and glanced at him again but his expression was masked. Could I have misread the situation? Was I imagining the spark of chemistry that fired between us? I raised my chin a fraction, my gaze steady on his. 'I thought you were going to kiss me.'

A half-smile began to play about the corners of his mouth. It made him look even more devastatingly attractive and irresistible, especially as it set off a diamond-bright glint in his blue eyes. 'Do you really think I'd complicate things by doing something like that?'

I gave a one-shoulder shrug. 'I don't know you well enough to answer that question.'

Suddenly he wasn't standing two metres away but was right in front of me. I had to crane my neck to maintain eye contact. I had to control my ridiculous urge to wrap my arms around him and bring him even closer. I had to stop myself from staring at his mouth but looking into his eyes was worse, much worse. A girl could drown in those blue eyes with their ink-black pupils. Pupils that were flaring like spreading black pools just as I assumed mine were doing.

'How about you answer this question instead?' His voice was low and deep, his eyes with their flecks of blue and grey mesmerising. 'Would you *like* me to kiss you?'

Okay, so maybe I overstated my skill at lying a little

bit. There was no way I could say 'no' and sound convincing. I was caught between a rock and a hard place. Me being the rock and Grayson being the hard place. He was standing so close I could just about feel his hard place. I was imagining it thrusting into me with vigorous energy. God, how I wanted to feel him deep inside. What was wrong with me? I am not the sort of girl to jump the bones of men I barely know, and especially men I don't even like. Especially men I'm not supposed to like because his grandfather ripped off my poor dead father.

'What do you think?' I asked instead, insanely proud of myself for evading a direct answer.

Grayson moved a couple of centimetres closer. I could smell his aftershave, and I had to stop myself from swaying towards him to breathe in more of that intoxicating scent. He lifted his hand to one of my dangly earrings and ever so gently toyed with it, running it over his finger. He didn't touch me at all, only my earring, but a riot of tingling sensations flooded my entire being.

'I think it would be crazy for us to go there.' His voice was so low and husky it sent a shiver across my skin.

'Go where?'

'Anywhere that involved touching each other.'

I could safely say I had never wanted a man to touch me more. It was ridiculous because I had once been engaged to be married and yet I had never fancied my ex as I fancied Grayson.

'You're touching my earring.' I injected a touch of

asperity to my voice to disguise my wayward drives and urges.

His hand fell away from my earring and he gave a lopsided smile. 'My self-control had a moment.'

My self-control was having a moment too. A big moment. A moment I wasn't sure I could handle without a block and tackle or other industrial equipment. How was I going to keep my hands off Grayson Barlowe? Especially when he smiled in that self-deprecating way? I gave a stiff no-teeth-showing smile and stepped back but I could still feel the magnetic force of him.

'So, what are we going to do?' I glanced at my watch and winced at the time. 'It's getting late. We can hardly barge into Ethan and Niamh's room at this time of night. They might be...be...asleep.' There was no way I was going to say anything remotely sexual.

Grayson ran a hand through his hair and sighed. 'You're right. We'll arrange to meet them for breakfast instead.'

'We?'

'We have to be united on this, Ash.' It was the first time I had heard him say my preferred name and it sent a skittering shiver down my spine. When he had been talking to his mother, he had used my full name. At various conferences and awards nights in the past he had always been more formal, addressing me as Ms Clancy. Him using my shortened name made me feel as if we had crossed an invisible boundary line. A line I wasn't sure could be uncrossed so easily in the future.

Besides, he had touched my earring. That was big. Not my earring, but you know what I mean.

'I am absolutely with you on this,' I said. 'I can't bear the thought of Niamh making a huge mistake. Marriage is a big deal, it's not something anyone should rush into without careful consideration.'

'I couldn't agree more,' he said. 'Look, I think it's best if we arrive together tomorrow. I'll pick you up at half-six.'

Half-six?

'Just as well I'm a morning person.'

'I'm an early riser too.'

I was almost certain there was a double entendre to his statement but I was determined to ignore it. He'd said we were not going to touch. I agreed with it… sort of. Although my mind had already run wild with images of him rising early, his gloriously naked body unfolding itself from his million-thread snowy white bed linen that contrasted brilliantly with his deep tan. Yikes, be still my pulse…well, slow down a little at least.

'Where do you live? Oh, and you'd better give me your phone number in case we need to communicate,' Grayson said, taking out his phone again.

I rattled off my details and watched as he entered them in his phone with his two strong thumbs moving over the keys with such rapidity it made my single finger pecking look infantile. He pinged me a text and I then had his number. I felt a strange sense of accomplishment at having it in my possession. I was probably never going to be on his speed dial, nor he on mine, but still. At least I could contact him in an emergency.

On the way back to our cars a short time later, we

walked shoulder to shoulder in the cool night air. It
had finally stopped raining and the air smelt of summer stocks and jasmine and damp earth. The moon had
peeped out from behind the clouds, casting a silvery
glow over the wet pavement.

'What will you do if Ethan doesn't answer your
text?' I asked. 'I haven't been able to contact Niamh.
I think she's turned off her phone.'

'I got a reply from him when you went to the bathroom just then.'

Okay, so I didn't really need to take a leak, but I did
want to peek at the penthouse bathroom. I wasn't disappointed. It was stunningly appointed with brass and
Italian marble with ideal configurations for someone
with limited mobility.

'Oh, what did he say? Is Niamh with him? Is she
all right?'

'They're both fine and they've agreed to have breakfast with us,' he said, stopping as he got to my car.

'Well, that is good news.' I unlocked my car but
before I could open the driver's door Grayson's hand
moved past my body to do it for me. 'Oh, thank you...'
I know I should have got in the car and shut the door
but I stayed where I was—in the space between the
open door and his strong tall body. I slowly brought
my gaze up to meet his and my stomach did a complicated somersault that would have scored a perfect ten
at a gymnastics event.

Our eyes locked. My mouth went dry. My heart rate
soared. A car horn bleated, jarring me out of my stasis.
'Gosh, that was loud.'

'Yes, it was.' Grayson looked down into my upturned face, his eyes moving between each of mine before flicking to my mouth. I couldn't stop staring at his mouth and the rich dark stubble that surrounded it. I wondered what it would feel like against my skin. I had to curl my fingers into my palms to stop myself from lifting them to his face to find out.

'Erm, so half-six then, right?' I sounded like a nervous teenager agreeing to her first date with the high school heartthrob.

His eyes were still on my mouth. 'Yep.'

I let out a shaky breath and stretched my lips into one of my tight no-teeth-showing smiles. 'Well, goodnight.'

''Night.' He stepped back and I did a pretty ungainly job of getting myself into my seat. I admire the royals and celebrities who have mastered the art of entering and exiting a car with such elegant grace.

Grayson closed my door and stood back and watched me do an even worse job of getting out of the tight parking space. I stalled the car and ground the gears and gritted my teeth until my jaw clicked. I caught a glimpse of him in the rear-view mirror, still looking at me inscrutably as I drove off.

I tried to go to sleep as soon as I scrubbed off my make-up and brushed out my hair and flossed and cleaned my teeth. I counted sheep and cows and chickens to no avail. I was too wired for sleep. Too wound up with desire for a man I knew I should keep well away from. I don't do playboys. I don't do one-night stands. I don't do mortal enemies. But then, since I broke up with my ex, I haven't done anyone. Maybe my long period of celibacy was why I was reacting to Grayson in such an out of character way.

But I must have finally drifted off because when I woke it was six-fifteen. I sat bolt upright in my bed, my eyes still gritty from my poor night of sleep, my hair in such a tangle it made a rat's nest look neatly coiffed. I swore and threw off the bedcovers and rushed to the shower. There wasn't time to wash and blow-dry my hair, so I put on a shower cap instead.

With four and a half minutes to spare, I checked myself in my full-length mirror. My dark brown hair was pulled back from my face in a smooth tight chignon at the back of my head. I was wearing white jeans with a silk shirt in a smoky grey. My make-up was understated but I'd highlighted my eyebrows with a kohl pencil, swiping a bit on my eyelids as well. I put on another pair of dangly earrings—I have lots of them in my jewellery kit. I have a skinny heart-shaped face so dangling earrings work well on me. Well, that's my story and I'm sticking to it.

I painted some lip-gloss on my lips and slipped my feet into a pair of high heels. I grabbed a jacket but from the look of the bright sky outside I probably wouldn't need it.

The doorbell rang and my heart leapt to my throat. I drew in a calming breath and walked to the door to check the security camera panel. Grayson looked disgustingly refreshed, as if he had slept as soon as his head landed on his feather pillow, although his hair was still damp. He had shaved too, highlighting the chiselled planes of his lean jaw.

I pressed the intercom. 'I'll be down in a tick.'

'No problem.'

I wanted to ask him up but I knew that was asking for trouble. The sort of trouble I wanted to stay away from, especially this early in the morning when I was tired and not in full working order. I needed a double shot of caffeine. And fast.

To my utmost surprise, Grayson had two takeaway coffees waiting in the car. The delicious aroma swirled around my nostrils and my mouth watered. I put on my seatbelt and glanced at him once he was behind the wheel. 'Is one of these for me?'

'Yep.'

I cocked my head at a suspicious angle. 'How do you know how I take it?'

A ghost of a smile flirted with his mouth. 'I took a guess. Long black, double shot, no sugar. Am I right?'

He was right, but I didn't want him to be. I needed to keep my distance and how was I to do that when he did thoughtful things like bring me coffee first thing in the morning?

'Yes.' I reached for the coffee and breathed in its delicious aroma, then took a sip. It didn't surprise me that the quality of the coffee was excellent. I had always known Grayson Barlowe had high standards—his body of award-winning work attested to that. The way he dressed, even when dressed casually as he was this morning, spoke of a man who valued quality.

I flicked my gaze his way again. 'But seriously, how did you know how I have my coffee? Do you have special mind-reading powers or something?'

His smile tilted one side of his mouth, making him look less serious and forbidding. His more relaxed features made my heart pitter-patter and my pulse race, as if I had downed the whole coffee in one swallow. And chased it with a couple of energy drinks.

'I overheard you order one at the design conference in Bristol last year.'

I gave him an arch look. 'I'm surprised you even noticed me. I seem to remember you were busy during the coffee and lunch breaks with a flock of young female architects who wanted to take a selfie with you.'

Ack. Why had I revealed that I had even noticed him with his entourage of adoring women? It made me look like I'd been following his every move at that wretched conference. The fact that I had was only because he was hard to ignore, even in a crowd. He was always head and shoulders over everyone else and had an arresting and commanding presence that drew my eye from way across a room.

Grayson gave me an inscrutable sideways glance and I could feel my cheeks heating under his scrutiny. 'You're hard to ignore.'

'Why's that?' I do not flirt. I do not fish for compliments. So it was kind of weird and out of character to hear myself ask such a flirty question.

He turned a corner at a busy junction and I watched his broad-spanned hands control the steering wheel with competence and skill. I tried not to think of those hands competently and skilfully caressing my body. Tried but failed. I took another sip of my coffee, hoping it would redirect my wayward thoughts. It didn't.

Grayson focused his attention on the traffic in front of us. 'You're dedicated, hard-working and talented.'

'And that makes me stand out in a crowd?'

A fleeting smile traversed his lips. 'I could list all your other assets but that would be crossing a line we said we weren't going to cross.'

'You only said we weren't going to touch.' My gaze drifted to his muscular thigh so close to mine. I could have reached out and touched him right then and there. I wanted to but somehow I resisted the urge. Maybe my self-control wasn't as out of shape as I thought. Go me.

He drove the car into the valet parking bay at the hotel, then turned to look at me. 'So I did.' One of his hands was still on the steering wheel, the other grasping the gear stick. Was it my imagination or was he holding them a little *too* tightly, as if he was trying to stop himself from touching me? His gaze went to my mouth and I held my breath. I held it for so long I thought I might faint. Or maybe that was because his eyes were so sexily hooded and his mouth so gorgeously sculpted I could think of nothing else but how it would feel pressed to mine.

I let out my breath in a shuddering stream. I licked my lips. I stared at his mouth, then flicked my gaze to meet his. 'You haven't changed your mind, have you?' I asked.

'It takes a lot to get me to change my mind.'

I twisted my mouth in a wry fashion. 'You sound a bit like me. Niamh is always calling me stubborn.'

He looked at me for another long moment without speaking, his eyes moving back and forth between each of mine, then over my face as if memorising my features. The curve of my cheeks, the arch of my eyebrows, the ski slope of my nose, the shape of my mouth.

'Stubbornness can be a weakness but it can also be a strength.'

'How so?'

'Someone who is stubborn is usually someone who stands by their convictions. They're steady and reliable.'

'Yes, well, I wish I'd been a bit more reliable twenty years ago,' I said before I could stop myself.

Grayson frowned. 'What happened twenty years ago?'

I bit my lip, wishing I hadn't let my guard down. I can't remember the last time I told anyone about the playground incident. I hate talking about it. I hate being reminded of how I ruined my sister's life. I glanced at the clock on the dashboard. We had ten minutes to spare, but I didn't want to be tempted to tell him my deepest darkest secret.

'Shouldn't we be going in? Ethan and Niamh might disappear again if we don't show up on time.'

'We've got plenty of time.' Grayson placed his hand on mine, where it was resting on my right thigh, and a jolt of energy coursed through my flesh.

I looked at his hand, his fingers so long and thick and tanned compared to mine.

'You're breaking the rules.' I tried to make my voice sound schoolmistressy, prim and proper. However, it came out kind of husky and breathless instead. But I didn't pull my hand out from under his. I couldn't. I liked the feel of his hand's warmth seeping into mine, the gentle squeeze of his fingers sending my heart rate off the charts. He had never touched me before, apart from toying with my dangly earring. This was so much better than that. His hand sent heat racing through my blood like tongues of flame.

Grayson slowly lifted his hand off mine, his mouth twisting in a rueful manner. 'Sorry. My bad.'

'It's okay.'

There was a beat or two of silence.

'I guess we'd better go in and get this over with,' he said, blowing out a breath of resignation.

'I can't say I'm looking forward to bursting their bubble.'

'But it has to be done. Ethan can't get married to a woman he has only known six weeks. I won't allow it.' The gritty determination was back in his tone, reminding me he was not going to change his mind in a hurry.

'Does he need your permission to marry? I mean, I know you're his custodian but he's an adult.'

'No, but I control the bulk of his trust fund.'

'Will you?' I asked, with a querying arch of my eyebrows.

'Will I what?'

'Make things difficult financially?'

A pleated frown pulled at his forehead. 'Not unless I have to.'

'So I guess Shakespeare was right in *A Midsummer Night's Dream*,' I said. '"*The course of true love never did run smooth."* You do realise by discouraging them it might backfire? Sometimes when we prohibit someone from doing something, the desire to do it is all the more fervent.' I was definitely speaking from experience—recent experience. I had a fervent desire to touch Grayson Barlowe and I didn't know how to quell it.

His eyes flicked to my mouth and back to my gaze, but his expression was mask-like. 'That's a risk I'm prepared to take.'

I followed him into the hotel a short time later, wondering if I was prepared to risk spending time with him in the quest to put the brakes on my sister's relationship with his brother. It was dangerous being around Grayson Barlowe. Dangerous and exciting and thrilling. I rubbed my left hand over my right where the skin was still tingling from his touch. He had set the boundaries down but I wondered if that was for his benefit rather than mine. Or was I being a fanciful fool for thinking he might be remotely interested in someone like me?

CHAPTER FOUR

GRAYSON GOT A security pass from reception to gain access to the lift that went to the floor where his brother and my sister were staying. His expression was grim as he came back to me with the security pass. 'They're in the honeymoon suite.'

The honeymoon suite? I chewed at my lower lip, wondering if Niamh and Ethan had consummated their relationship. Niamh knew the mechanics of sex because I had talked to her about consent and bodily autonomy even before she hit puberty. But she had never had a boyfriend before Ethan. I wondered if she was adequately prepared to deal with Ethan's physical limitations. But perhaps they were waiting until they got married. After all, six weeks wasn't a long time to wait. Maybe that's why they had decided on a short engagement. But... *the honeymoon suite?*

We got in the lift and Grayson swiped the pass over the keypad and pressed the floor to the appropriate floor.

'Are you okay?' he asked with a deep note of concern in his voice.

I hadn't realised I was frowning, and I tried to

straighten out the creases on my forehead. Unfortunately, I could do nothing about the hot colour I could feel pooling in my cheeks. 'My sister hasn't had a boyfriend before, so…'

'I'm sure Ethan would've been sensitive and put her needs ahead of his own.' His tone was calmly reassuring.

I disguised a swallow, feeling a fool for being so embarrassed at discussing our siblings' sex life with him. Seriously, I was behaving like an innocent Regency heroine instead of a twenty-first century career woman who'd once been engaged to be married. 'That's…erm…good to hear.'

'Ethan is a partial paraplegic in that he can still walk a few steps.'

I wasn't sure why he was filling me in on that detail, other than to assure me his brother was not as disabled as I had first thought.

'I didn't know that.'

'He had a stroke following the accident. A brain bleed took out his right side, but he worked hard at rehab and got a bit more movement, apart from his right hand.'

We arrived on the honeymoon suite floor and the lift opened with a whooshing sound. We stepped out of the lift but by tactic agreement stood in the wide corridor while the doors closed again behind us on another whisper.

'It must have been a harrowing time for you both, and, of course, your parents.'

A shadow passed over his features like clouds scudding across the sky. 'We could so easily have lost him. It still gives me nightmares about how close it was.' The gravity in his voice reminded me of my own visits to the ICU where Niamh was hooked up to a ventilator for weeks on end. The uncertainty was torture, each day unfolding with a new hurdle, a new drama to face. Then a flicker or two of hope, only to be dashed the following day.

'I understand. I know lots of people say that, but how can they if they haven't stood by a loved one's bedside, wondering if they would be alive the next day?'

Grayson's eyes held mine and I found myself unable to look away. 'What happened to your sister?'

I let out a ragged sigh. 'A head injury when she was seven. She fell off a swing and fractured her skull. She was in a coma for a month. When she finally woke up, she had no memory of the accident. No idea of how close we were to losing her.' I swallowed tightly and added, 'It was my fault.'

He frowned. 'How was it your fault?'

'I was supposed to be watching her.'

'How old were you?'

'Nine.'

'Isn't that a bit young to be responsible for a small child? Where were your parents?'

I let out another rough-edged sigh, wondering why I was unloading all this emotional drama to my sworn enemy. 'My dad had died two years before. My mother was still struggling to cope, so I used to take Niamh to the park after school to give Mum a break.'

Grayson's frown was still deeply entrenched on his

forehead. It gave him a severe and intimidating appearance, but when I looked into his eyes I could see a blue ocean that wasn't cold and icy at all. There were warm currents swirling in the depths.

'And all these years you've been blaming yourself?'

I shrugged one shoulder. 'Who else is there to blame? I was supposed to be watching out for her and I turned away to look at something, I can't even remember what it was now. I heard a scream and turned back to see Niamh on the ground, bleeding from her head and ears. It wasn't Niamh who'd screamed but another child who saw it happen. Fortunately, there were a couple of people nearby walking their dogs and they called an ambulance.'

'I'm sorry you and Niamh had such a terrible thing happen, but you really mustn't blame yourself, Ash.'

'How can I not? I changed the course of her life that day. Her potential was stolen by my inattention.'

Grayson placed one of his hands on my shoulder and a shudder of awareness coursed through my body. His touch was warm, anchoring, stabilising. Grounding me in a way I had not felt before. Our eyes met and, in that moment, I sensed that here was someone who truly understood the emotional trauma of watching someone they love hover between life and death.

'I blame myself too for my brother's accident. It was a snap decision to swap seats that night. He hadn't had much experience driving in the rain and yet I agreed to let him take over the wheel. It was the worst decision of my life.'

I placed my hand over his where it was resting on my

shoulder. I could feel the soft dark hairs on the back of his hand against my palm and fingers. I could see the anguish and guilt in his eyes that reminded me so much of my own. I gave his hand a gentle squeeze, marvelling at how broad his hand was compared to mine.

'I'm guessing you don't make snap decisions any more, right?'

His mouth twisted ruefully, and he lifted his hand away from my shoulder, taking my hand with it. 'Not usually.'

His thumb stroked over the back of my hand in a slow-motion caress that sent searing heat coursing through my flesh. His touch was so light, tender almost, and it should not have caused the riot of sensations in my body, but somehow it did and I—shame on me—did nothing to stop it.

Only the sound of the honeymoon suite door opening finally made me pull my hand out of Grayson's light hold. I turned to face my sister, who was dressed in smart casual clothes, her hair brushed and tied in a neat ponytail.

'You're late,' Niamh said, eyeballing me.

'Only five minutes or so,' I said, glancing at my watch.

She gave Grayson a hard stare and then turned and led the way inside the honeymoon suite. We followed her without a word and then Grayson closed the door, exchanging a brief raised brow glance with me that made something turn over in my belly. We walked to the sitting room off the foyer of the suite, where Ethan was seated on a plush sofa rather than in his wheelchair.

His expression matched Niamh's defiant you-can't-tell-me-how-to-live-my-life look.

'I hope you both realise the stress you caused us both last night by disappearing without telling us where you were going,' Grayson said in a stern tone that I knew was not going to work with my sister. And, judging from Ethan's expression, it wasn't going to work with him either.

Niamh sat beside Ethan and grasped his hand. 'Your reaction to our announcement was so upsetting.' Tears shone in her eyes, and she continued with a wobble in her voice, 'I thought you'd be happy for us and instead you tried to ruin what was supposed to be one of the most memorable days of our lives.'

Ethan seemed to grow a few centimetres as he held his older brother's gaze. 'I brought Niamh here to c-compensate for her disappointment in how you b-both reacted to our news.'

'Look, I'm sorry about that,' I said before Grayson could respond. 'But it was such a surprise to drop on us. We didn't even know you were seeing each other.' It felt kind of weird to be saying 'we' all the time as if Grayson and I were a couple.

Niamh met my gaze with her watery one. 'Is it because of what happened to Daddy all those years ago?' Her question was directed at both of us—me and Grayson.

'No,' Grayson answered.

'Yes,' I answered at the same time.

Grayson locked his gaze on mine, one of his dark eyebrows rising in an arc. 'Seriously?'

I straightened my shoulders and held his querying look. 'Our father would still be alive today if it hadn't been for your grandfather ripping him off in that so-called friendly merger. Any merger between the Clancys and Barlowes is to be discouraged, even romantic ones.'

Especially romantic ones that involved Grayson and me, but of course I didn't say that out loud.

A ripple of tension passed over Grayson's features and his mouth went into a straight line. 'I wondered when you were going to bring that old chestnut up.' His tone was ripe with derision. 'But perhaps you should get your facts straight before you start maligning my late grandfather.'

I gave him stare for stare, my blood pounding with anger. 'The facts are your grandfather reneged on the deal at the last minute and left my father practically penniless.'

The arch of his eyebrow went higher. 'Is that what you were told?'

A sliver of doubt got under the door of my dislike of all things Barlowe. It shone a tiny light on my beliefs and made me wonder if I had been told the truth or what my mother wanted me to believe. I had idolised my father and I had only been seven years old when he died. Details about business mergers were not exactly things I was interested in as a small child. I seemed to recall My Little Pony was front and centre back then. Could I have got it wrong about him? But why then did people in the architectural community still refer to Grayson's grandfather as a hard man who didn't suffer fools gladly?

But then another thought slipped into my head…
What if my father had been foolish in some way?

Grayson must have seen the doubts flickering over
my face for he turned and addressed his brother and
my sister again. I was incredibly grateful for the subject
change, but I dearly wanted to unpick the past with him
on some other occasion, preferably when we were alone.

'Whatever happened in the past has no bearing on
what's happening now. You both want to be together;
Ash and I are not in any doubt of that. But we want
you to slow down a bit before you take the next step.'

'What t-t-time frame are you suggesting?' Ethan
asked with a wary expression.

'Six months,' Grayson said.

'Three,' I said. I didn't want to look like I agreed
with him on every detail.

The young couple exchanged glances and then Ethan
said, 'One m-month and th-that's our final answer.'

I was secretly proud of Niamh's defiant stare aimed
at Grayson and me. And more than a little envious of
Ethan's proud glance at her and his warm, encouraging smile.

'Okay, so here's the deal,' Grayson said. 'In one
month's time, we'll regroup and assess how things are
going. If you still want to be together, we can talk about
what comes next.'

Ethan's expression became guarded again. 'Will you
promise to support us in our goal of getting married?'

Grayson's jaw worked for a moment. 'Why can't you
just live together to see if you're compatible in the me-
dium to long term?'

I folded my arms across my chest and gave Grayson a raised brow look. 'My, oh, my, you really do have a phobia about marriage, don't you?' I have to say, I rather enjoyed needling him a bit. It was only fair since he made my heart go pitter-patter and my belly flip-flop, and my common sense to go offline.

'I have nothing against marriage between the right people,' Grayson said.

'You don't think we're the right people?' Niamh's eyes shimmered with a fresh tide of tears. 'I know I'm not smart like you and Ash, but I love Ethan and I will do everything in my power to be a wonderful wife and companion to him.'

Grayson looked a little uncomfortable in the face of my sister's emotional outburst...or was he uncomfortable about her level of disability? Did he doubt she could be a loving wife and companion to his brother? Or did he still think she was a gold-digger, after his brother's trust fund? After all, Grayson controlled the bulk of Ethan's finances. There could not be a wedding without his say-so, or at least not the sort of wedding my sister had dreamed of since she was a kid. No Elvis impersonators for her. Niamh wanted one of those big meringue-like dresses with a long train and veil, and a church full of flowers and a choir, not a ten-minute ceremony in some dinky little chapel in Vegas.

Grayson let out a long breath. 'Let's see how things pan out after a month.'

'Will you promise to be s-supportive and open to us being t-together in the meantime?' Ethan asked.

'Yes,' I said, mentally crossing my fingers because

I still had my doubts about how a marriage between them would work. I did so much day-to-day stuff for Niamh. How was Ethan going to help her when he had his own needs to consider? But then I reminded myself—he could love her and that was what she wanted more than anything.

'There's one other thing…' Ethan added, grasping Niamh's hand again. 'We want you both to design a house for us. One that will suit both our needs perfectly.'

'Both of us?' I asked in alarm. I could not imagine working alongside Grayson Barlowe…well, not without being tempted to cross the boundary between professional and personal. It would mean spending even more time with him. Lengthy periods of time. Designing a house was not a weekend project. Some houses took weeks, if not months, to design according to the client's specifications.

'You're both award-winning architects,' Niamh said. 'We thought it would show your support of our relationship by designing our dream home for us.'

Grayson looked at me but his expression was as hard to read as a slab of marble. He turned back to eyeball his younger brother. 'What's wrong with your penthouse? It suits your needs, doesn't it?'

'It's a penthouse,' Ethan said as if that explained everything. 'Niamh and I want a house and garden. And we want to live in the country, not in the city.'

Grayson's jaw worked for a moment, which suggested to me his brain was filing through the arguments against such a move, but in the end he didn't say anything. He merely shrugged one broad shoulder and turned to answer a knock at the door.

Breakfast was delivered to the room at that point, but I didn't have much appetite. I picked at a croissant and had half a cup of coffee and watched as Grayson had even less. Ethan and Niamh tucked in, however, and Ethan seemed delighted with the enjoyment my sister was having in indulging in the delicious options on the trolley. Eggs Benedict, an artfully displayed fruit platter, little pots of yoghurt in various flavours, pastries and croissants with preserves, tea and coffee and freshly squeezed orange juice. It was a breakfast junkie's heaven, but I could feel myself sinking into a private hell of despair.

A house in the country? Co-designed by Grayson and me? How would my sister cope without me? We had lived together all our lives. My whole life revolved around her and work. I wasn't used to thinking only of myself. How would I fill the hours and days and weeks and months and years? And, more to the point, how would Niamh handle marriage to a man who needed so much help himself? The architectural project aside, if she married Ethan, Grayson would be her brother-in-law and it would not be so easy for me to avoid him. And I needed to avoid him, otherwise I was going to be in water deep enough to cloud my vision all over again.

Half an hour later, Grayson and I left the honeymoon suite and got back in the lift. The doors whooshed closed, and I met his gaze. 'So, that was a bit unexpected.'

His eyes glinted with cynicism. 'You think?'

I gave a shrug and toyed with the strap of my tote bag with my fingers. 'Well, at least they've promised not to get married for a month. That's a positive, right?'

One of his hands opened and closed, the other scraped a rough pathway through his thick hair. 'I hope a month is long enough for them to see the stupidity of getting married at all. And as to a house in the country,' he muttered a curse swear word and continued, 'that's even more preposterous.'

I cocked my head on one side and studied him for a beat or two. Unlike me, he didn't seem too fazed by my unwavering scrutiny. 'Are you worried about working with me on their house?'

A tiny muscle flickered near his mouth. 'I've done collaborative work before.'

'You didn't answer my question.'

'No, I'm not the least bit worried.' He enunciated each word as if speaking to a child. 'Are you?'

I twisted my mouth. 'It depends.'

'On what?'

'Whether we can work together without arguing over every light switch placement.'

'It won't be a problem.' His tone seemed to suggest otherwise, so too did the taut line of his mouth and the flicker of annoyance in his gaze.

'Back there, you said marriage between the right people was okay.' I raised my fingers in air quotes and said with a challenging note in my voice, 'Define the right people.'

The lift doors opened on the foyer level and Grayson

silently indicated for me to precede him. We walked along the marbled area for some distance before he spoke. 'Marriage can work reasonably well between two mature adults who have insight into their own psychodynamics.'

'You don't think your brother is mature enough for marriage?'

He gave me a sideways glance. 'Is your sister?'

My shoulders went down on a sigh. 'In some ways, yes, in others, no.' I stopped walking to look up at him. 'There's something I want to discuss with you. In private.'

He stopped in his tracks, his eyebrows lifting ever so slightly, and a glint came into his eyes. 'Oh?'

'It's about the feud between your grandfather and my father.'

The glint hardened to flint, and he resumed walking. 'It's in the past, it's best left there.'

I trotted to keep up with him and placed my hand on his muscled forearm to get him to stop. He stopped and glanced at my hand on his arm before meeting my gaze.

'I thought we agreed not to touch?' he said with a sardonic quirk of his lips that made me want to touch him even more.

I took my hand off his arm and let it drop by my side. 'I want to know more about what happened between your grandfather and my father. There seems to be some discrepancy between what I've been told by my mother and what you understand to be true.'

'Are you free for dinner tonight?'

The question utterly blindsided me. I stood there

with my mouth hanging open, unable to get my voice to work. Finally, I managed to croak in an incredulous tone, 'Dinner?'

'You're clearly not a fan of breakfast, so I thought dinner might be more suitable.'

So he had noticed my lack of appetite at breakfast. Interesting.

'I normally love breakfast but...' I chewed at my lower lip for a moment. 'Dinner as in a...?'

'It's not a date.' His tone was emphatic, annoyingly so. 'Call it a history lesson if you like.'

'A history lesson?' I knew I was parroting him but I couldn't get my head around spending more time alone with him—at his request. But I did want to hear his side of things about the leadup to my father's suicide.

'Okay. When and where?'

'My place.'

I frowned. 'Your place? Why not a restaurant?'

'You said you wanted our discussion to be private.'

'Right, well... Do you want me to bring anything?'

'No. And I'll pick you up.'

I was privately impressed by his chivalrous offer, but I didn't want to communicate it to him.

'Why? I'm perfectly able to get myself to your place.'

'I know, but I'd prefer to pick you up.'

'Is that so you can control when it's time for me to leave?'

He gave a ghost of a smile. 'I promise not to keep you long.'

Given he was a sleep-with-them-and-leave-them playboy, I could only imagine the ridiculously short timeframe on his relationships. I gave him a pert look. 'I bet you say that to all the girls.'

He threw his head back and laughed and I was totally blindsided again. I had never heard him laugh before. He had a deep rich laugh that made the fine hairs on my arms stand up at the roots. I wanted to hear more of it. I wanted to see his face relax in humour rather than tense up in stern disapproval. He was a stop-your-pulse-handsome man either way, but when he laughed it completely transformed him. It gave me a glimpse of who he had been before his brother's accident—a happy-go-lucky man who had no reason to frown.

'Shall we say eight p.m.?' he said, with a smile still curving his mouth.

'Fine. Eight it is.'

Seriously, if he had said two in the morning, I would still have said yes.

CHAPTER FIVE

MY WORK DAYS normally flash past but this day was as slow as a snail on crutches. I had trouble giving my clients my full attention. My brain kept drifting off to what I might wear for my dinner with Grayson. I mentally examined the contents of my wardrobe and decided I needed to hit the high street in my lunch hour. *Lunch hour, ha-ha.* I *never* took a lunch hour. I normally worked through because there wasn't enough time in the day with all I had to do for Niamh as well as work. But since she was still with Ethan, presumably at his penthouse apartment by now, I had more time on my hands.

After forty-five minutes of trying on clothes in various boutiques, I concluded I was a terrible shopper. I couldn't decide what to buy for my non-date dinner with Grayson. There was a part of me that wanted to wow him. I might not be supermodel material, but I can really rock a little black dress and sky-high heels. But another part of me wanted to keep things casual. I didn't want him to think I was hitting on him, especially since he was the one who'd orchestrated the no-touching rule. The rule I was having so much trouble sticking to.

In the end, I went for the little black dress. A new and ridiculously expensive one because I didn't want to wear anything I had worn before. Clothes can be as evocative as music. I got rid of a lot of my clothes when I ended my relationship with my ex. Most of my wardrobe represented my failure to see our relationship for what it was. And the one thing in life I try my best to avoid is failure.

It was bang on eight p.m. when my doorbell rang. I gave myself a quick glance in the full-length mirror in my bedroom. My hair was up in a bun that took me *ages* to appear makeshift and casual. My make-up was impeccable, my perfume subtle but fragrant. I wore my favourite dangly earrings—they were so dangly they almost brushed my shoulders and tinkled when I moved. My dress was worth every penny. It clung to my body in all the right places, making me feel feminine and attractive in a way I had not felt before. Or maybe that's what spending heaps of money on a dress does to you—it makes you want to believe it was worth it.

I opened the front door a short time later to see Grayson standing there looking handsome enough to stop my heart. My breath stalled, and my pulse went a little haywire. He was wearing a light blue blazer teamed with trousers in a navy blue and his shirt was white, highlighting his tanned complexion. His jaw was clean-shaven and his hair still damp from a shower, and I could smell his aftershave, an alluring mix of citrus and wood and country leather.

'Hi,' I said. 'I'll just get my purse and phone.'

He waited politely outside, which impressed me. Seems I wasn't the only one big on manners. I came back to him with purse and phone in hand and a stiff smile on my face.

'How was your day?' I asked.

'Busy. How was yours?'

'Long.'

He stood there looking at me for a long moment.

I smoothed my free hand down the side of my dress. 'Is something wrong?'

He rapid-blinked and smiled lopsidedly. 'You look very beautiful in that dress.'

'Oh, this old thing?' See? I am hopeless at accepting compliments. Not that many come my way, but still.

Grayson's smile informed me I hadn't fooled him one iota. For a moment I thought I might have left the price tag on, but no, I recalled I had snipped it off with some scissors.

'Love the earrings.'

I lifted my hand to toy with one. 'A client made them for me. They're my favourite pair. I only wear them on special occasions.' I suddenly realised what I'd just said and clamped my lips shut, furious for letting slip how much I was looking forward to this evening with him. I could feel my cheeks heating enough to put the sun out of a job. 'I—I mean, not that this evening is anything special, it's just I haven't been out in a while. I'm usually so busy with Niamh and work and stuff...'

I grimaced at the way I was running off at the mouth like a gauche teenager.

Grayson lifted his hand from by his side and gently flicked my left earring with his finger, the soft tinkling sound in the silence as loud as a gong. 'Are you nervous about having dinner with me?'

'No.' I could feel my blush deepening as if someone had turned up the thermostat in my body. My breathing was a little erratic, my pulse racing. 'Why would I be nervous?'

His hand went back to his side. 'You're entering enemy territory.'

'I—I am?'

His crooked smile tilted a little further. 'That's how you see me, isn't it? As the enemy?'

'Well, we're not exactly friends. We're business rivals.'

'The two aren't mutually exclusive.'

Somehow, I couldn't envisage him being a close friend to me. I had no doubt he would make a good one, but I needed to keep my distance.

'I have enough friends.' Not quite true. I lost a few friends when I broke up with my ex. People always take sides in messy breakups. And with my caring responsibilities with my mother and sister over the years, friends had often simply drifted away because I was so rarely available to hang out with them. I wouldn't describe myself as lonely, though. I am too self-sufficient for that. I have taught myself not to need people.

'You're never going to forgive me for winning that award, are you?'

I hated that he knew how much I had coveted that wretched award. It made me seem petty and childish, a sore loser.

'It wasn't that big a deal.'

'If it's any comfort, I think you should've won it.'

I looked up at him in surprise. 'Really?'

His expression was set in more serious lines. 'The McClean project was a difficult one and you handled it with a high level of creativity and skill.'

'But they gave the award to you.'

He shrugged one broad shoulder. 'You win some, you lose some. Awards don't mean much to me these days. They look good on the CV, but I don't need them to boost my ego. I know I'm good at what I do.'

I let out a tiny sigh. 'I envy your confidence...'

'You have no reason to doubt your ability.'

I gave a twist of a smile. 'That's two in the space of minutes.'

'Two what?'

'Compliments.'

His eyes held mine for a long interval. I found it impossible to look away. My heart was banging like a tribal drum, so too my pulse. I could feel its echo between my legs, an intimate beat that stirred my primal drives into restlessness.

'I could make it three, but you'd probably slap my face.' His voice was deep and husky, and it made my pulse race even more.

'Are you flirting with me?'

He gave another crooked smile. 'I'm trying not to, but you look good enough to eat in that dress. Speaking of eating—we'd better get going. I don't want the dinner I left cooking to set off the smoke alarm.'

I went with him to his car, which was parked outside my townhouse. I wasn't worried about his cooking setting off the fire alarm. My simmering body was probably going to do that all by itself.

Grayson pulled up in front of a gorgeous eighteen-forties mansion in Kensington and I had to stop myself from drooling. The five-storey house was white with a black wrought iron fence, which matched the iron lace of the long slim balcony that ran the width of the building on the second level. There were four topiary spheres in pots situated on the balcony and small lime-green neatly trimmed pines were in the front garden in a window box that jutted out from a window above the lowest level. Seriously, I was feeling like Elizabeth Bennet on first setting eyes on Pemberley in Jane Austen's *Pride and Prejudice*. Maybe I needed to rethink how much I disliked Grayson Barlowe...but *did* I dislike him?

My feelings were a little confused on that front. I wanted to dislike him. I wanted to keep him at a distance. I wanted to see him as my enemy because of the history between our families. But somehow it was becoming harder and harder to summon up that intense level of dislike. I had witnessed the care and concern he had for his brother. I had heard him laugh. I had felt his touch on my shoulder and my hand. And my earring. I could only imagine what it would feel like to have his lips press down on mine.

I pulled myself back into line. Kissing him was out of the question. It must *not* happen.

Because I was staring open-mouthed at his house for so long, I hadn't realised Grayson had exited the car and was now around my side, opening the door for me. I stepped out of the car with as much grace as I could muster, but my high heels caught on something and I pitched forward. I would have face planted on the footpath if he hadn't caught me by the arm. His fingers gripped me, and a shiver ran down my spine at the tensile strength in his stabilising hold.

'Are you okay?'

'I'm fine… I think…'

He kept hold of me until I was safely on the footpath. When his hand finally fell away from my arm I surreptitiously ran my hand over where his fingers had gripped me, and something in my belly softly unfolded like a flower opening its petals.

He laid a hand lightly to my elbow as we walked up the steps leading to the front door. I didn't object because, right then, I didn't think I was capable of walking unaided. My legs were feeling like soggy noodles and my heart was still hammering enough to send a cardiologist into a panic.

Grayson opened the front door, and I stepped past him to enter the Italian marble entrance hall. I swept my gaze over every angle, noting how the light came in, the sweep of the grand staircase, the priceless antiques and artworks that made the mansion such a showcase of design and upmarket taste without being too over the top.

'Nice digs,' I said.

'Thanks.'

'Have you lived here long?'

'Ten years.' Grayson closed the front door. 'Come through to the sitting room while I check on dinner.'

'Don't spoil my enjoyment of watching a man cook. Or did you get your housekeeper to rustle something up?'

He gave a rueful smile. 'My housekeeper is a terrible cook.'

'Then why do you keep her?'

'Him.'

I blinked in surprise. 'Him?'

'Romeo is great at cleaning and gardening, but he's got a way to go before I'll let him loose in the kitchen.'

'Romeo is Italian?'

'Yep, I met him when I was in Florence. He was looking for work, so I brought him home with me. He helps Ethan too. He lives downstairs but he's out tonight.'

I followed Grayson to the kitchen at the back of the house. 'So how old is he?'

'Nineteen but he's been here a couple of years now.'

'And his family were okay with him moving to London?'

Grayson pulled out a kitchen stool for me to sit on. 'He doesn't have any family, or at least none he wants to have anything to do with. He was homeless when I met him, begging for food.'

'Gosh, that's terrible. Poor kid. But great that you stepped in. But you were taking a risk inviting a teenager you didn't know to come and live with you.'

'I'm a pretty good judge of character. Besides, doesn't everyone deserve a chance to prove themselves?'

'I guess…' Somehow, I hadn't pictured Grayson as the sort of man to take in a homeless kid. Or maybe I had always been so heavily biased against him, I hadn't seen the admirable qualities he possessed. I do my bit for charity, and I can't walk past a homeless person without giving them money or buying them food, but I had never considered inviting someone to live with me. But then, I had the care and safety of my sister to consider. Or at least I had until now.

Grayson opened a cupboard where glassware was kept. 'What would you like to drink? Wine? Champagne? G and T?'

'White wine would be lovely, thanks.'

He opened a bottle of French white wine and poured some into two glasses, handing me one across the wide bench. 'Here you go. Cheers.'

'Cheers.' I clinked my glass against his, but I wasn't sure exactly what we were toasting. 'So, do you do all your own cooking?'

'I eat out a fair bit.'

'Yes, well, of course you do, being a playboy and all.'

He frowned and put down his wineglass. 'You know, the press like to paint a certain picture of me that's not always accurate.'

I toyed with the stem of my wineglass. 'How long do your relationships last?'

'Not long.'

'Why?'

'Because I'm not interested in settling down.' He turned away to stir something on the hob. I studied his strong back and shoulders and had to stop myself drooling again. The food smelled amazing, but it was his physique that got my attention.

I took another sip of wine. 'But you can't deny you've had a lot of lovers.'

'There're no notches on my bedpost. You can check if you like.'

'I think it's best if I stay out of your bedroom, don't you?' Two sips of wine and I was tipsy. Or maybe it was his company that was making me lose my head.

He turned around and met my gaze and a hot tingle rolled down my back and fizzed like a firework at the base of my spine. 'You don't seem the type of woman to get involved with a playboy.' He glanced at my empty ring finger before returning his gaze to mine. 'Or do you crave a walk on the wild side now you've set yourself free?'

I could not tear my gaze away from his if I tried. But then I didn't try. I wanted to stare into that blue-grey gaze and totally lose myself. Lose my sensible, rational side and play with capital D danger. There was a powerful energy crackling between his gaze and mine, an energy I could feel travelling through my body like a high voltage current. His gaze drifted to my mouth, and I couldn't stop myself from sweeping the tip of my tongue over my lips.

'How wild are you?' Was that my voice? That husky femme fatale voice I had never heard come from my mouth before.

Grayson walked around to my side of the kitchen island bench. My heart rate ratcheted up with every slow and purposeful step he took towards me. He took the wineglass from my fingers and set it down in front of me with an audible clunk that sent a shockwave of lust through my body. He swung me up on the stool so I was face to face with him, his legs either side of mine, effectively caging me. He didn't touch me, but he was close enough to and that was enough to send my senses reeling. I craved his touch like a drug addict craves their next hit.

'I—I thought we weren't going to do this.' My voice was thready and breathless.

'What do you think I'm going to do?'

'Kiss me?' I framed it as a question, almost like a command, only realising my mistake when he glanced at my mouth again.

'Is that what you want me to do?' His voice went down another couple of semitones.

I moistened my lips and swallowed. 'I'm tempted.'

A gleam of satisfaction shone in his gaze. 'So, what are we going to do? Stick to the rules or get up close and personal?'

'You're pretty close right now.'

'I can get closer.' The gravel-rough edge to his tone sent a wave of scorching heat through my lower body. Grayson lifted his hand to my face, one of his fingers tracing the curve of my right cheek all the way down to the base of my chin. His touch was light and yet electric and every nerve in my face reacted.

I closed my eyes as he sent his finger on a slow exploration of my lips. I tried to hold back a whimper of pleasure but wasn't entirely successful. No one had ever touched me with such exquisite tenderness, with such slow deliberation. I had no way of handling it other than to enjoy it. My lips tingled with each faineant brush of his fingers, my breath stop-starting as I tried to control my reaction. I had never considered myself a particularly sensual person. I hadn't hated sex with my other partners, but I hadn't loved it either.

But I sensed I would love it with Grayson Barlowe.

He would make sure of it.

He tipped up my chin with one of his fingers and I opened my eyes to find his gaze locked on mine. 'If we kiss, it's just a kiss, understood?'

'What? You think if we kiss I'll start sending out wedding invitations in the next post?'

He smiled at my attempt at humour. 'Don't even think about it. I have no plans to get married.'

'Nor do I.'

His hand came up to rest against the base of my neck. I had no idea my skin was so sensitive at my hairline, no idea how wonderful it felt to have a man's fingers splay into my hair. A shiver passed over my scalp like a Mexican wave and my insides coiled and tightened with sudden savage lust. His eyes lowered to my mouth and I held my breath, my heart beating so heavily I was sure he could feel it, let alone hear it. He brought up his other hand and traced a slow outline of my mouth with a lazy finger.

'You have a beautiful mouth.' His voice was low and

deep and sexy, so sexy it made every millimetre of my skin lift in a shiver.

I couldn't take my own eyes off his mouth. The shape of it fascinated me, the sensually shaped contours making me ache to feel them moving against my lips. I lifted my hand to his face and traced his mouth as he had traced mine, another wave of lust rolling through me as the rasp of his stubble grazed my finger.

'You're not burning dinner, are you?' My voice was barely above a whisper, my thumping heartbeat loud enough for the neighbours to hear.

Grayson gently tugged me off the stool so I was standing in front of him, close enough for our hips to meet. A bomb went off in my blood, an explosion of heat and fire that left no corner of my body unaffected. I yearned to move even closer, to press my pelvis harder against his, to feel the contour of his body rising against me. It was an urge, a primal drive I suddenly couldn't control. I placed my hands on his trim hips and leaned into him, a gasp escaping my lips as the heat from his hard body met mine.

His mouth came down and captured mine in a kiss that sent a shockwave of ferocious need through my flesh. I could feel the pulsing ache of my lower body, a secret ache that silently begged to be assuaged. His tongue demanded entry to my mouth and I opened to him on a breathless whimper of heady, blissful pleasure. Hot streaks of longing flashed through the core of my being, leaving fire trails in their wake. I was burning for him, on fire for the possession of his body.

Grayson shifted position to gain better access to my

mouth, his lips hard and yet soft and utterly irresistible. His hands came up to cradle my face and I shivered from head to foot at the sheer magic of his touch.
His tongue played with mine in a cat and mouse caper
that sent my senses reeling and my pulse racing off the
charts. It was a kiss of dominance and, God help me, I
submitted to it. Totally. How could I not? I was becoming addicted to the flick and dart of his tongue; I was
captivated by the firm exploration of his lips and the
explosive energy that generated between us.

His hands moved from cradling my face to hold
me by the hips. He pulled me closer to his body and
I nearly came on the spot. He was hard. Rock-hard.
So hard I could almost feel the thundering throb of
his blood. He lifted his mouth off mine and looked
down at me with his blue-grey eyes glinting with raw,
earthy lust.

'I was so determined to keep my hands off you.' His
tone had a generous hint of ruefulness and his mouth
twisted. 'Like that was ever going to work.'

I lifted one of my hands to the back of his neck and
played with the ends of his dark hair, my breasts pushing against his broad chest, my lower body humid and
wet with want. 'You're proving rather irresistible as
well.'

His eyes darkened as they held mine. 'If we were
both sensible, we'd stop this right now before things
get out of control.'

'Do you want to stop?' I could not believe how forward I was being. I'm no prude and I'm all for women
owning their body's desires and needs, but practically

begging Grayson to make love to me was a little out of character to say the least. He was my enemy, my rival. I didn't even like him…all that much.

But my body had other ideas. It liked him very much indeed. It desired him like it had desired no one else. It throbbed and ached and pulsed for his touch. I thought I was possibly going to *die* if he didn't kiss me again.

Grayson's hands tightened their hold on my hips and a shiver coursed down my spine. 'If we do this, it's only going to be once. To get it out of our system, understood?' His tone was adamant but something about the scorching heat in his gaze made me wonder if he was saying it more for his own benefit, not mine.

I raised my eyebrows in a playful manner. 'What if once isn't enough?'

'It will be.' He let out a short harsh-sounding breath. 'It will have to be.'

'Because?'

'Because I have a rule about mixing business with pleasure.'

I lowered my hand from playing with his hair and laid it flat against his chest instead. His heart was thumping hard underneath my palm and a frisson of delight rushed through me to think he was as attracted to me as I was to him. The sense of power it gave me went to my head. I straightened his shirt collar and then gave his chest a dismissive little pat and stepped back to put some distance between us. I had to before I was tempted to cross a line I hadn't crossed before.

'It's a good rule. But I have a rule as well.'

'What is it?' There was a guardedness about his

expression—a slight narrowing of his gaze, a tensing of his features.

I locked my gaze on his, determined not to be the first to look away. 'I don't do one-night stands.'

One side of his mouth lifted in a cynical fashion, but I was sure I saw genuine regret in his eyes. 'Then it seems we're at an impasse.'

'Because you won't change your mind.' I framed it as a statement instead of a question.

Grayson closed the distance between us and then picked up a loose strand of my hair and wound it around his finger, tethering me to him in a deliciously scalp-tugging, skin-tingling way. 'Are we a case of immovable object meets unstoppable force?' His voice was lightly teasing but there was a deadly seriousness in his gaze.

'Could be.' Another shiver rolled down my spine as his finger wound a little tighter. He was stirring in me a wild and reckless want that threatened to get out of control.

He slowly bent his head and lowered his mouth to the edge of mine. His warm breath skated across my lips and my insides quaked with longing. 'What if we just do this then?' He brushed his lips against mine, sending volcanic heat straight to my core.

I tried to suppress a whimper of delight but didn't quite manage it. 'F-fine...' I shuddered as his lips touched down on mine again. A feather-light touch that was no less arousing than his firmer kiss earlier. My lips tingled for more contact and my body throbbed hard and fast and furiously with need.

'It's been a long time since I kissed someone without it going any further.' His lips went on an exquisite exploration of my right cheek, his tongue darting out to stroke my skin, making my legs all but fold beneath me. My bones were turning to liquid, my ligaments loosening, my muscles melting.

I clutched at the front of his shirt, my mouth so close to his I could feel the soft waft of his breath against my lips. 'The self-discipline will be good for you.' Even if it was proving torturous for me.

He grunted in wry agreement and then his lips went to the side of my neck, his stubble grazing my skin in a toe-curling manner. 'You smell amazing.' His voice was lower than I had ever heard it, low and husky as if it was coming from beneath the floorboards.

I tilted my head to one side, the feel of his lips moving against the skin of my neck sending flickers of delight through my body. My dangly earring tinkled as he stroked his tongue against the cartilage of my ear. How was I going to resist him when he kissed and caressed me so exquisitely? I had never been so worked up before. It was like there was a unique alchemy between us, a chemical, combustible reaction that sent shockwaves through my female flesh.

'Grayson?'

He straightened to look down at me, his hands resting on my hips. 'Time to stop?'

I didn't want to stop but I had to exhibit some measure of self-control. I wrinkled my nose. 'Can you smell something burning?'

Grayson let out a swearword and released me to

check on the dinner. I let out a breath and tried to get my reeling senses back in order. I watched him move about the kitchen and did all I could to keep my hands off him. It would be so easy to close the distance between us and finish what we had started. But he was only offering a one-night stand and I had no intention of becoming one of his casual lovers.

But I wanted him and that was a problem. A problem I wasn't sure I knew how to handle. I was tempted to sleep with him to do as he said—to get it out of our system. But I had a feeling one night with him would not help in that regard but rather make me want him more. Have you ever tried to eat one piece of popcorn? Not possible, right?

One kiss from Grayson's firm mouth had stirred in me a desire for more.

Much more.

CHAPTER SIX

Grayson picked up the wine bottle that was sitting on the table during our dinner. 'Would you like some more wine?'

I put my hand over the top of my glass. 'No, thanks. I need to keep a clear head.'

His half-smile sent a shiver down my spine, leaving a pool of molten heat at the base. 'Because of what happened before dinner?'

I looked at his mouth and something in my stomach turned over. I could feel heat flooding into my cheeks and my lips began to tingle at the memory of his kiss. 'You know how you said you haven't kissed someone before without it leading to sex? Well, I haven't kissed anyone since my ex.'

He frowned. 'Do you regret breaking it off?'

'No, not at all. We weren't right for each other, but I couldn't see it.' I twisted my mouth and went on, 'I guess I didn't want to see it. There's a point in a relationship where you put so much time and effort in to keeping it on track that getting out of it seems more difficult than continuing it.' I shifted my wineglass and added, 'I think that's what happened with my parents too. My mother stayed with my father far longer than she should have.'

'They weren't happy?'

'Not particularly. They bickered a lot.' I frowned as I thought about my childhood before my father's death. Summoning up memories of my father made a crushing weight of sadness form in my chest. I had so many good memories of him and yet there were some shadowy ones I didn't like recalling. Memories of him shouting at my mother, slamming doors, and disappearing for days on end. 'I loved my dad, but he could be difficult at times.' I pushed a tiny crumb under the rim of my plate and then chanced a glance at Grayson. 'He was a gifted architect and loved his work. It totally consumed him at times. But I wonder if he was as honest with my mother about how things were going financially.'

'I know you were young at the time, but what were you told about the merger?'

I held his clear grey-blue gaze. 'My mother told me your grandfather had pulled out of the merger at the last minute. There was some disagreement about the terms of the deal and consequently my father lost thousands of pounds. After his death, we were left with virtually nothing. My mother blamed your grandfather to the day she died.'

Grayson was silent for a long moment, a muscle pulsing in the lower quadrant of his jaw. 'My grandfather was a hard-nosed businessman, but he wouldn't have ripped off your father.' The implacable edge to his tone made me uneasy. Had I got it wrong? For all these years I had blamed Grayson's grandfather for the destruction of my father. What if there was another side to the story?

'So, what happened to all my father's money?'

There was a long silence. A painful silence as the reality started to dawn on me. Grayson was not going to besmirch my father's memory by telling me the truth—I had to stumble on it myself. Some of those shadowy memories from my childhood surfaced—memories of arguments about money I didn't understand at the time. But I was starting to understand them now. It was a painful collision between the face-saving narrative my mother had spun and the cold, hard truth.

I swallowed a lightbulb in my throat. The same lightbulb that had just flicked on in my head. 'My father didn't have any money, did he?'

Grayson simply sighed as if he was reluctant to add to my pain at finding out my adored father was not the man I had thought him to be.

'For all these years, I've blamed your grandfather...' My voice trailed off as my mind drifted to all the conversations I'd had with my mother after my father's death. She hadn't got on with him while they were married, but in death she had glorified him, making him out to be the perfect husband. But I vaguely remember the arguments about his recklessness with money. Arguments that were conducted behind closed doors, so Niamh and I weren't privy to the details. In a child's mind, a parent can do no wrong, especially when they were a fun parent who was so generous with gifts and words of praise. But now I was seeing my father through an adult's eyes and what I had taken for spontaneity and generosity back then may well be seen as a lack of maturity and responsibility now.

I pushed back my chair and rose from the table, crossing my arms over my body, trying to contain my burgeoning emotions. 'I wish my mother had told me the truth after my father died. Surely, she owed me that?'

Grayson came up behind me and placed his hands on the tops of my shoulders. His touch was warm and grounding, and I was grateful for it as my world was still spinning on its axis.

'I'm sorry you had to find out this way.' His voice was deep and full of compassion, and it made it harder for me to find my dislike of him. But did I dislike him at all now? If his explosive kiss hadn't been enough to flick the switch on my feelings, his care and consideration over the last few minutes was enough to send me into emotional territory I had never been before. Not even with my ex.

I turned in his hold and looked up into his concerned gaze. 'You weren't going to spell out my father's wrongs, were you?'

His mouth twisted in a rueful fashion. His hands remained lightly on top of my shoulders, and I did nothing to move away. 'It's hard when those we love and admire the most let us down.'

'Your father too, huh?'

Grayson gave a grim movement of his lips. 'I was always closer to my grandfather, to be honest. My father wasn't and isn't reliable. He promised and didn't deliver. My grandfather, on the other hand, was honourable and true to his word.'

My gaze drifted to his mouth seemingly of its own volition. 'I'm sorry for thinking such bad thoughts about him all this time.'

Grayson smiled a lopsided smile and gave my shoulders a gentle squeeze. 'You were a kid. You believed what you were told. He wouldn't have held it against you.'

'I wonder why my mother allowed me to believe my father was betrayed so badly by your grandfather. I mean, she didn't have the most loving relationship with him. They fought all the time. But after he died, it was a different story. He was the most amazing husband in the world, blah blah blah.'

'Most mothers like to protect their kids from uncomfortable truths,' Grayson said. 'Grief can stir up a host of emotions, guilt being one of them.'

There was a beat or two of silence. A silence so intense I could hear the rustle of his shirt as he lifted his hand to my face. His fingertip stroked the curve of my cheek, and I shivered in reaction. What was it about his touch that put my senses on high alert?

'You're touching me again.'

'So I am.' His finger travelled down to my mouth, and I let out a soft gasp of pleasure as his finger brushed across the surface of my lips. 'Would you like me to stop?'

'No.' My voice was soft and breathless, and my self-control was missing in action. I moved closer to him at the same time he moved closer to me. Our bodies collided with a combustible impact I felt in every cell in my flesh. Scorching heat flashed through me, lighting spot fires in my blood. Our mouths came together in a desperate kiss, a kiss that spoke of primal yearnings that were no longer under control. His tongue met mine and the bottom dropped out of my stomach. His tongue was insistent, as urgent and passionate as mine. I could not get enough of his taste. I could not get close enough to the hard contours of his body. My blood was boiling with lust and there was nothing I could do about it.

'You have to tell me to stop.' Grayson's voice had a rough edge that sent another shudder ricocheting through my body.

'Maybe I don't want you to stop,' I said in a husky whisper, sweeping my tongue across his lower lip. 'Maybe I want you to make love to me.'

He held me in a tight grip, his fingers almost biting into the flesh of my upper arms. 'You'd agree to a one-night stand?'

I linked my arms around his neck, pressing my lower body to the burgeoning heat and hardness of his. 'Maybe one night won't be enough for you.' I injected my tone with flirty playfulness but inside I was praying he wouldn't settle for one night, that he would want more than a casual encounter. Not a long-term commitment by any means, just a little fling to scratch the itch, so to speak. And what an itch it had become. It was a fever in my blood and, if his hard body pressing against me was any indication, it was raging in his as well.

His eyes blazed with longing and my self-esteem

rose a few notches higher than it had ever been before. Had anyone looked at me with such raw naked lust? Had anyone made me feel more desirable? More beautiful and feminine? Not in this lifetime.

'One night. I can't promise more than that.' There was a hint of regret in his tone, and it made me even more determined to get him to change his mind.

I toyed with the ends of his hair at the back of his head, my chest pressed tightly against his. 'Then we'd better make the most of it.' I pressed my mouth to his but within a heartbeat he took control of the kiss. His lips crushed mine beneath his, the passion firing between us like highly flammable fuel. My spine turned to liquid and my insides coiled tight with need. His hands came up to frame my face, his lips still moving against mine with molten heat. His tongue commanded entry and I opened to him, my lower body tingling at the anticipation of welcoming his intimate invasion.

'God, I want you so bad,' he groaned against my mouth, his hands going to my hips, holding me close to his arousal.

'I want you too.' I was barely capable of speech, my breathing was so hectic, my pulse off the scale.

Grayson dragged his mouth off mine and grasped my hands in his, holding me apart from his body. 'Not here. I want you in my bed.'

I had almost forgotten we were still in the dining room with the remains of our dinner still on the table. I waved a hand vaguely in the direction of the table. 'Shouldn't we clear up first?'

'Later.' His mouth came down firmly on mine and I

was left in no doubt of his priorities. Clearing up after dinner was clearly nowhere near the top of his list of must-do tasks.

I barely remembered how we got to his bedroom on the next floor. Our journey passed in a blur of kisses and caresses that made the blood sing in my veins. He shouldered open the door of his bedroom and I followed him inside. He allowed me a few moments to glance around at the luxurious furnishings, not to mention the king-sized bed with its snowy white linen and array of pillows.

'Nice bedroom,' I said.

'It does the job.'

I arched a brow. 'For sleeping and sex?'

'Just sleeping.'

I frowned in puzzlement. 'What do you mean?'

He closed the door with a soft click, his eyes dark and lustrous. 'You're the first women I've brought home.'

'You've lived here ten years and never slept with a lover here? Are you flipping serious?'

He began to undo the buttons of his shirt, his eyes still holding mine in a lock that sent a delicate shiver rolling down the backs of my legs. 'I don't like sharing my space with strangers.' He shrugged himself out of his shirt and tossed it over the back of a carved walnut chair.

'So, you only sleep with strangers?'

'Mostly.'

'You know, a psychologist would have plenty to say about that.'

He gave a nonchalant shrug. 'They might have plenty to say about you remaining celibate since you dumped your ex.'

'Yes, well, I've been busy with work and stuff.'

He came over to me and lifted my chin with his finger. 'You can change your mind, you know.'

'About sleeping with you?'

His eyes glinted. 'I'm not sure we'll do much sleeping.'

I drew in a shaky breath, my body unravelling at the potent closeness of him. 'Good to know. I would hate to waste a minute in your bed snoring my head off.'

He grinned and reached for me, tugging me against his body. 'Why don't you get undressed?'

'Why don't you undress me?' Wow, who was this bold and brazenly flirty woman? I had morphed into someone else, someone I didn't recognise as myself. But I liked the sense of power it gave me to be open about what I wanted.

'With pleasure. Turn around.'

I did as he commanded. His hand went to the zip at the back of my dress, and he rolled it down slowly, so slowly I was quaking and shuddering by the time he pulled it to the small of my back. His warm fingers caressed my bare skin before he eased the straps off my shoulders, the dress falling in a black silky puddle at my feet. I was wearing a black strapless push-up bra and matching lace knickers and my high heels.

Grayson turned me to face him, his eyes feasting on my form, and I could not remember a time when I had felt sexier and more feminine or more powerful. 'You are so damn gorgeous.' There was a breathless quality to his voice that delighted me no end. Even though I knew he had seen countless women in nothing but their underwear or even less, I could feel myself glowing from his praise.

I placed my hands on his naked chest, revelling in the texture of his skin and the light dusting of his chest hair. 'Are you going to take your trousers off or will I do it for you?'

His hooded gaze smouldered. 'Feel free.'

My hands went to the waistband of his trousers, my heart thrashing around in my chest. I tried not to fumble but I was so turned on my fingers would barely co-operate. I finally undid the snap button and took the toggle of his zip between my finger and thumb. I gave him an arch look. 'I wonder what I'll find under here?'

'Only one way of finding out.'

I rolled the zip down and gazed in wonder at the considerable tenting of his underwear. My lower body grew damp with longing and my pulse pounded. 'Mmm... impressive.'

His hands came up to cup my breasts and even though I was still wearing a bra, I could feel the magical heat of his touch through the barrier of lace. 'I want to touch you all over.' His voice was gravel-rough, and it sent a shockwave of ferocious lust through my body.

'I want to touch you too.' I stroked my fingertip down the length of him through his underwear, and he shuddered and groaned.

His hands went to the clasp of my bra. 'May I?'

'Please do.'

He unclipped my bra and it fell away from my body and dropped to the floor. His eyes drank in my shape and then his hands gently caressed my breasts, sending shivers through my flesh. My nipples were tight buds, and he lowered his mouth to them in turn, the delightful sensations rippling through my body. He stroked his tongue over my breast, a light, barely touching caress, but it sent tongues of flame through my blood.

I whimpered in pleasure as his lips and tongue explored every inch of my breasts, never had they been subjected to such intimate attention.

Finally, he straightened and looked me directly in the eye. 'You still want to do this?'

'I do. You?'

His smile was crooked, and he tugged me against him, pelvis to pelvis. Heat coursed through my body in a scorching wave that made my legs tremble. 'What do you think?'

'I'm not sure I'm capable of thinking right now,' I said, relishing the rock-hard bulge of him against me. 'You've scrambled my brains.'

His mouth came down to just above mine, his warm breath teasing my lips. 'You've done a pretty good job on mine too.' And then his mouth sealed mine in a kiss that set my lips on fire.

But kissing wasn't enough for either of us. Within seconds his mouth was back on my right breast, licking and sucking and pleasuring my naked flesh until I was breathless with need.

Grayson walked me backwards to his bed and somewhere along the way I kicked off my high-heeled shoes.

His shoes and socks and trousers and underwear landed on the floor nearby. He laid me on the bed and stood looking down at me. I should have felt exposed and vulnerable under the searing heat of his gaze but instead I felt powerfully female.

'I need to get a condom.' He bent down to retrieve his wallet from the bedside table, deftly removing the protection from its packet and applying it to his swollen length. I could not take my eyes off him if I tried.

He came down beside me on the bed, leaning his weight on one elbow as he stroked his other hand down the length of my body, from my breasts to my thighs and back again. It was a slow, leisurely movement, as if he had all the time in the world, but my body was screaming for him in a silently throbbing ache between my legs that was almost like pain.

Grayson hooked one leg over one of mine, his mouth going back to my breast. I arched my back and gave myself up to the sensation of his lips and tongue on my skin. He moved his mouth down to the underside of my breast, his tongue moving in a slow stroke that made my toes curl and my desire for him skyrocket. He moved his mouth to the sensitive skin just below my ear and I shivered as his lips fluttered against me.

'You probably have no idea how long I've wanted to do this,' he said in a growly voice that sent another wave of molten heat to my core.

'Really?' To say I was a little shocked would be an understatement. I angled my head to look at him. 'You're very good at keeping your cards close. Just about every time I've ever looked at you, you were frowning.'

He pressed a brief kiss to my mouth with just enough pressure to make my pulse race. 'I'm not frowning now.'

I ran a fingertip around the gentle curve of his mouth. 'You don't look half as threatening when you smile. You should do it more often.'

He brushed his thumb across my lower lip, his gaze holding mine. 'So should you.'

I twisted my lips in a self-deprecating manner. 'I had crooked teeth when I was a kid. I guess I forgot how to smile, even when I got them straightened.' I waited a beat and then added, 'But then I didn't have too much to smile about after my dad's death and then Niamh's accident.'

Grayson stroked a wayward strand of hair away from my face, his expression thoughtful. 'I'm sorry life dealt you such a rough hand, but you mustn't blame yourself for either event. You were a kid. Sometimes bad stuff just happens.'

I didn't want to talk about my childhood and was annoyed at myself and embarrassed for bringing it up during such an intimate moment. I placed one of my hands on the side of his face, his light stubble tickling the flesh of my palm. I adopted a playful tone and asked, 'Do you have such deep and meaningful conversations with all your casual lovers?'

A flicker of something crossed his features like a sudden waft off air across a still body of water. 'Not usually.'

'What do you talk about?'

'Not much.'

'The weather?'

'Occasionally.' His gaze went to my mouth and my lips tingled in anticipation.

I brought my hand back down to his chest, laying in flat against his right pectoral muscle. His skin was like hot satin under my hand, and I longed to explore every inch of his body.

'Are you nervous?' His question caught me by surprise, mostly because I didn't think I had shown any sign of nervousness. But sleeping with a new partner was always a little tricky for me. What if I didn't turn them on? What if I made too much noise or not enough? And then there were all the body issues I had tried so hard to dispense with over the years. Somehow Grayson had picked up on my feelings and that was almost as threatening, *more* threatening, than him seeing me naked. I usually avoided emotional vulnerability at all costs. But being with him made me want to expose more of myself, my true self. My secret self.

I chewed at my lower lip, averting my gaze from his probing one. 'It's been a while since I...was with anyone...'

Grayson lifted my chin, so my gaze met his once more. 'Because you're not over your ex?'

I scrunched up my face at the ridiculous notion of me nursing a broken heart over Ryan. How could I ever have thought we had what it took to have a good relationship?

'I was over him the moment he made it clear Niamh

wasn't welcome in our lives going forward.' I sighed and went on, 'I should've seen it a lot earlier, of course, but I ignored the red flags.'

Grayson brushed another strand of hair away from my face. 'A lot of people don't understand how much we love and feel responsible for our less able-bodied siblings. It's more than blood being thicker than water. I don't think a day goes past without me worrying about Ethan's future.'

'Nor me with Niamh.'

He held my gaze for a long beat.

'We can't let them rush into anything they can't undo,' he said. 'A fling is fine; marriage is another thing entirely.'

'Yes, it is, but if we're too against them marrying it could backfire and make them all the more determined.'

His gaze went to my mouth. 'Like what happened with us?' He gave a slow rueful smile and continued, 'I told myself I wasn't going to touch you and look at us now. There's barely a part of our bodies that isn't touching.'

'You're not touching my mouth.'

'I can soon fix that.' He lowered his lips to mine, and I lost myself in the potent heat and fire of his kiss. After a few breathless moments, he broke the kiss to look at me through sexily hooded eyes. 'Anywhere else I've neglected to touch?'

I shivered at the rough edge to his voice and the determined glint in his gaze. 'I think you missed the side of my left breast.'

'I'll see to it right now.' He kissed his way down the side of my neck, covering every inch of my skin with soft fluttering movements of his lips that set my nerves dancing. By the time he came to my left breast, I was whimpering. His touch was so light and yet so electric, stirring my desire for him to fever-pitch.

'And I don't think I touched you here,' he said, moving his mouth down to my belly button.

I sucked in my breath and shuddered as his tongue circled the tiny whorl of my navel. He moved further down to the seam of my body, and I forgot to breathe when his lips and tongue explored my female flesh. Oh, and I forgot to think as well. Sensations I had never experienced before rippled through my body in crashing waves. I panted, I gasped, I cried, and I arched my back in ecstasy as the shockwaves coursed through me.

'Well, that's never happened before,' I said on an expelled breath of wonder.

Grayson shifted position so I was eye to eye with him. He stroked a lazy hand down the flank of my still quivering thigh. 'What do you mean?'

'I've never been able to come like that.' I lowered my gaze a fraction and confessed, 'I always used to pretend.'

He lifted my chin, so my gaze locked on his again. There was no judgement or criticism in his expression but rather a look of gentle compassion that totally ambushed my feelings. I was trying *so* hard not to be infatuated with him, to keep my feelings out of our one-night stand. But it was almost impossible not to open my heart a teensy-weensy crack.

'I'm glad you feel comfortable with me.' He stroked a slow-moving finger across my lower lip, sending tingles to my toes and back.

I threaded my fingers through his hair, my lower body aching for him all over again. 'I've thought of another place you haven't touched me.'

His smouldering gaze sent another wave of searing heat through my core. 'Really? How remiss of me. I must be losing my touch.'

Grayson Barlowe definitely wasn't losing his touch as far as I was concerned, but I was in danger of losing my mind, or worse—my heart. What came next was the most dazzling encounter of my life. He held me as I shuddered through another spectacular orgasm, and I held him as he shuddered through his own powerful release. We lay in each other's arms for a long time afterwards, neither of us speaking, our ragged breathing gradually returning to normal the only sound in the silence.

Finally, I found the courage to turn my head and look at him lying beside me. He had his eyes closed but as if he sensed my gaze resting on him, he turned his head and met my gaze.

'Hey,' he said in a gravel-rough tone, the fingers of his left hand entwining with the fingers of my right hand. He gave my fingers a gentle squeeze. 'You okay?'

'Why wouldn't I be okay? I've just had multiple orgasms for the first time ever.' I injected a playful note to my tone but inside I was still reeling from the passion that had transpired between us. The sort of passion

I had never experienced before. Passion that left my body singing and tingling and fizzing in the afterglow.

Grayson rolled onto his side and leaned his weight on one elbow, his gaze still trained on mine. 'You're a very responsive lover.' He slowly circled one of my nipples with his finger and I trembled anew.

'Who knew two enemies could get it on with such success?' I was still determined to keep my playful persona in place, but it felt odd, like wearing a jumper back to front and inside out.

His finger traced a circle around my other nipple, and I bit back a tiny gasp of pleasure. 'Is that how you see us? As enemies?' he asked.

I gave a little shrug and shifted my gaze from the probing heat of his. 'We're not exactly friends, are we?'

There was a long beat of silence.

'We might have to be if Ethan and Niamh stay together,' Grayson said. 'Will that be a problem for you? I mean, after tonight?'

I worked hard to school my features into impassivity. 'No. That was the deal, right? One night only.'

His gaze drifted to my mouth and my pulse began to pound. 'I should take you home.'

I had no idea of the time, but I knew it was way past my bedtime. 'You should.'

'But I'm not going to.'

'Oh, really?'

His eyes glinted with unbridled lust that reignited my own. 'I'm not finished with you yet.' And before I could think of a response, his mouth came down on mine.

CHAPTER SEVEN

I WOKE TO the sound of the morning chorus of birds in the trees outside Grayson's bedroom window and the hum of traffic and it took me a moment to reorient myself. The bed was empty beside me, but I could see the imprint of Grayson's head on the pillow next to mine. My stomach hollowed out at the memory of all we had done together during the night. I stretched my legs out against the silky sheets and breathed in the scent of him like I was breathing in a potent drug I couldn't resist.

But I *had* to resist.

We had made an agreement and I was not going to be the one who begged for him to change it.

I threw off the sheet covering me and began to search for my clothes. They weren't on the floor where I had last seen them but were now neatly folded on the walnut chair. I snatched them up and put them on with as much haste as I could muster, given I'd only had a couple of hours sleep, if that. There wasn't time for a shower, although I would have loved one. I had to put my game face on and get the hell out of Grayson's house before I was tempted to pop a toothbrush in his bathroom.

I opened the bedroom door to leave just as he came

in carrying a tray with a mug of coffee and some toast on it. I was in such a rush, I collided with the tray and the mug toppled over, splashing coffee all over the front of my dress. Lucky it was black—the dress, not the coffee, although that too was black—but the coffee was steaming hot, and I yelped and pulled my dress away from my stomach.

'Are you okay?' Grayson asked, putting the tray to one side.

'You could have knocked before you came in,' I said, throwing him a glare so icy it should have frozen him on the spot.

'Last time I checked, it was my bedroom.' His tone was as snippy as mine but then he let out a long uneven breath. 'Sorry. That was uncalled for. Blame it on the lack of sleep.'

'Well, that's your fault too.' I wasn't angry about the coffee. I was angry I was so touched that he'd brought it to me. It didn't seem to fit with the one-night stand arrangement we had made. No one had ever brought me coffee and toast in the morning, not my ex, not even Niamh, mostly because I was always up first.

'Did I burn you?' The concern in Grayson's voice and in his expression dissolved my anger on the spot and opened the teensy-weensy crack in my heart a little further.

I released a sigh. 'No, I overreacted. I'm sorry. You just surprised me, is all.'

He placed a gentle hand on the top of one of my shoulders, his eyes holding mine in such a tender lock my breath caught in my throat.

'You surprised me too.' His voice was deep and husky, and I wasn't completely sure he was talking about the coffee incident or not. Something about the glint in his grey-blue eyes made me wonder if he was recalling every passionate moment we had shared in his bed.

I could feel a blush flowing into my cheeks. Some of those moments in his bed were pretty damn hot. It would probably take me months to forget about them. Years, decades, a lifetime.

'I'm going to be late for work if I don't get a wriggle on. Thank you for…dinner and…erm…' I couldn't finish the sentence and instead forced my lips into a vestige of a smile.

Grayson brought me a little closer, the warm, clean, fresh scent of him making my senses do cartwheels. How could he look so good after so little sleep? 'Are you free tomorrow night?'

I blinked like an owl. 'Why?'

'We should at least put some ideas on the table for Ethan and Niamh's house.'

I had forgotten all about my sister and Ethan's dream house to go with their dream relationship. But would working with Grayson be a dream or a nightmare? Especially now we had done the once-only deed.

'Oh, right, yes, I guess so.'

His hand fell away from my shoulder, but he was still standing within touching distance.

'I figure if we show we're willing to work at it together, it might make them less defensive and more introspective about their plans to marry.'

'Building a house together is a big commitment. Does Ethan have the money to do it? Niamh has some savings but nowhere near enough to—'

'He has plenty of money. I oversee the bulk of it, but he has the freedom to spend his allowance and the income he gets from working for me as he sees fit. It helps him feel more independent.'

'So, he has a real job in your company? Not just a token position?'

A frown pulled at his brow. 'But of course. He'd have been insulted if I had given him anything less than a real position. He uses some quite complicated computer software with our design team. It takes him a little longer than he'd like but we make allowances for that.'

'He's so lucky to have you in his corner.'

A fleeting shadow passed through his gaze. 'We're lucky to have him. It could've been so different.'

'Yes…' I chewed at my lower lip and lowered my gaze, thinking of how different my sister's life would have been if I hadn't been distracted at the playground. How could one tiny mistake have such irreparable consequences?

Grayson's hand came back down on my shoulder. 'Hey.'

I raised my gaze to mesh with his. I could so easily drown in those eyes. I could so easily lose myself in a fantasy of being with him longer than one night. I could so easily fancy myself falling in love with him. I slammed the brakes on the thought and gave him a stiff smile and turned for the door. 'I must go. I have a client waiting.'

'I'll drive you.'

'No, it'll be quicker on the Tube, but thanks anyway.'

'Ash.' The sound of my name on his lips was almost my undoing. Almost. His voice reverberated in my body, sending my blood racing. But I had to be strong. I had to steel my resolve to keep my emotions out of our 'working' relationship.

I turned to look at him, schooling my features into an impassivity I was nowhere near feeling. 'Yes?'

His eyes were unwavering as they held mine. 'It's probably best if we don't mention what happened be-tween us last night to Ethan and Niamh.'

'Of course.' I made a zipping motion with my hand across my mouth and added, 'No kissing and telling from me.'

One corner of his mouth lifted in a half-smile. 'Where would you like to meet to discuss the project? My office or yours or somewhere neutral?'

'Your office will be fine.'

There was an infinitesimal moment of silence.

'Checking out the enemy territory?' There was a teasing note in his voice and a glint in his eye.

'You betcha,' I said and, giving him a finger wave, turned on my heel and left.

I got home that night after work to find Niamh there. A couple of days ago that would have been entirely normal, but since she had announced her engagement to Ethan she hadn't been home at all.

'Where's Ethan?' I asked, putting my briefcase down. 'I thought you two were inseparable.'

'He has a late gym session today. I thought it would be a good chance for us to hang out and discuss the wedding. I have some ideas for my dress. Do you want to see?' She scrolled through her phone and then turned the screen so I could see it. 'What do you think?'

It was exactly the sort of dress my sister adored—snow-white with lots of tulle, and a classical bridal veil and a train that was metres long.

'Mmm, lovely.'

Niamh tilted her head and studied me for a moment. 'Are you okay?'

'I'm fine.' I ran a hand through my hair and let out a sigh. 'It's been a long day.'

Niamh sat beside me. 'Where were you last night?'

'I was…out.' I didn't want to blatantly lie to my sister, nor did I want to tell her where I had been. I could barely think of where I had been and who I was with and what we had done without a whole-body blush.

'Out *all* night?'

I blinked. 'How did you know I was out?'

She lifted her phone and clicked on the app that tracked her whereabouts and mine. Funny, but I had forgotten she could check where I was at any time of the day. 'You were at Grayson's house last night.'

How could I deny it? She had seen the evidence on her phone. 'Yes, well, we had things to discuss, so—'

'Like what?'

I rose from the sofa and smoothed my hands down my dress. 'You and Ethan for one.'

Niamh's eyes took on a stubborn light. 'You don't

think I'm ready for marriage but I am. I love Ethan and he loves me.'

'I'm happy for you, I really am. It's just I agree with Grayson that you're rushing it a bit.'

'Is it because of his disability or mine?'

'No, of course not. But both must be factored in when you plan your life together. Relationships are hard at the best of times, but you and Ethan have other obstacles most people don't have to face. You have to be realistic about what to expect. You'll need support.'

'But we'll have each other.'

'It might not be enough.'

Niamh picked at her fingers—a nervous habit she had developed since the accident. 'But you'll be around, won't you?' She was looking at her fingers rather than meeting my gaze.

I bent down in front of her where she was sitting on the sofa, and I put my hands on both of her knees. 'I will always be around to support you.'

Her gaze met mine briefly and then shifted back to stare at her hands. 'But what if you fall in love and get married one day?'

'I am *not* going to fall in love and get married.' I may have sounded a little too adamant about the falling in love bit because… Grayson. I couldn't get him out of my mind. I could still feel the press of his lips, the stroke and glide of his hands, the powerful, passionate possession of his male body in mine.

Niamh's gaze met mine. 'Why don't you want to fall in love again? It's the best feeling in the world.'

I took one of her hands and held it in mine. 'I wasn't

in love with Ryan, I just thought I was at the time. That's why it's so important not to rush things.' Who am I to talk after sleeping with Grayson Barlowe last night? If that wasn't rushing things, I don't know what was, but I couldn't help myself.

'You were with Ryan for three years,' Niamh pointed out. 'How could you not have known you weren't in love with him?'

I released her hand and straightened with a sigh. 'On one level, I think I probably did realise it wasn't the real deal, but it took a lot longer than it should have for me to admit it.' I painted a smile on my lips and added, 'Now, enough about the past. Are you staying for dinner?'

Niamh got off the sofa. 'No, I'm meeting Ethan back at the gym, his session will be over soon. I just wanted to pick up a couple of things and check on you.'

I frowned in confusion. I was the one who checked on her, not her on me. 'Why would you feel the need to check on me?'

She gave me an unreadable look that was slightly unnerving, to say the least. 'You spent the night with Grayson Barlowe.' Her tone didn't contain any hint of disapproval or accusation but rather was stating an indisputable fact.

I licked my suddenly dry lips. 'We had dinner and talked about stuff.'

'You must've had a lot to talk about. Every time I checked my phone, you were still there.'

I could feel heat storming into my cheeks and other parts of my body. But I comforted myself that Niamh couldn't have possibly checked her phone all through the night. She had to sleep after all.

'It was a late night,' I said. 'But I managed to avoid getting into an argument with him.'

Niamh tilted her head and narrowed her gaze like an inquisitive bird. 'So, you're starting to like him?'

I pursed my lips for a moment, wondering why my sister was so interested in my feelings about her fiancé's older brother. I expelled a short breath and decided to lure her away from the conversation. 'Do you need a lift to the gym?'

'No, Ethan booked a car for me. It should be here any minute.' She glanced at the rideshare app on her phone and added, 'It's just pulling up outside now.' She came over and gave me a hug and a kiss. 'Can you and Grayson come to dinner on Saturday night? Ethan and I would like to cook for you both.'

My sister wasn't exactly a gourmet cook, but then I had done most of the cooking for her. I only hoped Ethan had a few more skills in the kitchen than her. I suspected they were determined to show they could look after themselves, to convince Grayson and me that they were ready for marriage.

'That sounds…nice.'

'Great. I'll see you then.' Niamh grabbed her tote bag in one hand and another small bag of clothes in the other. 'See you on Saturday. Shall we say eight p.m.?'

'Eight it is.'

I turned up at Grayson's office the following evening, but his secretary informed me he was still with a client.

'He's running over time, but he shouldn't be too much longer. Would you like a drink while you wait?' she asked.

'I'm fine, thank you.' I sat in the waiting area on a butter-soft leather sofa and picked up one of the glossy magazines, leafing through the pages without much concentration. I was trying to be cool and calm about seeing Grayson in a work capacity, but it was hard to get the memory of his intimate touch out of my head. I put the magazine down and glanced around my sur-roundings instead. Fresh flowers were on the glass and marble coffee table next to the stack of magazines. Plush cream carpet covered the floor, and the furniture was modern and stylish and luxuriously comfortable. In fact, so comfortable, I had sunk so far down into the caramel-coloured leather sofa I was wondering how I was going to get out of it.

Soft carpet notwithstanding, I heard Grayson's slightly uneven footsteps coming towards me. I looked up and gave him a formal smile. 'How's your day been?'

'Busy. Yours?'

'So-so.' I tried to rise from the sofa without success.

'Here, let me help you.' He offered me his hand and, with only a moment's hesitation, I placed my hand in his warm strong one. A shiver cascaded down my spine and a flashpoint of heat shot to my core. His fingers were firm around mine—they had to be in order to get me out of the sofa—as he pulled me to my feet. I was standing almost toe to toe with him, and I forgot how to breathe. His aftershave teased my nostrils and

I ached to lean closer to feel his arms go around me as they had the other night.

'Thank you,' I said. 'Erm…you can let go of my hand now. I promise I won't fall over.' I'm not sure I could promise that—my legs weren't feeling too steady. Just being in his presence was enough to undo me, ligament by ligament.

'Oh, sorry.' He pulled his hand away as if he had forgotten he had been holding it. 'Come this way.' On the way past his secretary's desk, he said, 'You can go now, Caroline. Thanks for staying back.'

'No problem,' Caroline said with a smile that encompassed me as well.

I walked with Grayson down the wide corridor to his office. He pushed open the door and indicated for me to go in first and I stepped past him and swept my gaze over the layout. Floor to ceiling windows overlooking the River Thames took up one side of his office, and on another side was floor to ceiling bookshelves. A couple of pieces of artwork hung on one wall and his qualifications hung on the other, but somehow I suspected they were there to reassure his clients that he had the necessary qualifications, rather than from any personal pride in his achievements. I scanned every surface but couldn't see any of the architectural awards he had won.

'Would you like a drink before we get started?'

'Erm, what were you thinking of having?' I asked.

His eyes drifted to my mouth and my stomach somersaulted. 'If I told you that, we might not get any work done.' There was a gleam in his grey-blue gaze that sent another shiver rolling down my spine.

I moistened my suddenly dry lips, my heart picking up its pace. 'I thought we weren't going to mention what happened the other night.' My voice came out a little husky and breathless.

Grayson came to stand right in front of me. He was so close I could smell the sharp citrus notes of his aftershave and the clean laundered fragrance of his shirt. He picked up a loose strand of my hair and tucked it gently behind my ear and my legs almost folded beneath me at his touch. 'We can tweak the rules a bit.'

'We can?'

'If you want to.'

'Do you want to?' My voice was still too breathless, too husky, too desperate.

His eyes moved back and forth between each of mine before dipping once more to my mouth. 'I want to.' His hands came down to settle on my hips and he tugged me closer until I was against the firm wall of his body. 'God, how I want to.' And then his mouth covered mine.

It was a kiss that sent rivers of fire through my blood and flames of need through my body. His tongue flirted with mine in an erotic dance that stirred my senses into overdrive. I was addicted to the taste of him, the hint of mint and good quality coffee that was my new passion.

He groaned as he deepened the kiss, and I made some breathless sounds as his tongue mated with mine. He finally lifted his mouth away, his hands still holding me by the hips. 'I told myself this wasn't going to happen.' His voice was deep and rusty, his breathing almost as ragged as mine. 'I told myself it mustn't happen.'

'We're both consenting adults, right?'

His eyes held mine in an intimate lock. 'I don't do relationships. This can only be a fling.'

'I don't do relationships either.'

He studied me for a beat. 'I couldn't get you out of my mind.'

'Nice to know I left a lasting impression.'

He gave a crooked smile and tugged me even closer. I could feel the delicious ridge of his erection and my body secretly prepared itself. 'I want you.'

'I want you too.' I moved against him and added with a sultry smile, 'I'm just better at hiding it.'

He growled against my mouth, and I opened to him again. His kiss was even more passionate, and I was with him all the way. One of his hands slid up my ribcage to settle just below my breast. It was the most exquisite torture to have his hand so close to my tingling flesh. But I liked that about him, that he didn't rush things. He took his time unravelling me, as if it gave him pleasure to pleasure me. Somehow, we managed to get our clothes off, and I was shocked again at how comfortable I was with him seeing me naked. I couldn't hide anything from him, and nor did I want to.

'You are so damn gorgeous,' he said, roving his gaze over my body.

'You look pretty good yourself.' I pressed my lips to the base of his neck and began to work my way down his chest.

His hand came to rest in the small of my back and

I relished the delicious sensation of his long fingers splayed against my lower spine. 'Come back up here. I want to kiss you again.'

We kissed some more but I was becoming impatient. I took him in my hands and stroked his steely length. He groaned and moved against me in pleasure and my inner core grew hot and damp with desire. He tore his mouth away from mine and muttered something about getting a condom. Within moments he was back, condom in place, and I was laid back on his desk and he was between my open thighs. Not to possess me but to subject me to the most glorious attention from his lips and tongue. I closed my eyes and gave myself up to the rapture of it. It was intimate and erotic in a way I had never experienced before. I swear I rattled the pens on his desk when I came. It was an earth-shattering orgasm that swept through my body like a tidal wave. It left no part of me unaffected. My toes curled, my fingertips tingled, my back arched, and my heart threatened to pump its way out of my chest.

I lay gasping on my back on his desk, unable to move, unable to think clearly, unable to find my voice.

Grayson stroked a lazy hand along my thigh, and I shuddered under his caress. 'You looked like you had a good time.'

I leaned up on my elbows to look at him. 'Who knew desk sex could be so much fun?'

'You haven't had desk sex before?'

'No, my experiences in the adventurous sex department are, sadly, quite limited.'

A glint shone in his eyes, and I shuddered again. 'I'll

have to do something about that.' There was an erotic promise in his voice that set my pulse racing.

I scrambled to my feet in front of his desk, and he gathered me close, his mouth meeting mine once more in a spine-tingling kiss that left me in no doubt of how aroused he was. It stoked my own desire again and I was soon whimpering for more than a kiss.

Within a few moments we were lying on the floor in a tangle of limbs. Grayson entered me with a deep guttural groan of pleasure, and I relished the feel of his potent length. He set a slow pace at first, each thrust careful and measured, but I wanted him to lose control, to give in to the powerful urges that he was holding in check. I writhed beneath him, whispering my need for him to go faster, harder, and he increased his pace, carrying me with him on a rollercoaster ride of primal lust. I was aware of every part of his body where it was in contact with mine—his lips on my lips, his chest pressed against my breasts, his hipbones against mine, his intimate possession that stretched me, filled me, thrilled me. The sensations rolled through me, picking me up and tossing me about like a piece of flotsam on a raging sea. I cried out loud at the sheer force of it rippling and then rocking through my flesh. I lifted my hips on his downward thrusts, the connection as electrifying as two powerful currents meeting. Grayson suddenly thrust deeper, pitching forward as his own release powered through him. I held him as he shook and shuddered in my arms, wondering why I had allowed myself to be so short-changed with sex in the past. This was how it was meant to be—a mutual giving and taking of pleasure.

Grayson lay across me, his head buried against the side of my neck. 'Am I too heavy for you?'

'No.' I stroked one of my hands down the length of his spine and he shivered under my touch. I decided I liked the weight of him pinning me to the floor. I liked his legs entangled with mine. I liked everything about making love with him. I liked *everything* about him, which was a problem because I wasn't supposed to allow my feelings free rein during our fling.

After a long moment he propped himself up on his hands to look down at me. 'How about office floor sex? Have you had that before?'

'Nope.'

His sexily hooded eyes went to my mouth. 'I hope I didn't give you carpet burn.'

I linked my hands around his neck and gazed into his eyes. 'If you did, it was worth it.'

His smile made something fall from a height in my belly. 'Roll over and I'll check.'

I turned over and lay my head on my crossed over arms on the floor. Grayson stroked his hands down the length of my back and over my bottom. His touch set every nerve under my skin dancing, and a new flicker of desire ignited between my thighs.

'No, you're all good.'

'Does this massage come with a happy ending?' I adopted a playful tone.

'Do you want one?'

'At the risk of sounding greedy, yes, I do.'

He stroked his hand down from my neck to the curve of my buttocks and I shivered in delight. 'I need to get a new condom first.' He moved away to get one and I lay there tingling in anticipation.

I angled my head to look at him. 'Why are you taking so long?'

He stood looking down at me with lust shining in his eyes. 'I'm enjoying the view.'

Until that point, I hadn't noticed the scar that ran from the top of his thigh to the middle of his left calf muscle. It had faded to white, but it stood out from his tan like a zigzag of lightning.

I rolled over and sat up with my knees bent in front of me. 'Does it still hurt? Your leg, I mean.'

A shadow passed over his face like clouds across the moon. 'Not much.'

'It certainly doesn't hinder your performance in bed or on the desk or on the floor,' I said.

'Good to know.'

A small silence passed.

I rested my chin on my bent knees and bit down on my lower lip. 'Have I killed the mood?'

'What do you think?'

I ran my gaze over his gloriously aroused body and my pulse began to pound. 'I'm thinking no.'

His lips twitched with an almost smile, his eyes dark and gleaming. 'Come here.'

I came. In more ways than one… Just saying…

CHAPTER EIGHT

IN SPITE OF the earth-shattering lovemaking, we did try to get some ideas on the computer screen for Ethan and Niamh's house, but I sensed Grayson's heart wasn't in it. He didn't want their marriage to go ahead, so why would he want to design a house for them?

I pushed away the computer mouse and sat back on the chair he had placed in front of his desk next to his. 'This isn't really working, is it?' I asked.

He scraped his hand through his hair and sighed. 'It's so soon to be planning a house. They didn't know each other six weeks ago.'

'I've said it before—people can have instant connections.'

He turned his head to look at me and my heart fluttered. 'Do you think your sister really is in love with my brother?'

It was a hard question to answer. 'I think she believes she is.'

He pressed his lips together and looked back at the computer screen. 'They haven't given us a detailed enough brief. Normally, I spend a couple of hours or more with a client on a first consult. We iron out any inconsistencies or council or engineering limitations. It saves them time and money to get it right first time.' He waved his hand at the printed sheet on the desk in disgust. 'This looks like Ethan left it to Niamh to decide what goes where. He should know better; he's worked with me long enough.'

'Sometimes men in love do things they would never normally do. I think it's kind of cute, actually.'

Grayson turned his head to look at me again, his forehead creased in his signature frown. 'There's nothing cute about a house that is impractical for people with the kind of disability my brother has.'

'Maybe Niamh doesn't see Ethan's disability. She just sees the man she loves.'

'Or believes she loves.' His tone was rich with cynicism. 'I wonder if she would love him if he didn't have my grandfather's trust fund.'

I pushed my chair back and stood. 'I think it's time we called it a night.'

Grayson turned his chair to face me, his expression shuttered. 'You're angry.'

I blew out a breath of frustration. 'Of course I'm flipping angry. You keep accusing my sister of being a gold-digger. It's so insulting. I know her well enough to know money and status are not things that impress her. She loves Ethan because of who he is as a person and how he makes her feel.'

'But you said, only minutes ago, you thought she only *believes* she loves him.'

My shoulders went down on a sigh. 'Who can say

how anyone really feels? The signs are all there but...'
I left my sentence hanging.

'What signs?'

'People in love want to spend lots of time together.
They look into each other's eyes a lot; they touch and
mirror each other's movements.'

'It's hardly an exact science.'

'No, but it's not without some merit.'

There was a beat or two of silence.

Grayson pushed back his own chair and came to
stand in front of me. His hands reached for mine and
he gave them a gentle squeeze. 'Still angry with me?'

I gave him an upwards glance from beneath my lowered lashes. 'You haven't apologised yet.'

'I'm sorry.'

'Apology accepted.'

He tipped up my chin with his finger and meshed
his gaze with mine. 'Do you want to grab a late dinner somewhere before I take you home?'

My stomach chose that moment to audibly growl,
which made it almost impossible to say I wasn't hungry. 'That would be nice.'

He bent his head to plant a soft kiss on my upturned
mouth. Then he raised his head to lock gazes with me
again. 'We're going to have to be careful when we
have dinner with Ethan and Niamh on Saturday night.
We'll have to make sure we don't show any signs of
being involved.'

'Yes, I know, but Niamh already knows I was at your
house the other night. She tracked me via the app on

her phone. I completely forgot she could do that. I usually keep track of her, not her me.'

Grayson frowned. 'Do you think she suspects anything?'

'I don't think so. I played it pretty cool. I told her we had dinner and talked about stuff. But I do think she's keen for us to like each other because she hates conflict of any sort. It would distress her to think her relationship with Ethan was causing trouble between you and him.'

He placed his hands on my hips and brought me closer. 'It's going to be hard to keep my hands off you.'

I linked my arms around his waist, delighting in the hard contours of his body probing me so intimately. 'We can make up for it later when we're alone.'

He gave me a wolfish grin that sent a bolt of heat to my core. 'Good plan.'

We arranged to arrive at Ethan's penthouse separately to avoid any hint of anything going on between us. I arrived a little earlier to see if there was anything I could do to help Niamh, but she was determined to keep me out of the kitchen.

'No, Ethan and I have got this,' she said as she greeted me at the door. 'You go through to the sitting room with a drink and wait for Grayson. Oh, here he is now.'

I turned and looked at Grayson and mumbled an impersonal 'Hi' and he grunted something unintelligible in return.

Niamh shifted her gaze back and forth between us,

her forehead creasing in a reproving frown. 'Have you two been bickering again?'

I hastily smothered a laugh by pretending to cough, and Grayson answered before I could think of something to say. I could hardly tell her Grayson and I had been making love, not war, could I?

'We've established a temporary truce, haven't we, Ash?' There was a gleam in his gaze that thankfully Niamh couldn't see for he had turned to face me.

'Indeed, we have,' I said, keeping my expression neutral. Our temporary truce was the code name for our temporary fling. Nothing could be anything but temporary between us, even if Ethan and Niamh did marry.

'That's good because I don't want anything to spoil tonight,' Niamh said. 'Ethan and I have gone to a lot of trouble over dinner.'

Ethan came towards us in his motorised chair with a smile on his face. 'Y-you're t-too generous, babe,' he said, looking meltingly at Niamh. 'You've d-done most of the work.'

It was heart-warming to see the pride Ethan had in my sister. It made Niamh glow like I had never seen her glow before. It also made me feel a little envious. Apart from my sister, I hadn't had anyone in my life who was proud of my achievements. Even before my father died, I can't remember either of my parents being all that impressed by my academic success. And certainly, after Niamh's accident, there was no way my mother would ever draw attention to my stellar school record when my sister's abilities were so damaged. I was glad Niamh now had someone to be proud of her, to support her in any endeavour she made.

Grayson and I ended up in the sitting room with drinks in hand while Ethan and Niamh went back to the kitchen. I took a sip of my champagne and looked at the view over Finsbury Park. How was I going to make small talk with the man who had seen me in my smalls? Who had seen every inch of me? And made love to me for hours?

'You look stunning in that dress,' Grayson said from just behind me.

I turned around and breathed in the citrus scent of him, my heart tripping and skipping and flipping as his gaze ran over me hungrily. 'You're going to give the game away if you keep looking at me like that,' I said in a hushed tone, glancing nervously towards the sitting room door in case my sister or Ethan returned.

'How am I looking at you?'

'Like you want to peel this dress off me and ravish me.'

Grayson's lips curved in a smile, and he lifted his hand to my face and trailed a lazy finger down the slope of my cheek. 'That's exactly what I'd like to do.' His voice was so deep and low it sounded like it was coming from the core of the earth. Speaking of cores— my feminine core was pulsating with liquid heat at being so physically close to him.

My pulse was pounding, my heart hammering, my self-control wavering. I could feel myself swaying towards him as if my body was an iron filing and he was a powerful magnet. 'You'd better hold that thought until later.'

He stepped an inch or two closer and bent his head to brush my lips with a light kiss. Our lips met for the briefest moment, but it was like a match had been struck against bone-dry tinder. Heat, fire, flames, lust burned between our mouths in an explosive combustion. We both made desperate sounds in our throats and our lips and tongues met again. And again.

Grayson finally lifted his mouth off mine, his breathing laboured. 'I don't think I've ever wanted anyone the way I want you.' The gravel-rough sound of his voice sent a shiver down my spine, so too the dark gleam of lust in his gaze.

I reached up with my hand to wipe some of my lipgloss off his mouth. 'Same.' It was one hundred percent true. I had never felt anything like the level of desire that he stoked in me. Was it because we both knew it was a temporary fling? That it couldn't last, so we had to make the most of it? Was that what was driving us so wild for each other? The clock was ticking and, because of that, every moment we spent together was consumed with our desire to make the most of what we had while we could.

The sound of Ethan's chair approaching the sitting room made me spring back from Grayson as if I had been burnt. But then I had been—burned, singed, fried by a lust so consuming it was making me wander into dangerous territory. The territory of feelings and emotions that had no place in a fling such as ours.

Niamh came in with Ethan and she narrowed her gaze at me. 'What happened to your chin?'

I lifted my fingers to my face, confused by her concern. 'Nothing.'

'It's red like a rash or something,' Niamh said, coming closer to inspect my face.

My stomach dropped as I realised what had caused it—stubble rash. Those stolen kisses had left a red circle of evidence on my chin. 'It's the preservatives in the champagne.' I put my glass down. 'It'll fade in a while.'

'But you've never had a reaction before,' Niamh said.

No, and I had not been kissed so thoroughly before either. 'I've got some cream in my purse. I won't be a minute.' I left the room to go to the bathroom. I closed the door and walked over to the mirror over the basin and grimaced at my reflection. My make-up had been rubbed off, leaving a patch of red where Grayson's stubbly skin had grazed mine. I touched my fingers to the reddish patch and something hot and liquid trickled in my core.

It was like Grayson Barlowe had branded me as his.

I opened my purse and took out a sample tube of my foundation and applied a new layer to disguise the stubble rash. I reapplied some lip-gloss and popped the tube back in my purse, snapping it closed with a click. But there was no cover-up for the shining light in my eyes or the molten heat in my body.

By the time I came out of the bathroom, dinner was ready in the dining room. Niamh had even gone to the trouble of writing place cards, and I found that I was seated opposite Grayson. His eyes met mine across the table and I had to work hard not to show how much it affected me. But then I felt the gentle brush of his foot against mine and another wave of searing heat flowed to my core.

I found myself eating almost mechanically, saying all the right things in all the right places, such as what a lovely job Niamh had done and how delicious everything was. But, to be honest, I could barely taste a thing. I could only think about how much I wanted Grayson's mouth back on mine.

'Yes, indeed, it's wonderful,' Grayson said, putting down his cutlery. 'Did Ash teach you to cook?'

'Oh, no,' Niamh said with a little self-deprecating laugh. 'She always said I was too messy, or I would burn myself or something.'

'Well, I love your cooking and I think you're amazing at it,' Ethan said, reaching for her hand across the table, his expression warm and tender.

I was temporarily lost for words. Unusual for me, but still, it was a shock to see myself as others saw me—as an over-controlling big sister who was more concerned about keeping the kitchen tidy than whether her disabled sister learned to cook. Had I unconsciously held Niamh back out of guilt? Had I done too much for her to compensate for how I had let her down in that playground by not properly watching her? Had she missed out on learning important life skills out of my guilt?

And, even more important, was I *still* underestimating her capability?

'I'll go and get dessert,' Niamh said, rising from

the table. 'Can you give me a hand with clearing the plates, Ethan?'

'Sure.' Ethan rolled his chair away from the table.

'Wait—let us do that for you,' Grayson said, getting to his feet.

'No, absolutely not,' Niamh insisted. 'You're not to make allowances for us. We're quite capable of putting on a dinner party by ourselves. You and Ash can entertain each other for a few minutes. That is, if I can trust you not to be mean to each other.'

'We'll be on our best behaviour,' Grayson said, looking at me with a sardonic glint in his eyes.

'Yes, of course we will,' I said, forcing a smile.

Once Ethan and Niamh had left the room, I picked up my champagne glass and took a sip.

'Aren't you worried you might get another rash from that champagne?' Grayson's expression and tone was playful.

I gave him a mock-glare. 'You could have told me I had beard rash before Niamh noticed it.'

His smile curved one side of his mouth in a way that was devastatingly attractive. 'I like seeing the effect I have on you. It turns me on.'

I tried but failed to suppress a shiver of reaction. 'Stop it. They might suspect something is going on between us,' I said in a hushed whisper.

He picked up his own glass and took a leisurely sip, his eyes still holding mine. 'What are you doing after you leave here tonight?'

'I'll drive home, take off my make-up, undress, brush my teeth, go to bed. Why?'

His eyes smouldered. 'How about you do all that at my place? We can have a lazy lie-in tomorrow since it's the weekend.'

A lazy lie-in with Grayson Barlowe.

Seriously, if anyone had told me only a week or so ago that I would be excited and breathless about such an event I would have told them they were mad. But maybe I was the one who was mad for wanting it so much. I could feel the hot tingle of desire travelling through my body at the thought of sharing Grayson's bed for another night. I had no idea how long our fling was going to last. It could be days or a couple of weeks, tops.

I had to make the most of it, right?

CHAPTER NINE

I WAS FIRST to wake the following morning and I lay for ages watching Grayson sleep. He was lying on his side, facing me, his eyes closed, his breathing slow and even. I studied each and every one of his features—the long blade of his nose, the dark slashes of his eyebrows above his deep-set eyes, the eyelashes thick and black, the contour of his mouth with its fuller lower lip and the well-defined vermillion borders. His jaw was richly peppered with regrowth and his hair was tousled from both sleep and the play of my fingers during our middle of the night lovemaking.

I shivered as I recalled his urgent possession, the deep and powerful thrusts and the clever flutter of his fingers on my swollen centre that had sent me flying off into the stratosphere. I had to keep reminding myself this was only a fling. That, no matter how wonderful the sex was, it didn't mean our relationship could evolve to anything more lasting. Besides, I wasn't after the fairy tale. I wasn't interested in being someone's wife. Not any more. I had my career and Niamh to focus on. That was more than enough for me...

But in moments like this, with the smell of Grayson

on my skin and the taste of him in my mouth, I was tempted...so sorely tempted to dream of more.

Grayson opened his eyes, let out a sleepy sigh and gave a stretch that brought his hair-roughened muscular legs in contact with my smoother ones. 'How long have you been awake?'

'Not long.'

He took a handful of my hair and let it trail through his fingers. 'I can't remember the last time I had a proper lie-in.'

I tiptoed my fingers across the framework of his collarbones. 'What? No lazy lie-ins with your numerous lovers in hotel rooms all over the world? What sort of playboy are you?' I kept my tone light and playful but inside I was hating the thought of him going back to that lifestyle once our fling was over.

Grayson gave a twisted smile that wasn't quite a smile. And there were shadows in his eyes that reminded me of clouds scudding across the wide pavilion of a clear blue sky. His fingers were back in my hair, toying with it as if it was priceless silk he was weighing up whether or not to purchase.

'I'm probably not the most easy-going playboy around. I guess I like being on my own too much.'

I trailed my finger down his sternum, my eyes avoiding his. 'Would you prefer to be alone right now?'

Grayson tipped up my chin with his finger and meshed his gaze with mine. 'No.' There was a definitive quality to his answer that thrilled me to the core.

'I have to warn you, I'm not fully human until I've had caffeine.'

His glinting smile was crooked and did serious damage to the armour around my heart. 'You mean you want me to go downstairs and brew you some coffee before I even kiss you?'

'Well, when you put it like that, I guess one little kiss wouldn't hurt.'

His mouth came down to mine and I forgot all about my need for caffeine. I forgot about everything except the throbbing energy that flowed through my blood as his tongue met mine. His arms gathered me to the warmth of his body, his legs tangling with mine as his kiss deepened. He groaned with pleasure as my hands boldly explored him, the hot satin of his skin and the steel of his arousal exciting me beyond measure.

At the back of my mind, I wondered how I was going to make love to anyone else after Grayson and I ended our fling. Would I even want to? The thought appalled and sickened me. I enjoyed his touch so much; I couldn't imagine wanting anyone like I wanted him.

The sound of a phone ringing by the bedside made Grayson groan in frustration and he lifted his mouth from mine. 'Sorry, I should have turned it onto silent.' He leaned across me to look at the screen, his face screwing up. 'I'd better get this.' He rolled away and sat on the edge of the bed with his back to me. 'Mum?'

I know I shouldn't eavesdrop but it's hard not to hear every word when you're in the same bed as someone receiving a call. Well, that's my excuse and I'm sticking to it.

'Oh, Grayson, I knew something like this would happen,' his mother said. 'If only you and Ash had been a little more positive about Ethan and Niamh getting married.'

I sat up, my heart giving an extra beat at the worried sound of Grayson's mother's voice. Grayson rose from the bed and looked at me.

'What's happened?' he asked in a deceptively calm tone. Deceptively, because I could see the flash of panic in his eyes as they met mine.

'They've eloped,' his mother said.

'Eloped?' Grayson and I said in shocked unison.

There was a beat of awkward silence.

'Is Ash with you?' his mother asked in an equally shocked tone.

I winced and bit my lip. Grayson let out a short breath and answered, 'We're having a breakfast meeting about the house Ethan and Niamh want us to co-design.'

'On a Sunday morning?' his mother asked.

'We're both too busy with our clients during the week,' Grayson said with an eye-roll in my direction. 'Now, what's this about them eloping? We only had dinner with them last night. They can't have gone far.'

'They flew to Vegas first thing this morning.'

'Vegas?' Grayson and I were getting scarily good at the speaking in unison thing.

'Yes, and I blame you both for it. They wanted a lovely church wedding, but you and Ash were so against them even being engaged, they had no choice but to fly to Vegas. I don't even know if their marriage will be legal.'

'Mum, stop panicking. I'll sort it out.' He said a few more reassuring phrases that I barely listened to in my own swirling panic, then he ended the call but kept hold of his phone. 'We have to fly to Vegas and stop them.' He began to scroll on his phone, presumably to book flights.

I was so many steps behind; I was still reeling from the thought of my sister getting married in a Las Vegas chapel instead of the flower-filled church of her dreams. How had I missed the signs that this was what she and Ethan had planned to do? We had shared a meal with them only last night and I had not picked up a single clue that anything like this could happen. But then, I had been totally consumed by my lust for Grayson. I had been so busy trying to hide the truth about our relationship, I hadn't been aware of anything else.

'Fly to Vegas?' I gulped. 'Now?'

'Yes, we have to stop them making the biggest mistake of their lives.'

'But I need to go home and pack.'

'No time. We can buy you some clothes when we get there.'

'I don't have my passport on me.'

'We'll swing by and get it on the way to the airport.'

'But it's close to an eleven-hour flight to Vegas. How will we ever track them down in time?' I asked.

'I'll think of something.'

And by the look of grim determination on his face, I could well believe he could stop a boulder rolling down a mountain.

In a dizzyingly short space of time, we were on a plane to Vegas. I don't remember much about the flight other than my half-hearted attempt to watch a couple of movies. I tried to sleep but the time difference was already messing with my circadian rhythm…or maybe it was Grayson's stern and brooding presence beside me.

'Have you had any success tracking them down? What hotel and so on?' I asked as we came in to land.

'Yep. I tracked Ethan's credit card payments. I've booked us into the same hotel. They only had a six-hour or so start on us, so we should be able to stop them in time.'

'Unless they go straight to the chapel,' I pointed out. 'We're talking about Vegas, remember? I'm pretty sure you can get married at any time of the day or night.'

He glanced at me with a frown. 'Let's hope they have the sense to get over their jetlag before they do such a stupid thing.'

I let a small silence pass.

'Do you think your mother is right? That it's our fault? I mean, we were a little distracted last night.' I bit down on my lower lip, recalling how I had barely touched the lovely food Niamh had gone to so much trouble to prepare. I had been so absorbed by Grayson. Absorbed and bubbling with red-hot desire for him.

He held my gaze and then let out a rough-sounding sigh. 'No, I think they had already planned this—to elope. The payment for the hotel was processed hours before the dinner party.'

It was my turn to frown. 'Oh…'

He lifted my chin to bring my gaze back up to his. 'If this is anyone's fault, it's mine. You warned me from the start about being too against their plans and now look what's happened.'

Look what's happened, indeed. I was fast falling in love with a man I had told myself I hated. I had forbidden myself to think of him as anything but an enemy. A business rival I could not have any connection to, especially in a romantic sense. How could I have been so stupid? So foolish to think I could be immune to him?

I swept the tip of my tongue over my suddenly dry lips. 'We can still stop this. Erm…them, I mean.'

'Can we?' He glanced at my mouth and my stomach hollowed out. His thumb came up and brushed over my lower lip with the softest touch imaginable. 'Maybe some things are unstoppable.' His voice had dropped a couple of semitones, and my spine loosened like molten wax.

I was still trying to think of something to say when his mouth came down and met mine. His lips were feather-light at first but then the pressure increased as desire flared between us like wildfire.

The only thing that brought me back down to earth was the little bump as the plane landed.

Grayson brushed an imaginary hair off my face and gave me a crooked smile. 'Let's see if you're right.'

I couldn't hold back a puzzled frown. 'About what?'

'Let's try and pretend to be positive about Ethan and Niamh's relationship and see what happens.'

'Okay…'

He brushed his thumb across my lower lip again, his expression now cast in shadow. 'I've booked us separate rooms at the hotel, but they're adjoining. I didn't want Ethan and Niamh to know we're involved.'

'Right. Good plan.'

He lifted his finger to my face and smoothed the tiny frown I hadn't even realised was on my forehead. 'Does it make you feel compromised to be lying to your sister?'

'It makes me feel hypocritical.'

His mouth gave a rueful twist. 'Yeah, well, there's that, I guess. Do you want to end it now, before we get to the hotel?'

I couldn't look into his eyes so looked down at my hands in my lap instead.

'Do you?' I tried to make my voice sound casual, light, and not all that invested in how he answered but I couldn't quite pull it off. There was an undercurrent of despair I couldn't disguise, no matter how hard I tried.

He brought my chin up with the tip of his finger, gently turning my face to meet his gaze. 'No.'

'Really?' A bubble of hope rose in my chest. 'I mean, isn't that a little unusual for you, Mr Playboy-About-Town?'

'It is.'

'What do you attribute it to?'

His eyes kindled. 'You.'

'Me?'

His hand cupped one side of my face. 'You make me laugh.'

'What? No one's done that before?'

'Not the way you do.'

I stared at the contours of his mouth, my heart kicking up its pace. It was foolish of me to think he might be falling in love with me. As foolish and idiotic as it was for me to fall for him. But what if he was starting to rethink the timeframe on our fling? We had spent so much time together lately. It didn't feel like a temporary fling at all. It felt like something with the potential to be so much more.

I adopted a teasing expression and met his gaze. 'You'd better go easy on the compliments, or I'll start thinking you'll be booking a chapel as well as your brother.'

A flicker of something passed through his gaze, a slight disturbance like something dark and shadowy moving underneath a deep current of water. 'That's not going to happen.' His tone was adamant but there was a disconnect with the way he was looking at me, as if he was seeing the potential for more and weighing it up in his mind. Or maybe that was my imagination playing tricks on me.

I was saved from having to think of a witty comeback by the disembarking routine. But I was aware of every time Grayson looked at me. Aware of every idle touch of his hand, like when he placed it on the small of my back to guide me down the aisle of the plane. I got the feeling he found it hard to stop himself touching me. I know I found it hard to keep my hands off him. They seemed to gravitate towards him of their own volition. It was like we were programmed now to be physically connected. Our bodies had muscle memory of contact, sensual contact, and wanted more.

Some time later we were in the back of the car he

had organised, the driver behind a glass panel, on our way to the hotel. Grayson suddenly glanced at me with an unreadable look. 'You didn't answer my question earlier.'

'Which question was that?'

'On whether you wanted to end our fling now, before we see Ethan and Niamh. You deflected the question back at me without answering it yourself.'

I rolled my lips together, pretending to think about my decision, but I was pretty sure my delay in response wasn't fooling him. 'I think it's okay to continue it for a bit longer.'

'How much longer?'

'How long is a fling or a piece of string?' I quipped back.

His lips moved in the ghost of a smile, but it didn't make the distance to his eyes. 'Funny girl.'

I narrowed my gaze at him in a mock-serious way. 'You're not in danger of falling in love with me, are you?'

The faint disturbance was back in the swirling depths of his gaze. 'Whatever gives you that idea?'

I gave a nonchalant shrug. 'I thought you were always the one to end your flings, but you keep handing me the power to do that. Or are you so confident I'll be like every other woman you've ever dated and beg you to stay with me?'

'Firstly, you're not like anyone else I've dated. And secondly, I'm not going to fall in love with you or anyone.'

I had to act like a veteran thespian to stop myself from revealing how much his words hurt. He was ruling out the possibility of feeling anything for me but lust. His heart was locked away and I wasn't sure I could find the key—or even if there was a key.

'Aren't you worried you might be tempting fate to say that?' I asked with a teasing smile.

'Are you in danger of falling in love with me?' His expression gave nothing away, but I could sense a throb of tension in the air. Or was it fear? The fear of hurting me when that was the last thing he wanted to do. He might have a reputation as a playboy, but he didn't strike me as the sort of man to use women solely as sex objects. He certainly hadn't treated me like that. I had never felt more respected and equal in a sexual relationship before, which made it all the harder to exercise the power to end our fling before I got too attached.

But wasn't I already *too* attached?

CHAPTER TEN

WE ARRIVED AT the hotel and quickly checked in to our adjoining rooms, both of us keen to track Niamh and Ethan down. Neither of them was responding to calls or text messages, which only ramped up my panic. I couldn't bear the thought of my sister getting married without me there.

Was this *my* fault? Had I driven her to do something she might later regret, only because I was so against her rushing into marriage because, deep down, I was worried about her being hurt? But Ethan was so devoted to her and she to him. Yes, they were still in the heady early days of falling in love, but that didn't mean they couldn't have a lasting relationship. I had allowed my cynicism about relationships to influence my judgement, but what sort of authority did I have over being in love? I hadn't been in love with Ryan. I realised now I had settled for second best because it made me feel less guilty about Niamh's situation. My distorted thinking had been: how could I allow myself to fall properly in love if she never found someone herself?

But Niamh had found someone and with zero help from me. And if I didn't get there in time, she would marry him in a Vegas chapel instead of the flower-filled village church of her dreams.

Grayson and I made our way to the chapel situated in the hotel, our pace brisk and determined.

'Let's hope we can catch them in time,' he said, frowning heavily.

'Yes, but if we don't, I think we have to be as positive as we can. The last thing any couple wants on their wedding day is negativity.' I blew out a breath and added, 'I can't help blaming myself for this. I shouldn't have been so against them being together.'

Grayson sent me a sideways glance as we traversed another long, garishly carpeted corridor. 'If anyone's to blame, it's me. I hated the thought of Ethan going through another heartbreak.'

We came to the chapel before I could think of a response. Another couple was stepping away from the marriage celebrant, their faces wreathed in smiles. And next in line were Niamh and Ethan. I allowed myself a moment of relief to sweep through me before stepping forward with Grayson. At least they weren't yet married.

Niamh turned her head as we approached and glared at us. 'You can't stop us.'

'We don't want to stop you,' Grayson said in a calm and measured tone. 'We want you to do it properly, at home surrounded by friends and family.'

'Really?' Ethan said, with a surprised look.

'Of course,' I chipped in. 'This isn't the wedding day you've always dreamed of, Niamh. Let us at least give you both a wedding day to remember.'

Niamh exchanged a glance with Ethan before turning back to me. 'But we want to get married sooner rather than later,' she said, lowering her gaze from mine and chewing at her lip.

My sister was never all that good at delaying gratification, but who was I to talk? I had rushed into a fling with Grayson because I couldn't help myself. He was temptation personified.

'I'm sure we can organise a lovely wedding in a few weeks,' I said.

'No, we d-don't want to w-wait a few weeks,' Ethan said, stumbling over his words in his haste to get them out in a determined tone.

'Don't weddings take ages to organise?' Grayson asked.

'Yes, but I know of a good wedding planner that might be able to help,' I said. 'There's a company run by three best friends called Happy Ever After Weddings. I've read about their hugely successful business and seen interviews on various social platforms. But, of course, they are popular, so it might not be easy to engage them, especially with such a short timeframe.'

'Can we talk in private?' Niamh asked me with a beseeching glance.

'Sure, but you'd better tell the celebrant we won't be needing them,' I said.

Ethan and Niamh mumbled something to the celebrant, who didn't seem all that fussed with the sudden change of plan. But, judging from the queue of couples lining up to get married, perhaps he was confident the vacant space would be filled within minutes.

I took my sister by the hand and led her out of the chapel. I spied a café nearby and suggested we go there.

'No, I want somewhere more private,' Niamh said.

'Okay, we'll go to my room.' I led the way to the lift.

'You have your own room?' Niamh asked once we were inside the lift and zooming up to the thirtieth floor.

'Of course.'

Her forehead creased in a puzzled frown. 'But I thought you might share with Grayson.'

I could feel heat pooling in my cheeks. Not could I only feel it, but I could also see it because three sides of the lift were mirrored glass.

I gave a little cough of a laugh. 'Why on earth would you think that?'

'I see the way he looks at you. And the way you look at him.'

'Erm…well, he's… I'm…' What was I supposed to say? How could I explain our fling to my sister? What sort of hypocrite would she think me?

'Are you in love with him?'

I rapid blinked like I was a rabbit suddenly realising a speeding car was about to turn me into roadkill. Niamh's question blindsided me. I didn't want to think about my feelings for Grayson Barlowe. I didn't want to acknowledge I even had feelings for him. We were having a lust-fuelled fling. Emotions were not supposed to be part of the deal.

'Erm…it's complicated…' What a pathetic cliché to resort to, but it was actually true. It didn't get much more complicated. 'So, what did you want to talk to me about?' It was time to get the focus back on her, not me.

Now it was time for Niamh's cheeks to go pink. 'Let's wait until we're in your room.'

The lift doors pinged open, and we stepped out and made our way to my room. I glanced at Grayson's door next to mine and a hot shiver passed through my body.

I opened the door to my room and Niamh walked through. I closed the door and followed her to the sitting room that overlooked the colourful and busy Vegas Strip.

'So, what did you want to talk to me about?' I asked.

Niamh turned from looking out of the window, her hands twisted together in front of her body. 'I'm having a baby.'

I stared at her in shocked silence. My mind was spinning out of control like a Buick on black ice. Niamh was pregnant? She was going to be a mother. Ethan was going to be a father. I was going to be an auntie. Grayson was going to be an uncle.

'Aren't you going to say something?' Niamh was looking a little worried.

I blew out an uneven breath. 'Wow... I mean...congratulations. How many weeks?'

'Four.'

'Four?' I gaped at her. 'But you only started seeing each other, what, seven weeks ago now?' That meant she'd got pregnant at the very start of their relationship.

'Yes, but our connection was instant. I knew he was the love of my life the minute I met him.'

I sat down because my legs were suddenly strangely

unsteady. 'Wow, I can see why you both wanted to get married in a rush.'

I shook my head, trying to get my brain around this new development. There was so much to think about. How would my sister cope with the responsibilities that came with motherhood? Our own mother hadn't had any of the limitations Niamh had and she had really struggled with the day in, day out routine of providing for and taking care of her children.

'Aren't you happy for me?'

I painted a bright smile on my face and sprang to my feet and enveloped her in a hug. 'Of course I am. I'm thrilled for you and Ethan.'

Niamh finally stepped out of my embrace and beamed at me. 'Ethan will be the most wonderful father. He's so excited because he never thought he would have the opportunity. I know there'll be obstacles to face but I'm sure we'll face them together.'

I wasn't sure what Grayson would think of this new development. He was far more against their wedding than I was, and I was pretty determined against it. Now I couldn't wait for them to tie the knot.

But not here.

Not in Las Vegas.

Half an hour later, Niamh left to go back to her and Ethan's room to pack for the trip home. I had already emailed Happy Ever After Weddings and as soon as the time difference and travel distance allowed I would call into their London office in person. I didn't care how much it cost but my sister was going to have the wedding of her dreams.

There was a tap at my door, and I opened it to find Grayson standing there with a grim look on his face.

'You know?'

'Yes, Ethan told me.' He stepped through and I closed the door behind him.

'I hope you weren't too negative about it.'

He scraped his hand through his hair and let out a whooshing breath. 'This changes everything. My mother is going to be beside herself with joy.'

'And you? Are you excited about being an uncle?'

I studied his features, wondering what was going on behind the screen of his shuttered gaze.

'I haven't given it much thought. What about you?'

I rolled my lips together, not sure how to answer. I was still trying to get my head around my sister becoming a mother. She had always been my little sister, the person who depended on me for everything. But, in the space of weeks, I had been cast aside for her fiancé. Now they were going to be parents. So many changes in such a short timeframe.

'On one level I'm thrilled to be an auntie, but on another I'm worried how my sister will cope with all the responsibilities of motherhood.'

'Yes, well, every new parent goes on a steep learning curve, from what I've heard. But I'm sure Ethan will support her in every way he can. And my mother, of course.'

There was a beat or two of silence where we just stood looking at each other.

I couldn't read his expression and I desperately hoped he couldn't read mine. I was trying to hide my emotions. The emotions I wasn't supposed to be feeling. The emotions I had forbidden myself to feel. But I was feeling them all the same.

I'm not sure how it happened but I was in love with him. I loved so much about him. The way he supported and protected his brother, the way he worked hard at his career, the values he stood by and his strength of character and self-discipline.

And I loved how he made love to me.

'I've booked a flight for us all,' Grayson said. 'The sooner we get back to London the better.'

'You're right. It's going to take a miracle to get a wedding organised in a couple of weeks.'

Grayson stepped up close, so our toes were almost touching. He lifted a hand to my face and stroked the curve of my cheek with a lazy finger. 'I wish we had more time.'

'For?'

He leaned down so his mouth was just above mine. 'For this.' His lips covered mine and I was swept up in the magic of the moment. No one had ever kissed me with such tender thoroughness. No one had ever made my blood sing in my veins the way he did. It was a kiss that spoke of fervent passion and deep longing. I wound my arms around his neck, my body pressed close to the strong wall of his. I could not bear to think of a time when I wouldn't be able to do this—to be so close to him I could feel the thunder of his heart against me.

Grayson finally lifted his mouth off mine and gave

me a twisted smile. 'Hold that thought until we get back to London.'

I ran my hands down his chest and let them settle on his trim waist. 'I think Niamh suspects we're seeing each other.'

A flicker of something passed through his gaze. 'How? Did you say something to her?'

'No, but she noticed how you look at me.'

He frowned. 'How do I look at you?'

'The same way I look at you.'

He brushed the pad of his thumb across my lower lip, sending my senses into a tailspin. 'I guess it's hard to hide the sort of chemistry we have.'

I eased myself out of his arms. 'Yes, well, it's not going to last for ever, is it? These things have a habit of burning out over time.' I spoke with cool detachment but inside I was thinking the opposite. I knew it was not going to burn out for me. How could it when I loved him with every fibre of my being?

His jaw tightened as if he was thinking over an appropriate response. His expression was mask-like but I could sense movement at the back of his gaze.

'Is it burning out for you?' His tone was as cool and detached as mine.

'Not yet.'

His gaze lowered to my mouth and the floor of my belly shivered. 'Good to know.' His hands settled on my hips and he brought me a tiny bit closer. I could feel the press of his erection and my pulse began to quicken.

'Don't we have a flight to catch?' My voice was

shamefully breathless, my skin tightening all over with desire.

'It's a private flight—it won't matter if we're five minutes late.'

'Five minutes? You reckon you can get me to come that quickly?'

He gave me a wolfish smile and brought his mouth down closer to mine. 'Watch me.'

The next couple of weeks were nothing short of a whirlwind of activity. I had to juggle work with dress fittings and meetings with the team at Happy Ever After Weddings, who had kindly taken Niamh and Ethan on, due to another couple postponing their wedding due to the groom injuring himself in an accident.

It was so different from when I had planned my own wedding. For one thing, I hadn't been anywhere near as excited and happy as Niamh. I hadn't been glowing with love for my fiancé. I had simply been going through the motions, ticking the boxes that needed to be ticked. Find dress. *Tick*. Book church. *Tick*. Select reception venue and menu. *Tick*. It had been a long list of jobs to get done.

Witnessing my sister's joy and anticipation made me feel increasingly envious. I began to daydream about my fling with Grayson becoming something else. Something more lasting. Something that would lead us to plan a wedding one day. I could imagine my joy and excitement if I was engaged to Grayson. I could imagine wearing his ring and looking at him the way my sister looked at his brother.

I could even imagine carrying Grayson's child.

I placed a hand on my belly, as I had seen my sister do so many times over the last couple of weeks. What would it feel like to have Grayson's child in my womb? I pushed the thought away before it could get a stronger foothold. What was I doing? I was a career woman through and through. I didn't have time for kids. My career was too front and centre. So too was my commitment to Niamh. I had always put her before everything.

But Niamh has Ethan now.

The thought was reassuring and yet…and yet I was so used to being there for my sister. I didn't know any other way of living. For the last twenty years I had been there for her. I had overseen her education, her medical care, her social life—her everything.

Who was I without her needing me?

In amongst all the wedding preparations, Grayson and I were still meeting after hours to work on Ethan and Niamh's house design. Neither of us had told our siblings about our relationship but I was feeling increasingly uncomfortable about the secrecy.

It was Grayson's turn to come to my house a couple of days before the wedding. I opened the door to him, and he stepped inside and closed the door. He reached for me and dropped a firm kiss to my lips. 'I've missed you.'

I leaned back in his embrace to look up at him. 'But you saw me the day before yesterday.'

His arms tightened around me, and my pulse began

to gallop. 'I like seeing you every day.' His voice was husky and low, his gaze dark and glittering.

'I like seeing you too.' I stood on tiptoe to plant a kiss on his lips.

He groaned and pulled me even closer, his mouth taking charge. His tongue slipped between my lips and danced with mine. Heat exploded in my body, my legs trembling, my spine loosening, my heart racing. We stumbled to my bedroom, knocking against furniture as we went, our mouths glued together as the passion between us soared. It was always like this—a rush of desire that was so heady it made me dizzy. I could not get enough of this man's touch.

'I want you,' I said.

'I want you more.'

I smiled against the sensual texture of his lips. 'Prove it.'

And so he did.

CHAPTER ELEVEN

THE DAY OF Niamh and Ethan's wedding arrived and, miracle of miracles, it was a sunny day. As I was Niamh's bridesmaid and Grayson was Ethan's best man, he was standing at the altar with his brother in his chair beside him as I preceded Niamh up the aisle. The music was emotionally evocative, and I had to blink to keep the tears back.

I locked gazes with Grayson and my heart skipped a beat. He was looking at me with such glittering intensity, as if he was committing the vision of me in my silk shell-pink bridesmaid dress to memory. I could feel his eyes on every curve of my body—curves he had caressed with his hands and his lips and tongue only the night before.

Niamh had chosen to walk herself up the aisle, which was another sign of how she was growing more and more independent of me. I was proud of her and yet a little sad too. I was so accustomed to being included in every part of her life but now she had Ethan and he would be her mainstay, not me.

The church was awash with flowers and the fragrance was intoxicating. Niamh looked exactly as a bride should look—beautiful and happy beyond description. And Ethan looked exactly as a groom should look—proud and desperately in love. The ceremony was traditional, and I didn't bother disguising my tears at one point. The exchange of vows was so meaningful, and I had no doubt that this couple, in spite of all the obstacles they had faced in life to this point, would be happy and stay happy. For ever.

If only I could have the same with Grayson.

The church bells rang as the couple left the church. Grayson and I followed in their wake, and I was conscious of my shoulder brushing against his arm as we walked back down the aisle.

'You look very beautiful,' he said.

'Thank you. I wasn't sure about the colour on me, but Niamh insisted on it.'

Grayson smiled and my heart did a somersault. 'Are you wearing underwear under it?'

'No.'

His eyes smouldered and he gave a low and deep groan. 'You shouldn't have told me that.'

'But you asked.'

'I'm not going to be able to think of anything else now.'

'Careful. Some people can lipread, you know.' I smiled at the people in the congregation as we walked past them to the bright sunlight outside the church.

'Just wait until I get you alone.'

'Promises, promises,' I said in a sing-song voice.

The sunlight was blinding, so too were Ethan and Niamh's smiles as they greeted their guests.

Grayson's mother, Julie, came up to me, beaming with happiness. 'Wasn't it the most beautiful ceremony? I was crying buckets as soon as I saw Niamh. I'm so glad you supported her and Ethan in their relationship. And I'm so grateful you talked Grayson round.'

'I didn't really talk him round.'

'Don't be so modest. Of course you did,' she said, glancing at Grayson, who was a few feet away. 'He can be so very stubborn, but somehow you got him to change his mind.' She swung her gaze back to me. 'Anyway, it's lovely to have a daughter-in-law at last. And I'm so excited about the baby.'

'Yes, so am I.'

I did my level best not to look at Grayson. I was trying so hard to appear indifferent to him, but every time I happened to glance in his direction I found his gaze on me.

'So, you and Grayson will have to be friends now,' Julie said. 'We can't have the baby's uncle and auntie not liking each other, now, can we?'

'I'm sure we'll manage to be civil to one another when required,' I said with an on-off smile.

Julie studied Grayson for a moment, then turned back to me. 'I can't help thinking he's changed lately.'

'How so?'

'He's happier, more at ease. Or maybe that's because Ethan is finally settled with the love of his life.' She gave a sad little smile and continued, 'Grayson has always blamed himself for the accident.'

'It's hard not to feel guilty when things happen on your watch.'

'I heard about Niamh's accident. That must have been so hard on you.' Her empathetic tone was almost my undoing. Almost.

'It was…' I had to blink away another prickle of tears. 'It is…'

Julie put a gentle hand on my arm. 'It probably always will be. But it doesn't mean you can't move forward. Don't let the past dictate your future.'

I didn't get the chance to reply, even if I could have thought of a thing to say. The photographer directed the wedding party to assemble for the official photographs. Once they were taken and refreshments were being handed around, Grayson came over to me.

'How are you holding up?'

'My feet are killing me and my face aches from all the smiling.'

'I hope my mother wasn't too full-on,' he said.

'She was lovely.'

He grunted and swung his gaze to look at Ethan and Niamh, surrounded by the other guests. 'As long as she didn't put any ideas into your head.'

I stiffened. 'What ideas do you mean?'

He turned back to me and gave a careless shrug, his expression masked. 'Weddings do strange things to people. Make them get all sentimental.'

I wasn't going to admit to how sentimental I was feeling but I needed to counter-argue on principle. 'I don't think it's strange to feel sentimental at a wedding. It's kind of nice to see two people who love each other make a public commitment.'

He thrust his hands in his pockets and gazed again

at the assembled guests sipping champagne and eating canapés. 'Most people fall out of love before the honeymoon is over.'

'Don't be so cynical. Some people fall in love and stay in love for a lifetime.'

He glanced at me with an unreadable expression. 'I thought you were as cynical as me. What's happened?'

'Nothing. I just think there are other ways of looking at things.'

I saw Ethan and Niamh approaching at that point and I hastily painted a smile on my face. 'I don't think I've ever seen a more blissfully happy couple. Congratulations. It was an exquisitely beautiful wedding.'

Ethan's arm went around Niamh's waist, his expression so full of love as he looked up at her from his chair it was enough to make my heart contract. If only Grayson would look at me like that. Or was I wishing for the moon?

'We should have made it a double wedding,' Niamh said, grinning at us.

'What?' Grayson barked the word, clearly shocked by my sister's comment.

I was a little shocked too. Shocked that she had put two and two together in spite of my efforts to keep my relationship with Grayson a secret.

'Don't be silly, Niamh,' I said with a laugh that sounded tinny.

Niamh was undaunted by our reaction. 'You can't fool us. We know you've been together for ages. You don't have to hide it from us. There's nothing to be ashamed of in falling in love.'

'We're not in love,' Grayson said in a tone that was so adamant I couldn't help but feel crushed.

Niamh looked confused and glanced at me. 'But I don't understand...'

'No, you're the ones who don't understand,' Grayson said. 'It's not going to happen.'

'What's not g-going to happen?' Ethan asked, frowning.

'This.' Grayson waved his hand to encompass the church in the background and the assembled guests in the garden. 'Any marriage between us is out of the question.'

I was determined not to sabotage my sister's wedding day by demonstrating how hurt I was by Grayson's stance, but it called on every bit of acting ability I possessed.

'That's right,' I said. 'We had a little fling but it's over now.'

'Over?' Niamh and Ethan spoke in unison.

Grayson said nothing, showed nothing. It was like someone had poured invisible concrete over him, freezing him in place.

'Yes, over, but we're friends,' I said. 'And we're both looking forward to being uncle and auntie to your baby.'

Some other guests came over to speak to the bride and groom and I was immensely glad of the chance to escape. But I had only got as far as the lychgate when I felt a strong hand come down on my arm.

'Wait. I want to talk to you.'

I turned to look up at Grayson's frowning features.

'What's there to talk about? You've made it perfectly clear you see no future for us.'

He let out a breath and a curse word at the same time. 'We agreed on a fling.'

'Yes, and now it's over.'

'But I don't want it to be over.' The words seemed to be forced out of him, as if he had not wanted to admit his continued desire for me.

I shook his hand off my arm. 'It has to be over, Grayson. You know it does. I'm getting too involved with you. I don't want to get hurt.'

'How will I hurt you?'

I gave a sad smile. 'By not loving me.'

His brows snapped together, and his expression became guarded. 'Are you saying you love me?'

I so wanted to deny it. I could taste the word 'no' on the tip of my tongue. It was teetering there like a skier at the top of a steep run, poised, waiting to fly down. But I couldn't say it. I was tired of pretending. Tired of pretending to be someone I wasn't. I had done it for years, fashioning myself into a person I could barely recognise as myself any more. It was time to be honest about what I wanted, what I hoped for, what I deserved but had denied myself out of guilt.

'Yes, I do love you. I know we agreed to keep our feelings out of it, but I couldn't do it. You made it so hard for me by being everything I didn't even know I wanted in a partner. I started to realise I wanted what Niamh has. Someone to love her and be with her through whatever life dishes out. All this time, I've been thinking she was too immature, too inexperienced to handle marriage, but it's me that needed to grow up. Continuing our fling when there's no possibility of it ever being anything but a fling would be wrong for me on so many levels.'

Grayson's expression underwent a series of changes as I spoke. Shock. Distress. A flicker of anger. A stiffening of his features that looked like a drawbridge was being pulled up inside him. 'So, that's it? You want to end it?'

'It's for the best.'

'Do I get a say in this?'

I swallowed a thickness in my throat. 'Sure, but nothing you say will change my mind. Unless you were to say you love me and want a future with me. A future that included marriage and hopefully kids one day.'

'I've never wanted those things with anyone.'

'I know. You were nothing if not brutally honest with me.'

'Then why did you fall in love with me?'

I gave a frustrated laugh that wasn't really a laugh. 'Because you have so much to offer. You're a good person, Grayson. A strong and capable person who takes his responsibilities seriously. Everything you do, you do to a high standard. And no one has ever made me feel the way you do physically. I know sex isn't everything in a relationship but it's a pretty good barometer. But physical chemistry isn't enough. You won't allow yourself to love anyone because of what happened to Ethan. Guilt has tortured you as it has tortured me. But I'm not going to live my life under that dark cloud, pretending I don't want the things I really do want. I want the fairy tale that you don't even believe in, even when it's right in front of you.'

He paced back and forth until I was sure he was going to wear out the grass beneath his feet. His agitation was palpable, it made the atmosphere crackle like an approaching storm.

He suddenly stopped pacing and his eyes cut to mine, his mouth pulled tight. 'This is not how I saw us ending.'

'I know, because you're the one who's usually in control of your flings. Doesn't that tell you something? You need to be in control because it's too threatening to give others the power to hurt you.'

'You haven't hurt me. You've surprised me.'

I folded my arms across my middle. I was so tempted to cave in and go back to him. Every cell of my body was drawn to him as if pulled by an invisible force. But I had to be strong. I had to summon every bit of willpower in order to complete my journey as a fully evolved human being. No more self-denial. No more pretending. No more bending myself out of shape to be someone I was not destined to be.

'I really want us to be friends, Grayson. There are other people who will get hurt if we're not.'

His top lip gave the tiniest curl as if he couldn't help himself, and his eyes glittered with his trademark cynicism. 'You expect me to greet you with a chaste kiss on the cheek after you've come apart so many times in my arms? Just to give you the heads-up—that's what I'll be thinking every time I see you.'

I raised my chin a fraction, even as my traitorous

body throbbed and throbbed with longing. 'You'll have dozens, if not hundreds, of lovers after me. I'm sure you'll forget all about our time together.'

He grunted something unintelligible, his expression brooding. 'Why end it today of all days? Why not wait until tomorrow?'

'Because Ethan and Niamh's wedding vows really spoke to me,' I said. 'Every word was so meaningful. The promises they made to each other are promises I want to make to the man I love. That man is you, Grayson, but you can't love anyone because, deep down, you don't like yourself. You've not forgiven yourself for letting Ethan drive that night. Until you can accept you are human, just like everyone else, and that making mistakes is part and parcel of the human condition, then I don't think you will ever be truly content, much less happy. Part of the reason you work so hard is to fill in the empty spaces in your life. I've done it too, for so long I thought it was part of my true nature. But while I love my work, I can no longer be a slave to it and allow it to crowd out some of the most important things a human being can experience—connection, commitment, and lasting love.'

'Thanks for the free psychotherapy session, but I'm quite content with my life as it is.' His voice was cold and distant, his expression closed-off.

'You might be now, but what about in a few years' time? How long do you think you can move from casual lover to casual lover, never staying with them long enough to get to know them or for them to get to know you? How long is that going to be satisfying?'

Grayson moved away a short distance to rest his hands on top of the wooden fence that divided the churchyard from a park. He stared at the trees waving in the slight breeze, every muscle on his face taut with tension.

'Okay, you've said your piece. I understand you want more, but I did warn you from the beginning there wasn't going to be more.'

'I know you did.' I let out a wobbly breath and walked back to the other guests.

I was trying so hard to hold it together, trying so hard to be strong and dignified, but inside I wanted to shout, I wanted to scream, I wanted to beg him to love me. It was strange to be on the opposite side of a breakup. I was the one who had broken off my engagement to Ryan. Looking back now, I could have done things a little more graciously, allowed him some measure of dignity, but my protective instincts towards Niamh had taken over. I hadn't been in love with Ryan, and I suspect he might not have been in love with me either.

But I was in love with Grayson. He was everything I could ever want in a life partner. He totally understood my commitment to my sister because he had the same commitment to his brother. He understood the guilt I carried because he had experienced the same. During our fling I had started to hope he was developing an attachment to me that was deeper and more enduring than his past casual encounters. That I was someone special.

Clearly, I was wrong.

I wasn't anything special to Grayson Barlowe. I was just another lover, just another woman who had succumbed to his potent charm.

And now it was over.

I don't know how I got through the rest of Niamh and Ethan's wedding day. The reception seemed to drag on for hours…or maybe that was because I was doing my best to avoid Grayson. But escaping him was impossible because, as best man and the only bridesmaid, we each had roles to play.

One of those roles included stepping up on the dance floor to join the bride and groom in their first dance together. I stepped into Grayson's embrace and tried to block my body's reaction, but it was like trying to stop a wave from cresting. A rush of longing flowed through me, a deep and unsettling longing because I knew it could not be satiated. Not now. Not ever again. We had done many things together before, intimate things that were etched on my mind and my body, but we had never danced before. How bittersweet to realise we were so well matched in this way too. We moved together as if we had been dancing partners for years. It felt so natural and easy to glide with him across the floor. I breathed in his smell, committing it to memory, for I knew I might never have the chance to get this close to him again. In a way, our dance was a goodbye and that made it especially poignant.

Other couples had joined us and the dance floor was a little more crowded, so Grayson had to hold me closer to avoid any collisions. I was aware of the gentle press of his hand in the small of my back, aware of how close our hips were, aware of the grasp of his hand and how my hand was so small and dainty inside the firm cage of his.

'Ash…' There was a strange quality to his voice, a slight hitch in it that I had not heard before.

I looked up at him to find his gaze on me, a frown etched on his forehead.

'Yes?' I tried to remove the note of hope in my tone but I'm sure he could see it in my face. I'm a good actor, but not *that* good.

His eyes dipped to my mouth for a long moment and my heart skittered. 'Is it going to be difficult for you to work with me on Ethan and Niamh's house? If so, I can organise one of my staff to take over the project for me.'

I frowned. I had forgotten about the house we were supposed to be designing together. We hadn't got far with it, mostly because of the wedding taking up so much of our time recently. How would it be working alongside him now we weren't seeing each other any more? It would be torture, that's what it would be. Plain and simple emotional and physical torture.

'But they want us to do it. I'm sure we can both be grown-ups about this.'

One side of his mouth tilted in a half smile that didn't reach his eyes. 'You think I won't be able to control myself around you?'

'I'm sure you'll be the ultimate professional at all times.'

He held my gaze for a heart-stopping moment before

looking away into the distance. 'We'd better reinstate the no-touching rule.'

'Fine.'

'And that probably should include earrings.'

In spite of my heartache, I laughed. 'I'll wear studs, so you won't be tempted.'

He looked back at me again, his eyes dark and intense. 'I only have to look at you to be tempted.' His voice was rough around the edges and his hold on me momentarily tightened, sending waves of incendiary heat through my body.

I aimed my gaze at his bowtie, not trusting myself to look into those mesmerising eyes. But I was acutely aware of how close our pelvises were to each other. It seemed our bodies gravitated to each other of their own volition, like two magnets locking together.

'You have to stop looking at me like that,' I said, keeping my voice low so the other couples dancing around us wouldn't hear.

'How am I looking at you?'

'Like you want to whisk me away and make love to me.'

'But that's exactly what I want to do.'

'But you can't, not now. We're over.' I injected my voice with as much determination as I could.

'You really think you can turn off feelings just like that?'

I glanced up at him, my heart climbing up to my throat. 'But we're not talking about feelings, or at least you're not. Our fling was never about feelings for you. It was about lust. And yes, that can be turned off if you're strong enough.' I only hoped I was strong enough, otherwise the next few months, or even years, were going to be hard to get through.

He frowned and looked into the distance again but his hold on me remained firm. 'Why are you so sure you love me? What if you're confusing it with lust?'

'I know this is probably hard for you to understand because you won't allow your feelings to get involved in your flings, but as soon as you kissed me I knew I was in danger of falling in love with you. But it wasn't just about the physical chemistry. Your character spoke to me in a way no one else has before. You understood my struggles because you had experienced them yourself. I felt like you were seeing me, the real me, instead of the persona I've adopted over the years. I could be myself with you and I like to think you could be yourself with me.'

I don't know how it happened, but we were no longer on the dance floor and had drifted out to a balcony festooned with flowers. There was no one else out there, so we were finally alone.

Grayson lowered his hands from my body and stepped back a step, his expression as inscrutable as the stone wall to our left. 'It was never my intention to hurt you.' His voice contained a chord of gravitas that made me realise this was painful for him too, for different reasons but painful regardless. I knew it wasn't in his nature to be cruel. Cynical, yes, but not cruel.

I painted on a brave smile. 'I'll get over it.'

He stepped closer again and gently stroked my cheek with a lazy finger, his eyes locking on mine. 'Will you?'

'Of course.' I wasn't as confident as I sounded. Inside, my heart was breaking like a fissure in a rock.

'Am I allowed one last kiss?' The rough burr of his voice sent a shiver down the length of my spine.

'Do you think that's wise?' My voice was not much above a whisper and my pulse began to pound.

Grayson's eyes moved back and forth between each of mine, and then his gaze lowered to my mouth for a pulse-tripping moment. He slowly brushed the pad of his thumb across my lower lip, and I trembled from head to foot.

His mouth twisted into a rueful line and his hand fell away to drop by his side. 'You're right. It's not at all wise.' And then he turned and walked away without another word.

CHAPTER TWELVE

THE NEXT MONTH I spent catching up on work. I had a lot of clients on the go and a couple of big new projects that took up a great deal of time. But my work was no longer as satisfying as it had been. Or maybe it was because I had no work/life balance. I worked all day and came home to an empty house. I didn't socialise because I didn't have the energy or the motivation. I missed Niamh but I was happy she was enjoying her new life with Ethan.

And it goes without saying I missed Grayson.

I missed his touch, his rare smiles, his intelligent conversation—so many things that made him so attractive to me. I missed hearing the sound of his voice, I missed the smell of him on my skin, the taste of him in my mouth, the feel of his arms so protective and strong around me.

We hadn't yet met up to continue working on Niamh and Ethan's house. I had been too busy with other clients, and I heard via Ethan that Grayson was snowed under with work too. He also told me Grayson had flown to the US to check on a build that was part-way done. I tortured myself with imagining him hooking up with someone over there. No doubt he would go back to his playboy lifestyle and barely spare me a thought.

But a couple of days later I was helping Niamh shop for baby things, and she told me Ethan was worried about Grayson.

'Why?' I asked, picking up a lemon-coloured onesie.

'He thinks Grayson's not himself at all.'

I put the onesie down and picked up a tiny bonnet and mittens, trying to disguise my avid interest in Grayson's state of mind. Trying too to disguise how envious I was of my sister shopping for babywear. Would I ever have the chance to do the same? I couldn't imagine having anyone else's child than Grayson's. But he didn't want the things I wanted.

He didn't want me. Not for ever.

'He's grumpy and unsociable,' Niamh said, handing me a bundle of clothes to hold. 'He won't come over for dinner and he won't allow us to visit him. Even their mum is worried about him.' She looked at me with her big blue eyes and asked, 'Did you part as friends or as enemies?'

'Friends… I think…' I bent down to pick up one of the onesies that dropped to the floor and added it back to the tower of items I was trying to juggle in my arms. How could one small baby need all this stuff? I tried to think of the last time I had held a baby, but I couldn't remember doing so since I was a teenager. Now all I could think about was holding one of my own. Why was I torturing myself with these thoughts? It was pointless. Grayson was not going to change his mind. He had made his position crystal-clear, and I had to put my big girl panties on and accept it.

Niamh started sorting through some christening outfits hanging on a rack. 'Ethan and I have tweaked a few of our ideas for our house. Maybe you and Grayson could get together soon to go over them.' She glanced at me over her shoulder and added, 'Or will that be too awkward for you now you're only...friends?'

I fashioned my lips into a confident smile, but it was totally at odds with how I was feeling. I didn't know how I was going to be in the same room as Grayson without wanting to touch him. How could I work alongside him for months and not embarrass myself by begging him to reconsider?

'It won't be a problem.'

Niamh selected a long white, beautifully embroidered christening gown and held it up for me to see. 'What do you think?'

I reached out and touched the finely embroidered fabric, thinking of the little person who would wear it in a few months' time—my niece or nephew. It looked like a family heirloom, the sort of gown generations of babies could wear. Would I ever have a baby to wear it? Or would I always feel this crushing sense of loneliness and emptiness because the only man I could ever love didn't love me back?

'It's gorgeous.'

She lowered the gown to look directly at me. 'Ethan and I want you and Grayson to be our baby's godparents.'

I tried not to show my sense of unease. Not because

I didn't want to be a godparent—it was an incredible honour, and I wouldn't dream of declining. But it would be yet another permanent connection with Grayson. How was I going to avoid him when there would be so many events where we would both be present?

'Oh, that's so lovely of you both. I'd be honoured, of course.'

Niamh beamed and added the christening gown to the pile of clothes I was already balancing in my arms. 'That's settled then. Now, let's have tea and cake.'

I know what you're thinking. I don't drink tea, right? But guess what? Ever since I broke up with Grayson, I haven't been able to bring myself to drink coffee. I can't even bear the smell because it reminds me too much of him.

Speaking of smells—I still have his handkerchief. I know I can get a little preachy about always returning things you've borrowed but I kept hold of Grayson's handkerchief, even though I'd had numerous opportunities to return it before I ended our fling. I'd washed and ironed it and now I kept it under my pillow. I find myself reaching for it each night, clutching it in my hand like a child clutches a favourite toy. Pathetic, right?

The following Friday I went straight home after work rather than join my team for end-of-the-week drinks. I wasn't in the mood for socialising, and I found it hard to make small talk because my life was so boring compared to everyone else's. All I did these days was work and exercise. Okay, I lied about the exercise. If you can call running ten metres along the platform to catch the Tube three mornings this week exercise, well, I tick the box. The other thing I hated when going out was seeing all the other couples. It was like rubbing rock salt into the open wound of my broken heart. Why was everyone so damn happy when I was so utterly miserable?

I picked at some leftovers for dinner but ended up pushing it away with a sigh. I surfed the streaming platforms on my smart television but, in spite of the huge number of options, nothing appealed to me in this bleak mood.

I sat on my window seat and looked at the street below. More couples walking hand in hand, families taking the kids and the dog for a walk. A young couple taking their baby for a stroll in one of those old-fashioned prams with large springs and shiny spoked wheels. And elderly couple walking hand in hand. A tall dark-haired man with a slight limp, carrying a bunch of flowers, walking on his own...

I sat upright, my eyes narrowing to focus on that all too familiar figure. My mouth dried, my stomach flip-flopped, my pulse hammered.

The man looked up and locked gazes with me and my heart went into arrythmia. He gave a slow smile and I rose from the seat on legs as unsteady as a newborn foal's. It could only have been seconds before my doorbell rang but it felt like a decade.

I took a calming breath, not wanting to get ahead of myself, but it was hard to control the leaping of my pulse and the balloon of hope rising in my chest. I opened the door and Grayson Barlowe was standing there with a beautiful bunch of sweet peas in his hand.

'Hi…' I said, my nerves making my voice sound gruff rather than welcoming.

'Hi. May I come in?' His eyes had a light in them I had not seen before. A light that sparkled and shone and made him seem younger and less burdened than he had been in the past.

'Sure.' I stepped back and he came through the door, bringing his alluring scent with him, sending me into an instant swoon.

Grayson handed me the fragrant sweet peas. 'These are for you.'

'Thank you.' I took them from him and buried my face in the colourful sweet-smelling blooms. 'Mmm… these are my absolute favourite.' I raised my gaze to his. 'A lucky guess?'

His wry smile made my heart skip a beat. 'Niamh happened to mention you like them.'

'Come through,' I said with an on-off smile. 'I'll put these in some water.'

He followed me into my kitchen and I made a business of finding a vase, filling it with water and arranging the sweet peas. I was aware of him watching me the whole time, but I tried not to show how much his presence affected me.

'So, have Ethan and Niamh mentioned the godparent thing?' I asked, placing the vase of sweet peas in the middle of the kitchen table.

'Yes.'

I turned to look at him. 'It's a big honour. I've never been one before, have you?'

'No, but there's a first time for everything, right?' There was a definite twinkle in his eye and his tone was playful.

'Right.'

He came a little closer and I snatched in an even breath. Being so close to him tested my willpower. I wanted to throw myself at him, to wrap my arms around his trim waist and lay my head on his broad chest. But I didn't want to make a fool of myself. What if this was only a social call? Or a visit to talk about Ethan and Niamh's house? There could be any number of reasons he was here apart from the one I hoped.

'Erm…are you here about your handkerchief?' I asked.

He gave me a blank look. 'What handkerchief?'

'The one you lent me the evening we met Ethan and Niamh at the restaurant when they announced their engagement. I should've given it back to you before now.' I could feel my cheeks heating and wondered if he knew why I had kept it.

'I'm not here about that.'

'Oh.'

'I've missed you.' His voice was deep and serious, not hint of playfulness now.

I licked my suddenly dry lips. 'I've missed you too.' Okay, maybe showing a little vulnerability wasn't too over the top. But I was wary because what if he just wanted to be friends with benefits? I wanted much more than that. Much more. I wanted the fairy tale.

He reached out to take my hands in his and I had to suppress a gasp of pleasure as his fingers wrapped around mine. His gaze met mine and my stomach hollowed out at the desperate longing I could see in the grey-blue depths of his eyes.

'I don't think anyone has ever touched me the way you touched me,' he said.

'Yes, well, we did push a few boundaries in the bedroom.' Here's the thing—when I'm nervous I use humour to cover how I'm feeling.

Grayson laughed and tugged me a little closer. 'That's exactly why I love you so much. You constantly make me laugh.'

I stared at him, my mouth hanging open. 'What did you just say?'

'I said, you constantly make me laugh.' His eyes were practically dancing their way out of their sockets and his smile was wider than I had ever seen it before.

'The bit before that…' I moistened my dry lips again, my heart pounding like a drum inside my ribcage.

He squeezed my hands and brought them up to his chest, holding them against the solid steady thud of his heart. 'I love you, my darling.'

I blinked. I blinked again. Could this be really happening? Was I imagining this, or did he just say the words I longed to hear?

'That's what I thought I heard you say, but I wasn't sure if I was dreaming or not.'

'You're not dreaming. This is real. What I feel for you is real. I just wish I had realised earlier. I love you so very much. These past few weeks have been a living torture without you.' He brought his mouth down to mine and kissed me passionately, thoroughly, hungrily.

After a few breathless minutes he pulled back to look down at me again.

'When you said at the wedding that you thought I saw you, the real you, I wasn't ready to admit that you saw the real me too. We have so much in common and yet I was denying the connection from the start, even before we began our fling. I was determined to keep away from you because I think, on a subconscious level, I knew you spelled danger.' He wrapped his arms around me and held me close to his chest, his chin resting on the top of my head. 'I can't believe I let you go like that. I was so stubborn, so scared, to be honest. You threatened me because you opened your heart to me, and I didn't have the courage to open mine to you.'

I lifted my head off his chest to gaze up at him through shimmering eyes. 'I can't believe you love me. I think I fell in love with you when you first kissed me. I tried so hard not to fall for you. I knew it was not part of the deal, that we said no feelings were to be involved, but you made it impossible for me to resist you.'

He smiled and brought one of his hands up to cup my cheek, his eyes meshing with mine. 'I spent a lot of time over the past few weeks thinking about my life. The mistakes I've made in not facing up to what I really want. I'd told myself I didn't want to settle down. I'd seen my parents go through a bitter divorce; I'd seen good friends drift away after Ethan's accident.

Love didn't seem something I could rely on. I didn't want to rely on it and get hurt the way my mother and Ethan got hurt. The way I got hurt. But I realise now I need to take the chance because life is not always predicable. Love is what gets you through the unpredictability if you're lucky. And spending that time with you made me see how lucky I was to have you in my life. And I want to keep you in my life. For ever.' His hand moved from my cheek to take something out of his pocket.

I swallowed and stared at the velvet ring box with my heart leaping in my chest. 'Is that what I think it is?'

He grinned and flipped open the lid of the tiny box. 'This ring belonged to my grandmother. She wore it for sixty-two years and loved my grandfather for every single one of them. Will you marry me, my darling girl?'

I couldn't believe what I was hearing. The ring was beautiful—exactly the sort of ring I would have chosen for myself. 'Oh, darling, of course I'll marry you.'

He took the ring out of the box and slipped it on my left hand. I wasn't one bit surprised it was a perfect fit. It seemed to confirm our destiny to be together, the unification of two families who were once bitterly estranged.

'I have to tell you I'm not a fan of long engagements,' Grayson said. 'It only took a couple of weeks to pull off Ethan and Niamh's wedding.'

I laughed and flung my arms around him. 'I can't wait to be your wife. But I don't need a flower-filled church and a choir to be happy. I just need to be with you.'

'How about Vegas?' There was a teasing glint in his eye.

'Funny man. No, I think a beach somewhere with the sun setting in the background as we exchange our vows.'

'Sounds perfect.' He brought his mouth back down to mine in a kiss that was full of love and hope for the future.

After another passionate interlude, Grayson lifted his mouth off mine to gaze into my love-drunk eyes. 'There's another thing we need to discuss. Are we going to have children?'

'Would you like to have them?'

'I always told myself no, but I've been thinking about it a lot lately. Seeing my brother prepare for fatherhood has made me realise what a privilege it is to be a parent. I can't think of anyone I would rather raise a family with than you.'

My heart was so full of love I thought it was going to burst out of my chest.

'I would love that. I was the same, always telling myself I didn't want a family, but that was because I didn't feel like I deserved to have one after what happened to Niamh. But I'm learning to forgive myself. I was just a child and accidents happen even when a parent or other adults are around.'

Grayson held me close again and I felt so secure and safe, ready to face whatever life dished up. We would face it together, not alone. We would be a team working together.

'I'm proud of you for letting go of the past,' he said.

'I've had to do it too. I guess we will always have some measure of guilt about what happened to our siblings, but we can't let it colour our whole life. We owe it to them to live our best lives.' He eased back to look me in the eyes again. 'And my best life is with you.'

* * * * *

COMING SOON!

We really hope you enjoyed reading this book. If you're looking for more romance be sure to head to the shops when new books are available on

Thursday 6th July

To see which titles are coming soon, please visit

millsandboon.co.uk/nextmonth

MILLS & BOON®

Coming next month

THE MAID MARRIED TO THE BILLIONAIRE
Lynne Graham

"You took me by surprise… You shocked me," she muttered unevenly, struggling to catch her breath. She was thoroughly unnerved by the sensations that had shimmied up through her taut body and then down again to a place that had ignited with a burst of warmth, mortifying her to the very bone.

Enzo released his breath on a measured hiss. "Relax. For a moment, I was tempted. But nothing is going to happen unless you want it to. I'm attracted to you. I know I shouldn't be but I'm not perfect. In fact, it seems I'm all too human. But you are completely safe with me, *piccolo mio*."

"Maybe I don't need to be safe…with you," Skye said uncertainly. "You make me feel things I didn't expect to feel. You make me curious. I know, like you said, I shouldn't be in these circumstances. But the truth is, I am and I'm attracted too."

"So…" Enzo breathed a touch raggedly. "What do you want to do about this?"

"We—we could try a kiss…just *one*," she stressed.

Continue reading
THE MAID MARRIED TO THE BILLIONAIRE
Lynne Graham

Available next month
www.millsandboon.co.uk

LET'S TALK
Romance

For exclusive extracts, competitions and special offers, find us online:

f MillsandBoon

𝕏 @MillsandBoon

◉ @MillsandBoonUK

♪ @MillsandBoonUK

Get in touch on 01413 063 232

MILLS & BOON

THE HEART OF ROMANCE

A ROMANCE FOR EVERY READER

MODERN
Prepare to be swept off your feet by sophisticated, sexy and seductive heroes, in some of the world's most glamourous and romantic locations, where power and passion collide.

HISTORICAL
Escape with historical heroes from time gone by. Whether your passion is for wicked Regency Rakes, muscled Vikings or rugged Highlanders, awaken the romance of the past.

MEDICAL
Set your pulse racing with dedicated, delectable doctors in the high-pressure world of medicine, where emotions run high and passion, comfort and love are the best medicine.

True Love
Celebrate true love with tender stories of heartfelt romance, from the rush of falling in love to the joy a new baby can bring, and a focus on the emotional heart of a relationship.

Desire
Indulge in secrets and scandal, intense drama and sizzling hot action with heroes who have it all: wealth, status, good looks…everything but the right woman.

HEROES
The excitement of a gripping thriller, with intense romance at its heart. Resourceful, true-to-life women and strong, fearless men face danger and desire - a killer combination!

To see which titles are coming soon, please visit

millsandboon.co.uk/nextmonth

JOIN US ON SOCIAL MEDIA!

Stay up to date with our latest releases, author news and gossip, special offers and discounts, and all the behind-the-scenes action from Mills & Boon...

 @millsandboon

 @millsandboonuk

 facebook.com/millsandboon

 @millsandboonuk

It might just be true love...